"With sizzling chemistry, brilliant banter, and an unapologetically strong, feminist heroine, Harper St. George sets the pages ablaze!"

—*USA Today* bestselling author Christi Caldwell

"Fun, tender, and definitely sexy, *The Heiress Gets a Duke* is already at the top of my list for the best books of the year. Don't sleep on this refreshing and feminist romance."

—*BookPage* (starred review)

"Harper St. George just gets better and better with every book, penning the kind of page-turning stories that you will want to read again as soon as you finish each one."

—Lyssa Kay Adams, author of the Bromance Book Club series

"A rich, compelling, and beautifully written romance. St. George brings us the story of Violet Crenshaw, an American heiress with distinctly modern ideas about love and marriage."

—Elizabeth Everett, author of *The Love Remedy*

"Luscious historical romance."   —PopSugar

"Rich with period detail, *The Heiress Gets a Duke* brings to life the Gilded Age's dollar princesses in this smart, sexy, and oh-so-satisfying story."

—Laurie Benson, award-winning author of the Sommersby Brides series

"You'll sigh, you'll cry, and you'll grin yourself silly as this independent and cynical heiress finally gets her duke."

—Virginia Heath, author of *Never Wager with a Wallflower*

THE STRANGER I WED

HARPER ST. GEORGE

BERKLEY ROMANCE

NEW YORK

BERKLEY ROMANCE
Published by Berkley
An imprint of Penguin Random House LLC
penguinrandomhouse.com

Library of Congress Cataloging-in-Publication Data

Names: St. George, Harper, author.
Title: The stranger I wed / Harper St. George.
Description: First edition. | New York: Berkley Romance, 2024. |
Series: The doves of New York ; 1
Identifiers: LCCN 2023031479 (print) | LCCN 2023031480 (ebook) |
ISBN 9780593441008 (trade paperback) | ISBN 9780593441015 (ebook)
Subjects: LCGFT: Romance fiction. | Novels.
Classification: LCC PS3619.T236 S77 2024 (print) | LCC PS3619.T236 (ebook) |
DDC 813/.6—dc23/eng/20231016
LC record available at https://lccn.loc.gov/2023031479
LC ebook record available at https://lccn.loc.gov/2023031480

First Edition: April 2024

Printed in the United States of America
1st Printing

Book design by George Towne

*For Lois Glanzer, who was
always the heroine of her own story.*

We love you and miss you.

PART ONE

Men have everything, most women nothing
but what men give them. When women
want anything, be it bread or a kind word,
they must pay the price that men exact for
it, and it is nearly always "a pound of flesh."

—Susan B. Anthony

PROLOGUE

Upper East Side, Manhattan
Autumn 1877

FIFTH AVENUE WAS CORA'S BIRTHRIGHT, BUT THAT'S only if one adhered to biology rather than social expectation. People usually didn't, which is why she and her sisters had never been invited to any of the exclusive addresses on the street. They were illegitimate. Secrets to be whispered about, sometimes scorned by otherwise polite citizens, and flatly ignored by Charles Hathaway. Despite her best efforts, Cora had never quite figured out how to not let that bother her.

Her knees were shaking as the driver helped her out of the cab in front of the Hathaway mansion. He eyed her dubiously, uncertain whether to place her among the residents or the servants that populated the street. She couldn't blame him, because sometimes she didn't know, either. The serviceable navy dress she wore was more suited to a governess than a Hathaway daughter. She thanked him with a coin, which he palmed while tipping his hat to her. His eyes seemed to wish her luck.

She inhaled deeply and took in the mansion before her. It

was her first actual sighting of her father's house. Five floors of brick and limestone, the home was imposing but not gaudy, built to blend in with the brownstones around it. A tiny lawn of grass and shrubbery was neatly contained within a wrought iron fence. It was exactly what she had expected from the Hathaway family. Ostentatious displays of wealth were better left to the new money that bled through the city. Old families like the Hathaways had no need to prove their affluence, because that had been established two centuries ago.

Her knees continued to tremble as she took the steps that led to the front door. The door opened before she could ring the bell. The butler, an older man with pale skin and drooping jaws, looked down at her as if he was on the verge of sending her around to the servants' entrance. "May I help you, miss?"

Infusing steel into her voice to stop the inevitable waver, she said, "Good morning. I am here to meet with Mr. Charles Hathaway."

The lines in his forehead deepened and his lips flattened. "Not possible, miss. The household is in mourning. Mr. Hathaway is not home to visitors."

"Yes, my condolences. However, he'll want to see me. Please tell him that Miss Cora Dove is calling."

Her name didn't seem to mean anything to the butler. His expression was as skeptical as ever. "I'm afraid that is impossible."

Having anticipated this very reception, she withdrew the letter that had brought her here. She kept a tight hold on it but held it up so that he could see the Fifth Avenue return address on the envelope. Curious enough to not slam the door in her face, he withdrew a pair of half-rim spectacles from his pocket and leaned forward to read the text. It was from the late family matriarch, Ada Hathaway. The handwriting was spidery and frail, uneven from being written on the woman's death-bed, Cora assumed, but it was legible nonetheless.

Not above a little ruthlessness when the situation called for it, she said, "I know that Mrs. Hathaway and her children are not at home." The papers had written about how they had retired to their Westchester farm after the funeral. "I can return later when they are, if you'd prefer."

His eyes narrowed with a shadow of contempt. Ah, perhaps he did know her name after all. They both knew that Mr. Hathaway's wife would not like it that she was here. He gave a telling glance toward the street—so far, none of the people hurrying down the sidewalk had taken notice of them—and he loosened his grip on the door. "Come in, Miss Dove."

The house was the epitome of elegance. A thick Persian rug covered the marble floor of the entryway and led to a wide and curving staircase, the balustrade a gleaming mahogany carved with tiny rosettes. Two rooms flanked the hall, each of them furnished with sofas and chairs covered in rich textiles and cushions; tables were strewn with delicate baubles, and walls were adorned with priceless artwork. The windows were dressed in black crepe, but she suspected they typically bore stylish and copious drapery.

It was all very tasteful and moderately extravagant—they weren't the Vanderbilts, after all. The Hathaways were one of New York's oldest families. They hadn't earned their wealth through modern industry. It had been gained by new-world commerce—trading and importing—then inherited and reinforced through the generations by rising property values.

The butler indicated one of the drawing rooms. "Wait in here and I'll let Mr. Hathaway know you have come."

Cora might have done just that, but she spotted the portrait above the fireplace. Mrs. Hathaway stared out at her. She was a woman in her midthirties who might have been pretty had she appeared less severe. Her hair was pulled back so tight that it gave her a nearly cat-eyed appearance, and her mouth was held firm in disapproval. Cora almost felt as if Mrs. Hathaway were looking out at her, condemning her for daring to step foot inside her home.

The woman was seated, and standing behind either shoulder was a young boy and an older girl. From the papers, Cora knew the girl's name was Agnes and she was around fifteen, only a few years younger than Cora's youngest sister, Eliza. She stood tall behind her mother in a dress that probably would have supported Cora's family for a year or more. Her heart ached for all that her own little family had been denied. It was strange to think that if things had turned out differently, she might have lived here.

"No, take me to him."

The butler sputtered in protest. She insisted. She eventually prevailed when a young maid rushed into the hall holding a stack of linen, saw them, and scurried away. There would be gossip now, and prolonging their disagreement in the front hall would only make it worse if more servants came to gawk. He turned toward the deep recesses of the house with Cora on his heels.

The butler came to a stop at the back corner of the house and knocked at a set of polished mahogany doors. A voice inside called out, and he gave her a sharp look that held her rooted to the floor before he disappeared inside. He returned moments later and motioned her in before closing the door behind him with a slam that was a smidge harder than strictly necessary.

She paused to gather herself, taking in her surroundings, not ready to look toward the figure waiting on the other side of the room. Her courage had yet to catch up with her bravado. The study was paneled in dark wood with hundreds of leather-bound books lining bookcases. Eliza would love this room. A fire crackled in the hearth; the scent of woodsmoke, not coal, mixed with the sweet pungency of cigars. Charles Hathaway rose from his place behind his desk, and she had no choice but to finally acknowledge him. He stood larger than life after all this time.

She had last seen him around twelve years ago, but he hadn't changed much. Silver wings now tipped his dark hair, and a few lines creased his face, only serving to make him appear more dignified. His looks perfectly matched his smart wool suit, his elegant home, and his disapproving wife. He was handsome in a bland and conventional way, as if his physical traits had come together to render him pleasing but never anything so garish as beautiful.

She'd only been eight or nine when she last saw him; now that she was older, she found herself looking for similarities. The middle Dove sister, Jenny, was their mother reborn, but Eliza had his strong chin. Cora had his eyes, grayish blue. She also recognized the slightly prominent slope on the bridge of his nose as a mirror of her own, though on a larger scale.

"Hello." For a moment, she forgot what it was she had come there to say.

He searched her features, puzzling them out as if he, too, were looking for signs of himself in her. "Cora."

Relief and welcome were evident in his voice, not the censure she had expected. Despite every other part of her vowing to despise him, the child in her that longed for a father stood up at that single word. He knew her name and had spoken it aloud. It was like stepping into a beam of healing sunlight after a long and bitter winter of darkness.

"You're here," he said as if he still couldn't believe it. "Has something happened? Is Fanny . . . ?"

"Mama is well."

He gave a slight nod, and they fell into silence until he motioned for her to take one of the chairs across from him. "How are your sisters?"

Did he remember their names? She didn't want to ask and risk disappointment.

Settling herself in the plush chair, she answered, "We are all well. Please accept my condolences on the death of your mother." Her grandmother, though no one had ever called her by that name in Cora's presence. If she had ever met the woman, she couldn't remember it.

His eyes widened slightly in surprise before he was able to rein in the expression as he sat. "Thank you. She had a good, long life." He searched her features again before settling on her hair. "You look like her a bit. You even have the same auburn tint to your hair that she had when she was younger."

Cora fingered the hair at the nape of her neck. They had always wondered where the distinctive color had come from. What else might she and her sisters have inherited from the family they had never known? They had been denied so very much. The anger she had carried around for as long as she could remember came seeping in.

"I wouldn't know. I never met her."

He had the gall to appear wounded. "Cora, I . . . I did the best I could."

She didn't agree but had not come to rehash the two decades of her life or expound on parental responsibility. Taking a deep breath, she pressed forward with the rest of the reason for her visit.

"She sent me a letter before her death." This time he wasn't able to get a handle on his surprise so quickly as she pulled the letter from her handbag. "It was delivered the day after her obituary appeared in the *New York Times*. She said that she had come to regret the way things were handled and she would leave an inheritance for me and my sisters."

Wordlessly, he held out his hand for the letter. Everything in her rebelled at handing it over. All he would have to do is toss it into the fire and there would be no evidence that Ada Hathaway had thought of her at all. She withdrew the paper from the envelope and handed it to him. At least the envelope would serve as some sort of proof if the letter within disappeared.

He perched a set of reading spectacles on the end of his nose and settled back in his chair. The letter itself was rather impersonal, written by a woman who obviously kept her feelings very close to herself. It merely stated her regret that things couldn't have been different and that she had left an inheritance and Cora should visit Charles for further information.

"I wasn't aware she had written," he said when he'd finished with the brief missive and given it back to her.

"Did she share her intentions with you?"

He nodded. "She did."

The tight pain in her chest was unexpected. "Were you planning to contact us?"

He sighed as if the subject was wearying for him. "Eventually, yes. I hoped to give things time to settle."

He retrieved a leather-bound folder from his desk drawer and opened it. After a moment flipping through papers, he pulled out a single piece of parchment. Scanning the page, he said, "She left you and your sisters a combination of shares in Central West Railroad and Hathaway Realty Investments. The shares earn roughly twenty thousand dollars a year. There is also a cash sum of two hundred thousand dollars each. All of this will be held in trust to be distributed to each of you upon your marriages."

Two hundred thousand dollars with an income of twenty thousand a year. They were rich! With that amount, they could each buy an estate and the annual income would be more than enough to sustain them. But they didn't have it yet.

She stared at him dumbly. "Marriages, not maturity?"

He shook his head. "She wanted to make certain you girls are provided for and set up for a stable life."

Odd, considering the woman had never particularly cared about their stability before. "What if we choose not to marry?"

"I cannot see all of you deciding to become spinsters, but those who do won't inherit the stock or the cash."

"That's preposterous." The woman hadn't given a fig about them until her conscience had finally caught up to her on her deathbed, and now she thought to dictate the rest of their lives.

"I realize it sounds that way, but it's for your benefit. We agreed that I should guide your choice of husband to avoid any sort of . . . well, inelegance in the situation."

"What does that mean?"

"I'm to help each of you find a man of suitable means and social position. Someone worthy of a Hathaway even though you don't carry the name."

"You mean someone like your daughter Agnes would marry."

He shifted uncomfortably. "Yes, but not someone from Manhattan, or anywhere in New York, nor Connecticut." He thought for a moment. "Not from New England at all, actually. Or Florida, and we do have acquaintances in San Francisco now."

She gave a dry laugh. "Well, now that we've ruled out the entirety of the United States . . ."

He chuckled self-consciously. "You can see how running in the same circles could lead to embarrassment for my family. I couldn't stand to bring further embarrassment to my wife or affect Agnes's chances for a solid match. And there are fortune hunters who wouldn't waste a moment's time in a blackmail scheme."

The chances of them ever collecting this inheritance were dwindling by the second. "Not every man would be looking to exploit the situation. There are noble men in the world."

His voice pinched in annoyance, he said, "Of course there are, but most wouldn't hesitate to take advantage." Pressing a hand to his temple, he said, "I warned her this was a terrible idea."

"A terrible idea to see us cared for?"

"No, for believing that a marriage of the sort she had in mind was possible."

Having spent her life feeling inferior and unwanted by her father's side of the family, that comment cut her to the quick.

She cast around mentally for some answer, but Mr. Hathaway had stricken practically all the men in the country from eligibility. There were noble men in the world. There had to be.

Noblemen. The Crenshaw sisters had famously married aristocrats from England a couple years back. Before them, Camille Bridwell, whom she had met as a child when her mother and Mr. Hathaway were still together, had married a duke.

"Aristocrats." She almost shouted, happy that she had come upon some idea he couldn't reject. More subdued, she said, "We could marry European aristocrats."

He chuckled. "Let's be reasonable, Cora."

His dismissal stung. "I am being reasonable."

But he wasn't listening, because he had pulled out a ledger and was perusing the columns of numbers. "I can give you a sum now to forget this foolishness." His voice was hard and clipped, all business now that he had disregarded his mother's plan as ill-advised. This was how he had disregarded them so easily, she realized. He slipped into a character. Or, maybe, his warmth and concern earlier had been feigned and this was really who he was. "Ten thousand dollars."

Disconcerted, she asked, "Ten thousand? Is that the going rate to buy your illegitimate children off so they leave you in peace?"

"Cora, no." He looked up at her with that wounded expression. His sleek eyebrows pulled low over his eyes. He appeared so regretful that she started to see the hold he might have held over her mother at one time. Whether it was true or not, he could make you *think* that he cared. "I understand your frustration, but, despite appearances, I don't have large amounts of cash sitting around."

Everything he wanted had been handed to him from the day he was born. She rather thought he couldn't possibly understand how she felt.

"I am doing my best to be fair. How about fifteen, then?" At her still horrified expression, he added, "Oh, come now, Cora. Be reasonable. I'll invest it for you and you'll have a proper income, enough to have a little room for yourself somewhere."

Is that what he expected of her? That she would hide away in a spinster boarding home accepting her allowance and causing no trouble for him? Meanwhile, his conscience would be clear. "That's a far cry from what your mother wanted."

He sighed. "Despite what you think, I am not a cretin. I want you to be settled in life."

"I want my inheritance."

"Cora—"

Led by desperation, she asked, "If I bring you an aristocrat, will you approve the marriage and release the funds?"

He laughed again, sending her anger bubbling higher. When he saw that she was serious, his amusement died away. "You have no family or name to recommend you. Do you honestly believe you stand a chance in hell of marrying an aristocrat?"

She hadn't when she'd suggested it. Not really, but she would be damned if she would sit here and allow this man to laugh at her as he was clawing back what was rightfully hers, all to save him and his *real* family a bit of embarrassment.

"Can you write a letter guaranteeing the dowries for all three of us?"

He stared at her in shock. "You're serious about this?"

Her spine ramrod straight, she said, "Yes, but I'll need proof of funds written in your hand."

"This won't work. You have nothing to recommend you."

She didn't answer because there was no refuting that. Instead, she did what she had learned worked on her mother when they were at an impasse. She stared him down.

"Oh, what the hell?" Bemused, he reached for a clean sheet of parchment from a basket on the corner of his desk. His name and address had been printed in embossed type near the top. "On the chance that it does work, an aristocratic connection could be very beneficial."

She had no idea how to start the search for a bridegroom, except to reach out to Camille for help and hope the woman remembered her from their meeting so many years ago. "You'll have to come to England or wherever we are . . . once we're successfully matched." The letter would only get them so far. He'd have to come and arrange things with the banks and the bridegrooms.

He chuckled without mirth as he wrote. "You find yourself an aristocrat, and I'll walk you down the aisle."

ONE

Oxfordshire, England
Spring 1878

TITLE-HUNTING WAS NOT FOR THE FAINT OF HEART. The occupation required a great deal of analysis, focus, and attention to detail, three qualities Cora Dove had no choice but to perfect. One had to be strategic when choosing the ideal candidate for a husband. Everyone knew that the perfect groom for a title hunter was a fortune hunter. However, it simply wasn't that easy. Too impoverished and the wealth gained from the marriage would drain away like water through a sieve.

Cora was determined that the man she married not be a gambler, at least not to excess. The likelihood of finding an aristocrat who did not gamble at all would be akin to finding a fish that did not swim. There were other considerations, too. In fact, she had made a list. Too young and he'd likely be brash and unruly. Too old and he could hold outdated ideas about a wife's role. Too temperamental or too wicked in his pursuits and he would be difficult to manage. Too attractive and heartache would inevitably ensue—this one had been the last to go on the list. Cora quite liked good-looking men and wouldn't have minded marrying one. Her sister Jenny, however, who knew more than she about the qualities of handsome men, had been insistent, so the condition had gone on the list. Only a fool would aim for the highest title and leave it at that when there were so many other considerations.

Cora was no fool. Not anymore. She had stepped off the steamer ship from New York with her mother and Eliza last week with her mission at the forefront of her mind. Find a titled husband and marry him by summer. Thankfully, she would not face the task alone. Camille, Dowager Duchess of Hereford, had agreed to act as a sort of agent to help the sisters find titled husbands.

"Camille, pardon my disbelief, but there can't possibly be suitors here," Eliza, Cora's youngest sister, remarked, her brow furrowed in distinct displeasure.

The three of them descended the steps of the train depot, umbrellas in hand to combat the spring drizzle. The train stretched out behind them on the track, belching steam into the cool air. They were in a small village—Cora had already forgotten the name—not far from Camille's country estate in Oxfordshire. The town was little more than a stop along the railroad, but it was quaint and picturesque, as Cora was finding most English villages to be. They possessed a charm lent to them by virtue of age that many of the industrial mill towns that had sprung up back home didn't have. The buildings, made of either stone or wattle and daub, had been standing for centuries longer than their brownstone back in New York. There was a security in that permanence that she found comforting.

"I quite like it," Cora said.

"As do I," Camille voiced her agreement.

Cora and her sisters had met Camille many years ago when Mr. Hathaway and Fanny were still an item, though their relationship had been in its death throes. Camille's father and Mr. Hathaway had finished some sort of business deal together, and they had been invited to spend a week with the Bridwells at their summer home. It had been an awkward week, and Cora now realized it was because Mrs. Bridwell hadn't approved of their presence there, even though Mr. Bridwell hadn't been above putting his company's profits ahead of what was socially acceptable. Cora and Camille had spent most of the time together outdoors swimming and playing on the rope swings. Thankfully, Camille remembered her and had been a wonderful source of support when Cora had contacted her with the marriage plan.

The duchess wasn't a proponent of the cash-for-class marriages that were becoming so popular between American heiresses and impoverished noblemen. Her own parents had all but auctioned her off to the highest title, and the marriage had been deeply unhappy until the much older duke had died and set her free. Now she was with Jacob Thorne, a man she loved. It had taken several letters and a few telegrams before Cora had convinced Camille that this marriage was what she wanted and that she was not being coerced by her mother. It was her negligent sire who had made this sort of marriage necessary, but Cora preferred not to dwell on that.

Instead, she devoted every waking moment to finding the perfect husband. She had a journal specifically for the task that she had diligently filled with notes about each man Camille proposed to her. She knew their ages, their immediate family members, and how they spent their days. Perhaps more importantly, she knew how their family had lost their own fortunes. That crucial bit of information could be the difference between a comfortable future and one spent scraping pennies.

Unlike the other American heiresses who came from new money families with industrial interests that kept their pockets deep, Cora and her sisters were illegitimate. They weren't marrying for mere social status, though that would be a boon; they were marrying for the very survival of their small family.

"Then you can marry any gentleman who might reside here. I'll choose one who lives in London." Eliza nodded her head in finality and Cora hid her grin. If only it were that easy of a choice.

"I understand the conditions are not ideal," Camille said, leading them around the muck and mud of the road to the higher-packed earth along the edge. They didn't seem to be heading toward the center of town but in the other direction along a narrow lane that followed the tracks before turning away. "But being able to observe these men outside of normal social conditions will give you rare insight. Since they don't know you yet and don't know that you're watching, they'll be more inclined to be themselves. Once at the house party, they'll all be on their best behavior, and you'll only see what they allow you to see."

That was certainly true. Of the ten men Camille had invited to the upcoming house party at Stonebridge Cottage, they had been able to observe five without them being aware. First, they had gone to the Lakes, where they had discreetly assessed two of their suitors who were participating in an angler tournament. They were two of the most boring individuals Cora had ever encountered. Since boredom hadn't made it onto her list, they had passed the test. Then, they had gone to a lecture at the British Museum to locate a third who had been a bit argumentative with the lecturer. She had drawn a line through his name. She wouldn't countenance a rude husband. From there, they had quietly observed two others at Hyde Park. Both were a bit snobbish in their bearing, so Cora had put a question mark by their names. Today was their last jaunt before the house party began early next week. They were here to watch a football game.

"I'm afraid the match has already begun, but we'll be able to see enough to judge their sportsmanship. I know that's not on your list, but you can learn a lot from how a man treats his teammates and adversaries," Camille continued. "Perhaps we can pop over to the public house and watch them after, though that might be pushing things."

It wouldn't do to have anyone recognize the duchess. Once they heard the sisters' American accents, their disguises of plain clothes would be quite useless to hide their identities from their prospective suitors. All objectivity would be gone, and they would lose their chance to observe them unaware.

"Perhaps we can watch for a time," Cora said.

They rounded a corner after a row of tiny houses onto a narrow dirt lane that led to a field. It did appear the game was already in progress with roughly two dozen men on the pitch. Half wore green shirtsleeves while the other half wore yellow. Both wore trousers or pantaloons that would never be white again with all the mud, along with high socks and leather boots, and their heads were bare. They chased a round leather ball across the field in a match that was much more physical than she had anticipated.

"Careful of your step, dear," Camille said, indicating a particularly deep puddle, and Cora lithely stepped around it. When she had righted herself, the duchess and Eliza were continuing on their way to the left where a robust crowd had gathered to cheer on the players.

Cora stood transfixed at the sheer physicality of the drama playing out on the field. One man hurried to kick the ball, grunting when another one ran into him, nearly sending him careening on the soaked ground. The ball had only been glanced, which sent it several yards toward the far side. Another man, his golden hair damp with sweat and rain and falling about his face, cursed and then let out a victorious yell as he ran through several opponents and managed to make good contact with the ball, kicking it in an arc, sending it farther downfield toward the goal. The players turned as one and hurried in that direction. If there was any sort of coordination among them, Cora couldn't see it. They all seemed madcap in their zeal to obtain the ball.

For a moment, she was struck by the sheer size and athleticism of the men. Without a coat to hide them, their shoulders appeared extra wide, the muscles working under the thin material of their shirts as they ran, the rain melding the fabric to them. Their chests seemed thick and strapped with sinew. It suddenly became apparent why good Society insisted on a man wearing his coat at all times. It might prove too distracting otherwise. Although, most Society men she had met had a bit of soft about them. Not like these men.

She smiled to herself and began to make her way over to where Camille and Eliza had joined the spectators. However, she couldn't stop herself from looking back at the one who had kicked the ball. He was tall and muscled, his jaw square and firm as his eyes narrowed, watching to see which way the ball would go when it finally broke free of the group. He loped easily toward his teammates, his long legs eating up the distance without making him seem out of breath. It was probably too much to hope that he would be one of her suitors, though the fact that he was so handsome meant he violated a rule on her list and she shouldn't consider him anyway.

As she stared at him, the ball suddenly broke free of the chaos on the field, hurtling in her direction. A player roughly her own size came rushing toward her, his eyes crazed with ferocity as he screamed with the triumph of a predator about to seize its prey. She barely got a look at him before the man she had been admiring yelled, "Briggs!" drawing her attention back to him. He'd picked up speed, running full bore in their direction, ostensibly to intercept his teammate from flattening her.

She sidestepped the ball, somehow managing to miss Briggs but stepping into the path of the golden-haired man. He tried to stop, but the change in momentum sent him skidding over a patch of mud and directly into her. Her breath rushed out of her at the initial contact, flinging her umbrella and journal in the air, and her own feet caught the mud and they tumbled to the ground together. He twisted, catching the brunt of the fall, but they rolled several more times before coming to a stop in the soggy grass. The players were still following the ball, and as they lumbered closer, sounding like a herd of cattle, she closed her eyes, expecting them to fall over her and the man. The anticipated disaster never happened as they continued running down the field. She opened her eyes to see his staring down at her. They were green like emeralds and intense with concern. She had never seen a color like them on anything but a cat.

"Are you hurt?" he asked.

She took in a breath, surprised to find that nothing was sore. "I don't think so." Her voice came out sounding winded.

He leaned over her as he ran a hand over her rib cage and up over her breast. She gasped as he pressed, no doubt looking for injury, but her nipple tightened beneath his touch just the same, and her blood warmed in a way that was unseemly. She sucked in a hard breath. "Excuse me!"

"You are hurt."

"No!" She wrenched his hand away.

His brow furrowed, flummoxed by her outrage. "No?"

Perhaps he hadn't realized that he had all but fondled her breast with his pawing. She took in another breath and managed to speak in a calmer tone. "I am uninjured." She attempted to sit up as embarrassment began to creep in, but she was stuck beneath the weight of his thigh over hers—his very large, very solid thigh. In fact, his entire body seemed very large and very solid above her. She ought to feel more put out, but suddenly, she didn't quite mind lying here like this beneath him.

"Let me help you up," he said just as she was becoming accustomed to his attentions. Removing himself from her, he offered her his hand.

She took it, still too aware of him in a physical sense. Her heart pounded as heat suffused her cheeks. At his full height, he stood nearly a head taller than her. His torso might well have been double the width of hers. Aside from a few dances, she had never been this close to a man before, and certainly not one so attractive.

"You might watch where you're going next time." She was struggling to catch her breath as if she were the one who had run across the field. Her hand shook when she took it back, so she wiped at the blades of grass stuck to her bodice to hide the tremble. His hands followed, helping her wipe the debris away and sending her nerve endings teetering wildly.

Before she could gather herself to protest—which may have taken a while, considering a very real part of her was enjoying the attention—he said, "You might have stayed off the pitch."

His words cut through the havoc within her. "I wasn't on

the pitch. I was off to the side. Your friend, Briggs, was outside of the boundary."

"You play association football, do you?" His gaze narrowed in obvious irritation.

"No, but every game has a boundary line. I was outside of yours." She turned to indicate that fact, but there didn't actually seem to be a line designating any boundary.

His brow rose dubiously.

"Are you blaming me for the fact that you ran me over?" she asked.

His lips tightened in what might have been a suppressed grin. "No, of course not."

"Good." She wiped at her skirt.

He walked the few steps necessary to pick up her journal and umbrella, handing them back to her. After she took them, he scraped his hair out of his face, sending rivulets of water running down his cheeks. She couldn't help but watch one make its way to his mouth, where it slid smoothly over his bottom lip.

"Perhaps the next time you see the ball and an entire team of men coming toward you, you might consider removing yourself from the field of play."

There was a spark of humor in his eyes that somehow softened his words. The result was that she felt mildly annoyed but greatly intrigued. "Perhaps you might consider keeping your ball and your men on the pitch."

He smiled, but only for a second before someone called out, "Dev!" and his head swiveled in that direction.

He sobered a bit, the spark of mirth dying out as he glanced toward Camille and Eliza, who were hurrying toward them, before asking, "You're an American, are you?"

Damn. She'd forgotten all about not talking to anyone. "Yes, I'm visiting friends."

He seemed to size up Camille and then glanced at Cora once more. With a tip of his head, he ran back out onto the field to join the fray.

"Cora!" Eliza ran up and held her umbrella over them both to block the sprinkle of rain.

"That looked horrific. Are you hurt?" Camille wiped at the grass and mud on Cora's skirt with a handkerchief, nearly losing her hat and veil in the process.

"Not unless you count my bruised pride." Cora smiled and led them away from the field.

"He might have broken your ribs," Eliza said, somewhat indignant on her behalf.

"But he didn't."

"Thank goodness for that," Camille added, standing to her full height, her attention back on the game still in play. "He hasn't yet confirmed his attendance at the house party. If he broke your rib, I suspect he wouldn't come at all."

Cora whipped around to look at her friend before finding the man called Dev among the players. He whooped and raised his hands above his head in triumph as his teammate scored a goal. "Dev," she whispered. Then louder, "Devonworth?"

"Yes, that was the Earl of Devonworth," Camille confirmed for her.

That name was in her journal. She had written down his family members, his family history, and the fact that he was passionate about his seat in Parliament. She had thought he might be an ideal candidate for husband because he met all the requirements. Except now she knew he was handsome. Too handsome, really. He completely violated the last rule.

For the first time, Cora understood why Jenny had insisted on that rule. It would be terribly difficult to divorce a man so tempting.

TWO

INVITATION TO HOUSE PARTY

Esteemed gentlemen and lords,

I am writing to request the pleasure of your company at Stonebridge Cottage for a small gathering. The guests of honor are very dear friends visiting from New York. They are respectable young women who intend to make suitable matches. However, as they are Americans and unaccustomed to London entertainments, I have proposed to introduce them to a small pool of exceedingly qualified company before their London debut.

    Mr. Thorne and I regard you with the highest esteem as men of character. It is my sincere hope that you will grace us with your honored presence. Since the company is selective, I must insist upon your complete discretion. Please reply at your earliest convenience.

Regards,
Camille
Dowager Duchess of Hereford

Montague Club, Bloomsbury, London

THE DUCHESS DID NOT PLAY FAIR. SHE WAS PROPOS-
ing to make marriage matches all while giving very little
information about the intended brides. One never knew about
these nouveau riche Americans. Any man in his right mind
would avoid such an obvious attempt at title-hunting. Every
firstborn son who stood to inherit a title had been warned
from birth about the dangers inherent in their positions. They
had been cautioned that women of unfortunate character
would be looking to bait and trap them. That they should always be on guard against such an occurrence. No one had
thought to counsel them on how to find a wife when the title
wasn't enough.

The fact of the matter was that Leopold Brendon, Earl of
Devonworth, was inching closer to insolvency day by day.
Every highborn family in Britain knew this and, title be
damned, did not want their daughters to go down with the
proverbial ship. On an intellectual level, Devonworth understood this. It stung, but he would have cautioned his own
daughter—if he'd had one—against a man such as himself.
His income simply wasn't enough to defray the expenses, despite the fact that he had curtailed them extensively since
inheriting. As it stood, his life was falling apart and only
money would help put it back together.

He crumpled the duchess's invitation as he put it back inside his coat pocket, still disgusted that marriage to a stranger
was something he was seriously considering. The invitation
had arrived several weeks earlier. He had not expected it
nor had he initially given it any serious thought. His first in-
stinct had been to write a pithy reply declining. Parliament

was sitting, which meant he was too busy for any amusements save for the social functions customary to his position, more obligation than entertainment. To be fair, the invitation was also not meant as an amusement. It was a business proposition. He already had a mother harping on about marriage and lineage, so he did not need the interference of a duchess—a title-hunting American duchess at that.

Several events had occurred that greatly altered his view on the matter. The first, chronologically, was an unprecedented March snow that had killed over two hundred and fifty sheep on his estate. Timberscombe Park had suffered, as well. The roof on the north wing had been damaged to such an extent that it was in danger of caving in. The place had been a collar placed around his neck from the very moment of his birth, limiting his options, ensuring any freedom he believed he had was only an illusion. Now it had grown unbearable, tightening to a choke hold.

The second, and by far the greatest need, was that his younger brother had managed to get himself into trouble again. This time, Harry owed a very large debt to an unsavory chap who lived and preyed in Whitechapel. What his brother had been thinking wagering at gaming houses run by those notorious gangs, Devonworth couldn't fathom. The very idea of such recklessness was beyond his comprehension, but here he was, left to clean up the mess . . . again. He had known for years that his time was running out, but he hadn't expected doom to settle on his doorstep all at once.

The third was that he believed he had already met one of the Americans. He was almost certain the woman who had got in his way at the football match was one of the heiresses. Wealthy Americans didn't generally roam around the English countryside untethered from a retinue of admirers. The village was located in the vicinity of Camille's country home. He would have sworn the figure veiled in black was the dowager herself. It was reasonable to assume that she had brought them out to preview the goods offered to them at the house party. The redhead hadn't been objectionable. To the contrary, she'd been intriguing.

An heiress would solve his problems, but marriage would mean letting another woman into his life. The acceptance of that was a bitter pill to swallow. But he'd finally concluded that if marriage was inevitable, why not choose an American? They all seemed very eager to offer their hands in exchange for titles. No properly raised Englishwoman would dare to marry him given his dire circumstances. He had learned that lesson with piercing clarity.

Rubbing his hand over the invisible bruise around the vicinity of his heart, he stood, no longer able to deny the nervous energy demanding an outlet. He circled the private room at Montague Club like a caged animal. He *felt* like a caged animal and had every day of his life. Pausing before the mantel, he pulled his timepiece out of his vest pocket. The sleuthhound was late. A fire crackled in the hearth where two large wing-backed chairs sat facing each other, a small table between them. It was bloody hot in here. Too hot for a fire. He gripped the knot of his tie and pulled it loose.

The door finally opened to reveal the investigator, a tall man with a well-kept beard and wearing the exact same sort of black, nondescript costume he'd worn when Devonworth had hired him. His eyes glistened in the light of the gas sconces that framed the door while he surveyed the room as a predator might scope a clearing before entering.

Deeming it safe, he said, "Milord." He spoke with a slight East End accent, though his vowels were clipped, and he gave an abbreviated bow that was barely more than a tip of his head as he closed the door behind him.

"Vining," Devonworth said by way of greeting.

The investigator carried a Gladstone bag. Devonworth had to force himself not to fixate on it too much, even though it very likely contained the keys to his future and that of his entire family.

"Apologies for my tardiness. I assumed that you would prefer me to be discreet, so I came through the back and took the servants' stairwell, careful not to be seen."

That explained why he still wore his winter coat and hat, instead of handing them off to a valet. Devonworth gave a nod of acknowledgment, his shoulders loosening the tiniest bit. "I understand now why Cavell recommended you."

Devonworth had gone directly to the club when he had returned to London from surveying his damaged estate. After he had explained in the broadest terms his need for an investigator, Cavell, the club's manager, had suggested hiring Vining. While Devonworth believed Camille had good intentions with presenting the heiresses, he wanted to make absolutely certain of these women before considering marriage. Secrecy was the very reason Devonworth had held both of his and Vining's meetings here at Montague Club in a private room on the second floor far removed from the gaming and discussions downstairs.

"Would you care for a brandy?"

When the man declined, Devonworth offered him a chair and took the one facing the door. Vining placed his hat and gloves on a table but kept his coat on when he sat. Glancing again at the leather satchel Vining rifled through with brisk efficiency, he said, "I presume your investigation has been fruitful."

"Indeed it has, milord." He took out a thin stack of papers

and set the satchel at his feet. There was the hint of arrogance about his face, as if he were proud of what he had been able to accomplish in a mere sennight. "Shall I begin?"

"Go ahead." Devonworth leaned forward, unwilling to miss a single detail.

"The young women in question are the Dove sisters: Cora, Jenny, and Eliza. Their father was Jeremiah Dove. His family dealt in coal, and his uncle was a state senator for Vermont. He himself was a theater owner of some renown. He operated several theaters across America."

A theater owner. Though the man was from a political family, it wasn't ideal. "Please continue." He waved a hand. "You referred to Dove in the past tense. Has he died?"

Vining nodded and replaced the last sheet of paper at the bottom of the stack. "He passed from heart failure some years back when the girls were young. He was sixty-six years of age. I found a short write-up in the *Times*." He produced an aged clipping from the London newspaper.

Devonworth glanced at it before handing it back. "There's no mention of his family." There were only two lines about his death that seemed to paraphrase a longer obituary, perhaps from an American newspaper.

"No, but that's not uncommon. He was little known here; however, his name is familiar to certain people in the theater community."

"You mention his uncle was in politics. Is the family respectable, then?"

"Well enough. The Doves were from the Albany area, not New York City. Wealthy." Vining made a show of skimming another sheet of paper. "The theaters undoubtably raised eyebrows, but they all seem to be of the opera house variety. He reportedly opened the first opera in San Francisco in California. I have wired New York for more information, but it seems he would have counted the American elite among his friends and investors."

Devonworth closed his eyes as he imagined what his mother might say to a future daughter-in-law who came from a family of theater owners. Dove would be respected by most everyone except for those of Devonworth's class. Still, it was enough respectability for him.

"And their mother?" he asked. It was almost an afterthought. The Americans would be tolerated because of their money, not their pedigree.

"Fanny Dove. She is something of an unknown entity. No maiden name could be found, or marriage record for that matter. She hails from Chicago. When my contact found no record of the marriage in New York, he wired Chicago only to find that there had been a fire some years back and the courthouse had burned, destroying many records from the time they would have married. He did verify that their home in Manhattan was titled to Dove. Witnesses claim they lived together briefly when Dove was alive."

It was disappointing. The mother could be anyone. Still, he wasn't marrying the mother. Any potential questions could be put to rest, if needed.

"What can you tell me of the sisters?"

"The middle sister, Jenny, has trained in opera in Paris for several years. She is a soprano, though she has not begun to tour widely. She lives in Paris still with a friend of the family." Vining produced a sketch from the stack of papers.

"I can assure you physical appearance is unimportant." Beauty tended to complicate matters.

"I promised your lordship that I would be thorough in my investigation. I always keep my word."

He spoke with such determination that Devonworth accepted the sketch from him. The girl was drawn with an expert hand that revealed an exceedingly lovely face and figure. Her features were even and proportionate, with perfectly arched brows and a pretty bow mouth tilted in an easy smile. Written next to the drawing were the words *brown hair and brown eyes*. He'd lied to himself, it seemed. Physical appearance mattered. Devonworth would not spend his life fighting off her lovers, nor would he allow himself to be brought under the spell such looks could cast.

"Will she be in attendance at Stonebridge Cottage?" Only two women had accompanied the dowager duchess to the football match.

"Yes, milord, she's arriving late, but slated to attend," the investigator answered.

"What have you found out about the others?" he asked.

Vining handed over two more drawings. "I solicited drawings of the other sisters, as well, since they are residing with the duchess in Oxfordshire. They recently arrived with their mother. They sold the Dove home in the once fashionable Bond Street area of Manhattan, though the area has declined in recent years as the more affluent families have moved uptown. From interviews with neighbors, my associate there found that the family solicitor recently arranged for the sale of their home."

He stared at the more rudimentary images, hastily drawn in pencil. Beside the one labeled *Cora Dove* were written the words *red hair*. The one labeled *Eliza Dove* had the words *brown hair* written at the bottom. They were adequate likenesses but did nothing to capture the personalities of the women.

He barely contemplated them as his attention was drawn

more to what Vining had found. The more affluent families? "Are they not wealthy?"

The man shrugged. "I have someone delving into their financial situation. According to interviews, both young women were known to aid their mother in providing music lessons to some of the neighborhood children, but as the area changed, one might presume the need for those lessons did as well."

Music lessons? "Why the devil would heiresses be in the business of giving music lessons to neighborhood children?"

"Heiresses, milord?"

Devonworth clamped his mouth shut. He hadn't shared with Vining that he suspected the women were title-hunting. In their initial meeting, he had merely asked the man to investigate the mysterious guests planning to attend the Dowager Duchess of Hereford's house party. Devonworth had been reluctant to say more, not wanting news of their arrival to get out. He'd been told Vining could be trusted, but one could never be too careful when talking about fortunes to be had. There was certainly no fortune to be found in England that the Americans weren't bringing with them. Or were they even, in fact, bringing a fortune? What game were they playing?

"Given their friendship with Her Grace, and her origin, I naturally presumed that they were . . . similarly endowed," he explained carefully. The duchess couldn't be planning to introduce them to Society without proper funds. It would be an embarrassment of epic proportions.

Vining gave a nod of understanding. "One could presume that the girls' mother has found herself in dire straits since her husband's death, what with the selling of their home. I'm told the brownstone had fallen into a state of near disrepair."

That did not sound promising. "Then why come to London now?"

"I cannot say for certain and can only offer speculation."

"Then please speculate." Devonworth was running out of patience.

He hadn't wanted to marry, but it had been a timely choice considering his dire financial situation. Now that the choice might be snatched from him, he was very much annoyed.

"My contact was able to ascertain that a"—Vining paused to check his notes—"Mr. Charles Hathaway has served as a protector of the family . . . a godfather for the children, if you will. Hathaway is from the well-known Manhattan Hathaways."

The Hathaways were one of the founding families of New York, having owned real estate there for centuries. Their reputation was alongside that of the Astors with their name showing up in the newspapers from time to time, usually due to financial endeavors but sometimes the odd scandal.

Protector was a loaded word. It might mean that as a friend of Dove he had taken it upon himself to see to the little family's welfare. It might mean more. "Does Hathaway have anything to do with the women coming to England?"

"'Tis certainly possible, milord. My contact found that he has booked passage on a steamer bound for Liverpool and will arrive in April. One can presume he intends to come to London, but I haven't yet found accommodations arranged for him here."

"But the sale of their house . . . would it be enough to finance hefty dowries?"

Vining shifted. "Not likely, milord."

He shot to his feet, his fingers sliding through his hair in a bid to tamp down the nervous energy threatening to consume him. "Are you saying they do not possess wealth?"

"I wouldn't know, but if I have more time, I can determine that. My associate is looking into their private accounts but hasn't yet found anything. All we know is that they sailed first-class in two adjoining staterooms on the *Lady Amelia*. I interviewed a maid who served in first class. I am told they were friendly but kept to themselves. Their clothing was modest but well-kept. They were agreeable."

"Agreeable but possibly poor," he said through the fingers that now covered his mouth as he stared into the flames.

The sleuth shifted, cleared his throat, and then shifted again.

"Yes, Vining?" It was clear the man was fighting not to talk.

"I believe there is more here than we yet know. Something tells me there is more to the Hathaway connection. I am known for my sense of people."

"Are you? What is your sense of me, Vining?"

The man's lips quirked, and he took hold of the leather bag, placing the stack of papers on the table between them. "With respect, I was not paid to investigate your lordship."

Devonworth smiled. "Are there copies of these?" He indicated the stack of papers.

"No, milord, I never leave a trail."

Satisfied, Devonworth nodded. "Good evening, Vining. Continue your investigation, quietly, of course, and contact me if you have any further information."

"Very well, milord."

The moment the door closed, Devonworth scooped up the sheets and fed them into the fire, one after the other. The sketches he folded and put in his pocket. He would go to Stonebridge Cottage and find out from the sisters and their mother how exactly they intended to fund their dowries.

If they could adequately explain, then he would offer for one of them. It was far superior to the alternatives, which were to marry a cousin or live a life of genteel poverty with the shame and embarrassment that accompanied that sort of life. That didn't even account for what would happen to Harry.

THREE

THE NEXT EVENING, DEVONWORTH ARRIVED AT Heathercote, the family seat of the Duke of Strathmore. Devonworth was there to see the duke's brother and his close friend, Lord David Felding. Caffrey, the butler, had taken his coat and hat and cordially asked him to wait in the drawing room, but Devonworth didn't have time for that.

"Where is he?" he asked.

Not that he didn't have a guess. All of London was wagering on the activity in which his friend was currently engaged. He'd been told a bet had been entered in the ledger at White's.

The butler actually flushed. "My lord, if you will but wait, I can get him."

Devonworth sighed and charged upstairs. Caffrey rarely blushed, so it could only mean his master was occupied with her. He should have known. That damned woman and David's reprobate tendencies were going to get him in trouble.

"I will find him. Thank you, Caffrey." He didn't pause to hear if the man replied as he took the stairs two at a time.

He had met David back in their schoolboy days and had spent countless summers and holidays roaming the vast estate. He knew every room as if it were his own home. He also knew that his friend had disappeared from London and would likely be found entertaining the wife of a man in the Prussian ambassador's entourage who had gone missing around the same time.

The stairs led to a lavish but tasteful landing on the first floor with statuary set into built-in nooks framed by Ionic pilasters. Gaslight sconces flickered with subdued light that made the Greek gods appear particularly menacing, or perhaps that was Devonworth's mood.

The door to David's suite loomed before him at the end of the corridor. Devonworth managed to keep his anger in check as his strides ate up the distance. Knocking briskly on the door, he said, "David, I need to talk to you." He waited precisely five seconds for a response before he pounded again. "David!" His knuckles smarted from the impact. Five seconds passed. "Damn you, come out now or I will come in there."

He reached to take hold of the doorknob, but a muffled sound from within checked his hand. Footsteps followed by curses that gradually got louder came from inside the room before the door opened to reveal his friend, bedraggled and in need of a shave. He wore a hastily donned dressing gown, and his dark hair was sticking up in all directions. His normally tanned skin had a bit of a sallowness to it.

"Fucking hell, man," David said, glaring at him through slitted eyes. "What?"

"I'd like a word." It was too dark to see anything in the room beyond vague, furniture-shaped shadows. A rustling sound came from farther in the suite, and a cloyingly sweet perfume wafted out into the corridor. He didn't have to ask to know the missing woman was in there. "Downstairs in the study. I'll have Caffrey send supper in while we talk."

David stared at him as if he'd lost his mind.

"You look like you haven't eaten," Devonworth continued. The alcoholic vapors were practically leaching off him. "A quarter hour, say?"

Devonworth walked away while David stared after him. By the time he reached the stairs, the door had slammed behind him. Devonworth should feel badly for interrupting them, but the truth was that simply laying eyes on his friend had made him feel better. The idea of marrying one of the Americans had rattled him more than he wanted to admit. He kept second-guessing the decision, which was a rare occurrence for him. Once he made up his mind on something, he always followed through with it and rarely ruminated over it.

But this was different. This felt more profound. That was the problem. He was typically able to remove his emotions from the equation and make decisions guided by logic and reason. Yet this situation involved a wife and probably children in the future. The near future. There would be no turning back from this. His entire life would change, and he was having trouble grappling with that. He'd already made the wrong choice with a woman once; he didn't trust himself not to do it again.

After relaying the request for supper trays, Devonworth settled himself in the study with a scotch. The fire was starting to blaze cheerfully when David swaggered into the room like a petulant child. The dressing gown he wore was buttoned tight. He'd donned trousers and slippers, and his hair had been combed. He wore the forlorn expression of someone who found himself greatly put-upon.

"That was faster than expected," Devonworth said, tipping

the cut-crystal glass to him. He'd half expected to return to the suite's door at least once.

David glared at him as he poured his own scotch and then slouched into the chair across from him. The fire in his eyes didn't diminish as he took a drink and rolled it around his mouth before swallowing. Finally, he leaned forward and rested his elbows on his knees, the glass held loosely between them. "Why in bloody hell are you here?"

"I'm getting married." He said it with the cool assurance that he was nowhere near feeling.

David stared at him. The words took a moment to penetrate the hedonistic fog he was laboring under. When they finally did, he said, "Fuck off."

Devonworth wished he were joking. "It has been brought to my attention that perhaps a wife is in order."

David laughed. "A wife?"

Devonworth shifted. "A wife. We all knew it was bound to happen one day."

"It doesn't have to." David sat back in his seat. "You could leave it all for Harry to figure out." There was the teeniest bit of resentment in his voice.

David's older brother, the Duke of Strathmore, was a confirmed bachelor who had on numerous occasions let it be known that he intended never to marry so that the dukedom would pass to David. This was gradually accepted because Strathmore lived and traveled with his close friend, Christopher Warwick, and most suspected the relationship was much more than friendship. Strathmore had declared David his heir, and eventually, families had stopped pushing their daughters at him and had turned to the younger brother. This was the main reason David also eschewed the London Season and preferred married women. He knew he had to marry but would take his time in doing so. Devonworth had felt the same, but it seemed his time had come to an end.

After explaining the situation with Harry, he said, "I cannot see any other way forward than marriage. The estate is insolvent, and Harry is an idiot. I love him dearly, but he has to be brought to heel."

David was too quiet, his face a mask of concern. "Strathmore could loan you—"

"No. I won't take another loan. God knows I couldn't pay it back before I'm dead. I won't leave my children with such debt."

Caffrey entered the room with a footman trailing behind him. They each carried a tray laden with what looked to be pheasant, roasted potatoes, and brussels sprouts, with compote of fruit and vanilla cream. The room fell quiet as they laid out the supper on the table with surgical precision, complete with linen and a cabernet. Devonworth's stomach growled, reminding him that he hadn't eaten since midday.

"Will there be anything else, my lord?" Caffrey asked as he poured them each a glass of wine.

When David didn't answer, Devonworth said, "Please send a tray up to . . ." He didn't know how David had introduced the woman to the servants. "To Lord David's guest."

The butler waited a full second for David to intervene, and when he merely took another sip of his scotch, he said, "Very well, my lord," and gave an efficient bow.

"Thank you, Caffrey." After the door closed behind the servants, Devonworth asked, "You have been feeding her, haven't you?"

"Of course." David had the gall to appear offended at the suggestion, until he thought about it. "I assume so. I'm very nearly certain there was food yesterday. Caffrey is good about that sort of thing."

Devonworth took up a knife and fork. Everything smelled delicious. "It sounds as if you've gone beyond vodka. Not opium?"

They had tried the stuff in their youth and, aside from a couple of weeks that had been completely wiped from Devonworth's memory, had come out unscathed.

"God, no. Makes me nauseated to even think of it." David perused the selection of food. He popped a sliver of potato into his mouth. "She brought along a bottle of Vin Mariani. We fucked for eight hours straight, and that's the last thing I remember until you knocked on the door."

"Christ. *Eight hours?* You exaggerate." The drink was a concoction of coca leaves soaked in wine and touted for its ability to increase stamina in all things. Scholars used it to further their concentration in their studies. The pope swore that it brought him closer to God in prayer. Devonworth had tried it once but hadn't appreciated the nervous energy it caused.

"I wish it were an exaggeration. My bollocks have yet to recover."

"That's more detail than I needed."

"Then don't ask questions." David smirked. "Tell me more about this wife. Do you have someone in mind or is this a more general statement?"

An image of the redhead came to mind.

"Camille, Dowager Duchess of Hereford, is hosting Americans at her country home. Young women. They are sisters looking for husbands. One assumes they are heiresses." Though, after talking with Vining, he worried that all was not as it seemed with them.

David laughed. "Ah yes, the young women from New York." He rose and walked to a cabinet behind the desk.

Opening one of the small drawers, he pulled out a thick piece of creamy parchment that looked suspiciously like the one in Devonworth's desk.

"You received an invitation, as well?" Devonworth asked.

"Yes, but I hadn't planned to go, obviously. Isn't it this week?" David glanced down at the date written in Camille's hand.

"Yes." Apprehension drove him to his feet and to the scotch. "I've made up my mind to go, but . . ."

"But you don't really want a wife?"

"I don't want . . ." He took a drink and savored how the liquor burned across his tongue. Somewhere in the back of his mind, he understood that he'd been drinking too much of the stuff lately, but he liked the way the burn and the accompanying numbness took his mind off things, however brief the respite. "I don't want to wed a stranger," he admitted.

There was a brief quiet, heavy with the memory of his past. "Perhaps a stranger is best. Strangers rarely hurt us." David's tone was thick with meaning.

Devonworth managed not to wince. He had tried everything to deny that Sofia was at least partially responsible for how he was feeling. Whenever the idea of a wife had crossed his thoughts, she had been that woman. Though that had been before she had married someone else.

"You're right." He was surprised at how resolute he sounded. A lifetime spent avoiding the traps that came along with his title and he'd managed to fall into the biggest one. Still, he bolstered the thread of steel in his voice until even he believed it when he said, "It will be a transactional marriage. Who better than a stranger to carry out such an arrangement with?"

"Precisely," David agreed.

But even that wasn't the entire truth. Devonworth didn't want to marry a stranger, because even a stranger would eventually become someone he knew. Someone he might potentially grow to care about. It was inevitable in such an intimate relationship. He'd chosen Sofia and been utterly wrong about her. He didn't want to be wrong again.

"I'd like it if you would go with me," he said.

"You want *me* to go to a party filled with husband hunters?"

The image that conjured of David surrounded by women intent on forcibly dragging him to the altar made Devonworth choke on scotch as he laughed. "You don't have to marry one of them. You'll go for moral support and to make certain I choose wisely."

His friend shifted uncomfortably. "How many are there?"

"Three."

"That's a good number. There's bound to be an acceptable one."

"So you'll come?"

"I'll come," David said, and Devonworth relaxed immediately. "We simply need to find out how much they are offering. Titles don't come cheap these days. We've all learned from Churchill's debacle." Lord Randolph Churchill had married an American heiress a handful of years earlier and was still in debt.

Devonworth nodded. "Assuming their funds are adequate, my plan is to marry the one named Cora. She isn't quite a complete stranger. I met her once."

"Really?"

"I have reason to believe she was at the football match." He relayed the tale. David was a teammate and had played in the game.

"Intriguing. I faintly remember her. She was pretty in a very proper sort of way."

"Yes." Not that her looks mattered to him in the least.

"Strathmore will probably want to come, as well."

"Your brother will want to go to a house party?"

"No, but he'll want to see you betrothed to someone who meets with his approval." When Devonworth simply stared at him in shock, David rolled his eyes. "You know you're like a son to him. He won't stand for you to be married poorly."

He hadn't known that. Strathmore's manner was unreadable at best. It was why most of Parliament was terrified of him. "Fine, we'll go up at the end of the week." The idea of spending an entire week at the gathering was abhorrent, but he could manage one evening.

FOUR

STONEBRIDGE COTTAGE WAS A BEAUTIFUL AND charming estate nestled among the picturesque hills of Oxfordshire. Although it seemed incredibly unfair to refer to it as a mere cottage. Cora had spent the winter back at home in New York imagining a quaint limestone house with a thatched roof and a cozy fireplace. While the home did boast a stone facade, the roof was steeply gabled and consisted of four floors if one counted the cellar. The only concession to its cottage descriptor was the climbing ivy that obscured much of the stonework. It was like something out of a storybook; one of the darker fairy tales. Beautiful and serene but meant to bear witness to all sorts of unfortunate misdeeds. The house party itself might not qualify as one of those offenses, but surely any marriage that came of it would.

On the first day of the gathering, Cora had privately acknowledged that the actual marrying of a noble wasn't as neat and tidy as she had originally made it out to be. She had been struck by the plethora of gray hair and balding spots among the candidates. Cora had known that many of them were older. She had seen most of them in person over the past couple of weeks, but that wasn't quite the same as seeing them all together.

By the last night, she was forced to admit that she didn't particularly want to marry any one of them. The irony of that was she had planned for a very benign and decidedly not happy ending. She had known that she would marry a man she hardly knew and there would be no romance or tender feelings. The entire plan was written down in her journal. She had even used black ink to more formally convey her sentiments on the matter. She had been resolved and unwavering. But that had been when the plan was on paper and not playing out in front of her like a Shakespearean tragedy.

Tonight was the last night, and Camille had thrown a proper country soiree to end the festivities. Several of the surrounding gentry families had been invited to help fill up the dance floor. A lively tune drifted out to where she stood on the terrace with Sir Barnaby Twistleton. She could quote the information she had gathered on him from memory. Thirty-eight years old. Never married. Parents deceased. Receding hairline and questionable teeth due to an unfortunate tobacco habit. An avid fisherman who spent his days, well, fishing, meant frequent travel through the British Isles from one loch or river to another.

He was actually near the top of her list, because he would be gone for long stretches of the year, and he seemed to have a gentle disposition. What more could one want in a husband? She should be thrilled that he had arranged it so that he led her out here directly after their dance. She should be elated that he looked at her in the same way Eliza had looked upon that gutter cat they had saved when they were children.

But when he opened his mouth—she sensed a proposal coming—her stomach churned so fiercely she was certain she would be sick in the bushes.

"Miss Dove, I am aware that we were instructed to send offers to your mother after the gathering, and I agree that is the right and proper thing."

Oh, dear God, he *was* proposing!

He continued in a halting voice, nervous and uncertain. "I wouldn't conceive of offending you or impugning your dignity, but I simply could not wait. I want you as my bride, and I wanted to tell you that in person."

"I . . ." She couldn't manage to make any other sound. The chilly evening wind blew threads of hair tickling against her cheeks.

"Miss Dove?" At her continued silence, he said, "Dear me, I've shocked you."

Cora had set this plan in motion months ago, and it was too far gone now to turn things back to how they had been. They couldn't go back to New York. Their home was gone, sold for the land under it, which meant it had probably been demolished. Mr. Hathaway wouldn't be happy to see them return anyway. She would lose her inheritance. Marriage was the only way out of this tangle.

Say yes. Just accept now and be done with this.

She opened her mouth to do just that—after all, it didn't really matter which of the suitors she accepted; she would acquire a divorce, or at the very least live apart from him. However, her gaze caught on the spittle that always seemed to settle at the corner of his mouth. She would only have to stare at it for two years, three at most. Same for the faint odor of mold combined with sweat that seemed to follow him.

"Sir Barnaby—"

She couldn't do it. Her lungs felt empty, as if she couldn't get enough air, yet breathing in only made her feel lightheaded.

"Miss Dove?" His nasally voice, already high, rose a little further as he sensed her panic. He reached for her, hands fluttering uselessly, and glanced inside, looking for help.

Her eyes followed his. Another polka had started, and Eliza danced by in the arms of Viscount Mainwaring. He was one of the younger suitors at twenty-eight. They had observed him in Hyde Park and determined that he seemed a bit snooty, but beggars couldn't afford to be too selective. He had been polite if a bit cool, but his preference for Eliza was obvious. Cora was nearly certain he would offer for her sister.

She couldn't send Eliza to her fate alone. Her mind made up, Cora said, "Sir Barnaby, I wi—"

But a commotion cut her off short. The heads of every person on the dance floor in her line of vision swiveled toward the entrance. Several couples collided in their zeal to see who had walked into their midst. The ones who hadn't been aware of whatever was happening at the entry noticed *that*, and then they, too, stumbled in their steps. The musicians, who had kept playing, ended the song on a plaintive note.

From her vantage point on the terrace, Cora couldn't see who had come in. It was as if royalty had deigned to pay a visit to their little party.

"Who is it?" She immediately thought of Lord Devonworth, and butterflies took flight in her stomach. It couldn't be him.

"I do not know," answered Sir Barnaby. "Perhaps the duke has come. He lives up the road a piece, you know."

"Duke?" There was no duke invited, but from what she had gathered, dukes could come and go as they pleased.

"The Duke of Strathmore," he said, as if she should know who he meant.

Her mind was swimming with all the names she had memorized, so it took her a few beats to pull that one to the surface. Lord David Felding had been invited but had not sent any sort of acknowledgment. He was the younger brother and presumptive heir to the Duke of Strathmore.

Before she could comment, Sir Barnaby ushered her inside. Several well-dressed men stood at the entrance. One of them was Lord Devonworth. His hair wasn't wet and curled from the rain and his own sweat. He wasn't wearing shirtsleeves that were wet and clinging to his shoulders. Yet, he was just as handsome and alluring as he had been that day on the football field. The cut of his coat emphasized his strong shoulders and the trimness of his waist. His blond hair was long enough to curl against his collar, approaching wild while staying on this side of refined. Even from across the room she noticed the distinctive lines of his profile, and her stomach swooped.

His gaze traversed the room, moving from one couple to the next and then sliding over the women who had gathered in the seating area along the far wall. Her skin prickled with anticipation. He was looking for her. She just knew it. Finally, he found her inside the terrace doors, and his gaze settled on hers. Their eyes locked and she couldn't breathe.

Was this stranger the man she was meant to marry? Why else would he bother to put in an appearance if that wasn't his intention?

"It *is* the duke," Sir Barnaby whispered. "He's come."

"The duke?" She had already forgotten that Lord Devonworth had arrived with others.

Sir Barnaby nodded, or at least she thought he did. She was having trouble looking away from Lord Devonworth.

"There," he added. "Her Grace is greeting him."

A tall, handsome man in his mid to late forties stood next to Lord Devonworth. He had dark hair with narrow strands of silver streaked through it and deep-set eyes that seemed to take in everything at once. He looked over the room as if everyone here was one of his subjects and he found them all distinctly unamusing.

Camille approached them, welcoming the new guests. Mr. Thorne, her fiancé, was at her side. He had just arrived from Paris earlier in the day. They were the only two people in the room who didn't seem unnerved by the arrival of a duke.

This seemed to break the spell. The room became animated again as women raised their fans to whisper to one another and people shuffled apprehensively. Before she even knew what she was doing, she left Sir Barnaby and was walking across the room, not even bothering to skirt the dance floor. Not that anyone noticed, because everyone was too caught up in staring at the newcomers. Lord Devonworth watched her the entire time, his eyes appraising her. He didn't look away until she came to a stop before the group and Camille turned to her.

Unfortunately, Fanny had roused from her stupor and arrived at exactly the same moment. Etiquette dictated that Camille introduce Cora's mother to the duke first. The older man shifted to acknowledge the woman who thrust out her hand for him to bow over. Whether he had actually intended the gesture or not, he was left with no choice but to take it.

"Good evening, Mrs. Dove," the duke said. "Lovely to make your acquaintance." The vowels were clipped and the tone crisp in the posh accent she had heard spoken in London. Most of the countryside gentry and even Mr. Thorne, who lived in London, had a slightly more relaxed manner of speaking.

Fanny fell into a deep curtsy. It was obvious she was smitten with him by the flush of her cheeks and the way she couldn't seem to look away from him. "Lovely to make your acquaintance as well, my lor—erm—Your Grace. I am absolutely delighted that you have come to meet my daughters."

As greetings went, it was fine, but it was the way she delivered the last line that had Cora's cheeks burning. She had mimicked his accent so perfectly that the man was momentarily startled out of his aloofness. His eyes widened and he looked at her as if he couldn't decide if she had a bolt loose or if she was mocking him.

Camille laughed and Cora managed to gently nudge her mother in the ribs. Whenever she met a person with a new accent, she would often copy it back to them. This had been embarrassing her children for all their lives. Cora honestly didn't think Fanny even knew she was doing it most of the time. Perhaps it was the actress lurking in her soul.

"Well done, Fanny," Camille said. To the duke, she added, "You'll find that Mrs. Dove has a brilliant grasp of accents. She spoke with a perfect Scot's brogue yesterday after only a few words exchanged with the head groomsman."

"Indeed." The duke's tone left the implications of that word and his thoughts up to interpretation. Cora rather thought it wasn't favorable.

The corner of Lord Devonworth's mouth quirked upward. Cora was struck again by how handsome he was. His hair shone gold beneath the gas lamps, and his features were well drawn, distinct and strong, as if an artist had taken extra time with each one. His lashes were long and a light brown color, the same color as his brows. His lips were perfectly sculpted with two defined arches at the top over a soft bottom lip.

He must have noticed her scrutiny, because his eyes held

hers when she managed to drag her gaze upward. They were darker green tonight, like liquid emeralds. A flicker of heat came to life in her belly, and she struggled to catch her breath again.

"Strathmore, please allow me to introduce you to Mrs. Dove's daughters. This is Miss Cora Dove," Camille said.

Cora almost missed her cue, but she managed to curtsy as Camille had taught her.

"Miss Jenny Dove," Camille continued.

Jenny curtsied beautifully. Her smile was a perfect bow as she drifted downward, her ruby skirts floating out around her feet. She was the spitting image of their mother with her chestnut hair, porcelain skin, and voluptuous figure. Her face had been created to grace the portraiture of the great hall of some ancient estate. "Good evening, Your Grace."

Cora hadn't thought that Devonworth would come, so the possibility hadn't occurred to her, but now that he was here, she realized that it was possible he might forget about her in favor of Jenny. Men usually preferred her.

"And Miss Eliza Dove."

Eliza curtsied prettily. At nineteen, she was the youngest of them, and her wide brown eyes were betraying her youth at the moment.

After the duke acknowledged them, Camille took care of the other introductions. Standing on the duke's left was his friend the Honorable Christopher Warwick. Lord Devonworth stood on his right, while the duke's younger brother, Lord David, stood slightly behind the group but came forward when introduced. Lord David appeared quite a bit younger than his brother. Thirty at best. He had similar features but seemed to look out at the world through a veil of wariness and skepticism, if the slight curl of his mouth could be believed.

There was a glint of mischief in Lord Devonworth's eyes as he said, "I'm almost certain we've met before, Miss Dove."

She smiled, unreasonably delighted that he would tease her. "Have we? There have been so many introductions since we've arrived in England, I can't recall."

Lord David snickered and Lord Devonworth almost grinned. She was certain she saw his lips quirk. His gaze was warm on her face before he looked away, directing his next comments to Camille and Mr. Thorne. "Please forgive my tardiness. I wasn't certain I would be able to attend."

"No apology necessary, Devonworth. I know the timing is difficult with Parliament in session. I am happy you could join us," Camille said.

"Come, Strathmore, have a drink." Mr. Thorne waved to a footman who hurried over with a tray of fresh champagne.

The men moved to accept the glasses offered to them, except for Devonworth. "Thank you, Thorne, but I would like to dance first." Holding out his arm to Cora, he asked, "Will you join me, Miss Dove?"

She nodded dumbly, suddenly unable to form a coherent word. She really had expected him to turn his attention to Jenny. Cora glanced at her sister, only to have Jenny smile and nod at her in encouragement as she allowed Lord Devonworth to lead her onto the dance floor. Behind them, Lord David said, "Miss Jenny, you are enchanting."

The music hadn't resumed, but when they reached the middle of the floor, Lord Devonworth raised his hand and the opening strains of a waltz filled the air.

FIVE

DEVONWORTH DREW THE WOMAN WHO WOULD BE his wife into his arms. Couples shuffled into place around them, confusion plainly written on their faces. *Why was he here?* Devonworth made certain to keep his expression one of polite interest. Once they were betrothed, rumors of this night would spread like a midnight fire through the city. He wanted the story to be that the young couple was happy and affectionate.

With that in mind, he kept his attention focused on Miss Dove as they began to dance. Her hair appeared more russet and less red in the gaslight than it had outdoors. Her skin was as pale as he remembered, with a very light sprinkling of freckles dusted across her nose and cheeks. Her eyes were blue-gray and wide, her nose was straight if a bit pronounced at the bridge, and she had a perfect flower bud mouth. All told, she was pretty if not conventionally beautiful. It would be no hardship to call her wife.

He relaxed a little at that. The days since their first meeting had left him questioning if she was as he remembered her. She was, thankfully, complete with spark. It was only then that he noticed she was holding herself a bit stiff. It made her movements wooden and less fluid. Without breaking stride, he reached over and closed her fingers down over his hand. They had been standing up like tiny soldiers at attention.

"You're not a dancer, Miss Dove?" he asked, replacing his hand on her back.

Her eyes widened almost imperceptibly before a tiny furrow appeared between her brows. "Not usually, no. Is it obvious?"

"I only mention it because you seem tense." He could almost see her counting the steps in her head.

"Forgive me. Perhaps I'm merely hoping you don't tackle me to the ground this time."

A laugh escaped him before he could catch it. Several pairs of eyes turned toward them. "You *do* remember me."

She glanced up from their feet, her eyes smiling. "I had given up that you would come."

So she was happy to see him. "I suppose I should ask forgiveness. I startled you and then whisked you away to dance."

She was quiet for a moment as they took a turn around the floor. He looked away only briefly to see her sister Jenny watching them as David tried in vain to talk to her. He couldn't help but smile. Women usually fell over one another to talk to David. By the looks of things, she was not at all impressed that David's brother was a duke. For that matter, the Miss Dove in his arms didn't seem entirely impressed by his own title.

He glanced back at her, looking beyond the facade she presented. There was an intelligence in her eyes that he quite liked, but there was something fiery burning in their depths.

"You knew who I was . . . that day at the football match?" she asked.

"I assumed, yes. There aren't that many Yanks roaming the countryside, despite what the papers would have you believe about an American invasion of heiresses."

She smiled at that. Good, let people see that they genuinely liked each other, whether or not that turned out to be true.

"I assume you knew my identity?" he asked.

She nodded. "Not at first, but after. Camille thought it best to see as many of you as possible before the actual party. She thought we would get a better idea of your character."

"Ah, a scientific exploration; to see us in our natural habitat is to see us as we really are."

She laughed softly. "Something like that."

"Well, I am sorry to tell you, but the football pitch is not my natural habitat."

"No?"

"No. I enjoy the game and have played it since my days in school, but it's not who I am. I should arrange for you to come see me in Parliament. It will give you a better idea of my character if you are looking to make your decision based on that alone."

She stiffened, not enough to draw attention but enough to let him know that he had revealed his hand. "What decision would that be?" she finally asked.

He gave her a rueful grin. "The decision we all know you are here to make, Miss Dove."

"Am I mistaken, or should there be a question asked before a decision can be made?" she asked.

"Isn't the question a foregone conclusion?"

"Not at all. What if you don't like what you see?"

He laughed. "You forget, I already saw you once. I wouldn't be here if I didn't like what I see."

She blushed red to the roots of her hair. It wasn't fashionable in the least, but he found himself oddly fascinated. He liked the honesty and lack of contrivance it conveyed.

After a moment, she said, "But you haven't heard the terms."

"True enough, but I figure you wouldn't be here title-hunting if you weren't in possession of a reasonable exchange." As he waited for the pointed tip of that pronouncement to land, he held his breath.

She processed it slowly, her gaze searching his face. He didn't know what she hoped to find there, but finally, she gave a brief nod. "You're correct, my lord. I think you'll be pleased."

"Good." He tried to sound as unaffected as usual. He kept the expression of benign interest on his face, but his tongue felt thick and he couldn't have spoken another word. It wasn't precisely a marriage proposal but it was enough. His fingers pressed into the silk of her gown toward the warmth of her body beneath. This woman would be his wife. No matter how many times the thought repeated itself in his head, he couldn't hold on to it. It was unfathomable, but true.

Barring no unforeseen complications, obviously.

"Could we talk later tonight . . . privately about the matter?" he asked.

"Of course." Her chin lifted a notch in confidence.

He nodded, taking comfort in her assurance. "Good. After the party, then. I'll ask Her Grace to arrange a meeting place."

AFTER THEIR DANCE ENDED, LORD DEVONWORTH went on to dutifully take a turn with both Jenny and Eliza. Cora danced with other gentlemen, but if pressed, she wouldn't have been able to remember which ones. She had been floating in a cloud of what could most accurately be described as euphoria. She had left the Hathaway mansion months ago feeling vaguely despondent and wary of her ability to carry out her plan.

Their dresses and gowns had all been a few years out of fashion. The few social events they were invited to attend in New York were all because of the esteem held for their late stepfather Mr. Dove. These events were inevitably hosted by older matrons who themselves were out of fashion. Any that they might have been invited to because of Mr. Hathaway's influence had long since died away when it had become known that his esteem for her mother had died. To host the mistress of a well-known gentleman was to court intrigue. To host the ex-mistress of a well-known gentleman only brought scorn. As a result, the sisters' social skills were good, but not English ballroom ready.

They had bought new clothes and first-class passage with the sale of their shabby brownstone. Located off Bond Street, it was too close to the Bowery to be fashionable. Most respectable families had left the area years earlier. The roof was on the verge of collapse, which had forced them to close off the top floor several years back when the number of leaks had outpaced their ability to repair them. The expense of first class had hurt, but Cora had reasoned they could not have it known they had traveled second- or third-class. Any hint of scandal could ruin their chances for decent matches, and the Dove sisters came with enough scandal without courting more.

The past week had been less than ideal as the reality of what she was about to do set in. Then the earl arrived and everything seemed possible again. A genuine smile burst out of her as she looked over the ballroom. The women wore gowns in all shades of colors in glossy and fine satins and ruffles. People were chatting and laughing, their discussions ranging from art to family to politics. This might be their world from now on. The world they were meant to inhabit. If they could but cross this last hurdle.

A rustle of fabric interrupted her reverie. Eliza walked up beside her. She wore a satin gown in lilac trimmed with black lace. It was one of the few they'd had made before setting off from New York. Her dark hair was curled and pinned in an elaborate updo that reminded Cora how little they had had the opportunity to dress up over the years. The costume made her look older and more worldly than her nineteen years.

Eliza was beaming as she opened her fan to cover her words before she said, "I can't believe he came."

"Me neither. When Camille never heard back from him, I assumed he wasn't interested."

"He apparently is interested. I'm glad. He's charming and a very good dancer." There was a poignancy in her voice that had Cora looking over at her.

"Do you want him?" Cora was aware that she had spearheaded this entire idea of marriage. Her mother and sisters had seemed to readily agree, but now she wondered if she had pushed them into it without properly considering their feelings on the matter. The decent thing to do would be to give her little sister first choice of suitor. "If you do, I can stand aside."

Eliza smiled again and shook her head. "No, I don't want him. It's obvious he's here for you anyway."

Elation rose inside her again, but she forced herself to stay calm.

"You know I am happy to go along with this scheme of yours," Eliza continued, "but I do not intend to marry a country bumpkin old enough to be my father."

"I promise that won't happen." Cora ran a hand down her sister's back. "Viscount Mainwaring seems taken with you." He had been sulking as she had danced with the earl.

Eliza nodded, but she didn't seem particularly thrilled by the idea. "I think so."

"Are we divvying up the suitors?" Jenny hurried over to them, leaving the arm of Sir Barnaby, who did not appear pleased to lose her company.

Cora avoided the searching look he gave her. He was clearly hoping for an answer to his proposal. Instead, she turned her attention to Jenny, who could easily have any one of the men. She was an undisputed beauty with shining sable hair and a perfectly oval face that gained admirers wherever she went. So far, she hadn't indicated an interest in any one man. Cora found herself hoping she wouldn't choose Devonworth.

Cora shushed her. They weren't that far away from the groups of people around them. "Not now, no."

"At least your footballer came." Jenny grinned. "I'm still so sorry that I missed that particular outing, but he's here and he is every bit as handsome as Eliza claimed."

"He is." He might very well be the most handsome man she had ever seen.

"What is his name again?" Jenny asked. "His real name, not Devonworth."

"Leopold Brendon," Cora answered, her gaze automatically finding him in the crowd where he spoke with one of the local gentry couples. It was well past dark, but the gas lighting gave him a golden hour sunset glow.

"Leopold?" Jenny made a face. "He's much more a Leonidas, don't you think? An ancient Greek king rather than a . . . Wasn't there a Leopold from somewhere?"

She silently agreed. He might have been Apollo come to

life, but it would have been foolish to admit to such fancies aloud. He looked up then, meeting her gaze across the room. A flush climbed up Cora's face. Taking both her sisters by the arm, she hurried them to the other side of a copse of potted palms. "I think he might have proposed."

They both gasped. "You think? You mean you don't know?" Jenny asked.

Cora felt giddy as she explained what had happened between them during their dance. Her eyes found him again through the leaves of the palms. He seemed to be in the midst of a deep discussion. His brows drew together as he listened intently, nodding occasionally before replying. She was struck by how a couple more men joined the group, surrounding him as he talked. They seemed to be listening to him, concerned with whatever it was he had to say. It was obvious he had their respect.

Eliza giggled when she finished the story. Jenny didn't seem quite as pleased. In fact, she said, "You can never trust the handsome ones. He's too handsome to make a good husband."

This wasn't the first time her sister had warned against this, so it was getting tedious. She sighed. "Why don't handsome men make good husbands?"

"You don't want to spend your entire marriage worried about his whereabouts. He'll almost certainly be a philanderer."

She said it so matter-of-factly that Cora's stomach churned. Jenny wasn't usually cruel, but this hit too close to her own insecurities. Cora knew she wasn't a great beauty, but she was happy with what she saw in the mirror. "That's hardly a certainty."

Correctly interpreting how she felt, Jenny leaned in. "It's nothing to do with you. Look." She discreetly pointed across the room opposite where Lord Devonworth stood with the men. Several of the younger women had gathered and were doing what could best be described as gawking in his direction. "They won't stop doing that just because you're married. Most men in a privileged position like his aren't able to turn them down."

"Fortunately, I don't plan to be intimate with him." They both knew her plan to keep their marriage one of convenience only, for as long as she could.

"Just make certain that you keep telling yourself that and don't let yourself get too close to him."

Cora glanced back at him, wondering if she was already too far gone for that. "Well, the alternative is Sir Barnaby."

"Did he offer, too?" Eliza asked.

"On the terrace before Lord Devonworth arrived."

"Between the two of them, the decision is obvious." Eliza leaned forward to whisper. "At least it will be no hardship to consummate your relationship, if you ever change your mind about intimacy."

They all laughed at that, drawing attention to themselves. Fanny floated over carrying a crystal coupe of champagne. "What's so funny, girls?"

Eliza giggled. "Nothing, Mama, we're simply looking over the selection . . . as it were."

Their mother frowned. "Ah yes, I'd rather hoped the men would be younger. The later husband can be staid and boring, but you want your first husband to be young and robust. Like the duke's brother and the earl. Now those two are worth considering."

Fanny privately claimed to have been married and divorced before she met the man whose name they carried, Mr. Dove. She had been a fifteen-year-old struggling actress in Chicago when she had married a handsome young actor. The marriage had only lasted a handful of months before he'd run off and she'd been granted a divorce for desertion. Cora was never sure if it was her mother's upbringing in an orphanage or her time on the stage that had given her such a nontraditional view of marriage. Either way, such views would not be looked upon kindly in British Society.

"*Mother.*" Cora gave her a look that urged discretion. "Not here."

Fanny smiled serenely, but her words were a bit sharper. "Fine, I will continue to play along, but I will not stand by and have my darlings sacrificed like virginal offerings." She patted her on her cheek like she was five years old. "He shall be younger than me or you won't wed."

With that, she hurried away as a new song started. She had been out there for every dance so far and would likely be the last one on the dance floor. She was all energy, and Cora couldn't figure out where she stored it all.

"How long do you think she'll be able to play the role of genteel mother?" Eliza asked.

Cora's stomach twisted with a sickening anxiety. Their mother had agreed that it was best to keep her years as an actress a secret. If someone went looking, they would find the rare mention of her stage name, Fanny Fairchild, but there were no definitive sources tying her to that name. Mr. Dove's extended family believed she came from a well-bred Southern family named Smith that had fallen on hard times and died off long before the Civil War. The few times his relatives had come for short visits, she had played the part flawlessly.

"She knows our futures are at stake. I believe she can play it for as long as necessary."

Even as Cora said it, she didn't quite believe it. Their mother and their illegitimacy were the loose threads in this tightly woven tapestry. Certainly, her own history of writing for a forward-thinking feminist publication would never come up. She'd used a pseudonym.

SIX

CORA HADN'T EVER IMAGINED HERSELF BEING IN-volved in a late-night assignation, but here she was creeping down the stairs after midnight to meet Lord Devonworth. *Assignation* might be too strong of a word. It brought to mind lurid images of kisses and fondling, which is not what they would be doing. Although her stomach took a tumble at the memory of his well-formed lips. She probably wouldn't say no to a kiss.

The guests had begun to trickle away as the clock ticked toward midnight. They kept country hours here, so the soiree hadn't gone on nearly as long as Camille had warned Cora the parties in London would last. The locals had left for home while the prospective suitors and the female relatives who had accompanied them returned to their rooms. The men had been given accommodations in the old groundskeeper's cottage, which was another house on the property. It was nearly double the size of the brownstone Cora and her family had sold in New York, so she didn't pity them. To keep up an appearance of respectability, the women were the only ones who stayed overnight in the main house. Something told her that the "no men in the house" rule wouldn't apply to Mr. Thorne. He had hardly left Camille's side all night.

Cora paused at the bottom of the stairs to make certain that the main floor was at rest for the night. The longcase clock ticked into the silence. It was a quarter past one o'clock. He might already be waiting for her. Her stomach swirled in anticipation as she took quiet steps to the back of the house where Camille had told her they were meeting. The parlor was a scarcely used room that never saw company. It was an ode to comfort with blankets and cushions tossed casually on overstuffed furniture, the interior Cora had imagined a cottage would possess. They had used it often in the days leading up to the party while Camille prepared them with all sorts of knowledge about the British upper class, but the room had sat a bit fallow during the formality of the house party.

As Cora approached the room, a soft giggle broke the silence of the night. It was followed by a deeper masculine laugh and then the foreign but unmistakable sound of two mouths coming together. The door was cracked open enough that Cora could see Camille perched on Mr. Thorne's knee, his hand tenderly cradling her jaw. A fierce longing strong enough to hold her in place took hold of Cora as she stared at that touch.

What would it mean to be married to a man in an arrangement that was more business than personal? What if a man never looked at her with affection in his eyes? What if he didn't even like her very much? What if he refused to dissolve their arrangement and she never felt the tenderness of someone who loved her?

Standing in that hallway, she felt more alone than she ever

had in her life. That included showing up at Mr. Hathaway's house unannounced and unwanted. What had once seemed to be a very sure path was now crumbling beneath her feet.

"Cora!" Camille scrambled from Mr. Thorne's lap as she came to her feet. Mr. Thorne stood at a more leisurely pace, his expression reflecting amusement as he put his arm around his fiancée. "My apologies," she said.

"It's my fault," Mr. Thorne added. "I distracted her."

"I should apologize. I didn't mean to lurk. I only . . ." Cora had only been in the midst of an existential crisis, a common enough occurrence for her this past year.

"You did nothing wrong. We were waiting for you." Using the mirror on the wall near the door, Camille arranged her nearly perfect blond curls. She gave Mr. Thorne's reflection a harsh look that only made his eyes grow warmer with affection. "Come in, come in," she urged once she noticed Cora hesitating at the threshold.

Cora nodded and forced a smile. It wasn't as if she believed in lasting love anyway. Marrying for business was so much more reasonable. She told herself there was no reason to be envious of their relationship.

"The letter from Mr. Hathaway," she said, holding up the proof of funds that Mr. Hathaway had written out for her. She tried not to think about how important the document was to the future of this betrothal. If she didn't think about how it represented her only value to Lord Devonworth, then she wouldn't feel melancholy about it.

Camille took her hand and led her farther into the room. "I can't find the words to express how happy I am that Devonworth came tonight and has asked to speak with you privately. I can only assume this will lead to good news. He will be perfect for you."

"I hope so. He *is* very handsome."

"He is, but more than that, he's not a typical aristocrat. He has shown support for the rights of women and the common man alike. You'll be well suited."

Before she could respond, heavy footfalls came from the corridor and Lord Devonworth appeared at the door. He still wore his evening suit and looked as if he'd stepped off the dance floor. His hair was lightly oiled and swept back from his forehead, emphasizing the strong and aristocratic planes of his face. He was so handsome that her breath hitched.

"Devonworth," Mr. Thorne said as Camille turned to greet him.

After addressing them both, Lord Devonworth looked at Cora. "Miss Dove."

"Lord Devonworth." Cora didn't miss how his eyes gave her a once-over before settling on her face. His expression was warm, so she took that to mean that he liked what he saw. She might not be a great beauty like her mother or Jenny, but she was pleasing enough.

"We'll leave you two alone to talk, but we'll be right next door." Camille took Mr. Thorne's arm and led him to the adjoining room, which was a sort of gaming room with card tables and a chess set. She gave Cora an encouraging smile, leaving the door open a crack so they wouldn't technically be alone.

Camille and Mr. Thorne shouldn't be alone, either, but they were to be married later in the summer and Camille was a widow. He owned the infamous Montague Club in London and was living in Paris temporarily to open a new club in that city. Camille visited him there with her mother in tow, so Cora imagined they were desperate for time alone together.

With their absence, the room became heavy with silence.

She and Lord Devonworth stared at each other, unsure of the next step in this arrangement. Finally, he broke the quiet. "Would you care to sit?" He indicated the sofa.

"Yes, thank you." Her knees inexplicably trembled as she settled herself on one end. She expected him to sit at the other, but he took the adjacent chair instead.

"Thank you for meeting me. I regret that it must be in the thick of night, but we are due back in London tomorrow," he said.

"I understand."

They didn't acknowledge that it was better to speak late at night anyway so that no one would be aware they had met. If he found something to dislike about the terms and changed his mind, then there wouldn't be gossip.

He glanced at the door leading to the corridor, which remained partially open. "Shall we wait for your mother to arrive?"

"My mother isn't coming. It'll just be us."

He frowned and settled down into the chair. She couldn't help but notice how his shoulders stretched across the entire back of the piece of furniture. His wasn't a thick, brute strength, but lean and powerful nonetheless. She should probably spend less time noticing that and more time focusing her attention on their negotiations.

"Why is she not attending?" he asked.

The question threw her off for a moment. Cora had discussed the meeting with her mother earlier, but it hadn't occurred to either of them that Fanny should attend. That was simply how things were in their household. Cora attended to the business at hand, whether it was negotiating with the butcher or selling the family home, and Fanny handled . . . well, whatever held her interest at the moment, whether that be mastering the perfect soufflé or helping one of her theater friends prepare for a role.

A proper debutante would be expected to have her mother present. A sweat broke out on her upper lip. They had already committed a faux pas.

"Um, she had a headache and needed to lie down. I think she might have had too much champagne." Partially true. She *had* drank too much champagne, but when Cora had left them, Fanny had been dancing Eliza around her bedroom as she sang a bawdy tune about a randy fellow on the way to his wedding.

A look of displeasure crossed his face, but it was fleeting. He shifted in his chair and seemed genuinely uncomfortable with talking to her alone. "Perhaps we should postpone. Marriage"—her heart did a funny skip in her chest at that word on his lips, but she forced herself to continue listening—"is an important matter. This discussion has the potential to affect the rest of your life. Your mother should be present."

A part of her was touched by his concern. It was clear that he wanted to make certain she wasn't taken advantage of in this meeting. But she was tired of men—Mr. Hathaway came to mind—who always assumed they knew better about her life than she.

"I agree. Marriage is a very important matter. When will your mother be arriving?"

His eyes widened infinitesimally before the corner of his mouth quirked in that way she was coming to appreciate. "I only meant that the unmarried women of my acquaintance would never attend such a meeting alone."

"Would those young women attend such a meeting at all?" she countered.

"Fair." He shifted again and brought his hand up to stroke

his brow, regarding her thoughtfully as if she were a puzzle he was trying to decipher.

She rushed on so that she didn't give him a chance to turn her away. He was obviously uneasy. As much as she was coming to realize what she was giving up by this marriage arrangement, she stood to lose so much more if it didn't happen. "I admit this must seem strange, and probably unprecedented. You likely have many questions."

"A few. I don't wish to start this discussion with secrets, so I will confess that I had an investigator look into your identity before the house party."

Her blood froze. An investigator could have found any number of things Cora would rather keep from him and, by extension, Society altogether. Her entire little family had thrived *because* of secrets.

When she could finally move again, she turned her attention to the letter in her lap. "What did you find?"

She couldn't meet his gaze, so she slowly and deliberately removed the paper from the envelope and took great pains in smoothing out the lines. He was silent for so long she imagined she could feel his censure singeing the hair on the top of her head.

"I found that your father owned several theaters across America, and he died when you and your sisters were very young. His associate, Charles Hathaway, stepped in as a sort of family protector. What more can you tell me about that arrangement?"

She felt as if she were under some sort of legal examination. She licked the sudden prickling of sweat from her lip and repeated the facts she had practiced her entire life. "Mr. Hathaway and my father were close friends. After his death, Mr. Hathaway oversaw our care and my mother's allowance. Now that we are older, he is determined to help our mother arrange our marriages. In fact, we must find appropriate husbands as a condition of our inheritances." She handed over the proof of funds. "He has very exacting standards on what constitutes an appropriate husband."

He accepted the paper and read it quietly. His eyebrows rose in surprise before he managed to pull them back into line. When he finished, she said, "I hope the amount is sufficient."

He cleared his throat. "It's sufficient."

She had assumed that it would be, but she didn't really know what sort of fortune an earl might require. She felt herself relax into the cushions at her back. "Good."

"Will Hathaway be visiting London to . . ." With his pause, she understood how delicate this entire situation was for him. The money he needed for his estate was there in the letter, but such a fortune was a tenuous thing until it was in his account. "To validate the transfer of funds?"

"Yes, and he has plans to attend any eventual weddings." She would wire him first thing in the morning to make certain, assuming the rest of this discussion went well.

"Tell me about your mother's family. What do I need to know about her?"

She tensed again. She preferred not to explicitly lie to him, but she didn't know how else to explain the situation. The fact that her mother had been an actress would simply not be acceptable, never mind the fact that she had no idea who her family was. "She was born in South Carolina, but her family died when she was a child. Cholera. After that, she was raised by a distant cousin in Chicago. That's where she met my father."

In truth, Fanny didn't know her family at all. Her mother, probably young and unwed, had left her on the steps of a Chicago orphanage as a newborn. There she had been raised until she had run away at fourteen years of age to pursue a stage career. At fifteen, she had married a handsome young actor and divorced him almost as quickly as she had wed him. Then, a few years later, Fanny had met Charles Hathaway when he had gone to Chicago on business. Mr. Dove had introduced them, since he knew Fanny from his ties in the theater business, and he knew Mr. Hathaway from long-standing social connections. She had promptly become Mr. Hathaway's mistress and moved to New York.

Months after arriving in New York, Fanny had given birth to Cora and then Jenny and Eliza in rapid succession. Fanny talked of those years with fondness, as if they'd had some great romance. Cora supposed it had been romantic, since Fanny had allowed herself to fall pregnant so often. Her mother claimed there had even been talk of marriage once his parents could be brought around to the idea. They never approved, and he had married someone else, and Fanny and her children had slowly become weights around his neck.

Their love story had ended unhappily. Cora very much suspected that most great romances did. Eventually, the glamour wore off and everything else intruded. Romantic love wasn't meant to survive in the world. Once it became clear that Mr. Hathaway was not going to wed her, Fanny had insisted that he make some arrangement for her and the children. Eliza had still been an infant when they had moved into their brownstone. Mr. Dove had been a convenient husband. Cora didn't know what sort of arrangement Mr. Dove and Mr. Hathaway had between them to make the man take on the responsibility of their small family. But it hadn't mattered, because he'd died within a year or so. To be honest, Cora wasn't entirely certain that Fanny *had* married Mr. Dove. That might have all been a fabrication.

But, of course, she could mention none of this to Lord Devonworth.

He sat watching her dubiously, and for one fraught moment she was certain he was going to tell her that his investigator had found out the scandalous truth about them. Instead, he cleared his throat again and said, "You have shown me what you will bring to this arrangement and, as is proper with any negotiation, it is only appropriate that I show my cards. My line stretches back to the sixteenth century when Henry VIII granted my ancestor—"

"Oh, I'm certain you are qualified, Lord Devonworth. Camille wouldn't have invited you otherwise. All the suitors are qualified as far as that goes."

He made a sound of acknowledgment in the back of his throat. It was a very deep, very interesting sound that caused a pleasant prickling sensation to move across her scalp. She didn't want to think about that. Her physical attraction to him did not matter.

"Am I in competition, then?" he asked. "Have you another offer?"

"Well, yes, as of now, though they were all told to hold their offers until the end."

He rose abruptly and crossed to the hearth. This information seemed to unsettle him in some way. She realized then that he had thought he might be the only one to offer . . . or at least the only one she would want to accept. He hadn't expected competition. This could be good. He might make concessions he wouldn't have been willing to earlier. Concessions like a separation. Or divorce.

Suddenly, he swung around to face her. "Miss Dove, I know that you don't know me. You don't know any of us, for that matter. But I can promise you that I will treat you with honor and respect. I will do my best to consider your wishes in all things. I don't know you, so I can only assume a title is of the utmost importance to you and your guardian. If that's the case, I have two of them. Our son shall carry the second one at his birth. I don't think those men can offer you that. Any other children we may have can be assured of a good and proper education, a thoughtful and understanding fath—"

"Lord Devonworth!" She rose because she couldn't withstand his earnest expression as he pleaded his case to her. "I think we need to talk further." She moved toward the hearth, but not to look at him. God, she couldn't look at him. She was too aware of Camille and Mr. Thorne in the next room, and what she needed to tell him, she didn't want them to hear. "Please, before you go on, there is something I'd like you to understand."

He stared at her; she could feel his eyes on her as she fumbled with her own fingers. "I had hoped that whatever marriage I make would be in name only. I don't think it's fair to bring children into it."

He frowned. "In name only?"

"Yes, I hoped to secure a separation after a couple of years . . . or . . . or perhaps even a . . . divorce." There, she had said the word out loud for the first time. "Once the dowry has been funded," she hurried to add.

"A divorce?" His face reflected the incomprehension she had expected.

"You think I'm mad."

"No." But the word came too quick. That's exactly what he thought.

"I know that divorce here is complicated, but it's not unheard of. I have read there are a couple hundred divorces a year."

"How do you know that?" he asked, brows furrowed.

"I came across a newspaper story. Obviously, I don't know the particulars or how troublesome they are to coordinate here. I believe it must go through Parliament, which I assume you can arrange if needed. At home, there is a saying, 'Marry in New York, divorce in Newport.'" The quote didn't appear to alleviate his concerns. The trench between his brows only deepened. "The divorce laws in Rhode Island allow for terms such as desertion and incompatibility," she found herself rambling.

"Divorce isn't so simple here. Not among the nobility, at any rate."

"I assumed it wouldn't be." She felt him slipping away, so she forged ahead. "A divorce will allow us to go our separate ways with no entanglements. I know it isn't ideal in your world, or mine, either, honestly, but it does happen. People divorce every day. I had hoped we could come to some sort of arrangement about the dowry. Obviously, you would keep a large portion. Enough to support your family, your estates, or whatever you need the money to accomplish."

He bristled at that. It was crass to discuss money in such terms, but she could see no way around it.

"And you?" he asked after a moment. "What would you keep?"

"I would ask that you invest a portion for me, enough that will earn a respectable annual return. Once we divorce, you will sign that over to me in the settlement. I will retire from public life and live somewhere away from London. Believe me, I have no wish to make any sort of impact on London Society. I will retire to the countryside or somewhere in America, maybe. I don't know yet."

"Not New York where you're from?"

A hint of sadness shadowed her eyes. "No, not New York. I want to support my mother and my sisters if necessary, not spend the income on a lavish lifestyle. Somewhere quiet and stable will be enough for us." She wanted to start her own women's rights publication, a publication that would discuss the obstacles facing women and the unjust laws that fostered those boundaries. It would be modeled on the one she had written for in New York, but he didn't need to know that.

"And for this you want a divorce?"

"At best, yes; a separation if it isn't possible. However, I understand male primogeniture and how important that is to the way you do things here, so I think a divorce is ideal. That way you can remarry and have an heir."

He took in a long, slow breath through his nose as he regarded her with the wariness of a man weighing his future. It was not an unreasonable look, but it gave her pause. What would she do if he said no? She would either have to accept him anyway or settle for Sir Barnaby.

"You put me in a difficult position, Miss Dove. I have been charged with continuing my line. I have to produce the next Earl of Devonworth. If I neglect that duty, it will fall to my brother, Harry, a boy completely unequipped to carry out the duty."

"I'm sorry for that, my lord. Perhaps you will find that a financially healthy estate is worth that risk."

He stared at her a moment longer. "I can promise to consider a divorce, but they can be difficult to obtain, and with my political future to consider . . ."

Her heart leaped at the small concession.

"I will agree to a separation, but only after we've lived together and presented an ideal image of husband and wife for a period of two years. I think that should be sufficient."

She nodded, willing to give him almost anything. "Yes, that is reasonable."

"If a divorce isn't possible, then I will *need* an heir."

Something came to life inside her. The little flame burned deep in her belly, but she ignored it. "I understand."

He breathed out through his nose. "Five years, Miss Dove. It's all the time I can give you."

"Fine. I'll agree to an heir in five years' time if a divorce cannot be arranged." She held out her hand.

He stared at it before finally taking it in his. His palm was warm and his fingers were long but thick. She ignored how pleasant his hand felt in hers. She had a feeling she would be ignoring quite a lot in the next couple of years.

"Does this mean you will be my wife, Miss Dove?"

For the first time that night, all of the tension holding her stiff seemed to drain away.

"Yes, I will marry you, Lord Devonworth."

"Good, then we shall be married immediately after the reading of the banns. That will put us after Easter. You should meet my mother and brother before then, obviously. I'll arrange a dinner."

She took in a deep breath and nodded; words escaped her at the moment. In three weeks, she would be Lady Devonworth.

SEVEN

Several weeks later, the Doves met Devonworth's family on the eve of the wedding. Hathaway and Mainwaring were also in attendance. It was assumed by everyone present that the viscount would offer for the youngest sister, Eliza, that very evening because he had asked to speak with Devonworth and Hathaway privately after dinner. They all simply needed to survive the meal first.

Devonworth was becoming less confident as the night wore on that such a feat was possible. For one, his mother was looking paler and icier with every course. By dessert, he mused that she very well might expire from disappointment right there at the table. She had been relieved when he had announced his marriage and its financial ramifications and had proposed hosting the meal. He would have bet every last penny he stood to gain from the marriage that this would be the last such meal they all shared under her roof.

For one, his mother and Mrs. Dove were polar opposites.

His mother was the very image of a countess. She wore an elegant black gown trimmed in dove-gray satin with a high neck and modest sleeves. Her dark hair streaked with the silver to be expected of someone in their fiftieth year was worn up in a respectable style, each strand held in place by bandoline. Mrs. Dove, on the other hand, wore a burgundy gown trimmed with a darker wine-colored velvet that, while not indecently low-cut, was low enough to raise a brow, leaving her shoulders bare. It worked better for a ballroom than a staid dinner table. Her curled hair had been pinned up to fall in ringlets over one shoulder and betrayed not a shimmer of silver. It was anyone's guess whether this was natural—she was in her early forties—or the effect of dye. One look at his mother's face upon their meeting and Devonworth knew which she believed.

It had only gone downhill from there. Through the course of the meal, Mrs. Dove had spoken in no less than six different accents, most of them intentional, he believed, but a couple of them had seemed to take even her by surprise. Those had been later in the evening after she had finished off an entire bottle of wine on her own. Devonworth found her amusing. It was safe to say his mother did not.

The differences in their families didn't end there. The sisters and their mother were simply more animated and enthusiastic in their conversation. Years of breeding had made it so that his family and others like them dined with the utmost efficiency of movement, and they spoke the same way. He hadn't particularly noticed it before, but watching the sisters throw their heads back to laugh or exclaim at some new information made them seem more alive, as if they were living in the world. His own family, by comparison, seemed to simply exist, and the world operated around them. They didn't immerse themselves in joy. Amusement was displayed by fleeting laughs and smiles that barely creased their faces. Nothing was to be enjoyed or savored to any extreme.

For his part, Harry seemed to have noticed these differences as well. Oh, he pretended to be jaded and older than his twenty-one years, but the way he kept eyeing the family with fascination was plain to anyone who cared to notice. Perhaps it was more than fascination that kept his gaze going back to the younger Dove sisters. Devonworth made a mental note to fund the Continental tour his brother had been begging to take for months. It would keep him out of the way until the sisters were safely married.

"My lord?"

Devonworth was brought back to the present by a footman offering him a selection of chocolates. He shook his head, and the man continued to Miss Dove. His bride's eyes lit up as she accepted a few.

"Do you enjoy chocolate?" he asked in a low voice so as not to disturb Hathaway, who was telling yet another story about his travels.

It was odd to him that he knew almost nothing about her personally but they were meant to be married tomorrow. Many Society marriages were arranged, but the families knew each other, had known each other for decades if not centuries. His peculiar arrangement with Miss Dove was almost medieval. It made him feel protective of her.

She nodded. "It's my favorite." She brought one to her mouth and turned her attention to Hathaway farther down the table.

Devonworth allowed himself a moment to take her in. She wore an appropriate dinner dress of bottle-green silk. The color set off the red highlights in her hair attractively. Though not fashionable, her hair was quite possibly her most intriguing feature. He had found himself wondering more than once what it would look like unbound.

Her next most intriguing feature was her lips. They were unexpectedly sensual on a face that was otherwise pleasing but not quite beautiful. The soft fullness of them closed around the piece of chocolate, and an undeniable tug of arousal pulsed through his groin. He cleared his throat against the unexpected pull and drew her gaze. She caught him looking. He startled at his lapse in propriety and inclined his head in acknowledgment, and then forced his gaze if not his attention to Hathaway, who was now regaling them with his tale of a lion hunt.

"Perhaps, my lord, you might consider accompanying me on my next hunt," Hathaway said. "I am told you are a huntsman yourself."

"I hunt for food, not sport. I've no interest in eating lion."

"But there is nothing like the rush of stalking big game and—"

"Charles," Mrs. Dove intervened. "For the love of all that is holy"—his mother flinched at that—"no one wants to talk about your escapades in Africa. We are here to celebrate their upcoming nuptials. How about we do more of that and less of . . . you?" Mrs. Dove raised her wineglass in a mock toast to the table at large and took a swallow of her dessert wine.

He rather liked her gumption. Cora's eyes widened in alarm. Jenny covered a smile with her hand, and Eliza sat in wide-eyed silence as her mouth gaped open.

"I wasn't aware there was an embargo on the conversation, *Mrs. Dove*." Mr. Hathaway put extra emphasis on her name, as if to remonstrate against her use of his first name.

There seemed to be a strange and slightly acrimonious

relationship between the two of them. It made him wonder if they had been lovers at one time, but that line of thought would have to wait for later.

"Thank you, Mrs. Dove." Devonworth motioned to the footmen, who scrambled to pour the champagne that had been waiting on the sideboard. One of them put a glass into Devonworth's hand, which he promptly raised. "I would like to take this moment to propose a toast to my bride." The table came to attention, and he waited as everyone was handed a coupe. "You are very much not what I expected, Miss Dove. In fact, you are more than I could have imagined." She flushed very prettily, and he added, "You are lovely, kind, and intelligent. I could ask for no better qualities in my countess."

"You are a very fine man, my lord, and I can think of no one I would prefer to call husband."

"I look forward to our future together." It was all true, he realized. He enjoyed the twinkle of mischief in her eyes and the gleam of intelligence she didn't try to hide. Something about her drew him in, and he couldn't quite understand what it was, but he liked it very much.

"As do I, my lord."

He even liked the way she said that. She smiled and drank from her glass, reminding him that he had yet to drink from his own. He tossed back a swallow. There were murmurs of approval all around, and even Mr. Hathaway seemed pleased again.

"Shall we retire to the drawing room?" Devonworth said to no one in particular. The sooner this evening was done with, the better.

He held out his arm for Miss Dove to escort her from the room. Mr. Hathaway took Lady Devonworth. Fanny exited with Harry, leaving the viscount to escort both of the sisters.

Devonworth intentionally kept Miss Dove behind as the others disappeared into the drawing room.

"How are you?" he asked her.

She gave him a sheepish look. "I don't think your mother appreciates the finer qualities of my family."

He laughed. It was true, but his mother knew they had little choice. "I love my mother, but she can be a bit snobbish."

She laughed at that. "There will be no shortage of that, I'm afraid."

"Do you mean tomorrow?"

"I am anxious about the wedding breakfast."

They would be married in a small ceremony at St. James's with a handful of friends and family present. The wedding breakfast would be much larger with notable members of Society and Parliament attending to meet her.

"You've no need for worry. There won't be much conversation expected of you. We'll simply stand there and appear gracious as everyone lines up to wish us well in our marriage."

"Don't forget, there will be those who come to gawk."

He scoffed. "There will always be those. No doubt the papers will list a running tally of our wedding gifts."

She fidgeted with the ribbon at her waist, a nervous habit she seemed to do when in his presence. "That doesn't make me feel any better."

He took her hand without realizing he had done it until her fingers stilled beneath his. He liked how her hand felt in his palm. It was solid and warm with just the right amount of softness. "We should decide now that we won't let anything they write about us interfere with our relationship. All of that exists outside of us. What we have together is what matters."

"What do we have, my lord?" Her eyes were more blue

tonight than gray and filled with an uncertainty that brought out a tenderness within him.

"A friendship . . . I hope."

She smiled at him, and something inside him startled as everything else faded away except the two of them.

"I'd like that," she whispered.

"Good," he said, looking away before he became further enraptured by the depth of her eyes. He squeezed her hand and guided her into the drawing room. Starting tomorrow, it would be the two of them against the world. He barely knew her, but already he was prepared to defend her at all costs if it came to it. She was giving him and his brother a future; he couldn't do any less for her.

EIGHT

D EVONWORTH HAD ALMOST MANAGED TO CON-
vince himself that marriage wasn't a daunting prospect.
He had lived his life after arranging things with Miss Dove
much as he had before. His days were spent between his office
and roaming Lords, while his evenings were spent in his study
at home peppered with the occasional dinner out where politics was always the main course. That didn't leave much time
for ruminating over a future wife. Aside from the dinner last
night and having his housekeeper ready a bedchamber for her,
he hadn't done very much to prepare at all.

The self-deception that his life wasn't about to change had
worked right up to the point when Miss Dove had joined him
at the altar at St. James's. The wedding had been a small affair attended by close family, David and Strathmore, and a
handful of others. To say that it was understated would do a
great disservice to how very little fanfare had gone into the
whole thing. They had exchanged vows, and then the vicar

had pronounced them man and wife, which had been followed
by muted well-wishes.

Now, however, as he sat in his private carriage with her
making their way through the crowded streets of Mayfair, it
was impossible to ignore the fact that she shared it with him.
She would be sharing it with him for years to come. At least
two. She was his wife.

His wife.

She sat opposite him in the carriage with her face turned
toward the window. The air was softly perfumed with lavender, a scent he was coming to associate with her. Her alabaster
complexion seemed even paler than normal. The sprinkling of
freckles over her nose and cheeks stood out like gold dust
against the white of her skin. Her hands were clasped in her
lap so tightly that her gloves seemed to be stretched too taut
against her knuckles.

She was probably still anxious about the breakfast. They
hadn't spoken to each other beyond the vows. He should say
something to put her at ease. What did one say to a wife?

"Did you find the ceremony to your satisfaction?" It sounded
wooden even to his ears.

She stirred and set her wide gaze upon his. "Yes, it was a
fine ceremony." She looked as if the slightest jolt of the carriage could shatter her.

"I agree." It was a failed attempt that went nowhere. She
gave him the barest hint of a smile and then looked back toward the window.

He couldn't remember ever feeling this awkward around a
woman. His mind grasped at things to say to make her feel
comfortable, but nothing seemed right. Reminding her that
she had nothing to fear from him would lead to suspicion.

Usually, those who meant harm were the ones promising not to do any.

Perhaps a compliment would help. Every bride wanted to look beautiful on her wedding day. "You look lovely."

Her gown was a simple confection of white satin with a veil that had been pinned back from her face. The white was very striking against her hair, which appeared deep red in the watery morning light. She was actually quite lovely in a way that he found dignified. She wore her prettiness like a rose that had yet to unfurl. Her beauty was understated and contained, not ostentatious. Not like Sofia's.

Bloody hell. He would not think of that woman on his wedding day, and he absolutely would not compare his wife to her. Miss Dove deserved more than that. Despite the fact that their marriage was very much a transaction, he would extend her that courtesy.

She gave a small nod of acknowledgment as if his compliment had been expected. As if it were customary and not a sincere expression of his feeling. Both happened to be true. "Thank you," she said. "You look very handsome, as well."

"Thank you." He wore his blue morning coat.

She immediately looked back out the window, and he sighed inwardly. So much for conversation. His mother followed in her carriage along with Mrs. Dove and her two daughters. He hoped she was faring better. He'd bet anything that she was having the opposite problem. The Dove family tended toward conversation and mild theatrics—Mrs. Dove had loudly exclaimed how happy she was several times. His mother tended toward quiet.

Since conversation seemed to be out of the question, perhaps information would be more beneficial. Anytime he encountered a new situation, he gathered information and found it inevitably helped him to feel more at ease. Like tiny building blocks that made this new foundation more secure.

Clearing his throat, he said, "Hathaway and I spoke to Mainwaring last night after dinner, and it seems he's intent on marrying Eliza."

She nodded. "Yes, he sent a note over." He couldn't tell if this pleased her or not.

"I thought we would leave for my . . . *our* townhome after the breakfast to get you settled. We'll depart for Timberscombe Park later on after you've had time to settle in here in London. It will give you the opportunity to see the place, and I can see how the repairs are progressing."

"Repairs?"

Ah, he hadn't completely explained his need for the marriage. At their negotiation, she had brought up the issue of the marriage being in name only, and he hadn't properly given her the details after that. He was struck again by how vulnerable she had made herself with this marriage. There had been no one to advocate for her or even ask the right questions. Hathaway had signed all the required paperwork through his London solicitor, but he hadn't asked the questions that Devonworth thought he should. The questions Devonworth might ask on behalf of his own daughter or ward. Questions that would verify her future husband had taken her well-being to heart.

He briefly explained to her the bizarre March weather that had damaged the roof of his estate and how that had forced his hand with the marriage. "It's not much of a wedding trip, I know, but we can plan one for later in the summer anywhere you want."

"That's fine." She gave him a shy smile. "I don't need a wedding trip."

The declaration left him speechless for a moment. Yes, the wedding trip was about them getting to know each other, but perhaps more importantly it was a social convention that was expected. If they neglected to take it, people would find that noteworthy, which meant it would be gossip-worthy. His career couldn't afford the unnecessary chatter, not on top of the inevitable gossip this marriage would bring. His seat might be hereditary, but getting the votes to go his way required a reputation that didn't court scandal.

He cleared his throat as he debated how to explain things to her in the most delicate way. "We must go somewhere. It will make things easier if people see us doing the usual things that couples do."

"Oh." Her eyes widened before she closed them and nodded. "Yes, you're right. I didn't consider that. You must be especially concerned given how much your work at the House of Lords means to you. I wouldn't want to do anything to put that in jeopardy."

He relaxed against the seat. "I'm glad you understand. Our marriage will be enough fodder for the rumor mill. It's true that most marriages are still arranged; ours will be seen as a bit more . . . mercenary, if you will. We don't have to fool everyone that we're in love, but we do need to display a vague affection and like for each other."

"Of course. I'm very boring, so I think the gossip will die down sooner rather than later."

She might be boring, but her mother most definitely was not, which brought up another issue. "Will your mother be staying in London?"

"Yes, Camille has offered to have my mother and sisters stay with her in Town through the summer. Camille will be in Paris visiting Mr. Thorne much of that time."

Good. He shuddered to think that her mother might move in with them in the autumn, but that was a battle for another day. Perhaps her sisters would be married by then and one of them could take her in.

"Speaking of your mother. What is her maiden name? My investigator wasn't able to find it with her wedding certificate having burned."

She froze. It was nearly imperceptible, but there had been a momentary panic in her expression before she got it under control. He'd had a nagging suspicion that she hadn't been completely honest with him during their negotiation. Now he was certain. There was something in the woman's background that gave her some unease.

"Why do you need to know?" she asked.

"So that it can be recorded in the family book." That was one reason. The other larger one being that he didn't enjoy surprises. He planned to figure out what they were hiding before it was presented to him at a most inconvenient time.

"Smith," she said.

How fitting. "Thank you, Miss Dove."

She smiled, and this time it was truly genuine. "You probably shouldn't call me that now that we are married."

He felt himself blanch. "Quite right. I had nearly forgotten." It felt too intimate to refer to her by her first name, but there was no help for it. "Cora."

"What should I call you?" she asked.

"Everyone calls me Devonworth."

"Your title? That seems rather formal. What does your mother call you?"

"Devonworth." His wife hadn't yet learned how starchily formal everything could be here. It must seem strange given how very casual her own family was with one another.

"Your mother calls you by your title?" She frowned, displeased by this.

"My father died years ago, so I inherited the title as a child. Everyone calls me Devonworth."

Her brow furrowed in distress. "It seems so . . . impersonal. Would it be all right if I call you by your name? Don't you think the informality will go a long way toward making that affection you mentioned seem real?"

She made a good point. "Fair enough. You may call me by my first name."

She smiled again, and it was so bright that his breath caught. A warm, comforting feeling seeped into him, and he made a mental note to try to make her smile at him like that again.

"Good. Leonidas it is, then."

He laughed. "I'm afraid that would cause considerably more talk than Devonworth."

She stared at him in question before realization overcame her. "Leopold!" She spoke through the hands covering her face in shame. "Your name is Leopold, not Leonidas." Then almost absently, she added, "That's worse than Devonworth." Her hands moved to cover her mouth, horrified that she had said the thought aloud. He burst into laughter. "I'm sorry. I didn't mean that. It's a very fine name," she hurried to add.

"No, you're right. Leopold is an old family name, which makes it stuffy and pretentious. I never cared for it, if I'm being honest. Leonidas is rather kingly." He couldn't seem to stop laughing, and after a moment more, she laughed, too. It was soft and breathy. He found it so pleasant that he vowed to make her laugh again and soon.

"Perhaps Leo, then?" she asked.

No one had ever called him that. For the amount she had paid him for this marriage, he was willing to let her call him almost anything, but he found himself agreeing because he had genuinely enjoyed this exchange and he wanted her to feel comfortable. Unexpected as it was, he liked his wife.

He took a deep, settling breath. There was hope that with a little time, they would find their way together. Marriage didn't have to be a terrible curse. Before they could talk further, the carriage came to a stop in front of Sterling House, the Duke of Rothschild's home in Town. The duke and his duchess, an American heiress he had married a few years back, had offered to host the wedding breakfast as a show of support for the marriage. Devonworth believed it was the intention of August and her sister, Violet, who had married the Earl of Leigh that same year, to take the Dove sisters under their wings to help ensure their acceptance into Society. He hoped to God it worked. Those vultures might eat her alive otherwise.

He disembarked and reached back to offer Cora his hand. She accepted it and stepped down, her expression tight with nerves. His mother's carriage pulled up behind them. The moment the door opened, chatter spilled out followed by his mother and then the Dove family. Cora's sisters hurried over to her while Mrs. Dove walked slower, her head swiveling as she took in the exclusive neighborhood. The houses here were larger than the terrace homes found in other parts of Mayfair and home to many notable people. The prime minister himself lived just down the lane.

"What a charming street," Mrs. Dove proclaimed as she approached. She was dressed more appropriately today in a high-necked walking dress that had been styled to complement his mother's. They were both light shades of blue with darker blue buttons and trim. "In New York, newer is better. I never considered that age could lend such beauty."

"And character," his mother added in a tone filled with meaning. "Age should lend character."

"Shall we . . . ?" He held out his arm to his new wife only to realize her sisters had swept her up between them and intended to see her inside.

She gave him a sheepish glance over her shoulder. "I need a moment to freshen up before the guests arrive."

Before he could reply, Harry approached. He had ridden with David, Strathmore, and Warwick in the carriage behind the Doves. He and David had stood up with him at the ceremony. Harry had the look of their father with his brown hair and eyes. He also had inherited their father's nose, which was much too large for his face, but he carried it off with a devil-may-care attitude that charmed many women. Mrs. Dove was one of them.

"Lord Harry, darling," she said with the faintest hint of an upper-crust London accent. "See me inside, won't you?" She attached herself to his arm before Harry could answer and began walking up the steps. His brother didn't seem to mind as he pointed out the finer aspects of the Georgian facade of the home.

"What manner of woman have you entwined us with, Devonworth?" his mother whispered at his side, leaving him wondering if the comment was prompted by Mrs. Dove's faux pas in addressing Harry by the wrong title, a conversation they'd had on the ride over, or the more general eccentricities that were Mrs. Dove.

He honestly didn't know how to answer her. Instead of addressing her question, he turned to her and said, "You look lovely today, Mother."

It was true. She was still considered one of the beauties of the ton. He had been lucky to inherit her bone structure and high cheekbones.

She gave him a quick glance of censure, aware of his attempt to change the subject, before taking his arm and following the group up the steps.

"I am certain you'll find Cora more to your liking," he said. "I've found her to be intelligent and thoughtful. Do not hold your resentment of Mrs. Dove against her."

His mother sniffed. "I should hope she is both of those things, but she is not who I wished for you. If your father—"

She broke off and her eyes shimmered. There was no use in going down that line of thinking. If his father hadn't died so young, if he'd made even half of the investments that had been presented to him, if he'd done *anything* to modernize, then they might not be in this situation. Sofia might be the woman he had wed this morning. Despite how he'd left things with her, he couldn't stop himself imagining her as his bride. The fact that she wasn't left a bitter taste in his mouth no matter how he tried to dismiss her from his thoughts.

"Forgive me." She pulled out a handkerchief from her sleeve and dabbed the corners of her eyes. "This is not what I wanted for you."

"I understand, but this is how things have to be." Taking her hands, he said, "Cora must be made to feel welcome. None of this is her fault. In fact, without her, we would be in more trouble than you know." He hadn't dared share Harry's gambling with his mother. "Can you help me do that?"

She nodded. "I won't do anything to make her feel unwelcome. That is all I can promise."

It would have to be enough.

NINE

"I CALLED HIM BY THE WRONG NAME!" THE WORDS tore out of Cora as soon as she was safely ensconced inside the bedchamber that had been designated for her to use before the wedding breakfast. Her sisters had accompanied her upstairs.

"You did what?" Eliza looked horrified, her eyes wide with disbelief.

Jenny giggled but quickly pressed her lips together to smother the sound.

"I don't know how it happened." Cora blindly felt her way to the settee before the window that faced out over the street. She was vaguely aware of the lavish trappings of the room: white moldings, an expansive Oriental rug, crimson textiles, and a fireplace that was so tall she could have walked into it. Any other time she might have looked around in awe, but she was too busy cringing against her own stupidity.

"What happened precisely?" Jenny asked, coming over to put a comforting hand on her shoulder. She wasn't smiling now, but there was a suspicious twinkle in her eye that indicated she was enjoying this far too much.

"He referred to me as Miss Dove, which we both realized is ridiculous since we are married now, so then he called me Cora. I"—even thinking about it made her face flame—"for reasons I don't completely understand, called him Leonidas."

Jenny let out a shout of laughter before she could slap her hand over her mouth. Eliza shook her head in sympathy, but even she was smiling now.

"*You did this*. You put that name in my head," she accused Jenny.

This only made her sister laugh harder. "I'm sorry! I didn't think you would actually call him that."

Cora held her head in her hands, her anger taking flight as quickly as it had come on. It wasn't really her sister's fault. Cora had been the one to say the wrong name. She was so discombobulated by this whole wedding day that she didn't know which end was up. "He's going to think he married a complete fool."

"He won't think that." Eliza was quick to comfort her. She sat down on the settee beside her, gently brushing the skirts of Cora's wedding gown aside. "If anything, he'll believe you were nervous. Besides, he thinks you're beautiful. Doesn't he?" She looked up at Jenny for support. Their sister nodded in eager agreement, so she turned her attention back to Cora. "We watched him closely during the wedding. He seemed quite taken with you."

"It's true. His face lit up when he first saw you." Jenny perched on the chair adjacent to the settee in the small sitting area and took Cora's hand. "I'm certain he doesn't think you're a fool. You barely know each other. Things like this happen."

For the millionth time that day, Cora wondered if she had

made a mistake. She had married a stranger. He could take her home tonight and do whatever he wanted to her and no one would or could intervene. But what use were thoughts like that? The deed was done now.

Her thoughts must have shown on her face, because she caught her sisters giving each other a concerned look. She felt worse for causing them even a second of distress. This had been her idea, after all. "We did share a laugh together about it," she said to smooth things over, although that didn't preclude him from thinking her a fool. "I don't think he's taken with me. It's a business transaction, but thank you for trying to make me feel better."

"It might be a transactional marriage, but that doesn't mean he didn't appreciate your beauty in that gown. You look stunning." Jenny smiled at her and brushed the veil back from her face. The sides had fallen forward.

Cora gave her sister a genuine smile. She had thought she looked pretty in the mirror at Camille's townhome that morning. It didn't matter in the least to their marriage, since they had decided to keep it a marriage in name only, but she liked the idea of him being attracted to her. She had been too nervous to notice much of anything at the church, but the very thought of him looking upon her in appreciation made her stomach swirl with a pleasant sensation.

"Come, let's do something about that veil. You don't want to have to keep pushing it out of your face all day." Jenny grasped her hand and led her to the vanity in the corner of the room. Cora took a seat, and her sister set about removing the hairpins and arranging her hair.

"Speaking of handsome men and their interests, did anyone notice how Lord David couldn't keep his eyes off Jenny?" Eliza teased.

Her sisters had stood as her bridesmaids, while Lord David and Devonworth's brother had stood with him.

"I did notice that," Cora said, happy to have the focus off of her. She wasn't used to being the center of attention. There was always her mother or one of her sisters to attend to. Through the mirror, she watched Jenny roll her eyes.

"I would not consider Lord David even if he did offer for me, which he hasn't yet and isn't likely to. Camille said he's shown no interest in marriage," Jenny said.

"Why wouldn't you consider him?" Eliza asked, leaning against the window jamb.

"Because he only wants to bed me. Even if he did propose marriage to get that, he'd be in some other woman's bed before the week was out."

"And that would bother you?" It wasn't something that Cora had allowed herself to think about, but there was no denying that something twisted painfully inside her when she thought of Devonworth—she couldn't even think of him as Leo with her mortification still fresh—with another woman. She had no claim to him besides their paper marriage, so it didn't make sense and wasn't particularly fair. He might have a mistress, for all she knew. *God, please don't let him have a mistress.*

"Yes . . ." Jenny hesitated and added, "I don't know that I can go through with a transactional marriage. I've given it a lot of thought, and I think I want more. I want a true marriage . . . whatever that means."

They had almost nothing to go by. Their own mother had never remarried after Mr. Dove, who had died so long ago that Cora wasn't certain if her faint memories of him were real or inspired by the small daguerreotype her mother kept of him. Cora didn't know for sure but suspected that marriage had been transactional as well. Fanny's selection of friends had been mostly theater folk and spiritualists who floated in and out of their house intermittently based on when their travels brought them to the city. Some of them were married, of course, but she had never seen the home life side of those marriages. As their neighborhood had fallen into decline, their mother had kept them inside more, and most families they had known as children moved away. The widows left behind in their crumbling houses had spoken fondly of their husbands, but that was no model for marriage.

"But that might mean you'll lose your inheritance," Eliza said.

"It's true," Cora added. "Mr. Hathaway made it very clear that he wanted us away from New York. He won't agree to just anyone."

Jenny shrugged and shoved one of the hairpins back into Cora's hair a little too harshly. She winced but her sister didn't notice. "I've had my doubts about marriage now anyway. I want to sing, and no husband will allow that. Maybe I won't get married for years."

They were all silent for a moment as Jenny worked on her hair. She was arranging the veil to trail out from beneath the curls pinned on Cora's head and flow down her back. She took some of the orange blossoms from her own hair and tucked them into Cora's.

"You could arrange a marriage . . . followed by a divorce," Cora said.

Eliza looked shocked, as did Jenny until she said, "Is that what you've done? Arranged for a divorce?"

"I mentioned it. Devonworth is considering it."

"You didn't!" Eliza's eyes were wide again. Cora couldn't tell if she was simply surprised or outraged.

Cora turned to face them both. "Why shouldn't we? Mr. Hathaway made his stipulations for his own benefit. He didn't make them because he cared about us. He could have given us our inheritance outright, or at least upon our marriage to any man *we* chose, as I'm certain his mother intended, if he cared at all. He wanted us gone, and he figured we would be out of his way over here in England. I don't care if this makes me a social pariah. I wasn't particularly social to begin with." At least this way she would eventually have control of her own finances, which meant control of her own life.

Silence took over the room, heavy and cloying. A clattering outside finally broke through. Eliza glanced out the window and said, "We should get downstairs. Guests are arriving."

Cora stood and peeked out to see a stream of carriages coming down the lane, waiting their turn to discharge their passengers. The guests would all be Devonworth's acquaintances. None of the people they knew from home would be able to afford the trip across the Atlantic or even be welcomed if they did. She couldn't imagine the Kowalskis, who owned the butcher shop back home, stopping in to wish her well, even though the wife had invited her in for a chat on several occasions. Aside from her small family, she was alone here now.

There was a soft knock at the door, and Eliza went over to answer it. Camille smiled and stepped into the room. "Are you ready? Guests are arriving," she told Cora.

Maybe she wasn't alone after all. Camille had been nice to her, as had the Crenshaw sisters. Her life was simply changing, and she needed some time to figure out this new part of it.

"I'm ready."

The three of them followed Camille and found Devonworth waiting at the bottom of the stairs. Looking at him still took her breath away. He held up his hand for her, and she took comfort in his warm, strong grasp. He had given her no reason to distrust him, and despite her earlier fears and embarrassment, she would try not to.

He took in her hair, which was revealed more now with the veil pinned behind, before his gaze settled on her face. Her sisters were right. Now that she wasn't too anxious to notice, she did see approval in his eyes.

"Shall we go meet our guests?" His voice was smooth and rich, settling the nerves inside her.

She nodded, nearly overcome with the gratitude she suddenly felt toward him. He would stand by her and lend her strength.

And that's what he did. He led her to the drawing room, where several new people already waited. They stopped to greet each one, and he introduced her as his wife. By the third one, she had rediscovered her voice and managed to speak loudly enough the man didn't have to lean forward to hear her. Then her husband took her to the end of the room where they were to stand for the rest of the party.

An endless stream of people came to meet her and congratulate him. A buffet had been set up, and footmen moved through the crowd, offering glasses of champagne. It wasn't as terrible as Cora had anticipated, and she eventually found her smile. The whole thing seemed more subdued than the American Society weddings she had read about. Those celebrations were always capped off by lavish balls. Here it was more dignified, less celebratory, as if it were any other gathering. Aside from the occasional ribald comment a few men made to her husband with a titter, it might have been. The guests didn't even eat their cake at the breakfast. They took their slices home in white boxes wrapped in blue ribbon.

A few hours later, Devonworth was showing her around

her new home in Mayfair. The house was a beautiful Georgian-era home with a brick facade and matching dormer windows and a short wrought iron fence around the front. It was very stately and elegant, and the inside was no different.

The entry was paneled in rosewood with a marble floor. As they moved through the rooms on the main floor, Cora could tell that meticulous detail had been paid to the decor.

"Did your mother decorate?" she asked.

"Some, but generally it's only been added to over the years."

She could tell. Antiques collected over the decades took up every room with only one or two pieces looking modern. It wasn't cozy, but neither was it austere. It lingered in some in-between place. It was beautiful, but she already found herself missing Stonebridge Cottage with its overstuffed chairs and soft pillows.

"Let me show you to your room," Devonworth said with a stiff sort of formality.

She suspected he fell back on that when things became awkward, as they certainly were now. Aside from the butler, an elderly man named Edgecomb, she hadn't seen any servants and suspected they had been sent into hiding to be brought out to meet her later. The place was as quiet as a church. Her room was at the end of the hall facing the small garden at the back of the house. The room was sparsely furnished but well-appointed with a four-poster mahogany bed, side tables, an armoire, and a writing desk. It was decorated in shades of coral and forest green. Not precisely her taste, but it would do.

As if he read her mind, he said, "It's yours to do with as you please. I have accounts at the shops if you want to change anything."

"No, I'm certain this is fine."

He shook his head, stopping her. "I want you to be comfortable, Cora. The room hasn't been used in years. My mother moved into the dower house as soon as she could, taking most of her furniture with her. This has all been collected from other rooms." He indicated the furniture.

"If you're certain."

He smiled and walked to stand before her. His lips were almost indecently shaped, full and soft and putting her in mind of how they might feel, but she forced those thoughts away. She wasn't meant to notice things like that, especially here in her bedroom where she most definitely would not find out how soft they were. "I am. This may not be the marriage you dreamed of, but I want you to be happy. Please . . . make this your home."

She nodded because words were not possible. She didn't understand all the things she was feeling to even begin to sort through them.

"Ah yes, here it is," he said as he spied a sheet of paper on the writing desk. Retrieving it, he glanced over the missive briefly and handed it to her. "I opened an account in your name at my bank with your portion of the funds. It will be yours to take . . . afterward."

After their marriage, he meant. Something about that made her feel sad, but she didn't take the time to examine the feeling too closely.

The sheet listed her account details and the available balance. Everything was exactly as they had discussed. Only, his name was on it as well because, as a woman, especially a married woman, she wasn't allowed to have any funds in only her name. She read and reread the words, hardly able to believe that what had begun as a shot in the dark had finally come to fruition. She was married to a nobleman and well on her way to financial independence.

With this money, she'd be able to support her sisters and her mother if needed. They would not be at the mercy of any man ever again. Well, except for Devonworth, who was technically the owner of the account.

"Thank you." She could only whisper the words; they were too precious to say out loud.

She wanted to kiss the paper, but a brief knock at the door interrupted them.

"This is Polly," he said as if he hadn't handed Cora the key to her future a mere moment ago.

The girl gave a quick curtsy. She couldn't have been more than sixteen. She had her hair in braids tied up around her head and wore a nondescript black dress with an apron. "She's a chambermaid and has graciously agreed to act as your lady's maid until we hire you one, haven't you, Polly?"

"Yes, milord." She didn't look at him, but Cora didn't see fear in the girl's face. A blush stained her cheeks, making Cora suspect the girl was as taken by Devonworth as she was.

"I interviewed a few this week and hired one already." At his questioning look, she added, "Camille and the Crenshaw sisters support a local charity, the London Home for Young Women?" She wasn't certain if he'd heard of it.

"Ah yes, the home for unwed mothers."

"They sent over a few women who were interested in the position."

He nodded in approval, and a rush of pleasure warmed her. She had been a little concerned he wouldn't welcome someone into his home from that sort of background, which is why she had hired her before moving into his house.

They weren't all mothers at the home. Many women and girls came to them from troubled circumstances, and the home provided shelter while helping them acquire skills to better their circumstances.

"Eugenie Monroe will start tomorrow."

"Good, I'll tell Edgecomb to look for her." Silence overtook them for a moment before he turned toward the other door in the room and said, "My room is through here, our shared bathing chamber. I'll leave you to change and rest unless there is something else you need?"

"I've already unloaded milady's trunks and sent them to the attic," Polly offered.

"Good work, Polly," he said.

Cora shook her head to indicate that she didn't need anything further. She wasn't capable of doing more because she was still reeling from the fact that someone had referred to her as *milady*. As inexplicable as it sounded, she was a lady now. A countess.

"I'll see you at dinner," he said to Cora and hurried out of the room.

Polly murmured something and retrieved Cora's rose-colored dressing gown from the armoire. It was strange to see a garment so familiar to her in this unfamiliar place. Before she could think better of it, she hurried to the connecting door and locked it. Polly didn't appear startled. She simply said, "Shall I help you change, milady?"

"Yes, thank you." Cora's voice was soft but audible. The girl hurried forward and started unlacing the fastenings on the back of her gown.

It was as if she had woken up this morning as one person and now had become someone else. She supposed she had. She was Lady Devonworth now. If only she knew what that meant.

PART TWO

Womanhood is the great fact in her life;
wifehood and motherhood are but
incidental relations.

—Elizabeth Cady Stanton

TEN

THEIR MARRIAGE SETTLED INTO A NICE AND PRE-dictable routine over the next week. Cora spent her days either at the shops supplementing her sparse wardrobe or looking at wallpaper and furniture to decorate her bedroom. Devonworth spent much of his time at Lords, where she had visited him once. He had suggested the visit as a way to ease her into her new life, but she suspected it was also to show everyone that they were a real couple who was happily married. She had met his secretary, a man in his thirties named Beckham, and then had tea with her husband.

It quickly became apparent that her husband was more than a little obsessed with his role in government. It was very nearly his only activity, aside from his football practices several times a week. Even when he was home, he could usually be found in his study. She saw him for minutes a day, if at all. Though there had been a single piece of chocolate on the breakfast tray the housekeeper, Mrs. Anderson, sent up every morning, and she wondered if he was responsible for it, which meant he did think of her on occasion. She understood now why marriage had only become a priority for him because of financial concerns. He had absolutely no time in his life for a wife.

This was fine with her—or it should have been—because she didn't particularly want a husband. But it became lonely taking supper by herself every night at the vast table in the dining room. He had only joined her for the first two nights. She couldn't help but think it might be nice if he managed to make an appearance more often. Part of the problem was that she wasn't accustomed to being alone. Her mother and her sisters were spending some time in Paris, visiting Fanny's friend, Mrs. Wilson, who had taken Jenny in to aid in her opera singing aspirations.

Mrs. Wilson was a singer who had befriended Fanny when the girls were younger. The woman had then married a wealthy American diplomat who lived in Paris. They had stayed in touch over the years, and when Jenny began to show musical aspirations, Mrs. Wilson, who had been a widow by then, invited her to Paris to study the craft.

With her family gone, Cora didn't have anyone at all with her during these first days as a bride. The dowager countess had made herself scarce, visiting friends in the countryside. Cora believed their absences were an attempt to give the newly-weds time to adjust to married life, and she might have appreciated it had this been a true marriage, but it had left her lonely. The only one she saw with any regularity was Harry, who managed to come and go at least once every day or so.

In fact, she heard him now and pushed back from the dining room table, startling the footman who had been ladling soup into the bowl in front of her. Not even bothering to mark her place in the book she had brought for company, she hurried from the table and opened the door. Harry paused in the hall, bleary-eyed and a bit taken aback.

She couldn't tell if he was coming or going. His clothing always looked slightly disheveled, and there was a blue tinge beneath his eyes that she suspected could be chalked up to imbibing in too much alcohol. He had graduated university only last spring and had yet to "find his way," as her husband referred to his brother's wastrel endeavors.

"Come dine with me." When he frowned at her in a way that made her suspect he had either forgotten English or was evaluating her sanity, she stepped back to hold the door open wider. "Please? I'd like to get to know you better. You are my brother now."

He hesitated another moment before he nodded. "All right. I can spare a bit of time."

She felt as if she had won a victory and didn't move until he had entered the room and she could close the door behind him lest he slip through her very lonely fingers. "Oliver, please set Mr. Brendon a place at the table."

The footman murmured a quick reply and hurried about setting a place for Harry across from her. As her brother-in-law settled himself, she watched him discreetly. She was closer to Harry in age than her own husband. He was only a year or two younger than her, but there was something about his general demeanor of not engaging himself in his surroundings that made him seem younger, or at least more immature. Like a child who had no interest in the toys they had been given, he wandered through life a bit disconnected. Or that was her perception after their short acquaintance.

He didn't look very much like Devonworth. She had tried before and even now couldn't find many similarities between them. They were nearly the same height, and they might have been of a similar build, but Harry was almost gaunt in appearance.

"Do you have plans tonight?" she asked before taking a spoonful of her turtle soup.

She didn't. No one knew what to do with her. Hopefully, this would change soon when she was properly introduced at Lord and Lady Leigh's ball early next week. It was to be her first Society event. Now that Easter was over, the social season was in full swing.

"I am meeting a few friends at Montague Club." This was the club Mr. Thorne owned with his half brother, the Earl of Leigh.

"Oh, do you like it there?"

"It's all right," he said around the bite of soup in his mouth. "I'm told they allow women members. You should go see it for yourself."

"They do?" There were shockingly few places here where men and women could mingle together. Not that there were many places back home. "I suppose I could."

"We're planning our holiday abroad," he hurried on.

"Holiday?"

He nodded. "Leaving next week."

"Where will you be going?" This was the first she was hearing about his travel plans.

"The Continent. Greece to start and then working our way back. We'll be gone until the end of summer. Mainwaring will be going with us." He perked up when he remembered she knew the man.

"*Viscount* Mainwaring?"

"That's the one."

"But he's betrothed to my sister."

She didn't think a betrothal contract had been signed yet,

but the terms were all but settled. The end of summer was months away. She had assumed the wedding would happen before then.

Harry nodded and swallowed before he said, "That's right. The trip is a fine last to-do before he's shackled, don't you think?"

She nodded because she didn't want to get into a disagreement with him, but something about it didn't sit right with her. She supposed it was the very practical nature of arranged marriages. She had always thought that when her sisters married, there would be joyous occasions and their spouses would be like her brothers. But that had been before Mr. Hathaway and the ridiculous condition he'd set for their inheritance. Once more, the reality of marriage as a business arrangement was harsher in practice than in her head. She wanted something better for Eliza.

"I need to go. It was good chatting with you." He pushed back from the table.

"But you've only had soup." They had several more courses to go, and she hadn't yet broached the subject of her mysterious husband. Harry could be a wealth of information, but she actually had to get it out of him first.

"Don't worry. I'll see you again before I go. I'll be attending the ball and dance with you properly."

"I'll only see you at the ball?" She searched frantically for some other reason to see him. She needed at least one person in this family who wasn't a stranger to her. "Have dinner with me again? We can get to know each other." When he hesitated, she added, "You need to eat. I need to eat. It's logical."

That made him laugh, and something in his eyes shifted and warmed. "All right. I can stop by for the soup course."

She smiled and nodded. That would have to be enough.

"Go on, then. I suppose I need to make sure your brother gets fed in his study."

He rose but paused when she said that. "He's not in his study."

"What?" She had heard him in their shared bathing chamber earlier in the evening. When he hadn't appeared at dinner, she assumed he was working in his study.

Harry shrugged. "I went there earlier to discuss my allowance for the holiday. He wasn't there and his desk was neat, which means he hadn't worked there tonight."

She didn't know what to make of that, but her stomach twisted uncomfortably. "Well, until tomorrow evening." She managed to smile and bid him good night.

He paused at the door once more and looked at her. Perhaps she was imagining it, but she would have marked the expression on his face as loneliness. "Don't spend all your time wandering around this old house . . . It'll drive you to madness." He left before she could answer, but she suspected he was right.

She didn't feel like eating much after that, so she hurried through the rest of her meal and retired to her room. After Monroe, her newly acquired lady's maid, helped her change into her nightclothes, she settled into bed to read but couldn't concentrate on the words. She soon found herself rambling around the dark house, eventually stopping outside of her husband's study. The door was open, and he hadn't told her not to go in when he wasn't home—he hadn't told her very much of anything since their wedding—so she walked inside. It smelled faintly of sandalwood. His scent. A now-familiar and pleasant warmth tumbled in her stomach.

She turned on the desk lamp, illuminating a room that resembled a library, as there were two walls of shelves. One of them framed the hearth. A wall of windows behind his desk faced the side of the house, but heavy drapes covered them now. Harry had been right about Devonworth's desk. It was mostly clean now with stacks of papers and leather binders taking up the low bureaus behind it.

She walked around the room, removing the odd book, examining a small statuette of indeterminate identity, and opening a metal case that contained thin cigars. The sweet and pungent smell of tobacco filled the space. She hadn't smelled that scent on him before and wondered if he partook often. Closing the lid, she moved to the stacks of papers behind the desk.

The weeks before her wedding had been busy ones, but she had made time to get her hands on as many newspapers as she could find to learn more about him and his work in Parliament. His name didn't come up often, but there was the odd mention here and there in relation to a Public Health Bill. The articles she had read hadn't gone into detail, but the words on the top sheet of parchment caught her attention, *In favor of the Public Health Act.*

Without thinking, she sat and read the entire ten pages of the document. It seemed to be a speech or treatise of some sort, and it also seemed as if he was having trouble with it. Words and whole passages were marked out with illegible notes scribbled in the margins. The document was very cut-and-dried. It laid out the need for clean water in the dwellings of all of England. Villages had been plagued with cholera and other disease for decades. He took up a lot of space discussing how the goal could be accomplished, the technicalities, materials, and financials of such an endeavor, but he did not mention the human toll not taking action would mean. Other than giving the statistic of the people who had been sickened and those who had perished and how production had been negatively affected in the nearby factories, he didn't elaborate on the personal stories of those who had lost their lives or their loved ones.

Cora had always received good marks for her writing in the little boarding school she and her sisters had attended for a short while in upstate New York. A couple of years ago, she had written to the editor of a publication that championed the right for women to vote. Her letter had criticized an article they had published that had completely overlooked the negative effects of the policies of the local male politicians on women in the Bowery. The publication had printed her letter, and the editor had reached out to her to expand on her views in an article. She had used a pseudonym and written about how some of the women who had inherited their businesses from their late husbands were constantly in danger of losing them because their legal rights to own them weren't fully protected. If another male relative claimed ownership, the women had little recourse without an expensive legal battle. These women, in many cases, had worked beside their husbands to build the businesses, but could be forced out. That article had led to another several written under the pseudonym of Lavender Starling, but after everything that had happened with Mr. Hathaway, Cora had turned her attention to moving her family to England and hadn't written more. Her greatest wish was to one day write again to draw attention to important issues.

She fairly itched to fix Devonworth's draft. The statistics he mentioned were important, as were the steps needed to solve the problem. However, the human connection was missing.

His fountain pen sat in its holder. It was a very fine pen made of what looked to be sterling silver engraved with an eagle at the top. The slip-in steel nib seemed sturdier than what she was accustomed to using. She picked it up, tested the weight, and had written almost an entire page of notes before she realized what she was doing. He probably wouldn't appreciate that she had been snooping in his study, much less his personal documents. The tip of the pen hovered over the paper, leaving a blot of ink. No, she shouldn't involve herself in his affairs. She knew nothing about how Parliament functioned anyway.

Setting the pen back in its holder on his desk, she wadded up the paper and tossed it in the wastebasket. She was leaving the study when she heard movement downstairs. He had come home.

ELEVEN

THE STREETS OF WHITECHAPEL WERE DIRTY AND dark, and they stank of piss. The gas streetlamps that lined Mayfair were nowhere to be found. Open fires in alleyways and oil lamps took their place, which left the already foul air oily and cloying. Devonworth had lobbied for the streetlamps but hadn't been particularly surprised to have been outvoted. Politicians were ever voting for their own interests over the people they were sworn to represent. The gains flowing out of the hidden opium dens and illicit whorehouses were enough to keep them complicit. Some deeds were better left done in the dark.

He disliked the place immensely and was only here for one reason. James Brody ran Whitechapel. Once, the territory had been divided among several gangs, but the past several years had seen the area consolidated through brute force and bloodshed. The smaller groups that still operated here on the fringes paid him for the privilege. This was the devil that Harry had been stupid enough to become indebted to.

Devonworth drew his collar up toward his ears and reached for the revolver secured at his hip. He didn't draw it; he merely wanted the reassurance of its presence. The weight of the bills he carried in the inside pocket of his coat was why he was here. Harry's debt would finally be repaid, and then Devonworth would spend the rest of his life making certain Brody was run out of London.

"The Scarlett Cock is just ahead. If he's not there, word will find him that we're looking for him." Cavell spoke from his left side. He had insisted on coming, and Devonworth was glad to have his company. The man had been born and raised on these streets, so he would know them better than anyone else Devonworth could find.

Cavell had suggested Devonworth hire Dunn and Sanford, two men who worked security at Montague Club, and they followed behind, along with two of the men Devonworth usually called on when in need of security. As a sitting member of Lords, he could never be too careful. Any number of foul cretins would count their blessings to see him dead. Their group was six in all, a number that had felt robust at the start of this mission but seemed to shrink the farther they slunk into Whitechapel's depths.

There was no denying they were conspicuous as they marched through the filth of the slum. The pavement ahead of them cleared as they approached. Several men slipped into alleys while the other pedestrians ducked into doorways, anticipating trouble. One woman they passed called out to her friend, "Look here, Dottie. West End lads coming your way."

Up ahead, an old wooden sign with a faded red rooster jutted out over the narrow street. Another woman leaned in a doorway, the stairs behind her leading up to the first floor of the building that housed the pub. No doubt there were rooms there where the women conducted their business. The woman smiled at him, her face painted unnaturally white with bright red lips. "What'd'ya say, dovey? Want to tip yer prick in me honey?"

Devonworth would have moved past her, but she stepped into his path. "No. Thank you."

She laughed, tossing her head back. "Oi, he's a polite one, inni he, Mabel? A 'andsome one, too."

Movement in the shadows behind her reminded him just how dangerous this mission could be. Sanford moved up to block the unknown threat, but Devonworth held up a hand to stay him when the figure came forward into the light. It was another prostitute. This one was younger, but her eyes were already creased with lines, hollows shadowed beneath them.

"Give Janie a go. She ain't had a proper gentl'man yet." The older woman thrust the younger one into his arms. She smelled overwhelmingly of cheap perfume and liquor.

Devonworth righted her and held up a coin. "We are looking for Brody."

The smile dropped from her face and she shrank back. "You should go home."

"Is he inside?"

All pretense of her flirtation stopped. "Don't mess with him. Your face is too pretty." She stepped back, not even bothering to take his coin.

The younger one looked from her friend to him and gave the barest of nods. He tossed the coin to her and she grabbed it, tucking it into some unseen pocket in her skirt.

Brody probably already knew they were here. One of his henchmen had likely spotted them the moment they had stepped over Commercial Street. You didn't control a territory like this without sentries.

"Thank you," he said as the women let the darkness swallow them.

They had already discussed how best to proceed, so when they reached the pub, the two hired men waited outside the door to alert them if reinforcements came. Cavell's men followed them inside. The pub was two rooms joined by the rectangular bar. The first room was filled with men at community tables as a few women circulated with ale and food, sausages by the smell of it. Someone played a bawdy song on a pianoforte in the far room where the crowd was more boisterous. Several heads swiveled toward them when they walked in. One of the men behind the bar turned immediately and hurried through a door that led to yet another room. When Devonworth and Cavell went to follow him, two men stepped into their path.

"Where you going?" one of them asked. He was dirty and rank, and his breath smelled like days-old beer.

"We've come to see Brody," Devonworth answered.

The man grinned, revealing teeth so stained with tobacco they were nearly black in the meager lighting. "Who's that?"

"Give off," Cavell said, his old accent coming out. "Everyone knows 'im."

"Remind me. Maybe I ain't so smart." The man's infernal grin widened.

"Lookin' that way," Cavell agreed, which made the man scowl at the insult.

He reared up as if he intended to fight them, but then a whistle sounded from across the room. The barkeep had returned and waved them over. They went to move past the man, but he held his ground, evidently still insulted.

"Leave it, Jim," the bartender barked.

Jim spat a wad of tobacco at their feet as he slowly moved to the side.

The four men walked to the door, and the barkeep turned to lead them down a narrow hall. They left Dunn stationed at the entrance to the hall in case any of the men from the pub decided to follow. After a couple of turns that led them down-hill and convinced Devonworth they were under a street some-where, they came to an arched door. It must have served as storage at one point in its history, but it was now an office of sorts where Brody conducted his business out of sight. It couldn't be the only one. Brody would never allow them to find his hiding places.

Sanford stayed outside the door with the barkeep as Cavell and Devonworth went inside. Brody lounged behind a table with another man at his side. This one looked mean with a meaty bald head and slashes for eyes. Brody was a bit more polished. He wore a suit and his dark hair was slicked back as he smiled at them with a cigar clenched between his teeth. Piles of money were stacked on the table along with leather satchels Devonworth guessed were filled with opium.

"Welcome, milord . . . Cavell." His enthusiasm dimmed as he took in his former colleague. Devonworth didn't know the details of their history, but it didn't seem good. "Streets are fairly deserted. Took you longer than I thought." He spoke with the same accent as everyone else here, but it was a bit more polished, as if he wanted them to know he was better than the others.

Devonworth had assumed Brody's men had been watching their progress, but it rankled to know he'd been right. "I've come to pay my brother's debt."

"I know." Brody's self-satisfied smirk was almost more than he could bear. "Hadley, fetch the ledger."

His colleague reached beneath the table and extracted a worn, leather-bound volume and flipped it open on the table.

It was filled with nearly illegible scrawls through pages and pages of ill-gotten gains. Devonworth was angry that he was here; he was even more ashamed that his money would be contributing to this evil. Men and women were lying in alleyways, their entire lives destroyed by the poison Brody fed them. Children were left to fend for themselves or join in the business as runners and thieves to support themselves. Any money that made its way into Whitechapel eventually was funneled into Brody's operation. He wanted to rail at Harry all over again.

Brody made a show of turning to the right page and scrolling the columns.

"Ten thousand pounds," Devonworth said to put an end to the display.

He took the cigar from his mouth and flicked it onto the floor. "Eleven."

"It's ten." Devonworth spoke through gritted teeth.

Brody smirked. "It was ten, but now it's eleven. Don't fret, you can afford the interest now that you've wed your little heiress."

The fact that Brody had heard of his marriage wasn't a surprise. Everyone knew of the marriage because it was in all the newspapers and tabloids, along with the requisite biting commentary, but it disturbed him that Cora would be brought into Brody's world even tangentially.

At his hesitation, Brody added, "Tell me, what's it like to fuck an American heiress? There are so many around London now, but I regret I haven't had the chance to—"

"Here." Devonworth almost ripped the package out of his coat before tossing it on the table.

Brody chuckled and gave a nod of command to his underling. The man ripped open the paper it had been carefully wrapped in and began to count it. Devonworth had been expecting something like this to happen. Brody was not an honorable criminal. He'd have no compunction about changing the terms. Devonworth pulled out another wad of bills and tossed them on top. The thought of Cora in Brody's clutches made him feel cold and hot at the same time. She might be the wife he didn't want, but she didn't deserve to be brought to the attention of scum like Brody.

The bald man gave him a cutting look before picking up the wad and adding it to the total. "Eleven thousand."

Brody nodded. "Thank you for your patronage, milord."

Devonworth's entire body vibrated with his anger and the suppressed need to take his frustration out on the man before him. "Stay away from my wife and stay away from my brother."

"I don't make those sorts of promises. Besides, your brother came to me. No one forced him to play a game he couldn't win. Keep the child away from games he doesn't understand."

Devonworth took an inadvertent step forward. Cavell put a hand out to keep him in check. "If you come near my brother again, I'll make certain you suffer for it, Brody."

Brody shook his head, but he no longer tried to hold that he was amused by the situation. "Take him out of here, Cavell, before something unfortunate happens."

"Let's go, Dev. Nothing more can be done tonight," Cavell said, his palm pressing into Devonworth's stomach.

Devonworth knew he was right, but irrational anger was driving him now, leaving him rooted in place. It wasn't until Cavell stepped between him and Brody that he was able to turn and walk out the door. They had to leave. He could fight Brody, but even if he won, they wouldn't get out of the warren alive.

The group came back together as they made their way out

of the pub until they were six strong again. He had no idea if Brody had anything unpleasant planned for them, but it was best to get out of the area as quickly as possible. However, as soon as they passed the first alley, a man rushed at them out of the shadows. Devonworth jumped back, and Jim came into the light, his tobacco-stained teeth gritted as he lurched at him, undoubtedly still angry from the earlier encounter. It was the outlet his anger needed. Balling up his fist, he hit the man squarely in the jaw and knocked him to the ground. He stayed there, gripping his jaw and moaning, no doubt hindered by the drinks he had consumed in the pub.

A woman screeched and came running up to them. Cavell braced for her attack, but she only bent to check on the fallen man. "You've killed him." She looked up at Devonworth and he realized she was the young woman from the doorway.

"He's not dead. Bruised but alive."

She rose, her brow furrowed as she looked down at the man, uncertain how to proceed. It was only when she braced a hand against the swell of her stomach that he realized she was with child. He didn't know if Jim was her man or her pimp, or perhaps those meant one and the same here. He reached into his breast pocket and withdrew a card. She flinched when he pulled it out as if she thought it could be a knife.

He paused to allow her a moment to see in the dim light that he wasn't attacking her. "Take this." She reached out hesitantly, and he closed the distance and pressed the card into her hand. "You can find help there."

She frowned as she examined the small rectangular card, and he suspected she couldn't read.

"There's a map on the back to the London Home for Young Women," he said. She turned it over to reveal a sketch with streets labeled along with well-known landmarks and a big star marking the destination. "They help unmarried women in need of aid."

"I ain't unmarried." She glanced back down to Jim, whose groans had turned into snores.

"Doesn't matter," he said. "They'll help you."

Her lips tightened belligerently, but she didn't toss the card down as she might have. Instead, she tucked it into her skirts where the coin had disappeared earlier.

"Let's get the hell out of here," Cavell urged.

By now some of the deeper shadows had begun to get restless. Devonworth didn't know if they were Jim's compatriots or Brody's men, and he didn't want to find out. The six of them hurried down the streets, and he didn't draw a restful breath until he was climbing the steps to his home. Edgecomb met him at the door and took his coat, gloves, and hat.

"Good evening, my lord."

"Evening, Edgecomb."

"Would your lordship care for supper?"

"No, thank you. I ate earlier." He'd taken a meal with Cavell at Montague Club before they had set out. "How is her ladyship?"

"Well, my lord. Mr. Brendon dined with her briefly before he left for the evening," the butler said.

A twinge of guilt gnawed at him. He had been so busy this past week meeting with his solicitors and accountants to get his debts and investments settled and arranging for the refurbishments at Timberscombe Park that he had hardly seen her. She must think him the worst husband, but it couldn't be helped. Bidding Edgecomb good night, he hurried up the stairs but stopped at the top when he very nearly collided with Cora outside his study, which was the first door at the top of the stairs.

She stood in her rose dressing gown with her hair in a braid over one shoulder. His exclamation of surprise gave way to silence as he studied her in a more natural state than he had ever seen her. She wasn't bound up and was no doubt naked beneath the nightclothes. She appeared softer and more vulnerable this way. The lavender scent she always seemed to carry with her washed over him. She was fresh and clean and so pretty and soft he wanted to pull her into his arms. She was an unexpected balm against the ugliness of the night he'd just had. It shocked him how very much he wanted to hold her against him.

"My lord," she said, belatedly raising a hand to where the sides of her dressing gown came together at her neck.

"My apologies. I didn't think you would still be awake."

A light blush lit her face, a slow raspberry stain that mottled her cheeks. "I wasn't sleepy."

He glanced to the open door of his study, suddenly very certain that she had been inside. What would she be doing in there?

"Did you enjoy your evening?" she asked, her gaze taking in his rumpled appearance.

Something had ripped when he had punched the man outside the pub. Devonworth suspected it had been his sleeve, and his lapel had refused to lay flat since. He hadn't even thought to smooth his hair. He realized the young prostitute's cloying perfume still lingered on him the exact moment Cora's nostrils flared and her eyes widened. She thought he had been with a woman. He should set her at ease, but then she might wonder what he had been doing. Somehow it was easier to let her think that than to admit the truth. His shame at having to deal with Brody was too great to share with her. What would it matter to her if he had a mistress anyway? They were not intimate.

Not by his choice, he realized. He had agreed to her stipulation without giving any thought to what it would mean, but standing here with her in a state of undress, he felt real regret. It would be no hardship to bed her. Indeed, his entire body resonated at her presence.

"Well enough," he offered, not bothering to explain further. After a moment, she nodded and said, "Good night, then."

"Good night." She walked down the corridor to her chamber and didn't even look back as she let herself inside. The light from the sconce she passed under highlighted the shape of her body beneath her nightclothes, and he found himself watching the outline of her hips until she disappeared from view.

He took one step toward his room before turning to his study. He lit the lamp at his desk and surveyed the room. Nothing had been disturbed. It all appeared as he had left it. Perhaps she'd been curious about the books on his shelves. None of them appeared to be gone, however. He leaned down to turn off the light when he noticed a single ball of paper in the bin. Retrieving it, he smoothed it out on his desk and looked over the notes she had written in an attractive and orderly hand.

She had read his speech pleading for the passage of the Public Health Bill. He wasn't to deliver it until later in the summer before the break. No one had read it yet, not even Beckham. The knowledge immediately made him bristle, but he slid into his chair and read over the notations again, taking hold of his speech to reread the areas she mentioned. Her critique was thoughtful, and she made several valid points when she suggested he bring in firsthand accounts from villagers. Not only that, her writing flowed well and was conversational rather than scathing or cold. She was right. Personal stories would go a long way toward making the statistics mean something.

He laughed to himself at her verve and filed the crumpled paper in his desk drawer. Perhaps he'd ask her to share more of her opinions. Ever since that demonstration outside Parliament in February when Camille's suffrage group had been assaulted at their protest by criminals funded by her late husband's successor, the groups in Parliament had begun to pull ranks. Several backed Hereford, even though there was nearly indisputable evidence of his involvement, while several supported Devonworth. He was afraid the mess would sway voting on the health bill. God knows he needed all the help he could find to get the bill passed.

TWELVE

THE BALL THAT WAS TO INTRODUCE CORA AND HER family was held at the home of the Earl and Countess of Leigh in Belgravia. The London Season had officially begun, so a stream of carriages lined Upper Belgrave Street, their occupants waiting to get an exclusive peek at the new Countess of Devonworth. Cora had told herself that this wouldn't be any worse than the wedding breakfast, and she had thought it wouldn't be right up until they arrived.

"Are you all right?" Devonworth asked from his place across the carriage.

"I'm fine." She didn't know what had given her away. Perhaps it was how she clutched her skirts as if they were a lifeline. She released them and gently smoothed out the delicate silk.

Her family had returned from Paris the day before when her mother had surprised her with an original Worth gown. None of them could afford it, of course, so she had been suspicious of its origin.

"I can't wear this," she had said.

"You certainly can, my love." Fanny had pulled it out of the box she had placed reverently on Cora's bed and held it up to her. "Look at it! It's perfect for you."

And it really was. Lavender was her favorite color. It was why she had chosen that as her pen name. The gown was made of the richest lavender silk she had ever seen. Gold thread, the only embellishment, had been delicately woven through the fine material. Worth gowns were known for their extravagant ornamentation—jewels, crystal beads, and a rich blend of textiles—which made this one unique and all the more beautiful for its simplicity. The skirt was tie-back, which meant it wouldn't need a bustle and would conform to her slight curves. She had loved it on sight, and that love had only grown deeper when Fanny held it up to her and forced her to a mirror.

Her mother smiled in triumph. "See? It's perfect with your coloring. I knew it would be the moment I saw it on that model in the shop. Cora, you wouldn't believe that shop. They bring you champagne and trot out all these girls in these gorgeous creations . . ."

Fanny's voice faded into the background as Cora studied the gown in the mirror. She'd never owned anything so magnificent. "It's the most beautiful dress I've ever seen," she whispered in awe at her reflection. The shade brought out the red tones in her hair, which she usually hated, but this made the color seem beautiful. Desirable, even.

"Oh, good." Fanny clapped her hands. "I'm glad you think so."

"How did you get it so fast?" Cora couldn't stop stroking it, imagining how it would look on her, falling just off the shoulders to a cinched torso to a sleek waterfall of fabric that would end in a slight train where the gold thread gathered together like a sunburst.

"You won't believe it. I gave them your proportions, and they almost exactly matched the model. They had to take up the tiniest bit at the hem, but other than that it was perfect. With a few adjustments by Monroe, it will be all ready for you to wear tomorrow night."

"I couldn't possibly." But oh, how she wanted to. The very thought of refusing it made her chest ache. She turned away from the mirror to avoid the visual temptation of seeing it against her. "We can't afford this."

"You can afford things now, darling. You're a countess, remember?" Fanny patted her cheek and then set about returning the tissue paper to the box. "How is that going, by the way? Did you enjoy your first days as a married woman?"

"Don't change the subject, Mama. It was fine. But we need to talk about this gown. Do you want me to pay you back for it? I can, of course, but I'm not sure this is the best use of our funds." Cora was always conscious of having to save money for when she and Devonworth ended their marriage.

"No, I didn't mean that. You don't need to pay anyone back. It's a gift."

Something about the way she had said that raised suspicion. While her mother was a good actress, she was a terrible liar. Her voice took on a certain high tone with her lies.

"Who bought it?"

"Does it matter?" Fanny asked, moving the box from the bed.

"Yes. Who?"

Fanny sighed. "Mr. Hathaway, if you must know." Cora started to argue, instinctively pushing the gown away from her, but her mother hurried on. "Don't fuss, Cora. He owes this to you. He's also a guest at the ball. I simply reminded him how gauche it would be if his goddaughter"—this was the term they had taken to using to describe their relationship—"appeared at the ball in anything less than a Worth. People would talk. It doesn't matter anyway because Jenny and Eliza both accepted theirs, and how would that look if you show up not wearing one?"

House of Worth gowns were the most sought-after in American Society. Owning one, or several, was the epitome of having made it to the top. The newly wealthy were always looking for ways to show their money, and this extravagance was considered well worth the price. The quality and style of the house was so remarkable that even the women in Knickerbocker families had begun to covet them. Cora didn't know if the gowns had made their way through London Society, but she had heard the Crenshaw sisters mention the house. She assumed they wore them.

The extravagance had been out of her reach for so long that she had never considered she might one day possess one. Accepting anything from Mr. Hathaway was like making a deal with the devil, as far as she was concerned, which she'd already done once. She wanted to wash her hands of him, but he wouldn't be out of their lives until Eliza and Jenny were married, unless they chose to forgo their inheritances. If keeping him placated also gave her what she wanted, then so much the better. She had kept the gown.

"I needn't tell you that you look lovely, so don't concern yourself with that," Devonworth said as the carriage rolled to a stop again in the traffic. Several footmen were charged with unloading the guests, so they were moving at a fairly good pace.

She wouldn't mind hearing it, but she wouldn't stoop to fishing for compliments. He had met her at the bottom of the stairs at home, and she would have sworn his eyes devoured her on her way down. He'd raised his hand to take hers, and she thought he meant to tell her how beautiful he found her, but they had been swarmed by her sisters. His hand had fallen to his side, and whatever he'd been about to say was forgotten as he ushered them all out to their carriages. Fanny and her sisters followed behind them. Harry was with them since he would escort her mother into the ball.

"Actually, you never said if you like my gown." Maybe she wasn't above a little fishing.

"It's beautiful, as are you." He was back to his stoic self, the words almost perfunctory, so she couldn't tell if he really meant that. It was too bad their moment on the stairs had been interrupted.

"Thank you. I needn't tell you that you look handsome tonight." She smiled as she tossed his words back at him. It was true as always. His evening black set off his tan complexion and gold hair. It also somehow drew the eye to the smooth angles of his face and jaw.

His eye twinkled at her jest. "I hope you aren't worried about meeting everyone tonight. You look lovely, so that is half the battle."

"What's the other half?" That was the part that most concerned her.

"Appearing mild and biddable." The corner of his mouth quirked with a bitter sort of humor. "I won't fault you for it if you choose not to do that."

She bristled. "Mild and biddable?"

"As I'm certain you're aware, Society requires their young women to be pretty and obliging. They reward those who fall in line."

She watched him closely. "But you don't agree with them. What makes you different than others in Society?"

He shrugged. "I prefer to concern myself with different things. Things that make the world better."

Her heartbeat accelerated. "Then you believe women should enjoy . . ." She swallowed, hardly afraid to let herself believe that he might think women should be equal to men. From what she knew of him, he did seem to believe in fairness and equality, but plenty of learned men would say they believed the same then lacked the will to hold firm to those convictions.

"I believe that women have earned their say. After all, men walk the earth because women exist."

She wanted to question him more, but the carriage had rolled forward, and when it came to a stop, a footman opened the door for them. Devonworth stepped out and then helped her down. She was aware of her sisters and mother walking behind them, but her nerves were back.

He leaned over, and his warm breath at her temple caused a tremor to run through her. "All you have to do is murmur greetings at every introduction. No one expects more than that. We'll dance twice, no more. We'll leave in two hours. It will be done before you know it."

The evening was basically the same as the one at the house party, except this time the stakes were different for them both. She was his bride now and would need to find at least a basic acceptance among his peers. The prime minister himself would be attending, which meant she needed to put on a good face for her husband's career as well. Her mouth was too dry to swallow, so she fixed her face in a benign smile and hoped she could get through it all without embarrassing him.

There was a small line when they reached the ballroom, but they were announced in short order, followed by Fanny, Jenny, and Eliza. She had been told that there would only be a few hundred guests in attendance, and it looked like most of them

were already here. Some of them clearly took note of their
arrival, but several of the groups continued on in their conversation, which she appreciated. Leigh and Violet greeted
them, and then they were approached by Mr. Thorne and Camille. The familiar faces set her at ease until they moved on
and she recognized the high forehead and stern features of
Benjamin Disraeli.

"My lord, this is Miss Dove—erm . . . my wife."

The only sign of his embarrassment was the clench of his
jaw and the way his eyes widened slightly when he realized his
mistake. Perhaps it was her nerves, but Cora giggled. The
prime minister smiled. It didn't reach his eyes, but he was
clearly amused. "No need for such formality with your own
wife, Devonworth," the man quipped.

"Good evening, your lordship." Confused if she was supposed to curtsy or not—he had only recently been made a peer
but he was a prime minister—Cora compromised and gave
him an abbreviated one, which he seemed to accept. "It's an
honor to meet you."

After a quick introduction to her family, he moved on and
the moment was over.

"That was adorable." She smiled up at her husband. Whatever attack of nerves she'd been under had passed with his
error.

He grinned down at her briefly before schooling his features into his usual impassive facade. "What do you mean?"

"You know what I mean, *Leo*." She teased him with the
reminder of their conversation on the day of their wedding.
She hadn't actually found the nerve to call him Leo again.

"I'm afraid I haven't the foggiest notion of what you're referencing." His lips quirked, but other than that, he managed
to contain himself.

"Are you telling me you don't recall introducing me as Miss Dove?"

He scoffed. "That would have been horrifying . . . intolerable, even . . . if it had happened." He took in the crowd as if looking for someone.

"Is that how things are? We simply pretend unpleasantness doesn't happen?"

"It's worked for generations. Why change things now?"

She laughed aloud at that, and he flashed her a bright smile. For a brief moment, their eyes met, and she felt as if they were alone in the room together. It was them against everyone else. He squeezed her hand and pulled her forward to meet another lord. Soon, one gentleman blended into the next and she had trouble keeping track of who she had met. At some point, her mother and sisters broke off and she was left alone on her husband's arm to face the well-wishers, and she found she didn't hate it. He was funny when he wanted to be, and charming. He was a solid presence at her side as he showed her around.

Once when there was a short break between introductions, she said, "I feel better about calling you Leonidas."

"I have no recollection of that, Miss Dove." He winked down at her, and her belly swirled pleasantly.

They weren't able to talk again until he led her out for their first dance, Liszt's *Mephisto Waltz No. 1*. It was a favorite of the music hall Fanny liked to frequent back home, though Cora had never heard it with a proper full orchestra.

Her nerves returned the moment they were in position and couples began twirling around them. She knew the steps and had danced with him before, but the stakes seemed higher now. Literally everyone who would make up her life in the coming years in any meaningful way was here, and she knew they would be watching.

"Take a breath, Cora." He kept his eyes on hers and his expression pleasantly neutral. His voice was pitched low enough to be heard over the music but so that it didn't carry far.

She hadn't realized she had stopped breathing until he said that and she drew in air. Her lungs expanded and the tension in her shoulders eased a little. He guided them around the dance floor, and she settled into his smooth rhythm.

"Are they watching?"

"Who?"

She didn't want to look away and lose her count, which would knock her out of rhythm. "Everyone."

He chuckled softly. "No one is watching."

"That's not true."

"It is. The ones who aren't dancing are drinking or gambling in that salon downstairs."

She faintly recalled sounds of revelry coming from a room on the main floor as they had made their way upstairs. She smiled back at him. "Do you mean the men aren't watching?"

His brow creased momentarily. "I meant everyone. Why do you ask?"

It was only at that moment that she understood he really didn't know. "I suppose you don't realize, but many women watch you."

He laughed, but it was more of a scoff. "They've long since given that up. Their mamas take them aside at the beginning of every Season and tell them who they are allowed to covet. I have never made that list due to my unfortunate circumstances."

There was a bitter tone in his voice that she hadn't noticed before. How difficult was it to be a penniless lord? He'd had power and influence but none of the money that usually went along with those things. "I suppose that could be true, but that doesn't mean they don't watch you and mourn what they can't have. Surely, a few of their mamas would accept you for themselves."

He chuckled at that.

"You must realize how handsome you are." If she said it casually, acknowledged it, then this fascination she had with his appearance would go away, or so she hoped.

He gave a brief shake of his head and led her into a series of turns. When they came back together, he said, "I don't put much stock into superficial things, Miss Dove. Ledgers, clean water, a functional roof . . . those are things that concern me."

He seemed completely indifferent to his appeal to women, but he obviously concerned himself with sexual matters. The fact that he kept a mistress and Cora had all but caught him in the act had been needling her ever since that night. She didn't quite know why. He was entitled to his pursuits of pleasure, since that wasn't to be a part of their relationship. Yet, she had wondered all night if the woman was in this very room. Perhaps she was the wife of one of his colleagues, or a widow. She couldn't very well say any of this to him. Instead, she said, "What about love? That isn't superficial."

"Love." His tone was disinterested. "A fleeting and silly emotion."

They turned again, and she took a moment to collect herself amid her unexpected dismay. What did it matter that he was a cynic? She'd had that very thought more than once. Romantic love was a fleeting emotion. It didn't last. She did not fancy herself in love with him, yet somehow she found herself disappointed. "Fleeting?" she asked when they came together again.

"Yes, I'd put it along the lines of infatuation and sensual obsession. Impermanent and self-indulgent."

"What of familial love?"

"What of it? Those young women don't watch me because of familial love, now, do they, Miss Dove?" His eyes narrowed the slightest bit at her as if they were sharing some private joke. Despite how inappropriate it was, she found herself enjoying their exchange.

"No, I should say not, Devonworth." Only it wasn't the young women that concerned her. She could not imagine a man as principled as Devonworth would make a mistress of one of them. His mistress would be a woman older than a debutante. Perhaps someone who was watching him at this very moment. She started to look, but he spoke again.

"Before I forget . . . About my speech. I saw your notations."

She froze, but his hand at her back kept her moving along. Was he angry? He didn't sound angry, but then it was difficult to tell with him. She'd never seen him in a rage. He was probably the type to internally combust with only an expression of vague disappointment on his face.

"And?" she finally managed to say.

"And you made several excellent points."

"Oh?" That was unexpected.

"I'd like to talk to you about them later."

She nodded, but the music was already starting to fade. She managed to school her shock into a neutral expression and gave a brief curtsy to his bow. Harry appeared from nowhere and claimed her hand.

"Will you dance with me, sister?" He looked slightly less rumpled than normal with his hair sleekly arranged and his tie straightened.

"Of course, Harry."

Devonworth bid them goodbye and turned to stalk through

the crowd. Whether he realized it or not, numerous sets of feminine eyes followed him as he walked. Most were probably hoping for a dance, but he left the floor. She knew that she probably wouldn't see him again for some time, as most of her dances had been politely claimed as he had introduced her around. They were scheduled for a quadrille later, not long before they were to leave.

The music started again, and she settled into her dance with Harry. Although she found herself preoccupied with the idea of sharing her ideas with Devonworth.

THIRTEEN

DEVONWORTH LEFT HIS WIFE DANCING WITH Harry and made his way toward the very far reaches of the room where he knew his friends would have a proper scotch waiting for him. He found most balls to be cumbersome events that interfered with accomplishing any real work. He attended them as infrequently as he could, but even he could admit that this one had been necessary. There was no better way to introduce his wife into Society. His mother had impressed upon him the importance of this in the letter she had sent from the comfort of her friend's lavish country estate in Cornwall, but it was not lost on him that she had not bothered to attend herself. With the exception of Harry, who seemed to go out every damned night of the week spending money they didn't have, they were not a family of social butterflies.

Even tonight his mind churned with the meetings he had scheduled for the week and the plans for the refurbishment at Timberscombe Park. The architect had found other structural issues, so it had gone beyond a simple roof replacement, which was never simple from the outset when attempting to preserve the historical aesthetic of a several-hundred-year-old property. It was only when talking to Cora that things seemed to settle inside him.

Although something about that particular exchange bothered him. He paused to greet an associate and found himself looking back at her. She thought he'd been insincere with his compliment earlier in the carriage, but she really was stunning tonight. The dress was a work of beauty, and she wore it well. She fairly shone in it with the deep red tone of her hair and pale skin. Her breasts were fuller than he had realized them to be. Her wedding gown and the gown she had worn at the house party had been as modest as the clothing she wore every day.

He smiled as he remembered how she had felt underneath him on the football pitch. He had felt her breasts then, pressing against his chest and under his palm as he'd attempted to clean her up, and then all but forgotten. That woman from the pitch had stared back at him tonight during their waltz. He'd been afraid he'd only imagined her spirit, but she'd come out of hiding.

Harry swirled her into the waiting arms of another man as the lively dance required them to change partners, causing her to move out of sight. Devonworth continued on his way and was still smiling when he reached his friends.

"Dear God, he smiles." David gave a look of mock horror.

"I told you he needed a good lay." Prince Edward Singh, a childhood friend from Eton, handed Devonworth a snifter filled nearly to the brim. "Figured you'd need this, but something tells me marriage is agreeing with you."

"It's tolerable." He took a drink while he looked for a hint of her lavender gown through the throng. "Truth be told, hasn't changed much for me."

"He hasn't been fucked," David clarified to Edward. "He's still a monk. Right, Dev?"

Devonworth glared at his friend. "Sod off."

Edward laughed and asked David, "And how would you know?"

"Rumors, the best part of balls," David answered with a smirk.

"Do you mean to say that there are already rumors about the state of my marriage?"

"I mean to say there are already gossip columns written about the state of your marriage."

"What?" Devonworth was properly horrified.

"It's the bloody servants. You can't trust any of the lot. Always willing to sell a tale to a gossip sheet for the right price." David tossed back his drink.

The prince nodded his agreement. "There are even bets on when you'll consummate. The word is you haven't yet."

"And why would anyone care if we consummated the bloody thing?"

David shrugged. "Perhaps you haven't noticed because no one has written a treatise about it and handed it to you to read, but your marriage upset the delicate balance of female sentiment in our fair city."

Edward let out a bark of laughter. "What does that even mean?"

"It means that the unmarried ones are all green with envy that she"—he gestured toward the dancing couples—"shares your bed, and the married ones are all wondering how long until you stray so they might have a chance. Of course the gossip sheets will find it sensational if you haven't actually done the deed yet. Got to give the masses what they want."

Did the entire country have nothing better to do than speculate on what went on in his bed? Had Cora been right about the women watching them? He let his gaze roam as it would through the crowd, taking in each couple and group. It wasn't long before he locked eyes with a group of young women who had likely made their debuts within the past year or two. They giggled and closed ranks, the ones on this side of the circle giving him their backs.

He cursed under his breath. "What a ridiculous society we are."

That only made his friends laugh. "Sex makes the world go round," Edward said.

"Speaking of, if you'll excuse me, I have a Dove sister to go attend to." David nodded toward him and began to walk off, no doubt in search of Jenny. His mild obsession with her wasn't very subtle.

Devonworth felt the right and proper thing to do was talk his friend out of his lecherous designs on his wife's sister. "David, I cannot countenance that. As my sister by law, she should be off-limits."

"We don't deal in shoulds, you and I. We deal only in what can actually be accomplished." With that he disappeared into the crowd.

"Let him go." Edward laid a hand on his shoulder. "He'll only get a dance out of her in this crush."

Edward was right. Jenny was in no danger from David's attention in the crowded ballroom. Cora's distinctive gown caught the light, drawing his eyes to her. He followed her with his gaze as she danced before he was conscious of doing so.

The way the fabric clung to her breasts had him wanting to know the weight of them in his hands. His palms itched to caress her. All this talk of consummating the marriage had turned his thoughts in that direction, and he couldn't turn them away. Edward continued talking, something about mineral rights in Northumberland, but Devonworth could only nod vaguely as his eyes followed his wife.

He was coming to suspect that what had seemed like a perfectly reasonable term in their verbal marriage contract would become a bloody nuisance. He wanted his own wife.

T HE DANCE WITH HARRY WAS FOLLOWED BY ONE with Lord Leigh and then his brother, Mr. Thorne. By then, Cora was feeling much more confident, comforted by the support of the familiar faces, so the rest of the evening passed in a blur. It was some time later when she found herself in need of a break from dancing.

The last she had seen of her sisters, they had been talking with Viscount Mainwaring, but that was long ago. She hunted the perimeter of the room hoping to find them. Several people gave her cursory nods and greetings, but no one seemed interested in talking with her. A few of them gave her looks she could only describe as *knowing*, but whatever it was they knew, she couldn't fathom. Not finding her sisters, she moved to an open window to drag in a breath of much-needed outside air. The room inside was stuffy and hot from so many bodies.

"Surely, you jest!" A woman's slightly inebriated voice rose over the din of the crowd, and her companions dissolved into laughter. It sounded like they were just on the other side of the potted palm next to the window.

Cora frowned, but leaned forward toward the open window and tried to focus on how good the cool air felt against her face. She managed for a moment or two until the inebriated woman said, "Have you seen her?"

"Seen her? We met her," a man answered. He sounded as if he were on the upper side of middle-aged.

"Peculiar little accent, that one," the second woman, presumably his wife, answered.

Cora didn't know if they were talking about her, Fanny, or her sisters. There was no doubt in her mind it was one of them. She said a silent prayer that her mother had behaved and hadn't started talking in one of her accents.

"What was she like?" the first woman asked.

"How am I to know? She was a quiet, mousy little thing," the second woman answered.

They weren't discussing Fanny, then.

"Mousy? Yes, she did appear to have a certain charm about her." The man's smirk could be heard in the inflection of his words.

There was a round of chuckling. Cora was certain they meant her now and struggled to place their voices. She had been too terrified to offer much more than the most basic of greetings when Devonworth had introduced her around. The couple could have been almost anyone she had met that night.

"I am surprised," the first woman added, a thoughtful tone in her voice. "I suppose I imagined Devonworth with someone more like Lady Sofia."

The second woman lowered her voice, but it was still loud enough to carry to Cora. "Have you seen the middle sister? That one could be a match for Lady Sofia."

The other woman agreed, and Cora hardly had the chance

to feel the sting before the man broke in, "Ladies, it's a financial arrangement. 'Cash for class' and all that."

They all laughed as if he were so very clever. The phrase was a familiar one that the press had created to refer to the marriages between American heiresses and the aristocracy. It was classism at its finest, even as she admitted that some families were so desperate to rise in Society that it was applicable. It wasn't why she had married, however. She had simply wanted her rightful inheritance.

"Cash for class," his wife repeated before sighing in near despair. "Oh, I suppose that family will be at all the events now, won't they?"

Cora drew herself up to put in an appearance on the other side of the potted palm when the first woman added, "It would seem so. Although they say the marriage hasn't been consummated, so perhaps it will be annulled in short order."

"Where have you heard that?" the wife asked.

"Everyone is saying Devonworth hasn't bothered to bed her," came the answer.

People were talking about their marriage bed? Why would anyone care about that?

That was all she could take. She couldn't stand here and listen to them discuss her private life. Cora pulled her shoulders back and held her chin slightly higher than was strictly necessary and looked right at the group as she revealed herself. She recognized the man and his wife as a couple she had met earlier. She had forgotten his rank, but Bolingrave was his name. He was a stout little man with a pointy face and hard eyes who served in Lords with Devonworth. Her introduction to him had been somewhat reserved, leading her to believe they were not friends.

"Lord and Lady Bolingrave," she acknowledged them.

His wife paled, but he nodded back unfazed. "Lady Devon-worth."

Cora gave a tilt of her head in acknowledgment of the third person and made her way through the crowd. They devolved into furious whispering behind her.

She didn't really care about them and their mean-spirited gossip. She did, however, care about whoever this Lady Sofia was. Could that be the name of his mysterious mistress? Had she been someone he had cared about at one time and possibly still did? She needed to know, but didn't know who to ask. Thankfully, she came upon her sisters in lively discussion with a group of young women. She joined them and managed to smile and reply appropriately, but she grabbed them both and pulled them away at the first opportunity.

"Let's visit the retiring room. I need to talk to you both," Cora said.

"Are you enjoying yourself? Isn't it such a fun party?" Eliza asked as they walked, her eyes alight with joy.

Cora agreed and made benign observations about the ball until they were inside the room. It was some sort of salon made over with several privacy screens and conversation areas. A few women lounged about chatting. Cora nodded to them and then drew her sisters to a far corner. "Have either of you met a woman named Lady Sofia tonight?"

"No, I don't think so. Why do you ask?" inquired Jenny.

Eliza looked around as if the woman named Sofia might have been courteous enough to follow them into the room. She quickly told them what she had overheard, minus the unpleasantness about herself. "I wonder if she is someone important to him."

Jenny smiled coyly. "Do you mean important as in a very close childhood friend or something more?"

Cora shrugged. "I don't know. I assume something more."

"Why do you care? I thought you said the marriage was in name only."

"I *don't* care. I'm merely curious," Cora clarified. "Devonworth is intriguing to me, and I find myself wanting to know more about him."

"Hmm . . ." The sound coming from Jenny was a bit skeptical.

"Do you . . ." Eliza lowered her already lowered voice. "Do you suppose he has kept a mistress?" The last word was more shape than sound.

Cora debated how much to tell them, but quickly realized it hardly mattered. They knew her marriage wasn't a love match. "I suspect so. He came in late a few nights ago, and he was disheveled and smelling of perfume. I think he had been to see a woman. Now I wonder if it was this Sofia person."

"And you're fine with him keeping a woman?" Jenny asked, her voice dripping with skepticism.

"Why wouldn't I be? We aren't pretending to be in love. You are the one who seems to be particularly bothered by infidelity. I already told you it doesn't matter how handsome he is because we won't have that sort of relationship. I do not love him." She didn't know why she felt so defensive about this. Perhaps it was because she liked him more than she thought she would, but she didn't want to go explaining that to her sisters. Her relationship with Devonworth was already becoming more complicated than she had intended.

Jenny frowned and Eliza took over the interrogation. "But doesn't it feel like a betrayal?"

It shouldn't, but it did . . . more than she was prepared to admit.

Jenny noted her hesitation and jumped to the wrong conclusion. "It does, which means you've consummated the marriage!"

She spoke the last several words so loudly the other women in the room looked over. Eliza and Cora both shushed her.

"No, we haven't," Cora whispered.

Jenny had the nerve to look disappointed. "I suppose the gossip sheets were right for once."

"It's in the gossip sheets?" It was one thing to have people talking, but to have ink devoted to the topic was even worse. "You've read about this?"

They both shrugged with guilty expressions on their faces.

Cora brought a hand to her temple. It didn't matter. What they did or didn't do in their marriage was between them. When they separated or divorced it would cause a bigger sensation than this, so she might as well get used to it.

"Let's get back to the party. If either of you happen to meet Lady Sofia, please let me know?"

They both agreed and all made their way back out to the ball. Even though she knew it shouldn't matter, Cora couldn't help but look for a woman named Sofia the rest of the evening.

FOURTEEN

CORA NEVER FOUND LADY SOFIA AT THE BALL AND concluded she wasn't there. Naturally, she put the phantom woman out of her mind immediately. It was easy to do because her interest was only intellectual curiosity. She wanted to learn more about this enigma of a man she had married, and what better way than to find the one woman who had apparently piqued his interest. She'd heard how people referred to him as the monk. He was too studious and virtuous to be seen as anything else. They didn't know how he had come in late that night disheveled and reeking of perfume. Of course they didn't, because he didn't flaunt his mistresses like other men might. He took his pleasures quietly and privately because decorum was of the utmost importance to him. She liked that about him.

So she did not think of Lady Sofia much on their way home that night, or after when she lay in bed with her eyes closed remembering how Devonworth had looked at her with that intense gaze that had bordered on something more when he had seen her in her gown. She knew that she was probably misremembering the intensity, but what was the harm while lying in the safety of her own bed? She could imagine that he had wanted her just a little bit. She could remember how his hands had felt on her during their two dances. They had been warm and strong and lit up the parts of her body they had touched. She could even pretend that his fingers had grazed over her bare skin, leaving delicious tingles in their wake. She could imagine what it might be like if their marriage was real.

It was make-believe. An indulgence. It didn't have to mean that she wanted it. Fantasies were just that. Fantasy. A means to set her mind afloat in the deep of night so that she might find peace and sleep, which is exactly what happened. She most assuredly did not have dreams that involved her new husband entwined with her in bed. And she did not wake up longing for those dreams to be real.

The next morning, the house moved through its normal rituals. Footsteps padded down the corridor as the maids saw to their duties. Cora had slept late to recover from the evening and her slight overindulgence in champagne. She remembered everything about the ball, but her head ached because she was only accustomed to having a glass of wine with dinner.

Monroe came in with her breakfast tray and the chocolate and to help her dress. A small box sat on the tray, wrapped in plain brown paper. She unwrapped it and opened the lid to find a fountain pen sitting on a crimson cushion. It was similar to Devonworth's in that it was silver, but a sprig of lavender was engraved near the top. Extra nibs and a stand were hidden in the box underneath the little cushion. She couldn't help but smile at the sweet gift as her fingertips traced over the lavender. How did he know that she liked the scent? Had he noticed her wearing it?

What would he say if he knew about her pen name, Lavender Starling? She didn't waste a minute wondering if the pen meant he had found out. He would have told her had he found those articles, she had no doubt.

Excitement swirled inside her as she rose to dress. She chose her violet morning dress. Not because it was the prettiest and the closest in color to lavender but because it was the first one she saw in the armoire. It had the typical long sleeves and high collar of a morning dress, but she had always liked this particular collar in how it opened in the front and stopped just above her collarbones. Her neck was long and graceful, one of the few charms she'd inherited from Fanny. She did not let herself think that he might admire that part of her as she dabbed the lavender water to her pulse point.

She drank her coffee as Monroe arranged her hair. She had been listening for sounds from the bathing chamber she shared with Devonworth, but all had been quiet.

"Have you seen my husband this morning?" she asked, hoping to affect a nonchalant tone.

"I believe his lordship is at work in his study."

It was Wednesday, which meant Parliament was not meeting. Rain poured outside the window of her room, so he had probably decided not to venture out. Her stomach leaped in excitement because he had mentioned the notations she had made on his speech, not because she looked forward to seeing him.

When Monroe had finished and she was presentable, Cora made her way to the end of the corridor to his study. The door was open, a fire burned in the hearth, and the lamp at his desk was on, but the man himself was nowhere to be seen. Papers were scattered across his desk where he had been working. She couldn't resist looking them over, her gaze tracing the sharp lines of his handwriting. He wrote with the same efficiency with which he carried out everything else in his life.

Next to the parchment was a pile of newsprint. Her glance might have passed right over the stack had a phrase in bold not caught her eye, *Marriage of Concern*. A quick skim was enough to understand the unknown author was concerned by the state of an unnamed, unconsummated marriage. She feared it was hers.

Another newspaper was folded open to an article that began, **"His lordship has been repeatedly shunned by his American bride. The lady in question is a known shrew who would rather polish her newly acquired tiara than consider her duty to her husband."**

Nausea whirled in her stomach. The newspaper underneath that one was open to a page that was more ribald in tone.

Little Lady D—
Sat and drank tea
Whiling her hours away;
'Til Lord D— came beside her,
Offered to ride her
And frightened Lady D   away.

She recoiled from the vulgarity and pushed the paper away only to reveal several more. All of them were open to articles and letters that lamented, derided, or laughed at the fact that she and her husband had not shared a bed. It was horrifying.

"Cora." Her husband stood framed in the doorway wearing his shirtsleeves and waistcoat. His hair was slightly rumpled as if he'd run his fingers through it several times.

A swirl of pleasure moved through her at how handsome he was, but she couldn't indulge that now.

"What is this?" she asked. When Jenny had mentioned reading about her marriage, Cora had assumed that one lowbrow publication had printed something vulgar. She hadn't realized that there would be so many of them.

His furrowed brow of concern slowly changed to a look of resigned disappointment or maybe even regret. "I had hoped you wouldn't see those." He walked slowly into the room and approached her warily.

"I don't understand. Why would they print this?"

"Because they want to sell newspapers and advertising." He shook his head.

"I expected people to talk, but I never imagined this." She looked back down at the paper in her hand. "Did you see they made up a rhyme?"

He gently took the paper from her and set it with the others. Then he took hold of her shoulders. His eyes were solemn when he said, "I don't want you to concern yourself with this."

"But that one—" She broke off and withdrew the newspaper with a particularly concerning headline and held it up to him. "This one is a letter signed by *a concerned MP*. It's almost as if he expects there to be an international incident if we don't . . . consummate things. He says that it leaves the marriage open to risk of annulment and the earldom must be secured with an heir."

"Cora, please, it will all die down. This is what they do. They print things like this to get under your skin, but it will go away as soon as there's another marriage or scandal or ball large enough to give them new fodder. It's drivel." His thumbs brushed slow circles on her shoulders that were distracting despite her anger.

"But who would write such a letter?"

"It's not a real letter . . . probably."

She wanted to believe him. She wanted to think that the

paper had made up the letter and signed it as an anonymous member of Parliament, but the way his gaze suddenly wouldn't meet hers roused her doubts.

"Do you have enemies in Parliament?"

He dropped his hands from her shoulders and gently took the paper from her hands. "I don't want you to worry about this. I will take care of it, and it will go away soon if we don't feed the fire." Gathering up the other sheets of newsprint, he added, "I will, however, feed this rubbish to the fire, which is precisely where it is meant to go."

The flames burned brighter as he tossed the papers in, one by one, hungry for the fuel. The paper curled at the edges before succumbing to the heat and disintegrating to ash. Though the destruction was only symbolic—there were hundreds or possibly thousands of copies out in the world—it was cathartic. She was able to draw in her first deep breath since she'd found them on his desk.

He turned with a self-satisfied expression. "There."

"Thank you. I'm afraid I disagree on one small point."

He raised a questioning brow as she approached him. Now that she could breathe again, she noticed all the little details about him that she had been too upset to take in earlier. How his shirtsleeves stretched across his shoulders, for one. Or how the charcoal-gray brocade silk of his waistcoat made her fingers itch to smooth it against his chest. How the lock of thick blond hair that had fallen over his forehead made her want to brush it back. Would it feel coarse or silky?

There was one way she could find out. Not only that, but it would put to rest all the fantasies she'd had last night while dispelling all the rumors. The idea came to her so quickly that she had to wonder how long it had been hiding there in her subconsciousness. She told herself that what she was about to propose was merely logical, but even she couldn't deny how the thought of it made the blood sing through her veins.

"I'm not certain the gossip will go away so easily. Last night I overheard people talking about it."

"Who was talking about it?" His eyes narrowed, and the energy around him intensified so much she could practically feel it crackling around her.

It was not at all an unpleasant feeling. In fact, she liked it a little bit too much and took a step back. Goose bumps broke out on her skin. "I don't know if I should say."

"Cora," he said, exasperated. "I can't stop them if you don't tell me."

"You can't stop them anyway, which is my point. Not by confrontation, at least. I do believe we can . . . mitigate things."

"How?" His brows furrowed and his eyes focused on her so intently that she couldn't find her words.

It was only when she turned to face the fire with him at her side that she could say, "I think maybe we should just . . . do it."

"Do it?" He sounded genuinely confused, but she didn't dare look at him.

"Yes. Do the deed, so to speak."

There was a pause. "Do the deed?"

He was going to make her say it. Fine. "Yes, consummate the thing quickly and get it over with."

This time he paused so long that the delay made her look at him. His expression was serious, but he didn't appear horrified by the suggestion. The longer he stared at her with that furrowed brow, the more she wanted a hole to open up in the floor and swallow her whole. She couldn't tell if he thought she was an idiot or simply desperate.

"If we ever decide to *consummate the thing* it won't be because gossipmongers forced us into it nor will you want it *over with quickly*, Miss Dove."

No, she didn't think she would want it over with quickly. She didn't have very much experience with men, but she did understand enough to know that lying with him would be magical. Or at the very least, something she would remember the rest of her life. There was no way she wouldn't want to savor it.

"Are you offended?" she asked, when she could talk again. She wondered if he realized that he called her Miss Dove, but she didn't want to risk drawing attention to it and having him stop. For some reason she wasn't willing to examine, she liked when he did that. It made him seem ever so proper . . . and corruptible.

"I'm still deciding, but that's neither here nor there. You make a good point." He strode around her, and she let out a tension-filled breath. "We could make them *think* we've consummated the marriage."

That did sound more reasonable. She probably should have thought of that first even if the suggestion did leave her feeling disappointed. "How?" she asked.

"Think about it. They have no way of knowing for certain that we haven't. A servant must have told them that I never visit your room. I simply need to visit your room at night on a few occasions. Problem solved."

"Yes, that's very logical." So logical that she definitely should have thought of it before leaping to the more extreme solution. If her face could flame any hotter, she would be reduced to a pile of ashes. "Do you think my maid is the servant talking to the papers?" She didn't want to think so, but she couldn't deny that Monroe would be the one to suspect if they had slept together or not.

"I did, yes, but this morning I had Mrs. Anderson question the servants. We suspect it's Polly, the chambermaid who assisted you on your first day."

"Polly?" She had been so kind to Cora. Had that kindness been the mere nicety required of her position?

"Yes, Mrs. Anderson believes that she is in need of money. Something about a sick aunt."

Her indignation gave way to concern. "Perhaps we could help."

His lips flattened. "If she's done this, she'll be dismissed."

"That seems harsh."

"What would you have me do? I can't have someone in my household who I can't trust."

"No, of course you can't. She was obviously desperate. I just wish there was some way to help her."

A knock on the door interrupted them. "Come in," Devonworth said.

His secretary walked in carrying a small stack of newsprint. As soon as he saw her, he hid it behind his back. Her heart sank into her stomach. It was more gossip about the state of their marriage. It belonged in the fire with the other papers.

Devonworth cleared his throat. "If you'll excuse us, Beckham and I have more work to do this afternoon."

She nodded and left them to it.

"Cora." His voice stopped her at the door. "I'll see you later tonight."

The way he said it left no doubt in her mind what he meant. They would pretend to do the deed tonight. Her cheeks burned and she nodded. The very thought of spending time alone with him in her room made her body come alive in ways it never had before.

FIFTEEN

EVONWORTH HADN'T CONSIDERED HOW THE night would proceed until the very moment he knocked on the door to his wife's room. His mind had been consumed by work and the anger the damnable rumors swirling about their marriage induced. Her soft voice beckoning him inside had him realizing that he was out of his element. The huskiness of the sound in the stillness of the night roused things in him that were not meant to be awakened tonight. Or by her. He waited a beat, until the flutter of his heart settled, before turning the latch and stepping inside her room.

He had timed his arrival so that her maid would still be attending to her. It couldn't hurt to have the woman witness him in the room. While he despised the rumors outside his home, there was nothing he could do about the talk belowstairs. He trusted Mrs. Anderson to keep a tight rein on the talk so it didn't get out of hand. It was only natural for the servants to discuss things, even personal topics. As it happened, he needed them to talk about this particular night.

Once the consummation of their marriage was assumed, he'd dismiss Polly.

"Good evening," he said.

Cora looked over at him from where she sat at her vanity table. Monroe gave a brief curtsy and kept her eyes lowered. A blush made the maid's ears turn red. He'd come in wearing his dressing gown and slippers, but the girl had never seen him in anything less than his daily attire. It wasn't helped by the fact that there could only be one reason why he was here in his wife's room so late.

"Good evening." Cora smiled at him. To the maid, she said, "Thank you, Monroe. Go ahead and retire for the night."

Monroe inclined her head and bid them both good night before she hurried out of the room. After the door was firmly closed behind her, he said, "It's an odd feeling, isn't it?"

"What's that?" Cora rose from the low-backed chair.

She wore a blue wrapper that tied in the front over what appeared to be a white nightdress. It cinched in at the waist, revealing more of the shape of her body to him than he had ever seen before. That night in the corridor when he had arrived home late, her nightclothes had been more flowy than fitted. Her figure was slight, but attractive, with long limbs and a bosom that was pleasingly full. Corsets could embellish even the sparsest frame. When he realized he was a bit too preoccupied with the apparent softness of her breasts and the curve of her hips, he glanced downward. Bare toes peeked out from beneath the hem of the wrapper. It was that unexpected nakedness that made something like desire zing through his belly. She was nude beneath her clothes, he was here in her room, and they were alone.

And she was his wife.

No. This would not do. He dragged his attention away

from her and to the other side of the room. An array of wallpaper and fabric samples was laid out there.

He had to clear his throat before he could answer her question. "The feeling of relying on a servant to put gossip to rest while simultaneously not wanting the servants to gossip about us. The situation is unwinnable."

She laughed softly, and the very intimacy of the sound made the fine hairs on his body rise. Her tread was so soft across the carpeted floor that he didn't notice her approach until she spoke next to him. "I suppose I have to agree. I'm not used to managing servants or running a large household, so it's all new to me." Instead of looking at him, she stared at the samples. Her hair was in a braid that draped over one shoulder. The gaslight picked up all sorts of gold and red tones in the tresses.

"You didn't have servants in New York?" He was almost certain Vining had told him that they lived in a respectable, if unfashionable, home.

"We did sometimes, but it wasn't a very formal arrangement. Mrs. O'Brien was our housekeeper. Her nieces worked with us, too. Different ones during different seasons when there wasn't farmwork to be hired for in Pennsylvania and upstate New York. Once they married, it was just her until we sold everything."

"No footmen?"

"We hired a handyman for tasks we couldn't take care of ourselves."

"Your father didn't leave enough to see you comfortable?" Vining was still making inquiries, but nothing unusual had been unearthed. Devonworth couldn't get over the feeling that there was something more to her that he didn't know. But then, she was all but a stranger to him.

"We were comfortable. But no, there was no excess."

"Except for the dowries."

"Except for the dowries," she acknowledged.

He glanced back at the wallpaper. There had to be at least a dozen samples in various colors and patterns. One in particular drew his eye. "I like this one." He picked up a purple sample. It was similar to the color of her ball gown with a thin vine and leaf pattern running through it in gold. "It reminds me of your gown."

She smiled and blushed prettily. "You remember."

"It was only last night. I'm not so old that I'm forgetful, especially when you looked so beautiful in it," he teased her.

Her eyes widened at the compliment, and she seemed tongue-tied. "Thank you," she finally murmured.

She walked over to her writing desk, her hips swaying subtly beneath her wrapper. He had the urge to touch them, to span the breadth of her waist with his palms.

"Thank you for this." She picked up the fountain pen. "It was very thoughtful of you."

"I didn't think you had one. You'll need it when you help me with my speech. As I said, you had very good insights. Would you consider helping me add them in?"

Placing the sample with the others, he walked over to join her.

"Do you mean now?" she asked.

He shrugged. "Why not? I assume I'll be here for at least an hour. I can't have anyone thinking I don't do a thorough job of bedding my wife."

Her eyes widened, and something tightened low and deep in his belly. He was pushing things, he knew, but he didn't want to stop. Part of him wished he was here to properly consummate their marriage. "We can spend an hour or so together several nights a week."

"Yes, I'd like that." Her breath was shallow, and he was almost certain her eyes were dilated.

But that wasn't why he was here. He took a step back from her and said, "Wait here."

He hurried to his room, opening the door slowly to make certain his valet wasn't lingering about, and retrieved the leather case with his papers that he had left there earlier. When he came back, she was sitting at her writing desk. The only other chair in the room, a small wingback, had been moved to sit adjacent.

"Come sit." All business again, she indicated the chair. "Tell me why this bill is important to you."

He told her about the unprecedented growth of the urban population. People were leaving their homes in farming communities to move to the cities for work. As industry thrived, more work opportunities in cities brought men and women into the urban centers. More housing, typically in the form of terraced homes, had been built because they could accommodate the greater number of people in the smallest area. Often these had been built without thought to water or sewer access. To make matters worse, not many in government or those landlords in charge of building terraces seemed particularly concerned, due to the high cost of building and maintaining clean water access. He, along with several others in Parliament, looked to change that.

She asked a few appropriate and intelligent questions for more information, and then she said, "None of that answers my original question. Why is this important to you?"

"I should think that's obvious. I have a responsibility to make lives better for people."

"Obviously, I understand that, but from what I can tell, many of your associates don't agree, or at the very least are ambivalent. Why do *you* feel so passionate about it?"

He knew what she was getting at now. "I'd like to believe it's the fact that I have empathy for those who have no choice. Perhaps that is some of it, but I think it comes down to my father. I was only a few years old when there was a cholera outbreak in Soho in London. A Dr. Snow traced the outbreak to a well on Broad Street. Over six hundred people died, most within a radius of that pump. The others had access to the pump because they had passed through the area. No one believed the good doctor. At that time, most still believed that sickness was caused from vapors in the air or even the will of God. That He was punishing the working poor.

"The sad fact is that even when Snow presented his practical evidence, people chose not to believe him. Even when Pasteur's scientific evidence confirmed this new germ theory a few years later, those in power didn't want to go to the trouble and expense to change things . . . my father included."

"Your father?"

"By all accounts, he couldn't be bothered to care. He voted against any sort of measure that would change things. I suppose you could say that I've made it my mission to right all the wrongs that he made."

"I wasn't expecting that. I guess it's fair to say you didn't get along with your father."

He gave a mirthless laugh. "It's fair to say that, yes. I didn't actively despise him while growing up. I knew very little of him, to be honest. I saw him a handful of times during the year."

"What are your memories of him?"

"He was cold and a man of little humor. He demanded much from those around him, no one more so than me."

"I'm sorry. That must have been terrible to grow up with a father such as him."

"As terrible as having no father?"

She shrugged. "I think so. In many ways, I can make Mr. Dove into the sort of man I want him to be. I don't have many memories of him to mar that."

"Why do you call your father Mr. Dove?"

She glanced away, sheepish. "I don't know. I never thought about it. It's how my mother always refers to him, so it's how my sisters and I talk about him."

"Do you wish you would have known him?"

"Of course, but only if he was nice."

He smiled at that, taken in by the charm of her. She most definitely wasn't what he had expected, but she was entertaining, to say the least.

"I've been thinking," she said, and looked away again, unable to hold his gaze. "If we were truly consummating this thing . . . wouldn't there be sounds?"

"Sounds?" He glanced to the bed as he realized what she meant.

"Yes, sounds and other signs that we had enjoyed ourselves."

He laughed, but it was to cover up the visual in his mind. He wondered what she would look like lying beneath him. Would she close her eyes as he entered her or keep them wide open? What sounds would fall from her lips as her body clenched him intimately? He stood abruptly when his cock woke up at the musings. Perhaps David was right and he really did need a woman.

Walking over to her bed, he launched himself to bounce into the center, startling a laugh from her. "Like this?" he asked and bounced a few more times until the bed squeaked and creaked. She covered her mouth to keep her giggles contained. "I suppose we should muss the sheets a bit." He moved around until the sheets were well creased and tugged the blanket and counterpane from the end of the bed. Then he stood and surveyed his work.

"There. Now it looks like we've properly completed the task."

"You were very thorough, my lord . . . and quick," she teased.

He gave her a mock glare and took hold of the bedpost. He proceeded to rhythmically shove it against the wall lest anyone believe he had taken his pleasure too hastily.

She bit her lip and a blush stained her cheeks as she watched the bed doing what it would be doing if they were indeed having sex. It did nothing to lessen the state of his semi-arousal.

"There," he finally said, and turned to her to give a little bow.

She mockingly clapped at the performance as she approached him, making certain she wasn't too loud. "Very good. I think they'll have no need to question your fortitude after this."

"One more thing." He reached up and untied the ribbon that bound her hair. Her eyes widened, but she didn't step away or stop him. He did what he had been wanting to do for so long he couldn't remember when the urge had started. He freed her of her braid and ran his fingers through the silk of her hair. He loved how it felt in his hands. Unfortunately, so did other parts of his anatomy. He dropped it when a tug of desire pulsed low in his groin. If he didn't cease, he wouldn't stop with her hair. He'd have her hips in his hands to hold her as he pressed himself—

"There." He stepped away and slipped the ribbon in his pocket. "Monroe will have no reason to question things."

"I suppose not, but there is the minor issue of . . ." She looked at him as if he should know what she meant.

"Of what?" he asked when it became apparent that she wouldn't continue.

"The virgin's blood," she whispered.

"Do you think they'll expect that?"

She shrugged. "They might question . . ."

"It's barbaric," he muttered. Walking into the bathing chamber, he retrieved a cloth from the chest of drawers and wet it. Bringing it back to her, he said, "Can't we pretend that we tidied up?"

She nodded as relief spread over her face. "Yes, we can. That makes the most sense."

He, too, was relieved. There was no way in hell he was enacting the thing to that degree of authenticity. "Good." He tossed the cloth to the floor and bowed his head. "I'll leave you, then. It's been enough time. Keep my speech. Next time, we can go through the first couple of pages."

She nodded, too relieved to see him to the door. "I have more notations to make. Until next time, good night, Devonworth."

He hated that she had reverted to his title instead of the name she had selected for him. But it was that strong emotion that caused him to accept it. He couldn't bear to grow too attached to her. She had already made her feelings clear on the matter of their relationship.

"Good night, Cora." He retired to his room certain this had been one of the stranger but more delightful nights of his life.

SIXTEEN

THE CONSUMMATION CONSPIRACY—AS CORA HAD begun to think of their deception—had worked. Over the next several days, almost every paper that had seen fit to print anything about the state of their marriage had written that the union had been made official. Those headlines had been just as eye roll–inducing as the first ones. **"His just deserts at last"** and **"The lady capitulates"** were two of the more irritating ones that continued to grate on her. No doubt the rumors were helped by the fact that he had come to her room twice more since that first night over the course of the week. They spent that time working on his speech and discussing the sanitary needs of the country. It wasn't a very sensual topic, but she had found herself drawn to him even more. Those feelings were something she would have to put aside, however, for many reasons. Not the least of which was that he had no interest in her beyond their agreement.

To do that, she kept herself busy. Not only had she decided on the wallpaper for her bedroom, she had also ordered new drapery and furnishings. It was no surprise she chose the pattern he had liked. After all, he'd selected the best one. Now that she had settled into married life and had her introduction to Society, she decided it was time to confront life outside their home.

Her first social outing was a meeting of the London Suffrage Society. She attended with her sisters and Violet, Lady Leigh. The meeting was a monthly strategy planning session where the group would discuss their spring and summer events. Cora welcomed the opportunity to become involved with their projects. She still felt American, but there was no doubt that Britain would be her home for the coming years. She hoped to do what she could to help while she was here.

Everyone was very nice and welcoming to her, but something in the air changed when they began to discuss the upcoming demonstration at Parliament Square. It was planned to coincide with the debates on the Married Women's Property Act. There were approximately thirty people present at the meeting, mostly women with a few men mixed in. Every single one of them seemed to sit up straighter when the president of the group, Mrs. Burgess, spoke.

"We have made passing the Married Women's Property Act our next goal. I don't need to tell you that the odds are stacked against us, nor remind you of the dangers that stand in our way. The events of February are still fresh in our minds." A murmur of outrage ran through the crowd. Mrs. Burgess raised her hand for silence. She was an older woman with a shock of white hair and formidable presence. It wasn't so much that she appeared forbidding as it was that she held herself with confidence and gravity. When she spoke, it was important. The group settled down. "We will not allow detractors to stand in our way. To that end, we have planned another demonstration outside the walls of Parliament in support of our objective. We cannot rest until women are given control of their lives. The Property Act is a crucial step down that path."

The Married Women's Property Act was intended to give women control of the assets they brought into a marriage. Other measures had not gone far enough to protect them. It was one reason Cora herself had been so apprehensive about trusting Devonworth to allow her to keep a portion of her dowry. She trusted him, but there should be a measure in place that would legally ensure their agreement was honored. She was confused, however, about what Mrs. Burgess had said while mentioning the act.

When there was a lull as an audience member questioned the logistics of the planned demonstration, Cora asked Violet, "What happened in February? Was there some sort of danger at that demonstration?"

Violet leaned over to her. "The entire group of demonstrators was attacked." Cora gasped but covered the sound so as not to draw attention. Violet continued, "A group of men wearing burlap sacks over their heads came out wielding batons and firecrackers. No one was seriously injured. There were some falls and scuffles as our people fought back. It was a stunt to frighten us. Thank goodness several bystanders intervened along with several MPs and Lords. Your husband was one of the men who ran out to help."

Cora found herself absurdly pleased by this even though she hadn't known him then. "Were the police able to apprehend the men responsible?"

Violet shook her head. "One or two, but not all of them. I've heard that they've claimed someone of some influence hired them, but if it's true, he hasn't been punished yet."

"Who is it?"

Violet's voice lowered even further. "The Duke of Hereford. My husband can't say very much on the matter, so I only know what the papers are reporting, but they have gathered evidence against him and presented it appropriately."

"What a horrible man."

"Yes, he's living up to the Hereford title," Violet agreed.

Cora had only met Violet and her sister, August, upon coming to England, but they had welcomed her as if they had known her forever. It was why Violet had hosted the ball in her honor, and Cora had no doubt that this was why there had been a grudging acceptance of her among the ton. Someone else might have stopped short of mentioning Hereford in relation to the attack, but Violet was as honest a person as Cora had ever met. It made her think that she might be a great source of information regarding Devonworth. The LSS meeting wasn't the time or place for such a discussion, however.

The meeting ended soon after, and Cora and her sisters all climbed into Violet's carriage because the countess had offered to drive them home. Cora waited until after they said goodbye to her sisters outside Camille's townhome to ask Violet the question about her husband that had been bothering her all night.

The dim carriage lantern created a warm glow that spilled over the woman's lovely features. The way she sat now, less formal and more relaxed against the plush velvet upholstery, highlighted the barely noticeable bump beneath her dress. Whether she realized it or not, Violet rested her hand lovingly over the baby she carried in her womb. Cora felt a twinge of longing for a child of her own.

Life with her mother and sisters had been somewhat chaotic. Fanny was always getting into some trouble, whether it be with a bill collector or a jilted lover who showed up drunk at their door. Cora had spent too much of the past several years dealing with that while trying to stretch their dwindling funds to ever consider whether she might want a family. Once the inheritance had become a possibility, having a real family with the man she married had never once crossed her mind. But she couldn't deny that thoughts of carrying Devonworth's child had been pushing at the edge of her mind lately. He was different than she had imagined an aristocratic husband might be.

It was best not to think about that. Clearing her throat, she said, "I've heard a couple of people mention a woman named Lady Sofia in relation to my husband. Do you know who she is?"

Her sisters hadn't yet found out any information about her, and she was loath to pursue the topic in front of them because they would insist her curiosity meant more than it did. It wasn't that she cared if the woman was his mistress. It was that she wanted to know more about him. Camille was still in Paris, so Cora couldn't ask her.

Violet smiled. "Lady Sofia Jameson. I have met her a time or two. What would you like to know?"

What did she want to know? *Were they lovers?* came to mind, but she didn't know Violet well enough for that conversation. "Are they close?"

"I only know Devonworth through my husband. We've attended several of the same social events, but I don't presume to have his ear. I can tell you that it was widely presumed the two would marry."

That was more than Cora had expected. Her chest tightened. "Obviously, they didn't. What happened?"

"I'm not certain. They grew up near each other in Somerset. She's only a couple of years younger, and by all accounts, they were good friends. She had resisted marrying, but she's so beautiful no one dared use the word *spinster*. I suppose her parents indulged her in that. It was only a matter of time until she finally married. She married a very wealthy baronet, and they've been touring the world ever since. Needless to say, it was quite the subject of gossip when she chose him over Devonworth."

"Do you know what happened between them?"

"I don't. I don't even know if there was anything to the gossip that they would marry. He didn't seem particularly upset about her marrying someone else, but I suspect with Devonworth you would never know his true feelings. He could have been crushed and he wouldn't have shown it."

That much was true. Cora couldn't claim to know him well, but he was the most reserved person she had ever met. She had thought it was to be expected of his very British, upper-class upbringing, and that was likely part of it; now, she wondered if the other part of it was his way of protecting himself.

"That's true, he wouldn't." Did this mean there was yet another woman in his life, or was Lady Sofia in town? "Do you know if she's still away or has she come back to England?"

Violet thought for a moment. "I'm not sure. Our paths never crossed very much. I could find out if you'd like?"

"No, that's fine." She didn't need to go stirring up trouble when this really had nothing to do with her. "Thank you for telling me all of that."

A few minutes later, the carriage pulled up to her home, so Cora bid Violet good night and hurried up the steps. "Good evening, Edgecomb," she said as the butler opened the door.

"Good evening, my lady." As unflappable as ever, he stood at attention.

She still couldn't decide if the man approved of her or not.

"Is his lordship home?" she asked.

"In his study, my lady."

After handing off her outerwear, she hurried up the stairs. Monroe was waiting for her, and together the two of them made quick work of changing her into her nightclothes. When the maid would have stayed to put things away, Cora told her to retire for the evening instead. The odds of him coming to her tonight were slim, since it was so late, but she still hoped he might.

Once she was alone, she took a quick look at herself in the mirror. She had been noticing her appearance more lately when she thought she might see him. Nothing romantic would happen between them, but she still wanted to look nice. She dipped her finger into a small pot of lip rouge that Jenny had given her. It was a pale rose that would bring out the natural color of her lips; she generally saved it for special nights out, but she had taken to wearing it on the nights he visited her. She also made certain her hair was in place, but she left the braid in because she secretly liked it when he took it out.

The second night he had come to her, she had assumed his attention to detail wouldn't be as thorough as the first. She had been wrong. They had spent the entire hour he'd been in her room debating the need for personal stories to add to his statistics and other figures. He agreed to some extent, but they couldn't decide on which stories would be most needed. There was a fine line between exploiting people's pain and telling genuine truths that everyone needed to hear.

"But we must have it known that these people are suffering because of these policies. We must tell their stories." She had been leaning over the speech, making notations in the margins where she thought it pertinent to insert a true life account of a cholera patient. When she looked up, he had been looking at her. No, not at her, at her mouth. His eyes had been intense and vivid, alive with a heat that had stolen her breath.

She nibbled her lower lip nervously and tasted the rouge she had forgotten she had put on in a moment of madness right before his arrival. His gaze had jerked to hers as the spell had been broken. She smiled inwardly at the obvious effect she'd had on him.

"We should go to bed," he said, and her stomach leaped before she told herself he didn't mean together.

After they both rose, he turned her gently and began the process of taking her braid apart. It was a perfunctory act to make her seem disheveled to further their ruse, but his fingers seemed to linger at the task. He'd run them slowly through the waves left by the braid, as if he enjoyed the feel. She loved the delicious way her scalp would prickle in response.

Now, slicking the rouge across her lips, she rubbed the excess into the apples of her cheeks to add a bit of a glow. Finally, she loosened the tie on her wrapper to open the V so that the lace of her nightdress could be seen better. Not that he was coming. It was late. But better safe than sorry.

Her mind was too busy swimming in everything she had learned tonight, from the violence at the suffrage demonstration to Lady Sofia, so she decided to read before trying to go to sleep. Arranging herself in bed with her pillows propped behind her—taking extra care to appear to her best advantage, just in case—she reached for her book on the nightstand. *Pride and Prejudice* seemed like an appropriate title given the cool reserve of her husband. But the book wasn't there. She had been reading it earlier during her bath and must have left it in their shared bathing chamber. She rose with a sigh and padded to the door of the room.

The door was cracked open, but she hadn't noticed the lamp burning inside the room until she pushed it open a little more. The air was heavy and humid as if someone had run a bath lately. A sound she couldn't identify came from deeper in the room. It sounded wet and . . . masculine. Her skin prickled. Someone was in here. There was a charged feeling in the air, making it almost too heavy to breathe. She might have left and pulled the door behind her, but another muffled sound caught her ear. A grunt. Was Devonworth injured or in pain?

The water closet was to her right along with the lavatory, with the rest of the room to the left. The door to her husband's room was straight across from her, and it was closed. The sound had come from the side near the window. The claw-foot tub was set up on a marble slab and hidden behind a screen, but from this angle she could see the head, and it appeared to be empty. The screen painted with water lilies hid that entire corner of the room. A padded chair and mirror were placed next to the tub because it was generally where they would towel off and dress after getting out of the bath. The chair was hidden, but when she took a step farther into the room, the mirror in the corner came into view. The reflection she saw made her bring her hand to her mouth to cover her surprise.

Her husband was sprawled in the chair, towel around him as if he had sat down while drying himself. Only the towel had completely fallen open to reveal him fully to her. His hair was wet, darkened to a dirty blond, as if he'd come straight from the bath, and it was pushed back from his face. It made his handsome looks nearly devastating as it emphasized the planes and angles of his face.

He was as lean muscled and fit as she had imagined. A light dusting of tawny hair covered a chest that was broad and strong but not bulky, and it trailed down over his flat and muscled stomach to his sex. Her penis experience was limited to those found on statues and in medical texts. To a man, every one had been flaccid and not noteworthy. His rose from the nest of curls at the apex of his thighs toward his stomach, ridged with veins, with a bulbous pink head. It seemed to glisten with moisture as his hand worked up and down the length in a rhythm. Indeed, a pearly liquid wept from the slit in the tip.

She watched him, mesmerized. His thighs were wrapped in muscle that constricted and loosened with each pump of his fist. His bare feet were spread wide on the tiled floor, his toes clenched against the obvious pleasure. His head was thrown back, eyes closed tight, his lips parted on another grunt as he chased gratification. As attractive as he was, as alluring as the forbidden sight before her, it was that sound that touched her. It was as riveting as she imagined a physical touch might be. The gravelly tone burrowed deep inside her, making every nerve ending sensitive to him. He did it again—this time a groan—and his voice raked right over her. The small hairs all over her body stood up, and she felt hot, too big for her skin.

Before her eyes, his hand moved faster and his breath came harder. His hips jerked upward, and she knew he was close to something. Her breasts felt swollen, and something deep inside her clenched, begging to be touched. He gasped and her knees felt weak. She wanted to go over and touch him, to share in what he was doing, but at the same time she was petrified and uncertain. They had never crossed this barrier, and somewhere deep in her mind she knew that she shouldn't watch, but she couldn't move. Her feet were rooted to the floor. She was helpless before her own desire and her curiosity to see what would happen.

His hand faltered and her gaze jerked upward to his face in the mirror. Their eyes met and her heart stopped. She had been caught. His jaw was rigid, but she couldn't tell if it was due to anger or his own arousal. The moment seemed to be suspended in time forever. She was afraid to breathe even as her own decency screamed at her to leave.

"Cora," he whispered, and the sound was serrated and raw, filled with so much want that she nearly cried out from it.

Instead of leaving, her already jellied legs gave way and she fell back against the doorjamb. Her heart beat so fast that she might well have run a race. But through it all, she held his gaze until she couldn't bear *not* to look at him anymore. The moment her eyes roamed back to that part of him, he took himself in hand again. This time his grunts were louder, as if he weren't trying to hold them in anymore. His hips pushed upward with each pump of his fist, and soon he was crying out.

The first eruption of his release made her gasp out loud. She had never been told that such a thing would happen, even though she knew the general logistics of the act. The pearly white fluid painted his stomach in long streaks, and he kept tugging, wrenching every drop of it out until he slumped against the chair, spent and satiated.

It was only then that she could force herself to action. She pushed away from the jamb and hurried back to her room, closing the door behind her.

SEVENTEEN

SOMETHING STRANGE HAPPENED TO DEVONWORTH the moment he looked outside the carriage window the next night and saw his wife approaching. His breath caught and there was an odd sensation in his chest. He might have lied to himself and chalked it up to indigestion, but he had barely had time to eat all day what with the endless meetings that had started early that morning.

It was the first time he'd seen her since last night when she had walked in on him pleasuring himself to thoughts of her. That wasn't even the worst of it. He'd invited her to participate like some uncivilized cretin.

What did one say to the woman after that? Especially when it had appeared as if she'd enjoyed every single moment of it. Until the end. It was only as she'd slammed the door behind her that he realized he might have read the entire situation wrong.

But that didn't completely explain it, because tonight wasn't the first night he had experienced the strange sensations. They had been a nearly constant occurrence. The switch had happened around the time they had faked the consummation of their marriage. Every night that he went to her and they worked on his speech, he'd felt something like anticipation beforehand. While he was in her room, he was aware of her in a way that made it almost impossible to concentrate on the bloody speech.

Her expression was unreadable as she dashed down the front steps. Her hair was in an elegant roll, and the dark blue silk of her skirts peeked out from the bottom of her cloak. He shifted as she approached, adjusting his coat and wishing he'd taken a moment to straighten his hair before he'd rushed out of his office. Beckham had sent a note to her earlier in the day to remind her of the dinner they were having out tonight. Devonworth himself had not had any contact with her all day. He was half-afraid he'd become aroused at the mere sight of her now, and half-convinced she'd never want to see him again.

The door opened and a footman helped her inside. She didn't make eye contact right away, but instead set about arranging her skirts on the seat across from him. Her fresh lavender scent teased his nostrils and sent a thrill of interest down through his groin. His cock remembered everything, even if he wished to forget last night had happened. He cleared his throat and held out the carriage blanket for her, which she wordlessly accepted.

"Good evening, Cora."

"Good evening." She cast her gaze somewhere around the vicinity of his shoulder.

"I'm sorry to be late. I was detained unavoidably. Thank you for joining me."

"It's no bother," she said, her voice strained.

She hated him. Was likely sickened by him. Her disdain didn't stop him from noticing that she was almost unbearably pretty tonight. Though her hair wasn't down as he preferred it, the meager carriage light cast a burnished glow to the pinned curls. Her cheeks were rosy, and there was a certain glow about her. Even her eyes seemed more vivid, the blue-gray color deep and beautiful. The long line of her neck drew his eyes as it often did these days.

In their evenings working together in her bedchamber, he found himself staring at that part of her as she leaned her head to the side, poring over the words she wrote. It was an absurd part of a woman's body to become fascinated with when there were so many other livelier parts to appreciate. But here he was, obsessed with it. Her pulse beat there like the wings of a desperate bird. Would her skin be as soft as it looked?

Understanding that ogling his wife was probably not the best way to begin the night, he looked out to the town houses they passed on their way to the Mayfair home a few streets over. He cleared his throat again. "We'll be dining with Lord and Lady Albright, and Lord and Lady Bolingrave, whom you met at the ball. The guest of honor is Mr. Guo Song Tao, the Chinese minister to Britain. He's been made an official ambassador to France so will be spending the next several months in Paris. Tonight is a going-away dinner."

"Beckham's note explained. Is there anything I should know or anything more you think I should do?" It was her turn to look out the window.

"No, you're doing a fine job as countess. It's a lot of small conversation, I'm afraid."

She nodded and they fell into silence. The tension was nearly unbearable. They could not possibly go through an entire night of not looking at each other. Well, of her not looking at him. He couldn't stop stealing glances at her. He couldn't bear that he had made things more difficult for them.

"Cora—"

"Please forgive me," she began at the same time. He was startled mute, so she hurried ahead. "I know that I should have left. I had no right to intrude on your . . . your . . . private time. It was possibly unforgivable, but I hope you can—"

"By God, Cora. No." He leaned forward and took her hands and was gratified that she did not shrink from him or pull them away. "You have nothing to apologize for. I never meant to put you in that situation. It won't happen again."

She stared at him, but he couldn't quite understand the expression on her face. She was distressed, certainly, but whether that was tinged with anger or something else, he couldn't say.

He hurried on. "I can . . . keep to my own chamber."

"No." She shook her head, twin lines between her brows. "You can do as you wish. I shouldn't have stayed . . ." She looked down at their clasped hands, and now he understood that it was shame he had seen in her expression.

"I assure you no apology is needed." He paused. "'Twas no hardship."

Her gaze whipped up to his face and he saw it . . . that same hint of desire. Her nostrils flared slightly and her eyes darkened. The blush that stained her cheeks seemed to spread beyond what was revealed by her clothes. Suddenly, the air thickened with that slight acknowledgment of what had passed between them the night before. All he could see was the rosebud shape of her mouth. Her lips were parted and he wanted to taste them. He wanted to dip his tongue into her and learn the feel of her. It didn't make any sense. They had already discussed how things would be between them. There was no reason for him to have this fascination with her. The only other time he had had this preoccupation with a particular woman, it had ended badly.

Thank God the carriage rolled to a stop. He sat back and bolted out the door the very second it was opened.

CORA WALKED INTO THE TOWNHOME ON CHARLES Street on Devonworth's arm. She always liked how it felt to be escorted by him. When he entered a room, people took note. Everyone approached him with a sense of decorum and deference. Part of it was his title and the role he carried in the hierarchy here, but a larger part of it was how he carried himself. He was confident, and he had a reputation for honesty and integrity. That induced most people to present their best selves to him. Some of that leached onto her, and it felt nice.

Much nicer than the strange looks she and her sisters would get back home. The times they dared to go Uptown, someone would inevitably recognize them or their name. It would lead to whispers and long faces and disapproving looks. Even in their neighborhood, Fanny was a bit notorious for her eccentricities. Those looks didn't bother her as much, but it was a welcome change to lurk in the shadow of respect for once.

She tried to focus on that feeling. It was her favorite thing about going out into Society with him. Unfortunately, there was no room for that with the awareness buzzing between them. She had lain awake for hours last night remembering how he'd looked and the sounds he'd made as he found his pleasure. She had imagined all sorts of ways that she might have joined him. By the end, her hands had found their way beneath her nightgown to find her own pleasure. It had paled to what she imagined it might feel like when he touched her, but it had sufficed . . . until she had seen him tonight and every-thing started up again. She was like a fire that had merely been banked enough to simmer, waiting for the right tinder to set her off again. Seeing him had been enough, but then he had gone and acknowledged that he'd liked her watching him, and she could hardly see straight. *'Twas no hardship.* What was she supposed to do with that admission?

Their hosts, Lord and Lady Albright, greeted them once they were shown to the drawing room. Cora felt like an au-tomaton going through the motions. She had to force herself to notice the room. It appeared that everyone else had already arrived. Devonworth made their apologies as they greeted everyone. Several MPs were present with their wives, as well as Mr. Guo, along with another Chinese official and their in-terpreter. She was gratified to see that August and her hus-band were also present, but that happiness turned sour when she realized they were talking to Lord and Lady Bolingrave. The same couple she had overheard gossiping about her at the Leigh ball.

She managed to greet the group warmly, but Devonworth must have noticed something about her was off. As they left the quartet, he leaned down and whispered, "Are you all right?"

His hand pressed into the small of her back, and she felt his touch so much more than she should have through the layers of her clothing and corset boning. The caress of his breath against her temple was too distracting, probably causing her to say more than was necessary.

"Yes, it's just . . ." She glanced over her shoulder to see the older couple happily continuing their conversation with the duke and duchess. "I overheard them at the ball, discussing the *state* of our marriage." She hoped he got her meaning, because she could not say the word *consummate* in this company.

He stiffened and his eyes hardened as he looked back at them. "Bolingrave was a part of the discussion?"

"Him, his wife, and another woman I hadn't met."

A tendon in his jaw flexed as he looked away from the group. "I shouldn't be surprised."

She had to drag her eyes away from that bit of tendon. It perplexed her how she could find it so very intriguing. "Do you find yourself at odds with him often?"

"He's standing in the way of the Public Health Bill. He believes the expense it creates will put an unfair burden on municipalities and landlords. Unfortunately, he has several men under his thumb and enough MPs to hold things up."

"What a horrible man."

"Yes, I've thought worse many times."

Their eyes met, and while her wholly inappropriate attraction was still there, it was joined by a feeling of belonging. They had to get through the evening with the Bolingraves, and they would do it together. She smiled and he smiled back at her.

The butler announced dinner, and Devonworth's hand slid from her back. She thought he meant to offer her his arm, but his hand took hers. She stopped breathing for a moment when his fingers closed around hers, and it was all she could do to walk beside him without stumbling over her own feet. When they approached the table, he squeezed her hand gently before releasing it. She felt the echo of that long after they sat down.

Everything went fine with dinner until near the end when Lord Bolingrave, who sat across from her, said, "Her Grace tells me that you have joined the London Suffrage Society, Lady Devonworth."

She glanced to August, who sat a little further down the table. She was in deep discussion with Mr. Guo and his associate about railroads and the potential for bringing railways and telegram lines to China. Since the duchess was involved with her family's company, Crenshaw Iron Works, and they were heavily involved in railroads, she was knowledgeable on the topic and was in the midst of an animated discussion. This meant that she wouldn't be able to come to Cora's aid in this conversation, however unpleasant it may be.

Perhaps she was wrong, but Cora figured it was fair to assume that anyone who was against the idea of bringing clean water to the working class would also be against extending voting rights to them.

She managed to keep her poise and said, "Yes, I have. Suffrage is essential in any free society. Wouldn't you agree?"

He smiled, barely, and glanced down the table at her husband. Lord and Lady Albright followed the now-familiar custom of not sitting spouses together. It was supposed to foster conversation and, one assumed, give them a welcome break from the other. She could have used her husband's support at the moment. He was engaged in conversation with the older woman who sat between him and Bolingrave. She was on her own.

Cora wasn't accustomed to large dinners with important men in government. She was, however, accustomed to men talking down to her, so she wouldn't let this go easy for him.

"Suffrage, yes," he began, "but I believe it should be an earned right. Not everyone can understand the complexity of laws and their repercussions. Even those who have proven themselves astute can hardly be expected to have the time or motivation to educate themselves on the issues."

"Then what would you have these people do? Go about and allow others to make the laws?"

"Why, yes. It's worked well for centuries. I know you're not accustomed to how things are here, but it's actually very simple and much the same as America." He swirled the wine in his glass and said, "The system works because we have different roles to play. Laborers, farmers, and the like have important jobs to do that keep our people supplied and fed. The landowners are the caretakers, the stewards. Their role is to see that the country is prosperous. Then, of course, there is the landed aristocracy, the peerage, and while we are stewards, our roles are larger than that. We guide the country forward."

"Are you saying that it is your belief that the working class is only to labor and work beneath your superior intellect?"

"I didn't say that, my lady. I merely believe that some things are too complicated and, indeed, complex for the uneducated to partake. Do I believe that some of these people can rise above their births? Yes, I do believe that. We have seen it happen. But not everyone can be educated, because then who would labor and farm?"

"Where do industrialists fit in within this hierarchy?"

"Ah, now, there is a good question." He took a swallow of wine. "These modern times have changed things. I would go so far as to argue that the industrialists are the laborers who have risen to the challenge and surpassed their lineage. They have indeed earned the vote."

"And where do women belong?"

"In the home in service of their Lord and families. Females are the moral backbone of our great society, while males are the governors, the ones with the rational minds. We've already seen the tragedy that has befallen our families with so many women working in factories. Have you heard of these terrible institutions known as infant farms?"

Before she could answer, he went on to explain. Cora had heard the term thanks to her association with the London Home for Young Women. Originally, these farms were families that agreed to take in babies and young children whose parents worked in cities, usually in manufacturing roles. The adults on the farm raised the children until they were old enough to find work. As time went on, the family farms became money-grubbing machines that took in babies as their primary sources of income. Several of them had been closed down due to deplorable living conditions after many children had died from neglect while in their care. There was a significant outrage against the practice, though she understood it still carried on to some extent.

"These farms are what happens when women work and their focus is taken from the home."

"That's a fair bit of hyperbole from someone with a more rational mind." She winced inwardly as soon as she said it. This was not the time or place for personal attacks, though it was the truth.

He merely grinned as if he had expected such from her, as if she were a kitten and of course she would claw at him so he would humor her. As if he knew he held all the power here and nothing she could say would amount to anything. She hated him.

"Whether you accept it or not, it's true. Were women to go out into the world and take the places of men, society would collapse within fifty years at best."

"Then perhaps it is society that should evolve. It can adapt and change to allow women to live as they wish."

He laughed. "Dear lady, are you suggesting that everyone

simply change who they are to accommodate these *women*?" He said the word *women* as if he were talking about a few troublemakers and not actually half the population. He saw them as accessories to his life and not fully functioning people at all.

"I am suggesting that society has been structured in a way that has allowed inequity to flourish and it's time to address that. Change won't be easy, I'll agree with you on that, but it must begin or there will be a reckoning."

"That's where you're wrong," he said. "There are not inequities as you imagine them. These elaborate systems have evolved to meet the needs of a growing society and they have worked for centuries. Farmers farm, workers work, and landowners, with their education and time for critical thought, govern. Woman, in all her glory, maintains the home and produces children to further our great society. It is the natural order of things."

"There is nothing natural about suppressing the very real needs and wants of half the population all in pursuit of some ideal that isn't idealistic at all, but is instead a corrupt system put in place to keep a very few on top and the others in a constant state of servitude and obedience." Her voice trembled with suppressed anger.

"Hear, hear." August raised her glass of wine while giving Cora an approving nod.

That's when Cora realized that, while their voices were still civil, they had risen enough to be heard by at least half the table.

"Change will come whether you fight it or not, Lord Bolingrave," August continued. "The time has come for all to have their voices heard. Women and men who do not have a voice with suffrage will find it soon."

Bolingrave's chest rose in a silent sigh. "You will find"—he glanced at August—"Your Grace"—then he looked to Cora—"my lady, that Britain has thrived because it knows when to change and when to hold firm. While there are good men in Parliament, tradition will hold true."

"My husband is one of those good men, my lord, and very much concerned with the plight of those who have not been granted suffrage. He will fight for those without a voice." It wasn't until after she spoke that she realized she was speaking out of turn. She had no real right to speak for him, especially when he was sitting at the table. She looked to him, almost afraid that he might be angry with her, but the look on his face wasn't anger. He looked at her with abject approval and maybe even appreciation.

"Devonworth knows—" Bolingrave began.

"My wife knows that I have devoted my life to speaking for those without a voice. I will continue to do so in all things, Bolingrave, a fact of which you are very much aware," Devonworth said.

She smiled at her husband and he smiled back at her. For one brief moment, everyone else at the table faded to the background. She was surprised at her longing to reach out and touch him. To find solace in his presence. She hadn't expected to form any sort of real attachment to him, but it had happened without her knowledge or consent.

"Perhaps it's time for the ladies to retire to the drawing room and allow the men to smoke their cigars and discuss politics," Lady Albright put in good-naturedly.

Cora wasn't completely sure if she was being mildly reprimanded or if such conversations were appropriate and expected at political dinner tables. She rose along with everyone else and made her way with the other women. The entrance was on the other side of the room, so she walked around the table while the men stayed in place to resume their seats when the women were gone. When she passed near Devonworth, he reached out and stroked her arm. The touch was so unexpected and wildly pleasant that she nearly gasped aloud. He smiled at her, his eyes tender, and whispered, "I'll be with you soon."

EIGHTEEN

CORA HADN'T BEEN ABLE TO FORM A COHERENT thought after he had touched her like that. She knew that he did it because they were playing the part of an affectionate, newly married couple, but it had felt real. Perhaps it was. They had come together against Bolingrave. Their friendship was real. The confirmation of that kept her spirits high when it would have been easy to give in to the acrimony brought on by the earl's determination to keep with old-fashioned ideals.

No one brought up what had happened at the dining table, except for August, who came over to sit with her on the settee while they drank sherry.

"You held your own in there." The duchess spoke in a low tone to not be heard over the conversations around them. She was probably in her middle twenties and dressed stylishly. While attractive, she gave off the impression that she didn't spend very much time working on her appearance. Cora was certain that she had a lady's maid to help her dress, but her hair was pinned up in a simple twist, and she wore the minimum in jewelry—earbobs and her wedding ring. She seemed much more business minded than fashion conscious.

"Thank you. I couldn't sit quietly while he went on with that nonsense."

August smiled. "That nonsense is what keeps him feeling safe and secure. I'm not even certain he believes it."

"We can hope he doesn't."

"I'm glad you've decided to join us at LSS. You were eloquent in your argument, and we need more people like you on our side."

An idea had been forming in her mind ever since the meeting. "I've been thinking that perhaps I could contribute something for the quarterly newsletter. I don't know very much about British law, so it wouldn't be specific to that, but I could write about women's experiences." She told her about the widows in her neighborhood back home and how she had written about their plights. "I could interview some of the women who come through the London Home for Young Women. They would keep their anonymity, of course."

August seemed excited by the idea, and they spoke about that until the men rejoined them a little while later.

Soon, Cora found herself in the carriage with her husband on the way home. He sat across from her in the dimly lit carriage, his perfect jaw outlined in the gaslight. She wondered if that little start that happened in her stomach when she looked at him would ever go away.

"I apologize if I spoke out of turn with Lord Bolingrave," she said. While she would have stood up to the man, she could have done it more tactfully without challenging him.

He laughed, a husky sound that lived and died in his throat. It reminded her of the other low sounds she had heard him make last night, and a frisson of awareness crept over her.

How was she supposed to survive close confines with him now? The hand he had so skillfully utilized last night was currently resting on his thigh. Devonworth seemed blissfully unaware of how he and that hand had featured in her dreams last night.

"No apology necessary. Bolingrave deserves to be challenged when he speaks like a hapless idiot."

She couldn't help but giggle and dragged her gaze away from his hand. His hooded eyes were in shadow, but she imagined they were shining in his amusement. "You don't like him, either, then, for reasons other than the Public Health Bill?"

"That's an understatement. The man is convinced that his own opinion of himself is infallible."

She laughed again and enjoyed the way his eyes lingered on her face. She had admired his looks and then his mind for so long that she was accustomed to watching him. Now it felt as if he saw her more and more. He had acknowledged her frequently and eagerly accepted her help with his speech, but tonight was different. Tonight, a new sort of camaraderie had developed between them. The feeling of being in the closed circle of understanding with him was nearly intoxicating.

"Talking with him has convinced me that I've done the right thing in joining LSS. I need to do something, and it's a cause I am passionate about. I'll be thinking of Bolingrave when we're picketing. He's put a face on my anger."

His smile melted away immediately. "Picketing? They're planning another demonstration?"

Something was wrong. "Yes," she offered cautiously, and then wondered if it was supposed to be a secret. She hadn't thought of the fact that he would be one of the very men whose attention they were attempting to sway by the demonstration. What if finding out ahead of time meant that he tried to stop them? Could he do that? Did he have such power? She didn't know.

"You mustn't participate, Cora. I implore you. The last time—"

Relief filled her to nearly bursting. He was concerned for her and not attempting to stop the entire thing. "Violet explained to me everything that happened. I know there was a dangerous incident, but she assures me that Hereford is under suspicion and no one believes he'll try anything like that again."

"You're right. He is under suspicion and will face a hearing, but that doesn't mean he's been neutralized. He won't hesitate to try something again. In fact, I don't believe that Hereford is the only one to be concerned with. Plenty of powerful men do not want to see women get the vote. As it stands now, not even all men can vote. There is a concerted effort to keep the vote among the landowners and those who want to maintain power. You've seen this in America with the effort to keep men of color from voting. It's the same here but with all laborers.

"I don't want you to go. It's too dangerous."

"You're concerned about me?" She didn't want to like that as much as she did, but it made her feel warm inside and full in a way she hadn't in a very long time.

"Yes, very much so. Cora, you're my wife. It's my job to keep you safe and well."

She wanted to like that just as much as his initial concern, but she felt quite certain that he would say the same to any woman who filled the role of his wife. He was at his core a caretaker, and he would find it his duty to keep anyone in his family safe and well. She admired that about him . . . but she also wanted more from him, which wasn't fair at all. He had never offered her more.

"I'll be fine. They have hired security. More than last time, I'm told."

He ran a hand through his hair, appearing more agitated than contented with that. "That's good and well, but it doesn't mean there won't be violence or mistakes. It only takes a few to join the fray, and you could be injured or worse. I don't mind you participating with the group, but find a safer way."

"You don't mind? Devonworth, I thought we agreed in the beginning that I would be my own person and you could continue to be yours. I made it clear that I would continue my interest in women's rights. I haven't stopped you from your mistress or asked where you go at night. I should think you would extend me the same courtesy."

"My mistress? Cora, what—" But he stopped and understanding seemed to dawn on his face. "I don't have a mistress. I never have."

"You don't have to lie to me. We never made any sort of stipulation about lovers during our negotiation." Then she swallowed to moisten her throat and lied right to his face. "I don't mind."

"I wouldn't lie to you. I've no reason to stoop to such—"

The carriage swayed as it rounded the corner to their street.

"Really, Devonworth, I don't care." She did care, but to reveal that to him would be to reveal her jealousy, and she couldn't let herself be vulnerable with him. It was her own fault that she had developed an infatuation with him. This is why Jenny had warned her about marrying a handsome man, though it was more than that. Cora had prepared herself for good looks, but she hadn't expected him to have so many other admirable qualities.

The door opened, and he hurried out as he always did. Then he reached back to help her out, offering her his hand.

Not *that* hand, though she imagined this one would be perfectly adept. His face was carved from granite, his expression stony. It wasn't unusual for him, but this time there was a bit of pique in the mix. Safe on the sidewalk, she would have released his hand, but he closed his fingers around hers and gave them a squeeze and released her quickly. She was left to look down at her gloved hand, expecting to see some sort of imprint, but it was only her glove. She watched his back as his long strides took him up the steps and to the front door where Edgecomb waited.

When she stepped inside, Devonworth was shrugging out of his coat. She had always noticed his solid shoulders, but they seemed even more substantial now that she knew what he looked like beneath his clothes. The memory of those lean lines of muscle would stay with her forever. He didn't bid her good night when he finished. Instead, he waited at the base of the stairs for her to hand off all of her outer garments.

"Shall we?" He spoke with purpose as he offered her his arm.

She didn't quite know what he meant. Was this part of their ruse? Would the servants expect them to spend the rest of the night together, or did he intend to continue their conversation from the carriage? She nodded and walked beside him upstairs.

"I'd like to explain what happened the night you believe I returned from visiting my . . . a woman."

"Devonworth—"

"Please."

It didn't sound very much like a plea so much as an order, but she was curious, so she said, "Okay."

"Good."

Monroe was waiting for her in the bedroom. She stood up

and glanced at Devonworth with a curious expression before she lowered her gaze.

"You won't be needed tonight, Monroe. You may retire for the evening."

"Your lordship." The woman gave a quick curtsy but hesitated.

"Good night and thank you for waiting up for me," Cora said to relieve her.

Cora's skin buzzed with excitement as the maid hurried out of the room. Even though she knew that Devonworth didn't intend they share a bed tonight, she couldn't help but imagine it and that this is exactly how the evening might play out if they were indeed a newly married couple deep in the throes of affection. Also, someone would have to help her out of this gown, and the idea of it being him set her senses reeling. Her clothes were fancier now than they had been back at home. Apparently, that meant the fastenings got smaller and even more difficult to reach on one's own.

He walked to the window, hands on his hips as he stared out at the night. He was clearly bothered by this talk of his mistress.

"How did you know I thought you were with your mistress that night?" She assumed he meant the evening he came home late and they had run into each other outside his study.

"Your face. Your expression. I didn't know for certain that was what you thought, but at the time it suited my purposes to allow you to believe it."

Interesting. "And it doesn't now? What changed?"

He glanced over at her as if she should know, but she wasn't above making him spell things out for her, particularly when she was so apparently starved for little scraps of affection from him. "We're friends now . . . or at least I believe us to be." She nodded to encourage him. "It doesn't seem fair to continue any sort of subterfuge."

She swallowed against the sudden dryness in her throat. The only sign of her guilt that she hoped he couldn't see. He was right. Lately, it had felt very wrong to continue to keep her illegitimacy from him. It probably wouldn't matter, but the subject was a sore one for her.

"All right," she said and sat down on the small settee before the fire. It had been delivered only this week, a subtle gold to match the wallpaper that would be going up next week.

"I was in Whitechapel that night. Harry had got himself into a bit of trouble with his gambling. It's always been a vice for him. He'd gamble in school and even after. A hundred pounds here or there. His own personal items: a watch, jewelry, and the like. I don't know how he got himself involved with the club in Whitechapel, but he was in debt. Ten thousand pounds and the debt was only growing." He took in a breath as if the next words were particularly painful. Then he turned to face her. "It's one of the reasons I needed this marriage. I didn't have access to that sort of money, not with the devastation at Timberscombe Park. I didn't tell you that during our discussion the evening of our engagement, and I should have."

He never looked away from her the entire time he walked toward her and sat down on the settee beside her. It was a small piece of furniture, so his thigh touched hers. "Can you forgive me for that?"

"Are you saying you married me for your brother's sake?"

"Partially, yes." His brow furrowed as if he truly feared this might be some sort of mark against him.

She was silent for a moment as she allowed her thoughts to churn over the events of that night. She believed he was telling her the truth, but there was still that scent to explain. "I thought I smelled perfume on you?"

He nodded. "A prostitute eager to acquire a new client. I turned her down." When she didn't answer immediately, he asked, "Will you forgive me for not telling you about Harry's debt?"

She wanted to put her hand over his but held herself still. Touching him had become fraught with dangerous feelings she had no business entertaining. "Devonworth, I admire how committed you are to your family and those you've taken under your wing. There's nothing to forgive. You did what you needed to do to take care of your brother. Is this why Harry is leaving on his trip?"

"Yes, I thought it best to get him away from any danger that might arise. I paid the owner of the club off, but one can never be certain with those types."

"That's where you were that night?" Part of her still couldn't believe that he would put himself in such danger for his brother. "You were in Whitechapel paying off your brother's gambling debt?"

He nodded. "I had to see to it myself."

She didn't think it was possible, but she admired him even more. "You take care of him like he was your own."

"Like you take care of your sisters," he offered softly.

She smiled and admired how very green his eyes were. They were like pools of liquid velvet. "I guess we have more similarities than we thought."

"I don't find it so surprising. We were both charged with the care and welfare of our families from a young age. It's obvious that you've shared the role of parent with your mother when she couldn't be bothered to do the job."

"It's not her fault." Cora shrugged. "She's eccentric and never had a family. She loves us and does her best."

He nodded. "I know that she does, but you easily fill in the gaps. You've grown beyond your years because of it. I . . ."

His voice drifted off, and she found herself leaning closer to him, urging him with her body to continue. "You what?" she asked when that alone didn't work.

He reached over and brushed a lock of hair from her cheek with the very hand that she had been obsessed with since last night. Her soul rippled in pleasure beneath the touch. "I find myself wanting to take care of you," he continued. "Wanting to keep you safe . . . and happy."

She tried to convince herself that he meant that in a familial way, but she couldn't believe it. Not with how he was looking at her now. His eyes were hot, and she didn't think she imagined that he had looked at her lips when he said the last word. They were so close she could smell peppermint on his breath mixed with brandy. Her body felt achy and alive with sensation.

"I want that, too," she said.

"Good." His thumb brushed her cheek again, but he rose to his feet. "Come, let us get you undressed."

He said it so casually, but her nerve endings were fraying. When she was slow to respond, he grasped her hand and pulled her to her feet. She obliged him and even grabbed the bedpost for support when he turned her away from him to access the row of impossibly small buttons down her back. He seemed perfectly unaffected as he began with the buttons near her neck. "If I seem a bit put out by your talk of the demonstration, that's why. I can't bear the thought of anyone I care about in danger."

"You care about me?" she asked dumbly.

He quickly went through the first several buttons. "Didn't I just say so? You are part of my family now."

Right. God, how stupid she was to mix the two together. Although that look on the settee hadn't been brotherly, it hadn't meant he was ready to bed her. A thrill went through her when he tugged a particularly stubborn button through its loop, moving her along with it. His knuckles drummed against her as he worked, tiny taps of pleasure down her spine. She closed her eyes and rested her forehead against the bedpost, determined to get through this without giving away how much she was enjoying it.

"I've come to see your sisters as my responsibility as well. I've asked Harry to report back on Mainwaring. I'm not entirely convinced his intentions are good, though I can't say why."

"You mean he might have mercenary intentions, much like yourself?" she asked.

He gave a short laugh that was suspiciously close to a groan, the sound he made last night. Well, possibly not close at all, possibly it had just been a sound from him that had been contained in his chest much like the groan, and her traitorous body was interpreting everything wrong. She clenched her thighs together.

"Precisely, but I don't trust him like I trust myself. We need to be certain that he'll take care with her."

"Yes, I agree."

"I'm glad we're agreed . . ." His voice trailed off as he bent down to examine the fastenings at her waist. "What the devil?"

The buttons there gave way to metal hooks and the tiniest little metal loops that were sewn into the fabric. He jerked but nothing happened except her hips pulled toward him. She gripped the post harder.

"They can be tricky. Monroe keeps a tool—"

"*Bloody hell*." He rose and brought his finger to his mouth.

"Are you all right?" She turned around and grabbed for his hand. There was a pink line on his index finger as if he'd been pinched. A tiny bead of blood welled near the edge of his nail.

"It's fine," he said as she hurried to grab a handkerchief.

She brought it back and took his hand in hers, wrapping the thin fabric around his finger. "I'm sorry, I should have warned you. You'll need a plaster."

He shook his head. "It's minor. One would think I could figure out how to work a simple fastener."

Cora retrieved the little hooked tool that Monroe used and handed it to him. "Try this."

He accepted it and she turned to give him her back. After a couple of failed attempts, he figured out how to use it and made short work of the rest of the hooks. He lifted the gown over her head. All went smoothly until the lace hem got caught in a hairpin. By the time he got it out, she was left giggling and half of her hair tumbled down her back. He frowned as he draped the gown over the back of a chair, perturbed at his inability to complete the task efficiently.

"Don't pout, you've clearly never done this before. You can't expect to get it right the first time," she teased him.

"It's maddening how complicated it is. Women should have demanded simpler garments long ago." He looked at her chemise like it was a mathematics equation he had yet to solve.

"They did, but here we are, back to endless layers of undergarments and fastenings."

"You have my permission to say to hell with it all." He reached out and tugged at the lacings of the corset at her back.

She smiled and closed her eyes as she enjoyed how inept he was at the task. Somehow it pleased her that he had no idea what he was doing. It meant that he hadn't done this before with another woman. Not that *that* mattered, she reminded herself. Another spark of pleasure shot through her at every wrong twist and turn of a fastening until the corset finally loosened and she was able to take it off. That left her in her chemise, drawers, and stockings. She regretted that she could handle those on her own, even as she was aware that she was standing before him in her undergarments.

"Thank you," she said as she turned to him. His gaze settled on the chemise and her unbound breasts for the barest moment before he looked away.

"Do you need anything else?" he asked with a suspicious husk in his throat.

"No, I can manage the rest."

He nodded. "Before I go, my estate manager at Timberscombe Park has asked me to go out and look at some of the improvements. I plan to leave Friday afternoon and take the late train back on Sunday, and I'd like you to accompany me."

"Oh, that sounds lovely. I'd like to see your estate."

"Good, though I must warn you that my football team will be participating in a match. Some of the wives go, but you don't have to attend."

They had been married weeks now, and he had never invited her to a match. This felt significant. She was agreeing before she could even think about it. "I want to go. I've never seen a proper game before, not all the way through."

"Good." He smiled as if he were relieved. "Fair warning, my mother will be there."

Oh. Well, she would have to spend time with the woman eventually, even though she had a sneaking suspicion his mother didn't like her. "That's fine."

He gave her a nod. "I'll bid you good night, then."

"Good night." She was almost certain his gaze went back to her bosom as he left, and she was certain there was a suspicious stiffness in his walk. She smiled to herself as he closed the door behind her. When before she had wondered, she now believed he wanted her.

As she finished undressing, she couldn't help but ponder if she was brave enough to reach for what they both wanted. Or if it would be best to leave that part of their relationship alone. After all, nothing had changed. They would still go their separate ways.

But wouldn't it be better to leave him knowing what it was like to lie with him? She knew what Fanny would say on the matter. She'd tell her to be bold and take what she wanted. However, Fanny's reasoning couldn't always be trusted. Cora sat down and dashed off notes to her sisters. She needed their advice.

NINETEEN

THEY LEFT FOR TIMBERSCOMBE PARK AFTER LUN-cheon on Friday. Devonworth paced on the first-class platform at Paddington Station. Cora was to arrive with their luggage for their short trip to the country. She wasn't late by any means, but he found himself walking back and forth and checking the time repeatedly. He had been this way ever since she had seen him after his bath. He felt on edge and anxious. Every time someone walked into his study at home, he thought it would be her . . . *hoped* it would be her. He'd gone from having to relieve himself of an excess of arousal once a week to every bloody day, though he did it in the privacy of his own chamber now. It was the one place she had not graced with her presence.

But she was there in every other way. She was in his thoughts when he was awake and his dreams when he was asleep. He'd pocketed every ribbon that had tied off her plaits the nights he had gone to her to continue their ruse of sleeping together, so her scent was with him, too. In the morning, when he woke in discomfort, he'd take himself in hand and her lavender perfume would surround him as he found his release.

His near-obsession with her had come on much faster than he could understand. In the space of a fortnight, he'd gone from tolerating her presence to lusting after her. That last part was a novelty to him. The only woman who had come close to inspiring this intensity of feeling was Sofia. That had been understandable because he had known her for years. She was beauty and grace, and their affair had been somewhat inevitable.

The situation with Cora wasn't like that. He didn't know her as well. He had always felt *different* because he didn't enjoy the indulgence of casual sexual interludes. After a few vaguely satisfactory attempts in his youth, he'd not seen the point of risking pregnancy, disease, and blackmail for so little. Then Sofia had come back into his life.

She was only a couple of years younger than he and had lived on a neighboring estate, which meant they had known each other since they were children. As an adult, he spent most of his time in London and they had lost touch. It wasn't until he had reconnected with her during the London Season a couple years back that things changed from friendship to something much deeper. They had quickly become lovers, and when he asked her to marry him, she agreed. He was almost certain her parents intervened, because it wasn't a handful of days later when he read about her engagement to Sir William in the papers. She hadn't even had the decency to tell him in person.

Just when he thought he had rid himself of those feelings, that blasted weakness, here was Cora, presenting him with temptation. It made even less sense because he had chosen a wife who did not rouse those wild feelings in him. He had chosen her because he thought he could keep her at arm's length. But he had tried and failed. The worst part about that was he was slowly losing his grip on his determination to keep trying.

People bustled around him. Trains stood noisily on several tracks as they waited for passengers. Smoke billowed from the engine of the eastbound train that was pulling out of the station. It was a chaotic scene, but he was still able to pick Cora out of the crowd as soon as she stepped onto the platform.

She wore a traveling costume in navy with black velvet piping for the trim. A hat sat askew on her head above the mass of red hair she'd pinned up beneath it. Monroe followed along behind her with Crawford, his valet. A young Indian woman he had never met walked beside her. They were in discussion about something. The woman was dressed in a plain brown suit and looked to be around twenty years of age. She had what appeared to be a camera case looped over her shoulder. What was his wife up to?

He started toward the group. Before he arrived, they all went off to find their seats, leaving Cora standing there.

"Devonworth!" she called out to him, and waved as he approached.

She smiled and walked toward him, happy to see him. He found himself smiling back at her. This woman he had married was an enigma to him, but he liked that about her.

They both stopped when they reached the other, unsure of the newfound closeness of their relationship and how that translated to greetings at train stations.

"You came," he offered her.

She nodded. "I did. I said I would."

Perhaps it was the fact they were getting out of London, or it might have been whatever she had planned with the unexpected guest in tow, but she seemed to glow. Her happiness illuminated her entire being, and he found himself content to stand there and admire it.

"Do you have the tickets?" she asked after an absurdly long pause.

He patted his coat where the tickets were tucked away in the breast pocket. "Yes."

"Oliver is taking care of the luggage."

"Well, then, shall we board?"

She nodded and he reached for her valise and walked with her to the first-class car. All along the platform, people shifted and moved for them as they walked. As if they were a real couple. As if they were truly man and wife and meant to traverse the world as one. It was a simple but heady feeling, and he liked it very much.

Once on the train, she slowed. Several people were in the process of finding their seats, but no one was directly in front of them. A glance at her face confirmed that she studied the interior. Her gaze roamed from the plush seats upholstered in emerald-green velvet to the dark walnut woodwork to the brass lighting fixtures hanging from the ceiling.

"Have you never been on a train?" he asked, keeping his voice low and near her ear. It was hard to fathom, but possible.

She shivered and looked up at him, an attractive flush staining her cheeks. He felt an answering tug deep in his groin at how he could so easily affect her. "Yes, but . . ."

The second her eyes dropped from his, he knew the rest of the statement she had left unspoken. "But you've never ridden in a first-class train car."

"No." She dipped her head, possibly embarrassed by the admission.

A porter approached, effectively ending the exchange. He

took their bags, and it was only when Devonworth handed off their tickets that he realized they were not direct to Exmoor. Edgecomb had sent his and Cora's tickets over to his office earlier that morning, and he hadn't even thought to take them out of the envelope to check them. The man led them to their seat, and Cora gave him a speaking glance over her shoulder. She knew something he didn't. It must be to do with that woman with the camera case. Devonworth waited for Cora to settle herself by the window before he joined her.

When they were alone, he said, "The tickets are—"

"I've arranged for a stop," she explained, smiling up at him. "I hope you won't be angry. I thought we might take a couple of hours in Clarkston. You mentioned that town in your speech, and I thought it would be a good idea to see it and document the current state of things. I spoke to August since Crenshaw Iron has an iron works there, and she arranged for one of the managers to guide us around the factory. He also knows other workers in the area who are willing to speak with us.

"I brought a photographer, Miss Sharma. I met her at the London Home for Young Women. She's another volunteer there and has an interest in photography. I spoke with her about your speech and she was moved. She's brought her own camera to photograph the lack of sanitation and the living situation of the typical worker. I plan to take a lot of notes that we can use in your speech. Hopefully, by bringing in personal accounts, we can appeal to the empathy of those who will be voting."

"Cora . . ." He couldn't find any words that would adequately express how *not* angry he was. "Thank you."

"I know how important the bill is to you, and it's a noble thing you are doing. I want it to succeed as much as you do."

He couldn't look at her. Instead, he took in the bustle on the platform outside their window. Couples moved through the fray, sometimes followed by children. Groups of men in suits hurried about, undoubtedly on their way to or from a meeting to conduct very important business. This wasn't the time or place to give in to sentimentality, but he couldn't seem to swallow the lump in his throat or blink away the sting behind his eyes.

"Devonworth?" Her voice was a mere whisper as she gently put her hand on his cheek and turned his face toward her.

How had he ever thought her merely passably pretty? She had the kindest, deepest eyes he had ever seen. They were like a storm-swept sea, boundless, infinite in the secrets they kept. He wanted to discover every one of her secrets and savor them all. The prominent slope on the bridge of her nose rendered her unique and gave her a look of confidence he had come to appreciate more and more. Her mouth had a lovely shape. That morning he had found his pleasure imagining how those soft lips might feel on him.

She was beauty.

"Are you . . . ?" she prompted him.

"No," he finally managed, his voice rough as it scraped across the ache of his throat. "I'm quite all right." He turned his head and pressed a kiss to her gloved palm before he even realized what he was doing. She startled, looking at her palm. He gently took hold of her wrist and lowered her hand to her lap. He couldn't help but notice how she closed her fist around the kiss.

This was all wrong. This wasn't what they were.

He had to explain, but he was having trouble finding the words. Realizing he had somehow leaned indecently close to her in the ensuing minutes, he straightened and squared his shoulders so he faced front. His coat pulled, so he gave it a tug at the lapel to set it to rights. "I'm unaccustomed to people going out of their way to assist me."

"Beckham—"

"Yes, Beckham does an admirable job." He hoped it might end there, but she was too observant and curious.

"You mean . . . family?"

He nodded, cursing that damned lump in his throat.

"You take care of everyone," she continued. "No one takes care of you."

He couldn't look at her again. If he allowed himself to study the tender expression he knew would be evident on her face, he'd lose the battle of his composure. "I can hardly complain. Valets, footmen, housekeepers . . ."

"But no one who cares for you." She hit the nail on the head and then drove it in even harder. "No one helps you shoulder the burden."

How was he to last under this onslaught of caring? He stared at one of the brass buttons on the steward's livery. If he stared hard enough, the pain would ebb.

It worked and he was able to look at her without shattering. "Cora . . ." Inexplicably, that was all he could say.

She smiled at him and wrapped her arm around his, her palm settling on his forearm. Wordlessly, he covered her hand with his, and they sat there in silence as the train whistled its warning and slowly chugged out of the station.

CORA AND DEVONWORTH ARRIVED AT TIMBERscombe Park that evening. The sun had set but the moon was nearly full, giving Cora her first glimpse of the late medieval home. She sat up straighter in the carriage as they crossed the moat and passed the walls. They were mostly fallen into ruin now, but his father had put great pride into maintaining the stones near the drive. Devonworth agreed that driving through the high arch lent a certain ceremony to coming home.

The servants had come along without them, so it was just the two of them in the carriage.

"I wasn't expecting a genuine moat." Cora smiled as she craned her neck to see more of the estate.

They passed the old gatehouse before driving through a field with several barns and stone outbuildings in the distance. The house loomed before them, backlit against the moonlight.

"Is it a castle?"

"No, it was built in the late medieval period. Not a castle, but close. There's a great room and a courtyard with wings on either side."

Devonworth had spent a lot of time lamenting how much his father spent on the upkeep of the place. Most of his father's time had been spent courting his own ego, so it had been no surprise that most of the funds diverted to the maintenance of the estate had been cosmetic. He hadn't reinforced the structure on the north side where the rainwater had been diverting to the cellar. Devonworth had done that himself. His father hadn't spent money on roof repairs, preferring to fresco the ceiling of the solar and add new carvings to the wood ceiling and moldings in the great hall. His entire life had been making things appear one way, while they had been quite another, all to seem better than he was.

Devonworth had been left with the hard tasks. For the first time ever, he found himself thankful for his father's frivolity. If Cora liked the place, then it might be worth it.

The carriage came to a stop and he helped her down, watching her take in the house. The exterior was stone and brick with two gables on either end and oriel windows. She smiled up at him. "It's beautiful."

"It's yours now," he said, though he knew she didn't see it that way. She still behaved as if everything she used was borrowed, and he supposed it was, were they to adhere to their original plan. The problem was that he was coming to like her quite a lot. The scent of lavender brought her to mind. Any redheaded woman made him think of her. He had even started to dream of her. Saucy, naughty dreams.

The servants who lived on the estate had come out to welcome them. They lined up at the steps, and Devonworth took a moment to introduce her. They kept a skeletal staff in the country, particularly since one entire wing had been closed down due to the roof repairs. His mother waited at the top step.

"Mother." He greeted her with a kiss to her cheek.

She accepted this mildly and looked to Cora. "Good evening, Cora. Welcome to Timberscombe Park. Mrs. Sims will show you to your room. I'm certain you would like a moment to refresh yourself before supper."

Cora returned a greeting and accepted the offer. The housekeeper came to collect her and they set off. Devonworth regretted not being able to show her around himself, but he understood that his mother wanted to talk.

"You're very late," she said as soon as Cora had disappeared inside. The rest of the servants dispersed to get back to their duties.

"We made a stop."

The excursion had been a fruitful one. They had toured the

hastily built neighborhoods of terraced housing that had been
constructed over the past two decades. They were overcrowded
and often lacked adequate ventilation. Several families could
be found living in one narrow home. Miss Sharma had photo-
graphed one of the homes that had recently become vacant. It
was a dark and dingy place, and Devonworth couldn't imagine one family living there, let alone several.

Then they had toured the rubbish heaps that had been rel-
egated to the edge of the small manufacturing town. The
smaller ones were piled nearly to his shoulders with discarded
household items, scraps, and what smelled like sewage. The
sewer system had long been overrun with the rapid population
growth. A local authority had been put in charge some years
back, but the people they spoke with strongly hinted that cor-
ruption had led to funding being diverted. Oversight was
badly needed. The bill he was pushing would make certain
that happened.

The trip had not only solidified his determination to see it
passed, but also today, he had noticed Cora's resoluteness.
She had taken fastidious notes and asked all the right questions. He had expected a shallow wife when he approached
her. Someone who was willing to exchange her money for his
title. A fair exchange given how his own need for money could
be viewed as shallow on its surface. But he had got so much
more in the bargain.

Cora was everything he could have asked for in a wife. As
the day progressed, he'd found one particular thought nudging
at him. He wondered if he might be able to figure out a way to
keep her past the two-year deadline she had set.

His mother made a noncommittal hum and turned to go
inside. "Let us talk before we eat."

He rolled his eyes—he smiled as he realized it was a gesture he must have picked up from his wife—and followed her.

They settled in the small drawing room tucked behind the stairs. It had an arched window that overlooked the topiary garden and was a room his mother had claimed as her own years ago. It was where she kept all of her embroidery, her only known hobby besides churning the gossip mill. He loved her dearly because she had always taken care with him and tried to guide him in what was best, but they were not very close. She preferred to keep a distance between them, something he had always assumed he enjoyed as well. Until Cora had made him yearn for more.

"I've read the gossip sheets." She wasted no time in getting right to the point as soon as she sat down.

He took a breath to control his suddenly rising anger and shut the door firmly behind him.

"And?" he asked, but he knew.

"The consummation."

"That's old news, Mother."

She didn't care for his tone, that much was evident in the look she gave him. "I didn't see the papers until yesterday, but it's given me an idea. It's not too late to get the thing annulled."

He held up his hand. "It is too late, Mother. You haven't read the current newspapers. They would have told you it's all been taken care of."

She pulled a face and turned her head toward the window.

"You might as well come to terms with this marriage. The new roof is because of this marriage. The fact that our tenants won't starve, the fact that we can purchase new sheep is because of this marriage. Cora is not so bad. Give her a chance and you'll see."

"It's not Cora. It's that woman."

He sighed, resigned. "Fanny Dove."

"She is making a mockery of us. They say she broke out in song at the Hoffmans' ball, some bawdy tune I'm sure I cannot repeat. She overly indulged at the Ferguson dinner. She is trading in social favor because of our name, and they are only inviting her to see what spectacle she might pull that night."

"Well, which is it, Mother? Is it our name or the spectacle she creates that gets her invited to these things?"

Her eyes narrowed. "They say she is Bertie's mistress." She whispered the last word.

"The Prince of Wales?" He couldn't believe what he was hearing. "Mother, Bertie isn't even in town."

She waved her hand as if that was irrelevant. "They talk and people believe it. That's all that matters. Our respectability will mean nothing in the face of this . . . this . . . woman."

He sighed and sat beside her on the sofa. "If our respectable reputation as a family cannot withstand one brash American, then it was a questionable reputation to begin with. This will pass. There will be another marriage next Season and another family to enter the fray. There are more Americans every year."

She nodded, but she didn't look convinced. "There will be more to come from her."

"That may be, but Cora is my wife and I will stick by her. She has done nothing but support me, and I will do no less for her."

His mother frowned, but this time she appeared less angry and more intrigued. "You care for her?"

That moment on the train came back to him, bringing with it the tender ache in his throat. He wanted so badly for her to be happy here. "I do."

"Tread carefully, son. I don't know what it is, but there is more to that family than we know. Mark my words."

He wanted to ignore her, but he couldn't. There was something Cora wasn't telling him.

TWENTY

DINNER HAD BEEN A NIGHTMARE. IT WAS OBVIOUS to anyone who cared to pay attention that the dowager countess disliked Cora. She wasn't outwardly hostile. She said all the right things, when she spoke at all, and her eyes did not shoot daggers. The problem was that she spent the entire evening avoiding even looking at Cora. She trained her eyes over Cora's right shoulder when she deigned to look her way at all. As a result, the meal had been an awkward affair that had gone on entirely too long. To make matters worse, Cora had hardly been able to eat a thing. Her stomach had been in knots the entire meal, which is why she found herself tiptoeing through the house late that night searching for the kitchens. Her growling stomach would never make it to morning.

The house itself had been a pleasant surprise. It was cavernous with soaring wood beam ceilings, but still cozy. Her bedroom adjoined the master—she had heard Devonworth moving around in there, but the door had not opened. Her own room was well-appointed with bottle-green textiles and mahogany furniture with elegantly curved lines. There was even a window seat in the oriel window that overlooked the lawn. The window was made up of tiny diamonds of leaded glass, and she couldn't wait to see how the sunlight would sparkle off the panes in the morning. She planned to take back whatever food she could find and enjoy it right there.

But first she had to find the kitchen. She had started with the dining room and walked through the door where the footman had brought in their meal. There was no butler's kitchen or dumbwaiter in the next room, so she assumed the kitchen was on this floor. The problem was that the house was a maze of rooms, and she had gotten turned around so many times she didn't know where she was.

A light shining from beneath a door guided her to the end of a corridor. She had to step up to enter the long hallway, which suggested this area of the house was a late addition and not original. A metal clanging gave her hope as it echoed on its way to her. She gently pushed open the door to reveal gleaming tile countertops with a large stove set into one side of the room. A row of windows took up the other wall. A rack held rows of pots to her left, and that's where the noise had come from. Devonworth rubbed his head as he knelt to pick up two that had fallen, no doubt because he'd run into them.

She didn't try to hide her laugh, and he startled, looking over to her wide-eyed before settling again.

"Did you hurt yourself?" she asked, walking into the room.

"They're very heavy." He scowled but it lacked bite as he set the pots back on their hooks.

It felt odd, but in a good way, to be here alone with him with no one around. Half-afraid that he might leave now that she had arrived, she said, "I'm glad you're here. I can't stop thinking about your speech and had an idea." That much was the truth, but it was also the only topic she thought might keep him if he were inclined to leave. "What would you say to changing the beginning a bit? You could open with an anecdote."

"Why an anecdote?" His brow furrowed as he ducked under the pots, successfully this time, and took hold of the slab of cherry wood the cook used as a cutting board. "These men want hard figures. It's all they will respect."

He placed the serrano ham upon it and began cutting thin slices. Her stomach growled as she watched, reminding her why she had ventured downstairs so late at night.

"To help them find their empathy. Figures are easy to dispute and manipulate. But if you talk about Mrs. Jones and how she lost her husband to that lung infection, I believe people might feel empathy for a woman who has five young children to raise all alone, particularly when you argue that his death might have been preventable."

He nodded reflectively and indicated the pile of sliced ham. "Would you care to join me?"

Her stomach growled again and they both laughed. "Yes, if you have enough," she said.

He grinned and began slicing off a few more pieces for her. "I like the way you're thinking about this," he added thoughtfully, which made her feel warm inside. "But wouldn't they simply dispute the fact that his death was preventable?"

She watched him work. He set the meat slices on a platter and then picked up a brick of cheese and cut sections off one end. His hands moved with brisk efficiency, and she found herself wondering how he had become so adept at working a kitchen knife. Her husband carried an entire history that she knew very little about, and the more hints he gave her, the more she wanted to know.

"Yes, of course there are those who will dispute it. You'll then discuss the story of the young Mr. Campbell who barely overcame the wasting disease he caught working in the textile factory, and now bears the effects of stunted growth."

He set the cheese pieces on the platter and retrieved a loaf of bread, all the while thoughtfully mulling over her words. "And then I'll discuss the statistics we have of how many young men have been similarly affected?"

"Yes, and we can use those statistics to show the financial cost of ignoring the problematic conditions." She personally felt the fact that people were dying and having their entire lives negatively affected should be enough, but Devonworth had impressed upon her the need for financial numbers to drive the point home.

Bread sliced, he picked up the platter, indicating the table in the corner of the room near the hearth. There was no fire now, but she had wrapped her dressing gown around her and wore slippers, so she wasn't very cold.

"You make good points," he said, setting the platter down. "I'll consider your suggestion."

She sat in one of the ladder-back chairs and he took the other. It was a simple meal, but it looked like a feast to her. "I should have eaten more at dinner," she said. The cheese crumbled on the end of the cheese knife as she spread it on a hunk of bread.

"Was it not to your satisfaction?" He took a piece of the ham into his mouth. Even here, he sat with perfect posture and ate with the same care as if they were dining with a prince.

Something about that made her smile. "Yes, the food was lovely. I . . . wasn't very hungry at the time."

He frowned and rose. "Wine?" he asked as he walked into what appeared to be a pantry of some sort.

"Yes," she called out, and he returned a moment later with a bottle of red wine.

After retrieving two glasses, he poured her one and set it in front of her. She couldn't help but enjoy how he made her feel cared for. She'd never want for anything as long as he was around.

"My mother tends to do that to people."

He spoke with such calm sincerity she wasn't sure he was jesting with her until she looked up and caught the laughter lurking in his eyes.

"No, it wasn't her."

He laughed. "Liar."

She smiled, feeling her cheeks warm. "Maybe a little, then." More seriously, she added, "She disapproves of me."

He shook his head. "She doesn't know you."

"No, but true knowledge of a person isn't really required for them to disapprove of you, is it?"

He spread the cheese on a small square of bread and set it on her side of the platter. "No, it's not." He conceded her point.

Warmth filled her when she picked up the bread and cheese he'd made just for her. It tasted better than her own efforts, probably because he had made it, and everything that came from him was better in her mind. She was afraid she would be lost in him soon, and she didn't know what to do about it. That moment on the train when he had realized she had arranged that stop for them had nearly been her undoing. She had almost confessed to all of the complicated feelings she had about him and asked him to be her husband in all ways, not only in name.

Her sisters had been no assistance in helping her decide whether or not to take that next step. Eliza had gently encouraged her to pursue him, while Jenny had warned her of the dangers to her heart. Both were right in very different and contradictory ways.

He prepared his own piece of bread and then paused with it in his hand. "She needs time. I think it's very difficult for her to know that I had to marry for money. Most people we know think the word itself is vulgar. She's struggling to accept things. It's not you."

She nodded. "Do you think she'll ever be able to accept me?"

He shrugged. "She doesn't have to, though, does she? We'll divorce or separate and that will be that."

Her stomach churned unpleasantly at that reminder, particularly after the closeness they had shared earlier in the day. It was true, but she was quickly coming to enjoy having him in her life. What would her life look like without him in it?

"I suppose she doesn't. I just want her to approve of me. I've spent my whole life being looked down upon. I don't want to live that way anymore." Truly, being his wife was a heady experience.

She didn't realize she might have said too much until he was quiet a moment too long. He looked at her appraisingly. "Why would anyone look down on you?"

She swallowed and took a long drink of wine to cover the anxiety that was churning to life within her. All this time, she had led him to believe that she had grown up the daughter of a man from a well-to-do family. They traveled first-class when they traveled by ship. They wore Worth gowns. They had dowries. He was looking at her too hard. Lying to him, or not telling him the entire truth, had seemed easy. It *had* been easy back when she barely knew him and marrying him had given them both what they wanted. But now things were personal.

She liked him. She respected him. She was strongly beginning to suspect that her feelings were much more intense than that.

"We were poor. After Mr. Dove passed away, we were left with our home but not much else, a small income that didn't stretch very far among the four of us." The allowance Mr. Hathaway had permitted them. Her mother had been forced to threaten to go to his wife before he paid for them to attend a finishing school for two years. But that money had financed Jenny's trip to Paris. That money had bought them the extras that didn't include the basic food and fuel. "Not when you counted educating us and keeping us clothed."

He was silent again. She hated when that happened. He was entirely too intelligent. They had had enough discussions and pleasant debates about his speech that she knew a little about how his mind worked. He was turning over her words, looking for holes and weak points.

"Why do you call your father Mr. Dove?" He'd asked her that once already. It was a weak point in their story and this new information no doubt had him reconsidering her earlier answer.

"I don't know. Why does your mother call you Devonworth? It's odd, but it's the way it's always been." She placed the crust of bread back on the platter, unable to eat another bite. Guilt was filling her up. He stared at her, a deep crevice forming between his brows. It opened up something inside her, and she couldn't stop talking. "I don't have any memories of him. There is a portrait that hung on the wall in our parlor and a daguerreotype of him. Those are the only connections I have to him. Mama calls him that, and it just stuck."

His eyes softened but were still heavy with concern. It was

how he looked at her on the train. "Cora—" He sighed, the sound tinged with disappointment for her.

It was her undoing.

She couldn't take it anymore. She could not lie to him when he had been nothing but kind and giving with her. Not when he had kissed her palm on the train and surprised them both with his tenderness.

"I . . . I call him Mr. Dove because he's not my true father." Her hands clinched into fists and her whole body tightened, bracing for his anger.

His breath came out in a long and slow release of air. "Cora—"

But she couldn't bear to hear that disappointment in his words, so she pushed back from the table and said, "I didn't know for a long time." But she had known before their deal. Before their marriage—*years* before their marriage—and she had lied to him by omitting the truth. When that truth might have pushed him away from her and had him finding another wife, she had selfishly wanted him for herself. She couldn't face him, so she paced to the end of the hearth and back. "I know I should have told you the truth. You deserve to know, and it's unforgivable. I understand if you want to have the marriage annulled now. I'll tell the truth when they ask me if it was consummated. You deserve a wife who isn't a liar."

When she turned around, she would have run right into him if he hadn't caught her by the shoulders. "Cora, calm yourself."

He didn't look unduly upset, but he wouldn't, would he? One of those terrible gossip sheets had called him the Ice Prince. He never lost his composure. It was the weight of his disappointment that would break her, not his words. The tender concern on his face was still there, only now he wasn't trying to figure her out anymore.

"Is Hathaway your father?" he asked. She couldn't tell by his voice what he made of that.

She swallowed past the lump in her throat and nodded. "He arranged for my mother to marry Mr. Dove after we were all born. It wasn't long after Eliza's birth that Mr. Hathaway married his wife. She was someone his family chose for him." He stayed silent, taking it all in. His hands never left her shoulders. "There have been whispers about us ever since. Mr. Hathaway provided for our care, but that dwindled as we got older and Mama became unhappy with the arrangement."

The crease in his forehead deepened. "What happened?"

"One day she took us to visit him in Newport."

Fanny had said that they were going to visit Mr. Hathaway at his holiday cottage, but they hadn't. On their one and only morning there, all the people had stared at them from the moment they stepped outside the inn on the main street where they were staying. Cora still got a funny feeling in her stomach when she thought about it.

She was accustomed to the attention Fanny seemed to attract wherever they went. Her mother was beautiful. This was a fact, not the delusions of a daughter's fancy. It had happened too many times to be otherwise. But on that day, those stares hadn't been filled with admiration. They had been hard, almost mean. Fanny hadn't noticed, of course; she never did. She had smiled with her shoulders back and her chin level with the ground as they marched along the sidewalk. Cora remembered this precisely because she had been unnerved by the attention and had attempted to mimic her mother.

Fanny had paraded them into a sweets shop where they had been perusing the ribbon candy when a man dressed in a fancy suit had hurried inside, his face drawn tight with outrage. Cora had never seen him before, but there was something familiar about him. He looked similar to Mr. Hathaway. She had tried not to stare as he'd had a heated and whispered debate with her mother in the corner of the shop, but she was too fascinated to look away, leaving Jenny to guide Eliza in her selection. She had seen the man take a handful of banknotes from the billfold pulled from inside his coat and stuff them into her mother's hand. Fanny had rebuffed him right away, but he had been insistent. Feeling indignant on her mother's behalf, Cora had marched to her defense only to reach them as the man had turned to leave. He barely gave her a glance before he stormed out, the little bell on the door tinkling behind him. Fanny had stuffed the notes into her handbag, her cheeks flushed with embarrassment. They had left town soon after, and her mother had refused to discuss what had happened.

He was silent after that, digesting the scene she had shared with him. To fill the quiet, she said, "I know now that the man was Mr. Hathaway's brother. He's the one we dealt with after that day, and he despised Mama. Any request of an increase in our pitiful allowance was met with outrage from him. Eventually, the money stopped once I came of age."

His hands fell from her shoulders. She could not look at him and see the same disgust on his face that others had shown them.

"Then Mr. Hathaway agreed to pay your dowries? I don't understand."

She told him about her grandmother's will and how Mr. Hathaway had used it to his advantage to get them out of New York, seizing on her suggestion of noblemen to leverage connections in London.

He was silent for so long, only the sound of his breath reached her ears. When she finally found the nerve to look up at him, his face was devoid of all expression. Her stomach twisted with the anguish of losing her newfound friendship with him.

"Come with me."

He didn't give her a chance to refuse or accept. Instead, he grabbed her hand and led her from the kitchen. The efficient clip of his boots echoed off the flagstone floor of the kitchen and then the wide, wooden planks of the corridor. She could see now that the kitchen had once been its own separate building and the corridor built to connect it to the main house.

"Where are we going?" She had a vision of him presenting her as a charlatan to his mother. She didn't want that. Telling him had been difficult enough. "Devonworth—"

"Shh . . ." He clucked his tongue at her like she was a recalcitrant child. Oddly, that soothed her. Some might consider him still a stranger to her, but she felt as if she knew who he was inside. He wouldn't shame her.

She padded on her slippered feet behind him and wrapped her fingers around his hand. He squeezed her back gently. For once there were no gloves between their skin. They seemed to walk forever, but it could only have been a couple of minutes. They went up a separate set of steps than she had come down, and he led her into a salon of some sort. It was dark because it was a long room and the only window was at the other end.

"Wait here," he said, and disappeared out the door again.

The room was filled with paintings, though there were quite a few shadowed spaces that no longer held artwork. They had probably been sold in desperation.

A moment later, a gas sconce on the wall flared to life and he came back to her. Taking her hand again, he led her to two portraits next to each other. One was clearly his mother. She had the same frosty eyes and tilt to her face, though she was probably the same age as Cora was now. Her coldness did not compare to the haughty indignation apparent in the late earl's expression. His eyes were hard, as if the world was beneath him. Harry looked a lot like him with his brown eyes and hair and the nose that was slightly too big for his face. Harry made it work somehow, but she disliked this man on sight.

"Your father." She looked up at him for confirmation.

Devonworth gave a single nod. "What do you notice?"

She frowned, uncertain what he meant. "He doesn't appear like a very nice man."

"He wasn't. What else do you notice?"

"Harry looks like him."

"And I don't." He said it quietly but with meaning.

Her husband did not look like this man at all. Where his father was dark, he was light. Neither of his parents had green eyes. He might have gotten the shape of his eyes from his mother, but it was difficult to tell. He really did not look like either of his parents.

She gasped. "No!"

"They say he was Scandinavian, someone connected to a royal family, but Mother has never said. Supposedly, there was an affair. I don't know how it ended, but I was born eight months after my parents wed. She won't talk about it. My own father could hardly bear to look at me. He much preferred Harry, for obvious reasons."

She could see that it still pained him. His jaw was tense and his voice tight.

"You won't find any judgment from me," he finished softly.

"Oh, Devonworth." She leaned toward him before she could stop herself, and put her arms around him, her face pressed to his chest.

After a moment, he brought his hand up to her head and

rested it there, holding her close to him. "I thought you were meant to call me Leo," he whispered.

She smiled, imagining that he was teasing her, but when she looked up at him, there wasn't a shred of humor to be found in his expression. He stared down at her as if his very life hung in the balance. Slowly, so slowly she couldn't even be certain it was happening, he leaned down. His breath touched her cheek, cool in the late night air. His thumb brushed her temple, and he leaned down even more. She pushed up on her toes, and their mouths were melding together. He made a sound in the back of his throat, and her pulse beat in response. His lips were warm and soft, and when they parted, he tasted like wine. The brush of his tongue against her bottom lip had her pressing forward, chasing the hot, slick feel of him. Her fingers delved into the hair at the nape of his neck, but he was already backing away. A space opened between their mouths, and he took in a gulp of air.

He was as breathless as she was. "We shouldn't, Cora. We can't."

Before she could counter that with several perfectly reasonable explanations of why they should, he walked quickly from the room.

"Wait. Devonworth. *Leo!*"

He didn't look back.

TWENTY-ONE

✦

AFTER BREAKFAST THE NEXT MORNING, THEY SET off to tour the improvements. The dowager countess did not make an appearance at the breakfast table. Cora was told this was a usual occurrence as the woman preferred a tray in her room. Cora was glad to be spared her frosty conversation for a few hours longer. Her meal passed pleasantly enough until Leo walked into the breakfast room.

He was dressed in riding gear, looking every inch the country gentleman. There was a momentary hitch in his step when he saw her, but he merely offered her a greeting and walked to the sideboard where a selection of food had been laid out for them. The Ice Prince. He didn't mention the kiss or what they had revealed to each other the night before. Except for the brief hesitation when he saw her, it might not have happened at all.

He picked up a slice of bacon and asked, "Would you like to tour the repairs with me? I'm meeting Fraser now."

She agreed, and just like that, they set out as if last night had never happened.

The roof repair was in the wing where the ballroom and guest rooms were. It was closed off from the rest of the house, but the smell of fresh wood reached them before she saw the opening in the ceiling and sunlight streaming inside. The ceiling above the ballroom soared over two stories in height with a balcony on one end, which is where she assumed the orchestra sat. It was a lovely room with carvings in the dark wood moldings all around. Men and women in various classical poses looked down on them from their perch at the top of the room, except at the far end where the roof collapse had destroyed them.

As Mr. Fraser and her husband discussed the timeline for finishing the project and the need to reinforce the roof, Cora pretended to study the wallpaper, which was clearly ruined by the rain and weather. In reality, she couldn't take her eyes off of Leo. She liked that name so much better than Devonworth. His title was cold, and it kept him aloof from her. Leo was warm and intimate. She had spent the better part of the night reliving his lips on hers, and she had determined that keeping their relationship as it had been was no longer possible. She'd take Eliza's advice and try for more.

She wanted all of him. He wanted that, too. Something was keeping him from her, and she was bound and determined to find out what it was.

After the stop at the ballroom, he took her on a tour of the property. She didn't know how to ride a horse, so he drove them in a gig along the roads and trails that wove throughout the estate while Mr. Fraser rode along beside them on his mount. She had hoped to be alone with her husband, but the estate manager was an amiable fellow. He was in his sixties and had grown up on the estate, so he was well versed in its history. From an ancient Druid encampment to medieval battles, he seemed to know it all and kept up conversation as they toured.

The drive around the property was beautiful. Half the estate seemed to be moorland and heath while the other was forest dominated by oak. Winter had released its hold on nature, but summer had yet to arrive. The air was cool, but inviting, and while the sky wasn't a vivid blue, it had lost the drab gray of the past months.

"It's so different from my life in Manhattan." She had loved the city with its variety. There were different sorts of people on every street with accents and clothing from all over the world. Turning a corner could bring you to a nook or startling piece of architecture you might have walked by a hundred times and never seen.

But this was good, too. She stared out over a particularly striking bit of scenery where Leo had pulled the buggy to a stop. The land stretched out before them in gentle slopes for miles. A ribbon of water sparkled in the sunlight as it gave them glimpses of itself between the hills. The air was fresh, and one deep breath felt as if it could nourish her for days. "It's so peaceful and calm. Did you love it here growing up?"

He stared off into that distance with her, not speaking for a while. Finally, he said, "I didn't appreciate it as a child, but I'm beginning to." His gaze met hers briefly, and it was filled with meaning before he clucked his tongue and the horse took them onward back toward the house.

She wanted to ask him to elaborate, but Mr. Fraser was there. She wanted to mention the kiss that he pretended never happened, but she couldn't until they were alone. And it seemed they would never be alone today. They were going to eat with his mother and then leave for his football match. That talk would have to wait until tonight.

The next couple of hours passed with a quick luncheon, and then Cora changed for the match. When she came downstairs, it was to find that her husband had already left and she would be riding to the nearby village with her mother-in-law. It was a silent and tense trip. His mother hardly spoke to her and answered Cora's falsely enthusiastic questions with as few words as possible. In the end, Cora gave up and watched the sights outside her window.

The village was quiet and peaceful with a main street that consisted of a square and shops. They skirted the edge of that shopping district and pulled up to a field behind the small industrial area of town. It seemed like most of the town had turned out. The stands were already filled with people, and others milled about the edge of the playing field. Both teams were already on the pitch, preparing for the game.

"They've set us up over here." Lady Devonworth directed Cora to follow her to where two padded chairs had been placed on a rug a distance away from the crowd. Apparently, they were to enjoy the game in comfort and without the bother of other people.

Cora followed without complaint, but she searched the field for Leo. She found him almost immediately as he kicked the ball to a teammate far in the distance. He wore a green shirt similar to what he had worn on their first meeting. The breeches he wore came to just below his knees where stockings or high socks stretched over his muscular calves. He would have made a wonderful footman. She laughed to herself as she remembered Eliza had done a lot of reading on England before they came here. One thing she had read mentioned that footmen would sometimes pad their calves to make them appear more muscular and thus capable. Cora still didn't know if that was true.

His blond hair shone under the tepid sunlight, highlighting the gold streaks. She still ached to run her fingers through it. She pulled up short when she would have run into his mother's back. She had been too caught up in Leo's attractive lines to pay attention. It was exactly what had happened to her last time she'd seen him playing football. She tried not to laugh at herself, but it was impossible not to find humorous how attractive she thought her own husband and how there seemed to be nothing she could do about it.

When she glanced back, Leo met her gaze across the field. The corner of his mouth curled upward, and she wondered if he was remembering their first meeting. His mother didn't seem to notice, and they settled themselves. Cora spotted Lord David and Prince Singh, who had attended their wedding, on the field. They were her husband's teammates, but she hadn't registered either of them that first day. Her attention had been reserved solely for her husband. It still was. The match began soon after, and Cora couldn't take her eyes off him. The sheer athleticism of his movements fascinated her. She finally dragged her gaze away from him to try to make sense of the game. To Cora, it was still a rather rambunctious group of men chasing a ball on the field, so she leaned over, determined to form some sort of positive relationship with her mother-in-law.

"Do you know what is happening? I confess I have no idea."

The woman glanced at her coolly and then pointed. "Devonworth's team is in green. They move the ball down the field toward that goal. The other team, in red, tries to get the ball in that side."

It was a rather simplistic explanation, and Cora had already figured out that much on her own, but she thanked her anyway. As the game progressed, she asked several more questions. The dowager seemed frigid, at first, but as time passed, she seemed to warm up to Cora. She even offered several comments of her own by the end of the game. Leo scored twice, and Cora rose to her feet to clap for him both times. Her mother-in-law stayed seated but smiled more and gave Cora approving looks. It wasn't a lot, but all in all, Cora found the day successful.

After the game—Leo's team won—Cora hurried from her seat to her husband on the far side of the field. The team was finishing their celebrations and packing up their things. Leo had poured a cup of water over his hair and was pushing his hair out of his face along with rivulets of water as she approached. Her heart gave a little skip. He looked exactly as he had that night after his bath. She had seen just how muscular he was that night, enough so that watching his athleticism demonstrated during the game today had had her imagining all sorts of naughty things as he moved.

He caught sight of her and smiled as she came to a stop in front of him.

"Congratulations," she said. "It was a good game." She wanted to kiss him but wasn't brave enough, not with everyone around them. Instead, she settled for touching his shoulder.

"They put up a bigger fight than we anticipated." He leaned a little toward her and his fingertips touched her waist. "It was good to not see you on the pitch this time," he teased her.

"I was happy to see you stayed within the proper boundaries," she teased him in return.

He tossed back his head and laughed. She loved how rich and deep his laugh was the rare times he let it loose.

"Lady Devonworth," Lord David said by way of greeting as he walked up to them. He wore the same tired but exhilarated expression as her husband. He was also attractive, but she only had eyes for her husband.

"Lord David." She inclined her head to him but glanced back to Leo. "You both played well."

"Thank you. Married life seems to be treating you both well." He looked at them appraisingly.

"Well enough," she replied.

"We are going to the pub to celebrate, but we'll be home before too late." At her questioning look, Leo added, "David will be spending the night before taking the train in the morning. Will you wait up for me?"

Of all the things he might have asked, she hadn't expected that or the way his eyes softened as he looked down at her. Maybe he wanted to talk about their kiss. Or maybe he wanted to give her more of them. Either way, she would not refuse him.

LADY DEVONWORTH WAS CORDIAL TO CORA AT DINner that night. She had thawed considerably, even if she wasn't exactly friendly. She even invited Cora back to her private parlor where she showed her several of the impressive embroidery samples she had been working on. When Cora mentioned that she didn't know how to embroider, her mother-in-law immediately launched into lessons. The woman didn't say very much, but she regarded Cora with benign interest and seemed glad to share the pastime that she loved so much.

Afterward, they both retired and Cora spent a little bit of time working on Leo's speech, trying to incorporate the personal stories they had heard in Clarkston. She still hadn't been able to get the opening where she wanted it. No matter how hard she tried, it was difficult to concentrate. She would hear a step in the corridor and rush to her door thinking it might be Leo only to find a servant going about their nightly duties. Or she would get stuck on a particular turn of phrase, and that tiny break in focus would send her to the window looking for signs of his return on the drive below.

He finally came home around eleven in the evening. She heard the muffled voice of his valet and forced herself to ignore the excitement in her belly and read the page over again. But her ears were attuned to every noise beyond the closed door between them. Finally, a door clicked shut and the sounds died down. His valet must have left.

The door stayed closed, however, and she began to worry that he might go to bed. What if he didn't realize that she had stayed up? Nibbling her bottom lip to keep her nerves together, she knocked lightly on the door. She told herself that if he didn't answer the one knock, she would turn away and go to bed. Another, far wilder part of herself that she must have inherited from her mother demanded that she walk in if he didn't answer. He owed her some sort of explanation for that kiss. He had enjoyed the kiss. She had enjoyed the—

The door swung open and he stood before her in his robe. It was made out of a thick velvety material that caused his shoulders to look twice as broad. The gaslight behind him framed his hair in some sort of golden halo. He smiled down at her, and she would have sworn he looked at her mouth.

"Hello," she said, unable to get any other words to form.

"Hello." There was a tone in his voice that made it huskier than normal. She suspected this meant that he was slightly inebriated. "You waited for me."

She was reluctant to let him know how she anticipated this, so she indicated the desk. "I worked on your speech."

His smile brightened, but he didn't look at the desk. He only had eyes for her. She blushed under his perusal, and everything inside her went soft. When he leaned a shoulder against the doorframe, unwilling or unable to cross the threshold into her room, she put her hand on his chest. His heartbeat was fast but steady under her palm.

"Do you . . ." How was she supposed to talk to him about this when he looked at her as if he could eat her up? "We should talk about last night . . . our kiss."

He took her face in his hands, surprising her. Then he kissed her forehead. His lips were soft and warm, and now that she knew how he tasted, she wanted them again. "We should."

She found herself leaning up, her fingers gripping the lapel of his robe. He was so strong and warm beneath her hand. "I liked it."

A breath of air escaped him. "Cora," he whispered, and his mouth moved down to her temple and then her cheek. She turned toward him, her mouth seeking his. Their breaths mingled for a moment, whisky mixed with wine, but he pulled back to meet her gaze. "I liked it, too, but I don't think we should do it again."

Her heart sank. "What?"

"I like this . . . your friendship . . . We can't kiss again." He pressed his lips to her forehead once more and then closed the door in her face.

She had waited for him for *this*? Oh no, she would not take this proclamation from him without fighting back.

Opening the door, she crossed into his domain. His room was similar in color to hers, but there were heavier pieces of furniture, all carved from a darker colored wood.

"Leo," she called him. His bed was huge and it loomed behind him as he turned around to face her, eyes wide and lips parted in shock.

His surprise quickly melted into pleasure. "Leo," he repeated, turning the word over on his tongue. "Say it again."

The way he said that, soft and with a quiet authority that she found immanently attractive, had her knees going weak. She had to look away from him to compose her thoughts. "Leo." She said it to steady herself, not to please him. "I think we need to set some things straight. You kissed me, and I thought it meant that things were . . . well, changing between us. I thought it meant you *wanted* to kiss me more—"

Her voice broke off as he approached her so fast that she was certain he wouldn't stop in time. Indeed, he didn't. He took her head in his hands and walked her backward until she was against the wall and he was caging her in with his body. His eyes looked as if he wanted to devour her. The possibility made her shiver in delight.

And then he did. His lips parted over hers and his fingers clenched in her hair, holding her steady for him. She made a sound she didn't recognize in the back of her throat and held tight to him as he ravished her mouth. His tongue pressed inside her. The slick glide of it against hers was both silky and rough and made goose bumps break on her skin. She could have gone on kissing him forever, but he abruptly broke off.

"Cora, you have no idea what you do to me. I want to kiss you." He gritted his teeth as if he were in some sort of war with himself.

She wasn't letting him end what he had started so easily. "Then do it." Taking hold of his head, she pulled his mouth back to hers and kissed him again.

His hands went around her and held her closer for a moment, but then he pushed her back enough to break the kiss. His eyes were closed tight in what appeared to be agony, before he opened them and said, "I cannot. I cannot do these things with you and keep myself apart from you."

Her mind was swimming. Physical intimacy was never part

of the deal, but she had never anticipated feeling like *this*. Like it would be the greatest tragedy of her life if they didn't explore whatever it was that was happening between them.

She grabbed his robe and moved closer to him. A gasp escaped her as she felt the long and rigid evidence of how he did want her pressed against her stomach. And she wanted him. Couldn't it be that simple? "Why do you have to keep away from me?"

"Because it's too much. I can't."

She wanted to argue, but she was too confused and overwhelmed by the strength of the emotion he was keeping inside. He was trembling with it. "Leo, please."

An unexpected pain flashed across his face. "And then what?" he asked.

The sight of his discomfort brought her up short. She didn't want to hurt him, and she couldn't understand how she had. "Couldn't we have a night together without dissecting what it might mean?"

He shook his head and kissed the corner of her mouth. "Go . . . please."

Dismissed, rejected, and flailing in confusion, she hurried back to her room.

TWENTY-TWO

❧

DEVONWORTH BARELY SLEPT THAT NIGHT, AND when he did, his dreams were taken up with Cora. She was present every time he opened his eyes to the dark. He was very nearly consumed by her, and if he didn't work to put distance between them, he would be lost. There were two reasons that was problematic. The first was that she had made it very clear that they were never meant to have a real marriage. She would leave at some point in the near future. The second was that he had already suffered loss. Sofia had come into his life and he had never been the same.

He had loved her. It had taken him a long time to come to that conclusion, because he had spent a great deal of time hiding from that truth. He had loved her. A part of him still did. She would always hold a piece of his heart even though he had tried to cleanse himself of her. Because of her choosing that man—or his money—over their very obvious and deep affection, he could not—*would not*—entertain the idea of losing himself so completely again. That part of himself was meant to be closed off forever.

Or at least it had been until Cora had come into his life. She was very nearly perfect for him in every way, surprisingly. Regrettably.

He was drawn to her. Even as he ate his breakfast from the tray in his room and told himself he would walk out that door, have his final meeting of the trip with Fraser, and stop thinking about how it had felt to kiss his wife, he could not stop. He was attuned to every sound and murmur that came from the room next door. He sat at the small table by the window and chewed a sausage as he heard Monroe come into her room. He was drinking coffee when the lady's maid said something about the cold. He imagined Cora dressing for the day in a fine-spun wool traveling costume because the morning had dawned more frigid than yesterday. He had finished his breakfast when the door to the corridor opened and closed again as Monroe left.

Perhaps his wife had gone with her. Or perhaps she was next door, mere feet away, and he could go and kiss her. Comfort her and take the pain that his rejection had caused away.

"Bloody fucking hell," he muttered under his breath, and flung open the door to the armoire. He had told Crawford to come later after he'd enjoyed a leisurely breakfast, but he couldn't wait anymore to dress. If he didn't get out of this room, he'd go over to her, and he couldn't trust himself not to touch her again. He needed to dress and put distance between them.

Her laugh came barreling through the closed door. His skin bristled with the pleasant sound of it. It tinkled on a high note and then ended in a long husk. He resolved to ignore it, but as he reached for his trousers, it came again. Tightening the belt on his robe, he was all the way to their adjoining door before he realized he meant to open it and see her. He was barefoot and wearing drawers, but the robe covered him sufficiently. Still, his hand paused on the handle, aware that opening the door could be a colossal mistake. She laughed again and he pushed the door open.

He saw her perched in the window seat, facing the panes of glass with her knee pushed into the cushions. She wasn't dressed at all. She wore a modern combination ensemble. A pair of drawers attached to a chemise top. The lacy strap had slipped down over one shoulder. The way her knee pressed into the bench cushion left her somewhat exposed. The slit in the drawers was wide enough and long enough that it revealed the creamy skin of her inner thigh and the bare curve of one cheek.

He took in a long, slow breath at the sight. There was a tightening deep in his groin, and excitement swirled in his belly. She looked over at him . . . glancing over that exposed shoulder, and he imagined her naked, nothing between them as he moved over her.

The momentary pain that flashed in her eyes stopped the daydream from going any further. She was still hurt from his treatment of her the night before. He couldn't say that he blamed her. But instead of commenting on it, her eyes shuttered and she nodded toward the window.

"The pheasants have escaped. Come look." Her attention turned back to whatever was happening outside the window, and she gave another soft laugh.

He walked like a man under hypnosis, his steps slow and careful, but drawn relentlessly to the sight of her and not whatever was out that window. Reason be damned. The skin from her shoulders to her ribs was pale and flawless. The delicate bone underneath was barely seen until she pushed the curtain back more and her shoulder blade flexed. The line of her long neck was elegant and, he knew now, scented with lavender. Her waist nipped in only to flare out at the hips. The thin linen clung to them, and he knew that if she turned around, he would see the dark shadow of curls that hid her sex from him, that if he reached a little lower, he could slide his hand against her and nothing would come between his fingers and her slick heat.

"Cora," he whispered when he reached her. His voice was foreign to his own ears, husky and filled with aching need.

She glanced over her shoulder at him, her eyes flared slightly, but she turned away, nodding to the glass. "Look."

A comedy of errors played out beneath them through the small diamond-shaped panes. The pheasants ran amok as a stable boy, groom, and two kitchen maids attempted to corral them back to their coop, which was far away on the other side of the stable. The birds squawked and flapped their feathers as they protested the indignity. Fraser's hound didn't help. He alternately barked at them and ran away as a couple of the braver hens stood up to him.

Objectively, he knew that the scene was amusing. Realistically, he could barely pay attention to it, and was only dimly aware that it was happening. He was too consumed with his wife to care. He leaned over her with good intentions. It was the only way to get a clear look. But the moment he did, he became aware of her smaller body beneath his. Lavender teased his nose, and he had to violently strangle the urge to bury his face in her hair. Her round bottom was only inches away from him, and he wanted to press himself against the softness. His cock went from half awareness to full arousal in the space of a heartbeat as the blood in his body shifted from his head to pulse there, aching for her.

She stilled beneath him. Was she aware of how much he wanted her? The chaos continued outside, but all went quiet between them. He fought for control. This had been a mistake. He should have never crossed the threshold of her room. He wasn't able to withstand the temptation she unwittingly presented. She hadn't asked for his attention. He needed to go.

He shifted, to move away from her—he was almost certain—but the softness of her hip touched him. He was so aching and hard for her that a hiss of air escaped him. With Herculean effort, he kept his hips in check when they wanted to grind against her. Instead of doing that, he pushed himself bodily away from her with a hand on the window and the other pressed into the cushion beneath her.

"Leo," she whispered and wrapped her arm around his, her hand covering his on the window.

He froze, vacillating between answering the voice in his own head that urged him to get the hell out of there and the need in her voice. Her hip brushed into him again, and he realized that *she* had moved earlier, breaking those sacred few inches that had separated them.

"Cora—"

She didn't give him a chance to say all the reasons they shouldn't do this. "Please."

She pushed back into him and he was lost. Pleasure and need exploded within him. He was so hard for her that he could feel it leaking out of him. He thrust his hips against the softness of her arse, and sparks of sensation exploded along his cock at the delicious friction, so he did it again.

She made a soft sound in the back of her throat, and he imagined it was the noise she would make as he fucked her, as his cock slid into her, stretching her to fit him. Christ, the very thought of that had his hips bucking involuntarily. She gasped at the force of it and he was lost. There was no going back.

She guided the hand that had been on the window to her breast. He shifted his weight to the other hand and cupped her. She was small and soft in his hand. The nipple was a hard bead pressed into his palm. He needed to feel the silk of her skin, so he tugged at the linen. It didn't give way easily, and he was too far gone for rational thought. He felt ravenous for her. The delicate fabric tore with an obscene ripping sound, and she was suddenly bare to him. He savored the feel of her and buried his face in her neck. He cautioned himself to be gentle even as he bit at her delicate skin.

She gasped and reached behind her, blindly shoving his robe aside as she grasped for his length. Her small hand found him through the linen of his drawers and he trembled. He was so close to release, it would only take a few pumps of his hips and he would be done for. He refused to unman himself with such little provocation and squeezed his eyes closed to fight it. He wasn't ready for this to be over. Instead of giving in, he released her breast and moved down past her stomach to the patch of curls he knew would be drenched for him. An impatient flick of his hand had the linen parting, and his fingers found her hot and wet.

"Leo!"

She let him go and braced her hands on the cushions, holding herself up for him so that he could play with her unimpeded. She widened her stance and he found her clitoris. She was swollen with need for him. Every flick of his thumb had her hips moving in rhythm, but it wasn't enough. He needed to feel her around him. He sought out her opening and pressed a finger inside. She was so tight that he was almost certain no one else had ever been there. He didn't go very deep, just up to the second joint before he withdrew only to press inside her again in a very basic approximation of how he wanted to take her.

"How is that?" he whispered, but it was more of a growl.

"Good," she said.

"More?" *Please want more.*

"Yes." The sound was barely more than a gasp, but it was enough.

He pressed his second finger in slowly, allowing her to adjust to him before he fucked her in a gentle rhythm, curling his fingers toward that enchanting bit of rough inside her. He made sure the base of his thumb pressed into the swollen nub, creating friction against her every time he thrust his fingers.

She was getting close. Her body trembled and she jerked back against him. He couldn't control himself anymore and started rutting against her. He squeezed his eyes closed and saw stars as he held her imprisoned between his hand and his cock. He was so close. A few more thrusts and he would come in his drawers. It no longer seemed to matter that it would be with all the finesse of a schoolboy. She was gripping his fingers, sighing with pleasure as he brought her ever closer to her release. Nothing mattered but them. Not the chaos outside or the world waiting for them in London or the damned knocking on the door.

Nothing mattered, not even that the door opened and her lady's maid walked into the room and saw them. He was so drunk on Cora that he could barely see straight. He saw the vague impression of a woman framed in the doorway, her eyes wide with alarm.

"Leave us," he managed to growl out, and she was gone with a slam of the door.

Cora's hand gripped his wrist as if she was afraid he might

take it away. He couldn't make her come like this. He needed to see her. Withdrawing his fingers, he gripped her hips to turn her around. She looked like a wanton but also like his Cora, the woman he was coming to care for far more than he should. Her eyes were dilated with need, and the torn linen revealed her breast to him. It sat high on her chest, small but perfect, tipped with a pink nipple. The very second she was seated, he fell on her.

He took her mouth in a deep kiss, his tongue mating with hers in a duel that left them both breathless. Then he went for her breast. He needed to taste her skin and feel the bead of her nipple against his tongue. She cried out as he sucked, her fingers curling in his hair. But even that wasn't enough. He needed to taste her, the very essence of her. Pushing her thighs wide, he fell to his knees on the floor and buried his face between them. She cried out again and her thighs clenched around his shoulders as he lapped at the salty taste of her. Her hands gripped his hair hard as she pressed him closer. He could barely breathe, but it didn't matter. He'd die for this. For her taste on his tongue.

The ripples started almost immediately. She threw her head back and cried out into the room as her hips undulated, trying to get closer to his mouth. He growled as she came on his tongue, his need for her bordering on animalistic. He didn't want to stop even when her trembles eased. He wanted to keep pleasuring her, to spend the day, no, a week at least, learning all the ways her body would respond to him. But they couldn't do that.

He meant to let her go and walk away to find his own release in his room, but she had other plans. The second he released her, she fell to her knees beside him. Her fingers were greedy in their haste to get to him. She unfastened his drawers and pulled them down to release his cock, which stood upright and fully erect, the head glistening. She met his gaze, and he knew what she meant to do.

"Cora, you don't—"

He couldn't get any more words out before she was lapping at him, her tongue both eager and cautious from inexperience. He nearly died at the sight of her soft pink lips closing around the head. He longed to hold her there and watch her take him into her mouth over and over again, but he couldn't move. He was too shocked and too on the edge of release to do anything. She made another one of those sounds in the back of her throat as she took him deeper into her mouth, and the vibration undid him.

"I'm going to spend."

It was a warning. A plea. He could no longer control himself, and he gripped his length and pumped. His release came pouring out of him. She startled and looked up at him, but she didn't move away. He came on her tongue and her lips, painting her with his spend as she licked at him.

His release came harder than he could remember ever coming before in his entire life. His entire body shook with it. He stared down at her and knew that it was too late. He couldn't save himself from her any more than he could stop the sun from rising.

TWENTY-THREE

CORA HAD NEVER EXPERIENCED ANYTHING LIKE that in her life. It had been euphoric. She had heard women talk about sex before. Fanny's friends were progressive as far as that went, and Fanny herself had been known to indulge in love affairs. Jenny had written home to her about a particular man she had fallen in love with in Paris. She had known that sexual encounters could be pleasant, but nothing had prepared her for *this*.

Release had felt like she had come out of her body. From the look of him, her husband felt that way, too. He had fallen to sit on the window seat, his back against the panes of glass. His chest rose and fell with his breaths as if he'd come from the football pitch. The muscles of his chest and shoulders were on full display, and she immediately regretted not being able to feel them properly during the encounter. But there would be more. She was certain of it. No one could do what they had done so spectacularly and not want more.

His eyes were hooded as he looked at her as if he'd awoken

from sleep. He cupped her face in his palm, and his thumb traced her lips, spreading his semen. It wasn't until that moment that she realized it was still there and she probably looked a mess as she knelt at his feet. Her body was still thrumming pleasantly, so she hadn't even considered that. Her fingers automatically flew to her mouth. He sprung to action, leaning forward and using his robe to wipe her mouth and chin clean.

"Christ, Cora." He kissed her forehead and leaned back again, his gaze fixed on her face. "That was . . . unexpected."

She smiled up at him. "It was."

"I'm not typically so clumsy."

Her smile brightened at how he was completely undone. His composure was in shambles. She had never seen him this relaxed or at a loss, and she quite liked him this way.

"I didn't notice," she said.

His mouth tightened. It was her first inkling that she wasn't going to like what came next.

"Cora . . ."

"Leo." A bloom of dread opened in her stomach. If this was going to bring them closer, his tone wouldn't be so off. Something was wrong, and she had a suspicion he was regretting everything. But she didn't want to lose this closeness with him. The very idea of it made her feel sick.

He took in a breath through his nose, and the silence grew.

"You didn't mean for it to happen, did you?" she asked, hating what she knew his answer would be.

"It shouldn't have happened."

Nothing could have prepared her for the pain that sliced through her. It was the worst thing she had ever felt. Worse than the last night Mr. Hathaway had visited them years ago. That night flashed before her eyes and she was back there, hiding outside the door to their music room as he argued with her mother about money.

"You will not receive a penny more than the monthly allotment we've agreed upon. Not a penny more, Fanny." Mr. Hathaway's voice had rumbled through the wall. He might have also stomped his foot. Something shook the crystal drops on the table lamp in the hallway where Cora knelt listening through the keyhole.

"Keep your voice down, Charles. There is no need to wake the girls with your tantrum."

Fanny's voice was measured in a way that it hardly ever was, as if she was trying very hard to stay calm. That more than her godfather's raised voice had made Cora's skin prickle with cold. Mr. Hathaway's rare visits were usually in the mornings when she and her two sisters would be presented to him in their Sunday best. Strange that he was here now, late at night.

The silence in the room was thick like vapor. Cora could almost imagine it seeping under the door to stain the hem of her nightgown as she shifted to her knees and peered through the keyhole. She couldn't see anything except the box piano that stood in the center of the opposite wall between two windows.

"If you call this a tantrum, what in God's name do you call that stunt you pulled in Newport?" Mr. Hathaway's voice shook with his anger. "My entire family was there."

"You're right, for once your entire family was in Newport," Mama quipped. Her voice came from the left, which meant they were on opposite sides of the room.

"You know what I mean."

"There was a time when *we* were your family." Hurt had overtaken the anger in Fanny's voice.

"Things are different now," he said quietly.

There was a rustle of fabric, and Fanny's skirts came into view as she closed the distance between them. Her voice had softened considerably when she spoke. "They don't have to be." Sighing dramatically, she added, "This isn't about the money. I . . . I know I shouldn't, but I still love you, Charles. Even though you've married that woman and I feel cast aside."

He let out a sound that seemed half sigh, half torture, and said, "No! Don't say such things. That is in the past."

"It's the truth. Despite what you say, I know that you still love me. Otherwise, it wouldn't be this difficult. Just admit it. Say that you love me. Say that you wish you got to come home to me in your fancy Fifth Avenue home every night. Say that you wish it was me—"

"Damn you!"

For a moment, he took up the entirety of the view from the keyhole as he crossed to her mother. Cora had the horrible thought that he meant to strike Fanny or punish her for speaking to him that way, and she made to rise, but that isn't what happened. He grabbed Fanny, but only to pull her against him. They were kissing. Fanny was kissing him back. One of her slender hands gripped his hair so tight Cora winced, while her other clung to his shoulder as if she didn't want to let him go. They appeared frenzied, and he lifted her against the piano.

Cora fell back in shock, closing her eyes so tight that white spots danced behind them as she tried to make sense of what she had seen. It still didn't make sense when she opened them. Her heart pounding, she hurried on her tiptoes to the stairs, intent on hiding in her bed and pretending she had never come downstairs in the first place. She had only made it to the first step when the door to the music room flung open and Mr. Hathaway's heavy footfall sounded in the hall. Instead of hurrying up the stairs, which would surely get her caught, she sat on the step near the wall and hoped the shadows hid her.

It didn't work. He paused when he came abreast of her, his eyes widening in surprise. "Cora," he said, and for some reason the sound of her name in his voice was a surprise.

"Mr. Hathaway."

"I won't see you again for a long time," he finally said. "I am sorry for that."

She didn't know what to say, so she nodded.

"Charles . . ."

They both looked back to see her mother leaning in the doorway, as if standing took too much effort. Her eyes were glassy with unshed tears.

Mr. Hathaway drew himself up, as if gathering his strength, and the expression on his face shuttered. "Should you need me, send a message through my brother. As long as you don't contact me directly again, Fanny, your allowance will continue unabated."

He went to turn away but paused and glanced down at Cora. A spasm of pain crossed his face for a moment and then it was gone. He gave her a nod, his goodbye, and then walked the few steps to the front door.

He gave Fanny one last look. "You and I are finished with each other. For good," he added in case there had been any doubt.

The slam of the front door seemed to echo in the silence he left behind. Her mother approached silently and sank down beside her on the narrow stair. The heaviness she brought with her was the scariest thing Cora had ever encountered. Her mother was always happy and smiling.

"Never love a man, Cora," Fanny said and put her arms around her.

"I hate him." And she did. She hated him in that moment as she had never hated anyone before. Not even Jenny when she stole her hairbrush, the one with the pretty pearl inlay, and broke it.

That same cold ache spread over Cora now, and she recognized it for what it was: rejection. She wasn't good enough. She hadn't been good enough for her own father, and now she wasn't good enough for her husband. He had taken from her the same way Mr. Hathaway had taken from Fanny, and now he was discarding her.

It wasn't quite the same. She knew that. *She did*. She wasn't being cast away out of sight. She wasn't forced to watch him marry some other woman and raise children with her. But the wound of his rejection wasn't logical and it refused to see the difference. It hurt with the same desperate ache.

"I . . . I . . ." She couldn't push any words out past the lump in her throat. This wasn't supposed to be happening after the most intensely pleasurable experience of her life. Not with him. "Why shouldn't it have happened?"

"Because I can't do this." For the first time, he seemed to notice that he was still disheveled and exposed. He quickly wrapped his robe about him and stood, stepping around her and turning away to arrange his drawers.

The emerald and rose patterns in the carpet swam before her eyes. She refused to cry, but she couldn't look at him and keep her composure. Rage and anguish warred for space inside her, and one of them was bound to win.

"You don't want me," she said.

"No . . ." His hands took her shoulders, making her start because she hadn't heard him come back to her. He knelt before her. "That's not what I meant. I do. Obviously, I do. What I mean is that I cannot do this." His gaze was fixed to her breast, and she realized that when he had ripped it earlier, he had broken the strap, leaving it dangling. That side of her chemise fell down to expose her breast.

She reached for the linen with numb fingers and brought it up to hold over her nipple.

"We can be friends or we can be lovers, but we cannot be both. Forgive me for touching you. I don't know what came over me."

She shook her head. "Please don't apologize. I wanted you to do that." She had thought they were sharing something together. His apology now only made her feel even more alone.

He regarded her intently and then nodded.

"Why can't we have both?" she mustered the courage to ask.

"I cherish the friendship we've created." He took in a breath, and she emerged from the fog of her pain enough to realize that he was laboring to speak. He appeared pained. "I don't have many friends," he whispered in an admission that sounded costly. "If we become physical and things end, then I . . . I'll be . . ." Pain wracked his features. "Please don't ask me to give this up."

What was she supposed to say to that? "Okay, I won't."

He let out a breath, and she could almost see the tension leave his face. He gently squeezed her shoulders and then let her go. "I should go get dressed," he said after a long and awkward pause.

She nodded and waited until the door closed behind him to start crying.

PART THREE

Truth is the most valuable thing we have.
Let us economize it.

—Mark Twain

TWENTY-FOUR

THE TRAIN RIDE HOME TO LONDON WAS NOTABLY awkward. Lord David rode along with them, so the complete and utter silence she had dreaded was avoided. Leo was solicitous to her and behaved as if things were normal between them. Cora supposed they were. His cool reserve and her uncertainty were how things had always been. One weekend away where they gave in to their baser desires need not change that. Once or twice David studied her as if he suspected something was amiss, but other than that, she assumed she pulled off the ploy of aloof wife. Their conversation flowed until they began talking about players in their football league and she stared out at the countryside wondering how she would make it through the next two years. Her husband already had half her heart.

She took dinner in her room that night, claiming fatigue. Leo did not knock at her door. When she awoke the next morning, he had already left for his offices at Lords. Cora solemnly refused to cry again and set about her day. Her first task was to finish rewriting the opening of his speech. After luncheon, she planned to visit Miss Sharma and view the photographs she had taken to document the poor sanitation conditions in Clarkston, and then she'd pay a visit to her sisters. She hadn't decided if she would share with them everything that had happened with Leo. It seemed too personal to speak of, but she was so confused by everything, she wanted the comfort only they could provide.

There was an odd stillness in the house even as the servants moved about. She supposed it was her own pain that made it seem that way. Resolved to not allow her husband to hurt her anymore, she pulled her shoulders back and made her way into his study and the table where she had taken to working during the day. The waiting tray of tea and orange cream biscuits made her smile. She had first tasted them at the wedding breakfast and loved them. Mrs. Anderson took good care of her. There was always refreshment waiting for her.

Usually, the table was bare, aside from the tray, but today there was a stack of newsprint. Edgecomb typically sent a boy to collect several papers each day, so these must have accumulated while they were out of town. She picked them up intending to set them aside, but she remembered the horrible things that had been written in some of them earlier. It couldn't hurt to look and see what else might have been written since. Surely, the topic of the state of their marriage had been laid to rest by now.

Pouring herself a cup of tea, she settled herself and opened one of the newspapers. A quick scan yielded nothing about her or Leo. More confident now, she picked up the second. This one was not so tame. Toward the last page in a section called *Tidbits*, the unknown author elaborated on the dinner party she had attended with Leo last week where she had sparred with Lord Bolingrave.

Although it did not name her, it labeled her a "women's rights advocate" who spoke with a "passionate and misguided fever" and had hardly allowed the men to get a word in edgewise. Bolingrave was treated as one of the poor and unfortunate men who had been forced to listen to her diatribe. He had been interviewed for his opinion on the exchange and asked if he would like to reply, as he had not been given a chance to reply during the dinner conversation. He had submitted a letter to the paper.

It read:

Thank you to the editors of this esteemed newspaper for seeking my opinion on this matter. I will give it here as I have given it many times to anyone who will listen. This idea of the new woman and the theory of women's rights is not new at all. The theory will run its course as it has in the past. It is in direct opposition to human law and a man's duty to labor for his family. The woman's place in nature is that of carer and nurturer. Nature will always prevail. I will give the women's rights set their due, however, and concede they have the right idea in utilizing women to solve the problems facing us. Take, for instance, the sanitation concerns facing our great country. Many of these issues could be solved by our women would they only take their minds from dissonance to harmony. Women (traditional women) are homemakers while men are out in the world. Everyone knows that sanitation begins at home. Let this new woman be a sanitary reformer with a mission to ensure our homes are clean. Let her master physiology and use

modern advances to keep her home free of dirt and disease. Let her allow sunlight and fresh air into her home to drive out the dark and damp where disease flourishes. Let her labor to keep the pipes and sewers of her home clean. Let her master chemistry so that she may ensure the water she gives her family is clean. Let her learn the properties of food so that she might feed her children the most nutritious morsels. We have millions of women at our disposal for the task. Put them to work to bring cleanliness to all homes. We know more about sanitation than we ever have before. Instead of utilizing this knowledge, women are out marching and joining committees and educating themselves to take jobs from the men who depend on those jobs. The care of children and home is left to servants and elderly caretakers. Were women to spend their time in useful and wholesome endeavors, our world, and indeed their very health and happiness, would be better for it.

Cora was livid when she finished his letter. She could not—would not—let this go unanswered. She reached for a blank sheet of parchment and wrote her own letter to the editor of that newspaper. She wrote that the fact that he would blame the inadequate infrastructure of a rapidly changing population on women seeking to be seen as full members of society was abhorrent. He was fighting the sanitation bill that Devonworth and others were struggling to pass. He claimed it wasn't necessary and that the expense would be an unfair burden to place on landowners. She suspected he was being paid by those same landowners, but she couldn't prove it. Instead of claiming any sort of responsibility as a government official for the lack of infrastructure, he was laying the blame on women.

She stopped short of calling him any number of the names

that came to mind. She also did not include her husband's name. She only barely managed to not sign the letter Cora Devonworth. She wanted to, but doing so would cause more harm than good. She could not risk antagonizing him when Leo was still courting his unlikely vote. The name she used was the same one she had used back home when she had written for the feminist periodical. It had served her well then and it would do so now.

Lavender Starling had come back to life.

TWENTY-FIVE

THE DINNER WITH HATHAWAY HAD BEEN PLANNED for several weeks. He would be leaving for a tour of Europe tomorrow with the intention of returning for Eliza's wedding at the end of the summer. Devonworth, his mother, and Cora were hosting him in a small gesture of goodwill before he left. Mrs. Dove, for obvious reasons, had found herself otherwise occupied, and Cora had informed him before dinner that Eliza and Jenny sent their regrets. Devonworth couldn't blame them.

Learning over the weekend that he was Cora's father had significantly colored Devonworth's perception of the man. Where before Devonworth had found him mildly pompous and annoying, now Hathaway's actions were perceived through a veil of loathing. The man had abandoned his own children. Devonworth could not hold with that. He didn't like that Cora was put in a position where she had to pretend a civility toward him.

All through supper, he kept staring at Hathaway, waiting

for some inkling of paternal warmth to spark from him. It never happened. He greeted Cora upon arrival as any other gentleman would greet the wife of a man whose influence he was courting. During dinner, he listened politely as she spoke and then immediately turned his attention back to Devonworth. Devonworth brought her into the conversation often enough that it became obvious to anyone who cared to notice.

The experience reminded him painfully of his own father. As a child, he had wondered if his father knew he wasn't his true son. Devonworth had found out about his paternal heritage when he'd been seven or eight years old. He had come upon his mother and grandmother in the parlor tucked under the stairs, but their hushed voices had reached him outside the door before he revealed himself.

"You must never tell him," his grandmother had said. That bit of intrigue had stopped him dead.

"How can I keep his true father hidden from him? You mustn't ask me to do such a thing. 'Tis immoral," Mother said.

"Your adultery was immoral." The older woman's words were like chips of ice.

"We were not married."

"Betrothal is the same. A vow was given. You've asked the Lord's forgiveness and that is all you can do. You have played the cuckoo's trick on your own husband. Leave your son in peace. To lay this on his shoulders would be another wrong."

"But Viktor is in London—"

"The Scandinavian?" His grandmother's voice rose in panic. "Does he know?"

"No, I didn't know if I should tell him," came his mother's meek reply. He had never heard her so timid.

"Good. You will not mention it to anyone. We will never speak of this again."

The room had fallen silent except for his mother's muffled sob. Afraid of discovery, he had tiptoed away, the foundation of his entire world shaken. As time went on, he came to believe that his father knew. He was not given the same regard as Harry. When the heir was generally the pride of the father, the one doted upon, Harry had received that treatment. There was nothing his father could do about the title passing to him because of primogeniture. It went to the firstborn son of the marriage. With no evidence available to prove that Devonworth wasn't his biological child, his father was left to show his disdain in other ways.

It seemed that Hathaway was cut from a similar cloth. He didn't disdain Cora, but he certainly had no true regard for her. He was the cuckoo in the situation, laying his egg in another man's nest. It must have been easy for him to walk away.

"Ladies, let us retire to the drawing room and leave the men to their cigars," his mother said, drawing Devonworth's attention back to the table.

He stood as the women rose. Cora had barely looked at him all evening. She wasn't cold so much as distant. He despised that he had allowed himself to go so far with her at Timberscombe Park and that she was now very obviously hurt. It didn't help that he had to restrain himself from going to her every night. He didn't trust that he wouldn't try to touch her again. Was staying away from her worth this pain if they didn't have the friendship anymore that he had so wanted? There was no easy answer to that question. Instead, he waited, hoping that either his longing or his rationale would win out.

He could only watch her as she silently made her way past him. Her hair was pinned up, the thick curls gleaming under the gaslight. As always, her long neck drew his attention, only now he knew the taste of her skin and wanted to dip his tongue into the hollow above her collarbone.

Footmen cleared the table, and Edgecomb brought a tray of brandy. Devonworth waved away the box of cigars he offered. He didn't imagine he'd have enough time to properly enjoy one. Not with what he intended to say to Hathaway. Hathaway enthusiastically accepted.

Devonworth waited until he had the cigar lit and they had been left alone before he said, "I know that you are Cora's father." The man's eyes widened in response, and he coughed against the smoke he had inhaled. "She told me," he added in case Hathaway intended to deny it. Then he went silent, enjoying how the man stewed in his own guilt as he decided how to respond.

Eventually, he recovered and rolled the cigar between his thumb and forefinger, gliding the tip along the edge of the crystal ashtray set between them. "You must understand, my lord. I wasn't certain that she was mine. Not at first."

"But Mrs. Dove was your mistress?"

The man shrugged. "I suppose."

"What does that mean? Did you pay for her expenses, her home?"

The cold edge of his voice had Hathaway eyeing him warily—how had he missed that those eyes were so similar to Cora's? It was because they lacked all of the warmth hers contained. The older man's were flat, like flint. "Yes, we eventually came to an arrangement. When I first met her she was . . ." Hathaway's voice trailed off, and when he spoke again, Devonworth was certain he'd changed what he had originally planned to say. "She was involved with an acquaintance of mine. Their relationship soured and we became close. She fell pregnant quickly, and I didn't know the child was mine until

later. The resemblance was close enough that I felt comfortable supporting them."

Something about that turned his stomach. It sounded as if
Hathaway would have cast them out had Cora not resembled
him, casting a woman he had been intimate with and her infant to the streets.

"I hope you won't hold her parentage against her. She had
no choice but to turn to deception."

"I would never hold that against *her*." He said it so pas-
sionately that Hathaway had the grace to flush in shame. No,
he would save his wrath for the man sitting in front of him.
"But since you mention it, why would she be forced to turn to
deception?"

Hathaway's mouth rounded and then opened and closed
several times. "I—I could not publicly acknowledge her."
His eyes narrowed as he floundered for some sense of com-
miseration, hands gesturing wildly. "You know how these
things go."

It was on the tip of his tongue to admit to his own illegitimacy and how his path had been far different than Cora's, but
he couldn't betray his mother that way. People whispered, of
course they whispered, but there had been no proof or hint of
intrigue from his father's camp. Meanwhile, his true sire remained in Scandinavia. Devonworth didn't even know which
country the man named Viktor called home. He refused to
give Hathaway such ammunition to use against them in the
unknown future.

"I have no children, so I am afraid I do not."

The older man appeared frustrated, his mouth pulled into
a tight line. "It happens, particularly in your aristocratic circles. Jacob Thorne himself is the natural half brother of the
Earl of Leigh."

"Mr. Thorne's father, the late earl, acknowledged him and saw him and his siblings cared for. He was educated and inherited monies and investments."

"I educated Cora *and* her sisters, even though I was less certain of their paternity."

"Are you so uncertain of the faithfulness of every woman you lay with?"

The thinly veiled insult struck home, and the apples of Hathaway's cheeks turned red with hidden fury. He sputtered again, looking rather clownish with his glowing face. "We weren't married. I couldn't be certain she didn't see other men. She's very beautiful now and was even more so then."

Devonworth suspected his fear had more to do with his own insecurities than Mrs. Dove's beauty. "Did you promise to marry her?"

The man got very still. Shame tinged his voice. "My parents refused my request to marry her."

"Why?"

"Fanny's family was not known in our circles. She was no one, and they couldn't see the heir to the Hathaway fortune married to someone like that. At the time, I was bitter with them, but now that I have my own daughter approaching marriageable age, I understand their concerns."

"You mean your fourth daughter."

Hathaway gave a brisk nod, nostrils flaring. "I intended to elope with Fanny, to take her and the children to Toronto. I owned shares in a railroad there and figured I could make it on my own. Then the war came and everything changed. My father died, and I was suddenly in charge and working with the government in Washington to keep our troops supplied. That part of my life with Fanny and the children had come to an end.

"I sent money for their care. A friend, Jeremiah Dove, took them in and gave them respectability. Somehow word got out about them after his death. I have long suspected Fanny was behind it. She thwarted her own daughters' futures to smite me. I couldn't see them as much as I wanted because every time I did, the gossips got wind of it. You can imagine the shame and embarrassment they were to my wife . . . my mother. Finally, I had no choice but to cut off all contact."

"You wanted to forget about them." His voice was laced with absolute loathing, and he couldn't be bothered to care. "To abandon your own flesh and blood."

Would the man who had fathered Devonworth treat him so coldly had he known? Had his mother ever confessed the truth to the mysterious Viktor? He realized that he had never asked because part of him was afraid to know the truth.

"I did what I had to do for my family. They were hardly paupers or cast out into the street."

Rubbish. "As Cora's husband, I am Jenny and Eliza's brother by law and their closest male relative. I want you to transfer control of their inheritance to me."

"Out of the question." Hathaway's voice was whip sharp. Devonworth knew he had likely gone too far in showing his disdain when he wanted something from the man. It was a lesson he had learned several times over, but his anger on Cora's behalf had been too fierce. "My mother left that to them, and I could not see it controlled by anyone other than their husbands."

"Or is it that you would rather control their husbands?"

Instead of answering, Hathaway snubbed out his cigar and rose, pushing the chair back so fast that it scraped across the floor. "I should be going. I leave early tomorrow."

"No." Cora walked into the room, her chin parallel with

the floor and her eyes alive with suppressed fury. Devonworth was so startled by her entrance that he stumbled in his haste to get to his feet. "Answer him," she demanded.

Hathaway gave her the smooth grin he employed while trying to be charming. "Cora, dear, you and I both know that my mother—"

"Stop." She held up her hand and the older man was silenced. "You and I both know that your mother intended for my sisters and me to have inheritances, not dowries. You are the one who contrived to arrange things to your benefit. Let's not pretend that this is anything other than it is."

Hathaway's expression turned serious, and he glanced at Devonworth as if to plead with him to control her. But he could only smile at her bravado—Christ, she was something—and took the few steps necessary to reach her, where he put a supportive hand on her lower back.

"I don't know what you are going on about," Hathaway said. "This has all been settled."

"It has been settled, hasn't it? Everything has worked out for you as it always does. Eliza will marry, and then eventually Jenny, and you'll have us out of your way while gaining the influence of three prominent sons-in-law. That has all been settled. I would simply like for you to understand that we all see you for what you are."

Hathaway stiffened to his full height and looked down his nose at her. "And what is that?"

"A miserable, frustrated little man who will have to live his entire life knowing that he was too spineless to ever once reach out and take what he really wanted."

His face reddened. "I will not stand here and listen to this nonsense."

He made to leave, but Devonworth moved to block his

path. "I want you to consider my proposition very carefully while you are gone. Eliza and Jenny deserve better."

"Good evening, your lordship." The older man tipped his head, and Devonworth moved back to Cora's side, where they watched him leave.

The room was heavy with their silence. Finally, Cora turned to him. "Why did you do that?"

"I don't trust him, and I don't like the idea of him having any power over them."

She nodded, but there was a suspicious sheen in her eyes. "That's why you were so angry earlier."

"You noticed? Is that why you returned to the dining room?"

She shrugged. "I had a feeling you meant to speak with him, and I was curious."

"I don't like how he abandoned you and your sisters. I'm glad you won't have to deal with him anymore. I won't invite him back here if you don't wish to see him. Just say the word and—"

She reached out to touch him. It was the slightest press of her hand against his chest, but she might as well have touched him with flame. Every part of him lit up, warming, throbbing, burning for her.

"I appreciate that, Leo. I might take you up on your offer, but for now we can't cut him out of our lives. Not when Eliza's marriage could be at stake or even Jenny's . . . when she finds someone." Then she closed her eyes. "Or maybe I've already put them at risk. I shouldn't have said those things."

She started trembling, and he pulled her against him. His lips rested at her temple. "You had every right to say them. Unfortunately, everything you said was correct. He won't withdraw the funds because he wants the contacts those marriages will bring too badly. Your words smarted, but he'll recover by morning."

She nodded against him and drew in a stabilizing breath. "Yes, I suspect that's true."

He pulled back enough that he could tilt her chin up to make certain that she was better. "Are you all right?" His voice was husky with need.

It was difficult to be so close to her and not take more. He knew her taste and smell. It would be so easy to take her mouth and dip his tongue between her lips. They could be in his bed in under a minute. He could be inside her in a minute more. He had to grit his teeth against the wave of arousal that caused. This was not the time for that. Not with her so vulnerable. Not with him so very afraid of the great emotion lurking just below the surface of his heart. It could all come crashing open so very easily.

"Much better, actually. I've been wanting to say those things for a long time." She did look better. The anger had gone to be replaced by a peaceful joy.

He wanted her so badly. He wanted to bask in her peace and happiness. She smiled and took his hand, giving it a squeeze. "Come with me. I want to show you something."

He followed, part of him silently plotting to see every part of her that he had denied himself, part of him warning that he should never be alone with her again.

When they reached her room, she hurried inside.

"Would you return in a quarter hour?" She spoke to Monroe.

He couldn't hear the woman's muttered reply, but she came out a moment later and averted her gaze from him as she skirted around him. It would be years before they could look at each other again after Timberscombe Park.

"Sit down."

Cora indicated the chair he usually took and picked up the papers he recognized as his speech. Shaking them out, she said, "I finished the opening. Tell me what you think." Clearing her throat, she waited for him to settle before she began.

"Colleagues, friends, and . . . *bellends*." She gave him a mischievous smile that made him burst out into laughter.

"Where did you learn that word?" It was strikingly British, or so he had thought.

She raised one shoulder. "I thought it appropriate. Use it or not. It's up to you." She cleared her throat and continued on in a more serious tone. "Allow me to share with you the story of a family I met while visiting Clarkston, a village that, like many, has borne the brunt of our race to industrialization . . ."

He listened with rapt fascination and awe as she read the words he would say in a few short weeks. As he did, he knew that he was absolutely lost. They could not go back to being friends after all. He loved her.

He imagined evenings spent working on speeches or papers in the years ahead. Her beside him. Their verbal sparring as they discussed the best turn of phrase. He would kiss her neck, and the evening would slowly melt into night when he would carry her upstairs where he would bed her so thoroughly she'd fall sleep in his arms, too exhausted to retire to her own chamber. But that wouldn't happen. Not with her wish for a separation.

Unless he could change her mind.

The thought struck him from nowhere, causing him to physically jolt from it. Did he want to change her mind? Did he want to be so completely at the mercy of another woman who held his heart? He glanced away, lest everything he felt be displayed on his face.

She looked up, eyes questioning. "What do you think of the new opening?"

He swallowed thickly. "It's perfect," he said with polite applause. "Thank you for writing it."

She smiled, and his heart palpitated in the most alarming way. It was too late for him. Mild panic drove him to his feet.

"You're leaving?" she asked.

He gave a terse nod. "I've remembered that we left my mother downstairs. I should bid her good evening."

Her smile fell fractionally. "I forgot about her."

He could not leave without touching her, so he took her shoulders in his hands. "Are you truly all right?" When her brows drew together, he clarified, "With what happened with your father?" Her lips curved in that beautiful smile again, and he let her go to put distance between them.

"Yes, I'm glad to have said to him what I've been wanting to say for a long time. Thank you for standing by me." She closed the distance, and he kept walking backward until he ran into the door, where he put his hand on the latch as if it was a lifeline.

"Always, Cora." It was bloody true. He cleared the husk from his voice and attempted to set them back on a less emotional track. "Tomorrow is the LSS demonstration. You remember what I told you?"

She nodded. "I remember. You want me safe."

"Good." At the very least he could keep her safe until he figured out what the future held for them. "Good." Opening the door, he said good night to her and put much-needed distance between them.

TWENTY-SIX

CORA HAD NEVER BEEN TO A DEMONSTRATION BE-fore. The excitement in the air was palpable, as was the underlying sense of danger. Gaslight lamps lit the space, insulating the group of fifty or so protesters, but it also made the night beyond seem much darker. No one mentioned it, but the danger was there nonetheless in the forbidding faces of the men garbed in black who stood guard at the edge of the green space. The men were there to keep them safe in case someone decided to attack again. Thank God no one had . . . yet.

Several men, and a few women, in the crowd of passersby called out rude comments, but no one assaulted them as they carried their signs printed in red and blue around Parliament Square. There were two dodgy-looking characters who watched from the corner of a building. She'd look up and see them, a tall, thin man and a shorter, rounder one, both with dark hair and endlessly smoking cigarettes, and they would be staring back. She ignored them and instead focused on the importance of the evening.

The Palace of Westminster loomed in the distance where the men of both houses, including her husband, were debating the rights of women to retain control of the assets they brought into marriage. It seemed like such a simple idea, but the bill had come before Parliament in the past and been roundly defeated. Too many were afraid that giving way to this one thing would open the floodgates to more rights and eventually women's suffrage. They were right. Everyone believed it was one small step in correcting a long line of wrongs.

Near the end—the big vote would take place tomorrow when they would find out how much further they needed to go to reach their ultimate goal—Mrs. Burgess pulled her aside. "Lady Devonworth, I wanted to personally thank you for joining us tonight."

Her husband's influence was at work again and he wasn't even here. Cora smiled. "It is I who should thank you, Mrs. Burgess. The work you do is important to women and children all across Britain."

The woman nodded gratefully, but she was preoccupied. With a gentle hand on Cora's arm, she led her farther from the green, where everyone was beginning to load the signs and themselves into wagons and carriages. "I would never presume to come between a husband and wife, but I wondered . . ." Her voice trailed off, and she glanced over Cora's shoulder to the palace in the background, its windows alight with orange. "Forgive me, but Lord Devonworth has some influence, and I wondered if . . . if he . . ."

"He's very sympathetic to women's rights," she announced proudly.

They hadn't explicitly discussed it since the night of their marriage negotiation, but he was a good and fair man. It was that as much as his good looks that had won her over. Okay, maybe the good looks had a head start, but she was half in love with him because of the strength of his character.

Mrs. Burgess's face relaxed somewhat, though it was difficult to say, because she always carried herself very sternly. "Yes, yes, I assumed so, my lady. Perhaps you might convince him to join our cause, officially, in the coming months. Even in the event the bill passes tomorrow, it is but one stop on our journey. There will be several more before we reach our destination, and his support could go a long way."

Cora had never thought of asking him to join LSS. It had never even occurred to her. Would he? He was busy with his work, but it couldn't hurt to ask him. She agreed and then hurried off to find August, who would be dropping her off at the mews behind her home. Devonworth hadn't wanted her coming to this, and hoping to avoid a confrontation about it, she had decided not to take the carriage out. She would use the servants' entrance, and he would be none the wiser unless he asked her about it later. She wouldn't lie to him, but there would be nothing he could do about it at that point.

Twenty minutes later, she knocked on the kitchen door. Mrs. Anderson had been expecting her and let her in right away. "There you are. Welcome home, milady." Her face showed her relief as she quickly ushered Cora through the maze of corridors downstairs. She had been complicit in Cora's minor subterfuge.

"Is his lordship home yet?"

"Not yet, but he is expected any moment." Mrs. Anderson followed behind her up the stairs to the main floor. "I would suggest you get to your bedroom as quickly as possible, milady. It wouldn't do for him to suspect a thing."

Cora agreed. Things had been going well for them lately. His rejection still smarted, but they managed not to discuss that. She appreciated the way he had tried to intervene with Mr. Hathaway. Also, her letter to the editor had been printed yesterday, a fact she had not mentioned to him. She didn't think the pseudonym would ever come to light, but if it did, she wanted to keep things good between them.

"I understand," she said when they reached the main floor. "Take my things and I'll hurry up the back stairs." She shrugged out of her cape and handed off her gloves.

"Yes, milady. I'll send Miss Monroe up soon. She's finishing her supper."

"Thank you, Mrs. Anderson."

Cora hurried into the corridor, intending to turn up the servants' stairs, but muffled male voices caught her ear. Damn! It sounded like her husband talking to Edgecomb. He must have just walked in the front door. She waited in the small alcove near the stairs wondering what to do. The stairs shared a hallway. Even if she missed him downstairs, she ran the risk of running into him in the hallway upstairs. Even though she had relinquished her outerwear to Mrs. Anderson, the dress she wore was not one she would wear for an evening at home. She still wore her boots, the high, serviceable ones she reserved for rainy days. He would know what she had been up to the moment he saw her.

The voices faded. She hoped that meant he had gone to the drawing room. He sometimes did that when he came home, to get a drink. She peeked out of the little alcove and had the extraordinarily bad luck of locking eyes with him. He stood just past the foot of the front stairs as if he were walking down the corridor toward her.

Her heart jumped into her throat. His eyebrows rose in surprise, then the skin between them creased, which was followed by a full-blown mask of fury that crept over his entire face. *He knew.* He knew and he was angry. She didn't give herself time to think about it. She flew out of the alcove and turned the corner to the servants' stairwell. Holding her skirt up off the floor, she took the steps two at a time. He must have started running, too. She could hear his heavy footfalls echoing through the house.

She burst out of the stairwell on the first floor only to see he had been faster than her. He had taken the front stairs and was already halfway down the upstairs corridor coming toward her. She squeaked in surprise.

"Cora!" His voice was full of the authority she imagined him using on the floor of Lords. It sent a shiver of fear and something equally pleasant and disturbing in a completely different way coursing through her.

Instead of waiting, it only spurred her forward across the hall and into her bedroom where she slammed the door behind her. She let out a breath of relief when she turned the key in the lock. Safe at last. Only she wasn't, and she realized a moment later that the door to the bathing chamber stood open. She cursed and hurried to it, but it was too late. His footfalls echoed on the tile floor, and he reached the door at the same time she did. Only the door opened into her room, so he had the advantage. She turned to run back to the door that led to the corridor, and he slammed the bathing chamber door, trapping himself in here with her.

"Do not open that door." He didn't yell, but his voice was commanding nonetheless. She glanced at him over her shoulder as she fiddled with the key, her fingers too clumsy and wired with energy to turn it properly. "I have never taken you for a coward," he added, the insult settling around her as he no doubt knew that it would.

She whirled to face him, her shoulders pressed to the door. "I am no coward," she spit out.

"Then answer for what you've done instead of running." His breaths were heavy as if he'd run a race.

"What have I done?" She put her chin up. She wasn't a complete idiot. There was no use in answering for anything if he didn't know.

"You went to that demonstration after I told you not to."

"Yes, I went. I went because I am a member of the Society. We were letting our voices be heard to bring personhood to married women."

He stared at her, his jaw rigid with anger. "But I forbade you to go."

"You *forbade* me?" She drew herself up and took a few steps toward him. "Why on earth did you think such a thing would work? I am not yours to forbid or to grant permission to."

He ran a hand through his hair in frustration, leaving it mussed and quite attractive for it. She liked it when he was ruffled, his polish gone. Only now she was too angry to properly appreciate the effect.

"You are my wife. It is for me to keep you safe."

"That's right. I am your *wife*, not your property. It *isn't* up to you to keep me safe. You can provide me with protection, but ultimately, I am my own person. You cannot keep me locked away."

"I don't want to keep you locked away. I merely asked you not to go. People were injured at the last one. I did not want to be concerned about your safety."

"Well, you weren't concerned about my safety because you didn't even know I was there."

He literally growled at her and turned away, stalking to the far corner of the room. "That's not helpful," he said.

He turned to face her, and the fury in his eyes had changed subtly. She couldn't put her finger on what it was, but it was simmering there below the surface. She understood then that he wasn't simply angry that she had disobeyed him. He was frustrated that he couldn't have helped her had she needed him. He cared about her.

"Leo." He jerked his head to the left to look out the window. Her indignation slipped away from her as she approached him. "I know that you were only concerned for me. You didn't mean to sound like a dictator."

She came to a stop next to him, but he didn't seem inclined to acknowledge her. Instead, his brows lowered over his eyes and he kept his gaze fixed on something outside her window. She touched his arm to bring him back to her. He immediately looked at her hand before meeting her gaze. "If anything happens to you on my watch . . . I don't know what I would do . . ."

She smiled to break the sudden tension. Butterflies swirled in her stomach, but she kept her voice light as she said, "You'd be able to keep all the money."

His expression shattered. "I don't want your money." His whispered voice was raw and filled with an ache that twisted her inside. "I want you, Cora. To be safe, to be happy . . . to be loved."

The liquid emerald of his eyes shimmered down at her and she was lost. Before she could even understand her intention, she leaned into him and pressed up onto her toes. He met her halfway, his lips crushing hers, and she was lost in his kiss. She wanted to be loved. By him. His tongue pushed into her mouth, stroking against her own and sending a delicious shiver down her spine. Her body lit up, just like it had on the weekend when he had touched her in her room.

Her hands moved up his arms to his shoulders, but he grabbed her upper arms and pushed her away. It was only an inch, but it might have been a mile for all the space between them.

"No, Cora."

She hated how he kept doing this. "I'm not your plaything, Leo. You can't take your fill and then push me away when you've had enough."

"My plaything? You think I've had enough?" He brought his face down to hers so they were nose to nose. "I haven't had nearly enough of you."

She knew she was playing with fire, and for once she wanted to get burned. If he had his way, they would keep playing this game. She would walk through the flames of hell before she would go through her whole life not knowing what it meant to be with him. What if no one else could ever make her feel like he did? What if they were missing something really special because she had entered this marriage already looking for a way out, and he was too stubborn to ask for what he wanted?

"No? Then maybe you're the coward."

TWENTY-SEVEN

AN ARRAY OF EMOTIONS WASHED ACROSS HIS FACE: hurt, fury, confusion, and finally understanding.

"Cora." The word was a soft groan. "You don't understand what you're asking of me." Even as he spoke, he moved infinitesimally closer, leaning into her, the movement slow and measured. He smelled like sandalwood and heat. His body was rigid with tension, and that tension moved like a tangible wave from him to her, thrilling her and making the fine hairs on her body stand up. He was fighting a losing battle. She could sense his near capitulation, if she just waited.

She tried to pay attention to what he was saying, but he made it too difficult. Her gaze fixated on his full bottom lip. "I understand exactly what I'm asking." One of them had to say it, so she did. "I want you to make love to me."

His nostrils flared, and she wondered if he was scenting her arousal. The ache between her thighs had intensified. She pressed them together, certain that she could feel the liquid heat of her desire on her skin. She remembered how easily his fingers had moved inside her and wondered if that other part of him would as well. It was an accident, she was certain, but she pressed forward and felt him there, pressing against her stomach. He made a sound deep in his throat that her body answered with a throb.

His large hands grasped her hips, strong fingers digging in gently as he pulled her into him. It was her turn to sob gently as the full length of his erection nudged against her. She grabbed his biceps, and a secret thrill shot through her at how hard they were. He was that hard everywhere. She knew because she had seen him, and she wanted to explore every muscle in his body.

"We can still be friends after this," she said.

He growled again and covered her mouth with his. Releasing her hips, he buried his fingers in her hair, heedless of the pins, and cradled her head, tilted it upward so that he could better feed off her lips. His tongue pressed inside again, sparring with hers. The pleasure of his possession washed over her, turning her knees weak and making her throb with anticipation. His tongue had pressed inside her, between her thighs, in much the same way, and her body remembered. It ached for him as if he were doing that again.

Her fingers curled into the hair at the nape of his neck, and her tongue brushed his. She would not let him escape her. This time she would get what she wanted, which was everything. She wanted everything from him.

He pulled back a hair's breadth. His heavy breath filled the space between them. "We'll never be friends after this."

She gulped and for the first time had an inkling that he might be right. They were standing on a precipice, and whatever they did next would change everything. But it was already too late. She couldn't turn back. Much like in New York, she knew that the only answer was to charge ahead. Desperation had guided her then. Something deeper and infinitely more dangerous guided her now.

She cupped his face in her hands, noting the tender uncertainty in his eyes. She didn't want to turn back and give this up. "Then we'll be something better."

He groaned and crushed her to him. One hand tightened in her hair while the other moved around her waist, dragging her up against him. There was no room for questions and uncertainty after that. He lifted her feet off the floor and held her against him, kissing her as he walked toward the bed. Once there, he placed her on her feet and reached up to loosen his tie. Her own fingers were busy with the buttons on her jacket. They trembled, but what she lacked in grace she made up for in sheer determination. Shrugging out of her top, she made quick work of the fastenings for her skirt. He was faster, though. He'd already shrugged out of his coat and waistcoat and was working the buttons of his trousers when she stepped out of her skirt.

He left them on as he dragged her back up against him. She already missed the hot glide of his tongue against hers. She savored it briefly before she went back to work on her clothes. She wanted to feel his skin against hers and was convinced this was why society insisted on so many layers. This time his fingers joined hers and the corset loosened. It fell away to be replaced by his hands. They caged her waist, then roamed up her rib cage to her breasts. The linen of her chemise still separated them, but his palms were so hot on her skin that it almost seemed as if it had disappeared. The fabric was rough against her beaded nipples as he plucked at them.

She cried out against his lips and he did it again, over and over in an endless rhythm that sent darts of longing straight to her core. Just when she'd had enough and couldn't take any more, he pushed his hands inside the linen and dragged it down off her shoulders. When it stopped at her waist, hindered by her underskirt, he fumbled with the ties, ripping them and letting her mouth go long enough to curse under his breath. She couldn't help but laugh at his clumsiness and step back to help him.

The skirt fell away, and he watched with eyes wide and dilated. He seemed obsessed with looking at her, and she loved that. Had anyone asked her, she would have been certain that being nude before a man would be mortifying. But it wasn't. Not with him. She loved how he watched her. His gaze caressed each bit of newly exposed skin as if he was savoring the discovery. She tossed the chemise aside and reached for the tie of her drawers. He'd already seen her most intimate place, but she'd been covered otherwise. She pushed them down her hips and stepped out of them before sitting on the edge of the bed to untie the laces of her boots.

Except he went to his knees on the floor before her. He took over, his much less shaky fingers making quick work of the leather. When both boots had fallen forgotten to the floor, he gently rolled down her stockings. His mouth followed their path, kissing each exposed inch of her calf that he revealed. He tossed the stockings aside and turned the full attention of his stare to her. He kissed his way up her legs to her thighs and then the soft patch of hair between them. Her body clenched for him.

"Lie down," he whispered.

She moved farther back onto the bed, and he crawled over her, picking up where he'd left off. A quick stop to kiss her stomach and then he was lingering at her breasts. He laved a nipple with his tongue and then sucked it into his mouth, leaving it red and aching as he abandoned it and moved to her other one. He gave it that same attention before his teeth scraped over her neck, and then he was kissing her full on the mouth. She was finally able to indulge her desire to touch him. Her fingers roved over his broad shoulders and down the shifting muscles of his back to the coarse wool of his trousers. She nearly cried aloud at not being able to touch him. In desperation, she remembered he had unfastened the trousers and pushed her hands beneath the waistband, delighted when it gave way.

He shifted, helping her, and she was able to get the trousers down past his hips. The firm flesh of his buttocks filled her hand, but even more than that, the thick length of him pressed against her thigh. She shifted, seeking him, and he fell into the cradle of her thighs.

She gasped at the sensation of feeling that part of him *there*, firmly lodged against her. When he paused to look down at her, she smiled. "This reminds me of the first time we met." He'd been above her then, and though she'd had no idea of how good this would feel, her body had suspected. She'd come alive with him.

He laughed, the coarse, masculine sound vibrating through her. "I was fascinated with you even then." He pressed forward, nudging at her opening, and she cried out softly. "I imagined lying with you just like this." Their smiles slipped away. He stopped, holding himself against her but not breaching her, and wrapped a hand in her hair. The pins had been falling out by this time so that it half hung down around her shoulders. He pulled her head to the side, baring her neck to his hot, open mouth. She shifted restlessly. She could feel herself become wetter, more aroused from both the weight of him above her and the head of his cock nudging at her. He knew and hitched his hips, rocking forward to tease her.

"Leo," she gasped in frustration.

"Say it again."

She barely registered what he said. All she knew was that she ached and if he would just shift forward he could fill her so exquisitely. "Please." She pressed her feet to the mattress, widening her thighs and urging him to do more. But while her movements jostled him, the blunt end of his erection stayed seated *right there*.

He rose above her, one knee pressed into the mattress beneath them, spreading her even wider to him. He brushed the hair back from her face and stared down into her eyes. "Say my name, Cora."

Leo was the name she had given him. The one only they used. For some reason she couldn't fathom at the moment, that brought tears to her eyes. "Leo," she whispered. She might as well have said *I love you*. An expression of such profound relief and happiness came over his face. She did love him. There was no question in her mind.

He reached between them, dragging his fingertips down the center of her body until he touched her where they were almost joined. His thumb dipped into her, gathering the heat of her need for him and using it to ease the way as he gently massaged it over her clitoris. Her hips bucked upward, but he held her pinned down, so she could only accept the pleasure he offered. It was as heady as it had been just days ago, only now it wasn't nearly enough.

"Leo, please, I need more of you."

He smiled and she lost her breath. God, he was the most handsome man she had ever seen in her life, made even more so by the tenderness of his heart. She wanted to consume him. He moved over her completely then. Of their own volition, her hips pressed upward, seeking that wonderfully hard part of him.

"You're ready for me," he said, lying over her while keeping most of his weight on an elbow.

"Yes." As if there had been any question.

He was savoring this too much. The thick weight of him was pressed firmly against her sex now, and every time she moved, her body throbbed. In her mind's eye, she remembered him sitting in the chair pleasuring himself. His cock had been weeping with need, and she imagined it was doing that now, needing to burrow inside her as much as she wanted him to.

He guided himself to her. Notched inside, he held her hip firmly and pressed forward. The pleasure was too intense to be believed. He stretched her as he filled her, but it still wasn't enough. When he pulled back, she grabbed his hips and he whispered softly to her. She couldn't make sense of his words. He filled her inch by slow inch until they were joined completely, his hips settled into the cradle of hers.

She clenched her eyes closed against the uncomfortable pinch. It wasn't very painful. She remembered the telltale pink left on her inner thighs after he had brought her to pleasure in the window seat.

"Have I hurt you?" he whispered. He shifted a little, rocking against her, and she gasped at the sensation that gripped her. She opened her eyes and he looked down at her, concerned but aroused. The green was a mere sliver in his eyes because they were dilated with need. He was nearly drunk with it, but so was she.

"More," she whispered.

It was all the encouragement he needed. He gave a tentative thrust of his hips, and she gasped at how that made the pleasure in her belly spiral higher. It was more intense than she had imagined it could be. He did it again, and she couldn't stop the cry of pleasure that spilled from her. She wanted nothing but this, except he stopped abruptly.

"Wait a moment," he said and pulled out of her.

She sat up in bitter confusion as she watched him leave her bed and then the room. Her body was alive with need and aching for him. From his room she could hear drawers opening and closing, him cursing, and then a door slammed. Intrigued, but also mightily perturbed, she hurried through the bathing chamber that separated their rooms and through the open door leading to his chamber. She had never been in here before.

The bed was huge. Dark walnut draped with rich green bed coverings. A set of armoires took up the far wall, and that's where he was now, the strong line of his back and buttocks facing her. He had taken off his boots and trousers. He found what he was looking for. His hands were shaking as he tossed aside a small tin and worked a condom down his length. She had seen one before. Fanny had made certain to tell her and her sisters about them, particularly the new models made from galvanized rubber, but she had completely forgotten to think of the need for one. She was so mad from wanting him that she welcomed as many babies as he'd give her if it meant he would assuage this damnable ache inside her.

Finished, he came back to her. She barely had time to think before he lifted her against him.

"I wasn't thinking," he said by way of explanation.

She wrapped her legs around his waist and kissed him deeply, eager to continue things. He dragged the heavy velvet blanket that covered his huge bed down and laid her onto the sheets. The white linens were cool and crisp against her back and they smelled like him. If it were even possible at this point, being in his bed heightened her arousal. She was half-afraid he would tease her again, but he didn't. He settled over her and gently pressed inside. She groaned aloud at the pleasure, and he arched forward, the heavy length of him filling her completely. They settled into a nice rhythm, her body reaching for him and him thrusting into her again before she could miss him.

Finally, an exquisite aching desire pulsed through her. Her world got smaller until there was only him and the relentless need only he could fill. Soon, the pleasure in her belly tightened so much that she was certain she would explode, and then she did. She squeezed her eyes closed so tight that she saw pinpricks of light as the waves broke over her.

"Cora." He whispered her name against the shell of her ear. He drove himself into her over and over again until the wave had crested over her. Then his breath stopped and he shuddered above her, finding his own release.

TWENTY-EIGHT

EVERYTHING HAD CHANGED BETWEEN THEM. THE sex wasn't the reason; it was the symptom of a deeper metamorphosis that had been happening from the moment Devonworth had made her his wife. Never would he have believed that an illegitimate, redheaded American would be his perfect match. He believed it now.

They lay in the aftermath of what had transpired in his bed. He had disposed of the condom and promptly slid back under the blanket and pulled her against him. The very idea of being away from her for any length of time was so abhorrent that he planned to entice her to stay the night if she tried to return to her room. He had five other condoms on hand, and he'd swallow his pride and send Edgecomb for more if need be. But he didn't appear to be in any immediate danger of losing her.

She had snuggled into his arms and lay with her cheek against his shoulder. Her fingers absently curled through the hair at the back of his neck. He kissed the inside of her arm, wanting to taste her as the full gravity of what they had done washed over them.

"Did I hurt you?" he asked.

"No." She shook her head and burrowed deeper into him. He put both arms around her and tugged her closer. He loved the naked feel of her skin against him. She was silk and softness. "I think you were right, though." She glanced up at him, a worried wrinkle creasing her forehead. "I don't want to go back to being friends after this."

He could hardly speak past the ache that had opened in his chest. It had been like this with Sofia. Once they had crossed that physical threshold, there had been no going back for him. "I don't think that's possible for us."

"Then what does that mean?" She shifted to hold herself up on her elbow and look down at him.

A long, red curl flopped onto his chest. He wrapped it around his finger already knowing that it would smell like lavender when he brought it to his nose. Deep down he could feel anxiety trying to take hold of him at the intensity of his feelings for her, but it wasn't as strong as he assumed it would be. He was content to lie here with her all night. His mind conjured thoughts of them further into the future. He imagined her at his side at Timberscombe Park. They would spend their winters there. Eventually, they would have children.

"It means that I want you for my wife, Cora. In all ways." The panic threatened to rise to the surface, but he kept it at bay.

Her eyes widened. The light of the single lamp made them appear fathomless. "But you don't know very much about me."

He laughed. He knew everything he needed to know. "I know that you are kind and intelligent and strong in your convictions." He knew enough, and he intended to send a note to Vining to call him off the search for more information about her. Whatever he found wouldn't matter.

"Is that enough?"

"I don't know, but it's a start." He couldn't stop touching her. His fingertips traced over the line of her shoulder and down to the curve of her breast. She was small there, but perfectly formed. "Do you know enough about me?"

She nodded. "I know that you are an honorable man. I know that I admire your heart."

His breath caught, and it was a moment before he could speak. "Well, then . . . perhaps that's enough to start."

She smiled and pressed a kiss to his hand. He cupped her face, unable to stop looking at her. He loved the freckles on her nose and the way her eyes turned up subtly at the corners. The look she gave him when she had something mischievous to say. He loved her. He couldn't say it yet, not when he hardly dared to think it, but she had become extremely important to him in a frighteningly short amount of time.

"There is one thing I'd like to know." She paused, and he could tell whatever it was, it was difficult for her to say. She swallowed and her gaze fell to his chest. "Who is Lady Sofia?"

The pain that came along with that name was unexpected. It seared through him like a brand. He'd worked hard to get over that pain, but there it was. "How do you know that name?"

"Bolingrave and the women he was with at that ball. Someone linked her with you."

He wasn't surprised at Bolingrave's gossiping about him. He wasn't ready to reveal the depth of his feeling for Sofia, but he needed to tell her. She had a right to know about his past. "I was in love with her, and I thought she loved me, too. I even asked her to marry me. She married someone else instead. One of the wealthiest men in England. It turns out she preferred wealth to love. Or her parents did. I never had the chance to ask her. Their betrothal was announced in the *Times* and I never spoke to her again."

"Leo . . ." She cuddled close to him and put her arms around him. "I'm sorry." And then she asked very quietly, "Do you still love her?"

There was a part of him that would always think of her fondly, but the wound she had inflicted had only just begun to heal. He didn't know if he'd ever be able to forgive her for hurting him, but the imprint of her would always be a part of the shape of his heart. "No."

His breath eased out of him as he lay there with the truth of that single word putting him at peace. He had never admitted that to himself before. The days and months had passed without her, and he'd wallowed in his bitterness over the choice she had made. He'd come to realize that he hadn't really known her. The person he had known wouldn't have done that to him with such cold brutality.

Cora pressed a kiss to his chest. The slide of her lips against his skin had his cock coming to life again. She sensed the change between them, and her tongue came out to taste him. He wanted to spend the night inside her, but he had to make certain that she understood where this would lead them.

"Cora . . ." She looked up at him, and he pulled her over him. She settled above him, and he held her hips to keep her in place against his stomach, to keep the temptation of her luscious cunt away from him. "I don't want a divorce or a separation. If we move forward, I need to know that you want the same things I do."

"I want to see where this leads us, Leo." That name. It was like a balm spilling from her lips. "If it means that I'll want to spend the rest of my life with you, then so be it."

He rolled her over so fast that he surprised even himself. He wanted her with a ferocity that he had never experienced before. It was as though if he didn't possess her in that moment then he would die. Fortunately, she seemed to be suffering under a similar fate. She grabbed at him, and before he knew it, he was buried to the hilt inside her. Condomless. Again. His erection was already weeping for her.

"Bloody hell!" He withdrew and she giggled as he hurried for the little tins hidden away in the armoire drawer. This time he brought them all back to the bedside table.

"We'll get better at remembering," she teased him as she welcomed him back to bed.

He wasn't as certain. He'd never been so careless before, and he was afraid it was a testament to how far gone he was for her. That was a question for tomorrow. Tonight, they would lose themselves in each other.

D EVONWORTH LEFT CORA ASLEEP IN HIS BED. HE liked the sight of her there. Her auburn hair spread out across the white sheets like spilled wine. It had been all he could do to walk away from her. He wanted to spend the day with her, but he had to get to Parliament. He'd dressed quietly in the bathing chamber and then headed out. Today was the vote for the Married Women's Property Act. Hereford appeared intent on stalling the effort by using his power to influence enough votes to draw its passage into question. It was all in an effort to keep himself from having to answer for his actions during the February demonstration.

The day ahead might have seemed tedious and tiresome, but because of last night, Devonworth walked through the halls toward his office with a light step. He could still hardly believe how the night had ended. He had thrown his heart into danger, but it was too late to waste time on fear. No, he was too far gone for that. Cora was everything, and with her in his arms, he possessed all he ever wanted.

Beckham's desk was in an antechamber off the corridor. The man was usually writing away at his desk at this time of day, but it was empty. That should have been his first clue that something was awry. It wasn't until he had passed through and stepped into his own office that he realized he had a guest.

The pungent scent of pipe smoke filled the air. Beckham looked at him when he walked in, an expression of pure apprehension on his face. He stood adjacent to the round table where they usually took their luncheon. Sitting in one of the chairs and smoking the pipe was Bolingrave.

"Good morning, Devonworth. I trust you slept well."

"What do you want, Bolingrave?"

He smiled, calculated and bold. Devonworth knew he was in trouble, a feeling that was confirmed when Bolingrave said, "I've recently made a new acquaintance. I believe you know him . . . a Mr. Vining." When Devonworth only swallowed, he continued, "He has some interesting information about your wife . . ."

Bloody fucking hell . . .

TWENTY-NINE

CORA PASSED THE DAY IN A DELIGHTFUL HAZE. SHE had awoken alone in his bed and had debated staying there until the LSS meeting that afternoon. A fanciful thought, but her rumbling stomach had soon intervened. Before leaving his room, she had snooped in the drawer in his bedside table— what did men keep in there anyway?—where she had found every ribbon he had taken from her braid carefully stored away. She imagined him all those nights they had pretended to sleep together pocketing them and putting them away for safe-keeping. What did he want with them? She couldn't fathom, but knowing he kept them made her feel warm and cared for.

She carried that feeling with her throughout the day.

"What has you so chipper?" Eliza asked as she climbed into the carriage. She was accompanying Cora to Mrs. Burgess's home where they would await the results of the vote along with other members of the LSS. Jenny and Fanny were off attending a party, so they weren't able to come.

Cora smiled and attempted a shrug, but the smile expanded

until it felt like it took over her whole face and her cheeks burned. "Nothing," she said, but it sounded like a lie.

Eliza gave her a knowing grin as she settled back into her seat and the carriage jolted forward. "Cora Dove, have you slept with your husband?"

Cora didn't even want to deny it. "I'm not a Dove any longer. I'm Leo's wife now in every sense."

"It's Leo now, is it?" Eliza squealed and grabbed her hand. "Tell me everything. Was he gentle? Did he take his time with you?"

Cora laughed. She couldn't possibly tell her sister everything. What had happened between them was too special. Words wouldn't do it justice. Even now she floated in the remembered pleasure of the previous night. Not only the pleasure, but the certainty that she had found something rare and special with Leo. Leo, not Devonworth. That name was too cold and removed from what they were now, at least in private.

They were Cora and Leo. Leo and Cora. She had never imagined having a man like him in her life. She had thought that, on some level, most men were like Mr. Hathaway. They were ready to use a woman to their advantage and then leave her. But she had been so very wrong and shortsighted. Leo wasn't like that. It was early yet in their marriage, and her mother's warning about falling in love still nagged at her, but she was willing to risk it. This was Leo, her husband, not some nameless stranger anymore.

"Yes, he was gentle. He was everything I could have wanted."

She spent the next few minutes deftly evading her sister's questions until Eliza finally gave up. Staring out the window with a wistful look on her face, Eliza said, "Do you suppose it's bad of me to want that for myself?"

"To want a happy marriage? No, I don't think that's unreasonable."

Eliza looked at her with an expression that was far too wise for her years. "No, I don't expect that. Not if I want my inheritance."

Cora stilled. "What do you mean exactly?"

"Passion. I've never felt it and I want to."

"You don't think you'll have that with Viscount Mainwaring?"

Eliza shook her head. "He's not a very passionate man."

"Neither was Devonworth, or so I thought, but—"

"Cora, he's not like Devonworth."

Cora thought back to the man she had met only a few times. Mainwaring had seemed very reserved and well-mannered, the typical nobleman. "Then you don't have to marry him."

Eliza held up her hand. "No, I'm resigned to do what's right. We need to make certain Mama is provided for, and Jenny has all but said she won't wed any of them. It's up to you and me to keep their futures secure. My only sadness is that I will never know true passion."

Cora didn't know what to say to that. If she were being honest, it was very likely true. Mainwaring seemed the type that would keep a mistress for his baser needs once a wife had done her duty and given him an heir.

"I've heard rumors that he and his friends have made something of a tour of the Italian brothels. There's a bet about how many they'll frequent."

"Where did you hear this?" It certainly wasn't the sort of talk to be found in polite society.

Eliza sighed. "Mama took Jenny and me to have dinner with Camille and Mr. Thorne. His home is attached to Montague

Club, so I had a peek inside." At Cora's horrified look, she added, "Don't worry. No one saw me."

Cora had been too concerned with her marriage to consider how Fanny might be negatively influencing her sisters. If Mainwaring or anyone in Society found out that Eliza had been to the club, then the betrothal could fall apart. "Eliza, if you want this marriage, you cannot go back there."

The carriage turned onto Mrs. Burgess's street, which increased her sense of urgency that her sister understand how that behavior could destroy everything. She only had a minute or two to impress that upon her. "Women have joined the club. They are limited to widows, powerful women with powerful husbands, and middle-class women who are not constrained by the need to marry a nobleman. Mainwaring won't marry you if you develop a reputation."

"I know all of that, but I simply wanted to see. And it's good I did. They have a betting room there. There's a large board filled with bets written in chalk. Mainwaring's name is there, along with all of the men who went on this excursion. Even Devonworth's brother, Harry. They all had tick marks next to their name. A very helpful and inebriated man explained to me that each mark represented an infamous courtesan.

"So . . . I suppose what I'm asking is if he is having his adventure before our marriage, would it be so very terrible if I had one great passion, too, before we wed?"

The carriage rolled to a stop and the footman jumped down. "Eliza . . . I don't believe that—"

The door opened. Eliza smiled at her and accepted the footman's hand. "Just think about it."

Cora anticipated she would do little else, but as it turned out, even Eliza's disturbing revelation couldn't put a damper on her good mood. Eliza would find her own way. Cora had no doubt of that. Other Society members were arriving at the same time, so the next hours were taken up with small talk and discussion about their plans going forward, whether the vote passed or not. Through it all, she felt the imprint of Leo's hands on her skin and couldn't wait to get home to him later that night.

By early evening, everyone was crowded around tables in the drawing room taking tea and refreshments when the front bell rang, which likely meant the vote had finished. Mrs. Burgess had briefed them that she had a man inside watching the proceedings and he would dispatch a messenger the very moment there was news to be shared. At the sound of the tinkling, everyone became deathly silent; not even the sound of the wheezing Mr. Eversby, the man who sat beside her, broke the quiet.

Mrs. Burgess rose from her table and made her way to the open doorway. Murmurs broke out at the other tables. A messenger appeared and handed a folded note to the woman. She thanked him and took a stabilizing breath. Soft murmurs broke the quiet as everyone anticipated what was in the note. Several were certain that the bill would pass this time. Everyone knew that married women deserved the same rights as unmarried women. Several believed that they had years to go and an uphill battle to fight yet. The others were somewhere in the middle.

The older woman turned to the room, and everyone quieted again. To a person, they all respected her, and her general bearing demanded to be heard, but in this case they wanted to know what was in that note. "Whatever the outcome of the vote may have been, we can rest well knowing that we have done our best. I am proud of each of you for the time and effort you have put into the passage of this bill. We are a light of freedom to guide the rest of the world."

There were several hear, hears but mostly everyone was silent and anxiously awaiting the result. Mrs. Burgess closed her eyes briefly before looking down at the paper and unfolding it. When she looked up, Cora couldn't make out anything in her expression. It was exactly as reserved as it always was.

Finally, she said, "The vote was unsuccessful. We will not allow this to deter us." Her voice rose, its unquestioning authority ringing out over the space to be heard over the shouts of disapproval. "We will continue to fight this fight. It is an important step along the long road to suffrage, and we will not stand for its death."

She went on to say how they would redouble their efforts. They would work harder to petition every MP and sitting Lord. As she spoke, Cora imagined starting her periodical early, before her separation from Leo. Which, now, she was increasingly certain she didn't want to happen at all. Perhaps she could devote her first efforts to the passage of this act. She would interview the women she had met and would continue to meet as Leo's wife. She would keep them anonymous, of course, but hearing their thoughts could only help them next year when they pushed for the marriage act again.

Instead of feeling defeated, she felt hopeful as she left Mrs. Burgess's home later that evening. The bill's failure was a blow, and many women would continue to be affected by the unfair laws, but Cora believed this was only a temporary setback, as did Mrs. Burgess. The woman had given them a rousing talk, and Cora felt as if she might have a real purpose here in England. She expected nothing less than Leo's support. He had never once tried to hinder her except for the one time regarding the demonstration. She was certain they could come to some agreement about her safety. Eliza, too, was taken with the idea of the periodical, and so they spoke about that on the way to drop her off. Then on the way home, Cora thought of Leo and how they would spend the rest of the night.

D EVONWORTH WALKED UNDER THE WEIGHT OF HIS guilt as he made his way up the stairs. The house had been deathly silent when he'd arrived. He wasn't certain how he'd find Cora. She'd undoubtedly already heard about the vote.

She had probably not yet learned how he'd voted. He hoped she hadn't. He needed to be able to explain to her himself. Bolingrave had found that damning information about her and left him little choice in the matter.

Vining had given Bolingrave a payment receipt from a publication based in Brooklyn, New York, that had paid Cora for an article penned by Lavender Starling, a pseudonym. It had been for a radical essay espousing the benefits of Free Love, a concept that even members of the LSS weren't ready to embrace. Had it got out, not only would his wife be a laughingstock of the ton, but she would have likely lost her place in the group. He knew how important that was to her. If they had any chance of staying together in the long term, he knew that she needed to find a cause of her own. It would nurture her and help her feel at home here. He'd known for a while, and especially after last night, that he didn't want to lose her. He wanted her as his wife in all ways, for all time. The stain on her reputation would be so great that even his name couldn't save her. Her sisters would lose all hope of good marriages and likely lose the dowries Hathaway had dangled in front of them.

But now that he had done what he'd done, he didn't know if he'd condemned his marriage. She might leave him now. Thanks to his no vote on the bill for married women's property rights, the receipt was safely in the breast pocket of his coat where it would stay until he could burn it. He despised that Bolingrave had gone to such measures, and for what? The bill would not have passed even if Devonworth had voted for it. There simply hadn't been the numbers to see it pass. The bellend had done it out of sheer spite to get back at her for penning that rebuttal in the newspaper.

Devonworth had read the article written under the name Lavender Starling, though he hadn't made the connection to Cora until today when he'd seen the payment receipt. She had been articulate and had thoroughly annihilated every argument Bolingrave had made, and the man hadn't been able to let that pass unchecked.

He took the stairs slowly, worried that she would have somehow found out about everything and be ready to leave him. A light shone from beneath her door, so he knocked lightly. When she didn't answer, he carefully opened the door and found her room vacant, but the door to the bathing chamber was cracked open and the light was on. If she had heard, she was taking things exceedingly well.

With a prayer that she would forgive him, he stepped into the bathing chamber. She was in the tub, soapy water both concealing her and revealing her as it swirled around her. She smiled at him and held an arm out to him, and he knew without a doubt that she had no idea of his betrayal. Her pink nipples played with the water line, peeking out at him.

"Cora." His voice ached with what he had to tell her.

"I know about the vote . . . I was at the LSS meeting when we got the news."

"I am so very sorry." He walked over and sank down to his knees beside the tub.

"Don't worry," she said, touching his temple and smoothing her fingers through the stiffness of his hair.

He'd styled it with pomade, but that had been hours ago and some of it had flopped to the side. Blood rushed through his groin as he remembered how she had run her fingers through his hair last night and clasped them tight in the strands as she'd found her release beneath him. He closed his eyes in pleasure. This would all end when he told her the truth.

"The results weren't completely unexpected. Mrs. Burgess prepared us for this. Even if it had passed, it would have been by a slim margin. We'll try again and again until we're successful. It will pass eventually. I have no doubt."

"I promise I will do everything I can to help. I've already arranged for Mrs. Burgess of the LSS to have a meeting with the men who supported the bill." He'd spoken with Lords Burton and St. Michael and secured their agreement. "We can work together to plan a campaign that will see this pass in the next few years."

She gave him a look of utter adoration. "You would do that?"

"I would go to the ends of the earth to see you happy." No truer words had ever fallen from his lips. He was coming to need her in a way that was wholly unexpected and not entirely comfortable.

The fragrance of lavender touched his nose, and he turned to kiss the scent from her wrist, but he couldn't stop kissing her. He kissed the bend of her arm, the creamy skin of her shoulder, before taking her lips. What was meant to be a soft kiss of homecoming became deeper and harsher. The desperation that was always between them flared to life, caught like kindling. Their mouths and tongues met as if they had been apart for days rather than hours. Before he realized what he was doing, his hands dipped into the cooling water and his arms snaked around her.

She giggled against his lips as he lifted her out completely. "I'm getting you all wet."

"Not as wet as I'm about to make you," he growled against her neck.

He was greedy for her and this madness that existed between them. He told himself it wouldn't be so terrible to give themselves this one more night together before he had to ruin everything with the truth.

She laughed again and held tight as he took her to his room and dropped her on the bed. The sight of her, naked and wet on his bed, made him almost feral in his need. He tore at his clothes and left them where they fell as he climbed onto the bed and settled between her thighs. Her eager fingers found him and guided him to her. He drove inside her in one deep thrust as he took her mouth in a soul-searing kiss. He would never get enough of her. She was a powerful addiction from which he never wanted to be free.

THIRTY

ORA KNEW WHAT LOVE FELT LIKE. SHE HAD KNOWN
her mother's love as well as that of her sisters. It felt like
warmth and security. It was acceptance and approval. Their
love hadn't prepared her for what it felt like to be loved by
Leo. His love was all of those things and more because she was
secure in the knowledge that he was on her side. They were in
this together, and she would never have to bear the burden of
her family alone again.

She spent the night in his bed again. His valet woke him
very early the next morning when the gray light of dawn
peeked around the curtains. A furious and whispered conversation had happened, but she had been too sleepy to make out
the details. There had been something about a man named
Vining.

After the valet had gone, Leo had kissed her and said that
he needed to go to his office but that he would be back soon,
so she had fallen back to sleep. When she woke, she spent the
day working out ideas for the publication she had been planning.

It was past time to stop dreaming about it and to start putting her ideas on paper. She closed herself in Leo's study and set about writing out a business plan.

She didn't stop until Fanny and Eliza made an unexpected call around teatime. She assumed that Eliza had shared the news with their mother about the new state of affairs between Cora and her husband and her mother had come to congratulate her. She wouldn't put it past her, but she did not intend to discuss her intimate life with her mother.

Cora called for tea and joined her sister and mother in the drawing room. After a few preliminaries, their conversation came to a standstill and an awkward silence ensued. Silence was very unusual for her family, so Cora knew something was wrong. She looked back and forth between them and noted how subdued they appeared. They didn't quite make eye contact with her. "You're not usually quiet. Is there something the matter?"

Fanny set her teacup aside and pushed back a nonexistent strand of her perfectly coiffed hair. "No . . . Well, yes, but not if you're not upset by it."

Confused beyond measure, Cora asked, "Should I be upset by it?"

"You haven't mentioned it, so I assume not."

"Well, what is it?" Cora laughed.

Fanny shared a look with Eliza, and Eliza gave a brief nod, as if giving her permission. The crease between her mother's brows deepened, and she said very gently, "About Devonworth and his vote against the marriage act."

Cora stared at her, unable to comprehend what she meant. Finally, she glanced at her sister, who said, "It's true."

But Cora couldn't believe it. They had gotten things mixed up somehow. "You mean his vote *for* the marriage act?"

Fanny pressed a hand to her temple. "You didn't know?"

"What do you mean? He voted for the bill to pass." Of course he did. Anything else was absurd.

Neither of them seemed convinced. Fanny rose and started to pace while she wrung her hands.

"Did he tell you that?" Eliza asked. There was a slightly hardened gleam in her eye that was suspiciously close to anger. It was the first time Cora had ever got the sense that her sister might not like Leo.

He hadn't stated that he had voted for the bill, but he had led her to believe that he intended to. They hadn't spoken about much of anything after he came home last night. He'd made love to her three times, only the first time without a condom—she made a mental note to ask Jenny what she knew about diaphragms. She might need one. And then they'd fallen asleep.

"Why are you both saying this?" Cora sat upright. She was tired of all of these rumors swirling about her and her husband, and to know that someone was parroting lies to her own family was beyond the pale.

She also didn't like the look of pity Fanny shot her when she said, "Because it's true."

"It's not. You know he's a supporter of equal rights for women." He'd come home after the vote and told her how sorry he was. They had made love and he'd been so tender and understanding. She refused to believe it.

"Cora, darling . . ." Her mother shook her head and hurried over to her handbag. She pulled out a folded-up piece of newsprint. "Here, I brought this."

The sheet had been torn out of the *Times*. Under the headline referencing the bill, it listed all of the members of both houses with an *aye* or *nay* next to their name. Cora snatched the paper rather indelicately from her mother's hand to read it. There was a *nay* next to Lord Devonworth.

"This is inaccurate," she said, even though she suspected it wasn't. The *Times* wasn't infallible, but they wouldn't get something like this wrong.

Fanny stroked her shoulder. "I don't know why he didn't tell you, except maybe he didn't want your anger."

"Everyone knows about this," she whispered as a delayed sort of embarrassment washed over her.

Mrs. Burgess and everyone at LSS would know. He had voted no and hadn't even told her. Despite the evidence before her, a small part of her couldn't believe what she saw. He couldn't have done this.

"Everyone knows." This time the anger was readily apparent in Eliza's voice.

Fanny said, "I'm sorry he lied to you. It's what men do. I warned you not to fall in love with one of them."

Cora hadn't confessed her love to her mother. She had been holding it close to her, a secret she hadn't yet shared with Leo, but it must have been obvious. Somehow that only made her pain worse. "Please, Mama. Not now."

"I should go and let you talk to him," Fanny said. "I have a tea to get to anyway."

"Well, I don't." Eliza's hand rested gently on her back. "Would you mind if I stay and keep you company?"

Cora nodded and hardly noticed when Fanny gave her a kiss on the cheek and left them. Her mind was spinning. She felt hurt and betrayed and so angry she didn't know what to do. Underneath all of that was the feeling that maybe this was wrong. Maybe none of it was true. Maybe it was some elaborate prank orchestrated by Bolingrave. She wouldn't put it past him if he ever learned who Lavender Starling was. But even as she thought it, she realized how far-fetched that sounded. No one would connect that name to her, least of all Bolingrave, who had more important things to do than to concern himself with her. The fact that she was making up elaborate excuses served to bring her back to reality.

Leo had betrayed her. It was the simplest answer, which meant it was the one most likely to be true. She didn't know how long she sat there silently with Eliza in the drawing room until voices from the front hall drew her attention. She heard Leo's voice, but he wasn't alone.

She rose, and Eliza came to her feet as well. Together, they hurried to the door in time to see Leo halfway up the stairs on the way to his study. Two men were with him. They didn't seem like work associates. There was something a little rough around the edges about both of them. Eliza gasped, her gaze drawn to the one beside Leo, as if she knew him. He was young, maybe in his middle twenties at best. His eyes widened at the sight of her sister, but he quickly glanced away. Cora didn't have time to analyze what the silent exchange might mean. She was too focused on her husband.

"Leo?" She normally didn't use her pet name for him in front of anyone else, but she couldn't be bothered with formality right now. She needed to understand how the man she loved could betray her.

His face was set in firm lines, no doubt due to the seriousness of the discussion with his associates, but he paused to look down at her. He looked tired and slightly unkempt, which made her wonder what he must have been up to all day. He clearly hadn't been at his office. Something about her expression must have clued him in to her distress. He excused himself and made his way down the stairs to her.

Eliza quietly disappeared from her side to go back into the drawing room and give them time alone.

"What's wrong?" he asked.

"Is this accurate?" She held up the paper for him to see.

The momentary confusion on his face faded away as understanding dawned. He didn't look closely enough to see the *nay* written next to his name. He didn't have to because he knew what it would say, which meant it was the truth. Her heart fell.

"Cora, I had planned to tell you. I cannot—"

She interrupted him. "So it's true? You voted against it."

"I had no choice." He glanced over his shoulder to the men who continued on their way to his study. "Give me a few minutes to see them out. I'll explain—"

"I can't believe you didn't tell me."

"I meant to tell you," he said. Guilt made him flush and softened his eyes.

"I thought we had turned a corner in our relationship. That we could rely upon each other and be honest." *That* hurt even more than his vote. He'd taken her to his bed last night without confessing the truth, making her feel like a fool.

"We have. We can," he insisted.

But her newfound faith in that was shaken. The weight of it all threatened to swallow her whole, and she felt that same suffocating feeling she had experienced with her inheritance dangled just out of her grasp. It was a loss of control, she recognized now. Someone else held the strings, and she had no choice but to dance as they wanted. He had taken what he wanted from her without giving her his honesty in return.

She turned away, but he took hold of her arm. "Cora, please let me explain. I promise I will. After they leave, we can spend all night talking about it."

Would it always be this way? Men telling her or *not* telling her what they pleased to get the right response out of her?

She nodded, but she hadn't really heard what he said. She must have convinced him she had, because he kissed her forehead and returned to the men upstairs. She wandered back to the drawing room door, viciously hurt by his betrayal. He hadn't trusted her and had chosen to allow her to believe a lie.

Suddenly, it was too much to face Eliza, who would only offer her comfort. Cora was supposed to be the one who comforted her sisters through their scrapes. She needed time to get herself together first. She needed to take a walk to gather her thoughts and the armor she used to wear to shield her from these sorts of hurts. She grabbed her cloak and gloves.

Edgecomb found her in the front hall as she opened the front door. "My lady, may I call the carriage 'round for you?"

"That won't be necessary. I'm walking to the park."

"But Miss Eliza . . ." He gestured toward the drawing room.

"Leave her be. I'll return soon."

He muttered some objection, but she closed the door before he finished his sentence. Hyde Park was only a few blocks away. The cool evening air would clear her head. She didn't want to argue with Leo, and she knew that she would if she spoke with him now. She had already closed the door when she realized she had forgotten her hat. She felt quite naked without it, but it couldn't be helped. No doubt Edgecomb had raised the alarm and she'd lose her chance at solitude if she returned.

She hurried blindly down the sidewalks, and a few minutes later she found herself crossing Park Lane and almost running into the deep recesses of the park. She dodged the few pedestrians who were out walking and hurried across the horse track. The lampposts were starting to light as darkness descended, creating that gray haze that made it slightly more difficult to see in the moments before full dark. She followed a narrow footpath through some trees before finally coming to a stop. Tears had begun to fall, but she hadn't even noticed them until that moment. She furiously wiped them away. It was stupid to cry. She refused to shed any more tears, but more continued to fall.

She was so wrapped up in her sobbing that she didn't hear the men approach her until one of them said, "Lady Devonworth?"

"Yes?" She looked up to see two roughly dressed men walking up to her. They were so close by the time she had noticed them that it gave her a start and she backed away. She realized too late that they were the same strange men she had noticed watching her at the demonstration. "What are you—"

Her words cut off in a scream as one of them lunged toward her. The other one caught her as she leaped away, dragging her arms behind her. A hand covered her mouth, and between them, they were able to lift her off her feet. She had no doubt they had followed her from her home and waited for the perfect opportunity to take her. From the corner of her eye, she saw the hulking outline of a carriage lurking in the shadows of the trees. If they got her into that vehicle, she might never get free.

THIRTY-ONE

❧

R ELEASE MY WIFE."
        The fiery rage that filled Devonworth was fueled by
fear at the sight of Cora in the despicable grasp of those ruf-
fians. He knew immediately who they were. He'd seen them
both on his trip into Whitechapel to pay Harry's debt. The
man who held her arms behind her back was named Jim. He
was the same man Devonworth had been forced to pummel.

Jim's eyes widened before they settled on Devonworth and
narrowed in unadulterated meanness. His companion quickly
dropped Cora's legs and whirled to face the oncoming threat.
Cora renewed her efforts to escape, but Jim's fingers bit into
her cruelly as he tightened his grasp.

"Can't do that," Jim said, but he was caught and everyone
knew it. One slip of his grasp and Cora would gain her freedom, so he couldn't reach for a gun, assuming he had one on
him. His companion was clearly too afraid or too inept to do
anything but look out with a slack-jawed stare.

Devonworth couldn't blame him. The men were clearly

third-rate criminals, and Devonworth hadn't come alone. When Cora had left so abruptly, Edgecomb had sent the footman, Oliver, to follow her in case she might need some assistance. Certain that something was wrong with his mistress, who was usually so self-possessed, the butler had stood watching from the front door long enough to see the two dangerous-looking men fall in line behind her. He had immediately called up to Devonworth, who had never once in his entire life heard the older man raise his voice.

As luck would have it, Cavell and his man Sanford were already in his study. Cavell had spent the previous night looking for Vining. He'd sent word at the break of dawn that he had him at Montague Club, which is where Devonworth had gone that morning. Together with Sanford, they had gone to Vining's flat and found the notes and correspondence the sleuth had uncovered about the Dove family. That had included information about Mrs. Dove's life as an actress and an alleged previous marriage. The documents were safely in Devonworth's study now where he planned to destroy them in the hearth.

The criminals were outnumbered. Devonworth, Sanford, and the footman numbered three. Neither man knew it, but Cavell had gone around the trees and was approaching from behind them. For her part, Cora wasn't making things easy on Jim and his friend. "Let me go!" She struggled and stomped on his foot, eliciting a groan.

Jim jerked her, shaking her so that Devonworth could hear her teeth clack together. To his companion he said, "Get my gun from—" His words cut off abruptly as whoever had been driving the carriage lurking under the canopy of trees took off at a fast gait, leaving nothing but dust in its wake. Jim muttered a curse, and his friend immediately looked around as if getting ready to run. "Blast you, Willy, grab me gun from the holster!" yelled Jim.

But Willy wasn't listening and Jim was getting desperate. Devonworth and the men had been slowly walking forward, closing in as they spoke. "Take one more step and I'll break her bloody wrist," he said.

Devonworth paused and motioned for Sanford and Oliver to do the same. The man was daft enough to try it. He wouldn't have her injured. Her eyes flared in despair, and he tried to communicate to her that everything would be fine. Cavell had slowly crept out of the copse of trees behind them, revolver in hand, and would be upon them soon. But before that could happen, she stomped on Jim's instep and he loosened his grip enough that she was able to elbow him in the ribs. She might not have got far on her own, but it was enough. Devonworth sprinted forward and managed to grab her just as her shoes were slipping on the mossy ground. Cavell hurried forward and pressed the revolver into Jim's back.

"Make one wrong move and I'll put a bullet in your back," Cavell warned, his voice low and menacing.

"You wouldn't shoot a man in the back." Something like hope filled Jim's voice, but it was quickly extinguished when Cavell laughed.

"There are no scruples where we're from, Jim."

Willy had taken off at the first hint of a struggle between Cora and Jim, but Sanford pounced on him, aided by Oliver.

For the first time, something like relief poured over Devonworth. Cora was in his arms and she was whole. Her body trembled against him, and she held him tight. Her fingers clutched at his coat. He buried his face in her hair and whispered, "Are you injured, love?"

"Shaken, but I'm not injured."

He held her close to his heart for another moment. It was all the time they could steal, because already people were calling out, having been alerted to the danger by the disturbance. Edgecomb had gone to collect the police, and they should be arriving any moment.

He looked up to see gentlemen converging on them from the nearby paths that meandered through the trees and offering assistance. He kept a firm hold on Cora's hand as he assured the men they had everything under control. The next few moments were fairly chaotic as men stepped forward to help detain Jim and Willy until the police arrived.

It seemed interminable, but it wasn't more than an hour later before they were back home. Eliza had been there wringing her hands in worry. After a brief reunion where Cora assured her sister she was unharmed, Devonworth had carried his wife upstairs to his bedroom.

"Did he say why he'd done it?" Cora asked after he'd set her on her feet.

"I met Jim that night I went to Whitechapel to clear Harry's debt." The shame of bringing that trouble home to his wife was one he wouldn't soon forget. She deserved better. "Jim is one of Brody's men. He and Cavell had words, and later he charged at us. I hit him, embarrassing him in front of his lady friend. He must have wanted to humiliate me in return. What better way than getting to my wife?"

Devonworth rubbed salve on the abrasions left on her wrists by Jim's meaty hands. He'd dismissed Monroe and stripped Cora out of her soiled dress and down to her chemise, drawers, and stockings, all by himself. He'd wanted to make certain that she really was fine. Now that the danger was over, he was coming to grips with how close he might have come to losing her. The very moment he'd seen her reddened skin, he'd felt anger flare within him and he'd reached for the salve.

"Don't blame yourself." She gave him a timid smile and brushed her fingertips against his cheek. "You did a brave thing for your brother."

Securing the lid back on the jar, he set it aside and stared down at his wife. "Why did you run from me, Cora?"

"I didn't run. I took a walk to clear my head. It never occurred to me that horrible men would be waiting to take me." She hesitated. When she spoke again, he knew why. "I saw that man . . . Jim . . . He was at the demonstration watching us, but I never thought he would come after me. I suppose I should have listened to you about not attending the demonstration."

"My God, Cora." He pulled her into his arms again and closed his eyes. He wanted to somehow make her a part of him even more than she already was. He wanted to make it so that she would never face danger again. He hadn't thought his trip to Whitechapel would have followed him to Mayfair, but he'd been wrong and it had almost cost him dearly. He'd find someone to accompany her at all times now that he knew the risk. Jim had been biding his time all these weeks, waiting for the one day she went out alone.

"No, you can't blame yourself," he said. "This is my fault. He was using you to get to me. My apologies for that. I was careless with you."

"No." She gripped the lapels of his coat and looked up at him. "It's not your fault."

It was, but he wouldn't debate that with her. Instead, he said, "I love you, Cora. I would die without you."

"You love me?" Her cheeks turned a pretty shade of pink and her eyes softened.

"I do, yes. Wholeheartedly. I'm sorry I haven't said it before now."

She still seemed to be in awe, and he found he couldn't hold her gaze. It felt too raw, as if she saw too much of him. He hadn't been this open even with Sofia. Their love had been understood. He'd never felt the need to declare it.

"How long have you known?" she asked. Relentless.

"Timberscombe Park . . . perhaps sooner. It all started for me when we began working on our speech together. I might have realized then had I been less of a blockhead."

She laughed softly, and her grip on his lapels tightened, possibly ruining the wool forever with salve, but he didn't care. She leaned forward and pressed a kiss just above his heart and his breath stopped.

Slowly, reverently, he took her face in his hands. There was still an uncertainty deep in her eyes, and he wanted it gone. He needed it gone so they could get back to how things were last night. "Let me explain to you why I voted the way I did."

She nodded.

He didn't want to hurt her, but there was no way around it. "Early on when Camille first invited me to the house party, I hired an investigator to research you. At that time, I didn't even know your names. He found out a little information. Your names. The fact that your father, Jeremiah Dove, had died. The fact that Hathaway was some sort of benefactor. Only the most basic of facts." He paused to see how she received that. He had confessed this first part to her on the night he'd proposed, when it hadn't meant anything. But now, there was no denying that his meddling in her background had led to Bolingrave having the upper hand.

"Go on." Her brow furrowed, but that was her only expression.

"I told him to keep looking, because I didn't want any surprises. After we met and negotiated our marriage, I suspected there was something you were not telling me. Then you admitted that you were Hathaway's child, and I thought that was what I had been missing. I meant to call the investigator off, but I never sent the letter. It turns out he kept looking and Bolingrave found him. Apparently, he was willing to pay Vining a lot more for the information."

She stiffened in his arms. "This investigator gave Bolingrave the secrets you had him dig up about my family?"

"I have reason to believe that he only turned over one."

"Which one?" she asked, her face tense with fear.

"Bolingrave had a receipt for a payment you received for an article you wrote for a feminist publication." She took in a harsh breath. "They found your pseudonym, Lavender Starling. It was the same pseudonym you used to dispute Bolingrave in that London gossip sheet. Why didn't you tell me?"

She turned away, dislodging his touch, her brows drawn together in pain. "I don't know. I didn't know if I could trust you then." Glancing back at him with solemn eyes, she said, "I do now, Leo."

He nodded. He was familiar with the feeling. "I don't fault you for it, but if I'd had warning, I could have planned. It gets worse. The article you wrote promoted Free Love."

"The articles I wrote demonstrated the need for women to be able to leave relationships when they need to. They often need to be able to access divorce for their own safety. Free Love simply means that they can do so without barriers put in place by family and government. Women are free to love at will and move on to another love or to freedom if that time ever comes."

"I understand your position, but that's not how it would

look if Bolingrave and his ilk had a chance to present it to the world. He insinuated that you argued for sleeping with a different man every night. Many people believe that is what is meant by Free Love. I couldn't allow you to go through that. Especially not after we've had to face down the ugly rumors about us. You'd be an outcast. Even the LSS would throw you out. Worse, your sisters would have no chance at securing husbands. Mainwaring would have had no choice but to break the engagement with Eliza."

"Is that why you did it? He told you he would keep my secret if you voted no on the property act?"

He nodded. "The bill wouldn't have passed regardless of my vote. We didn't have the numbers. Bolingrave has been playing this dangerous game with other men for their votes. He promised to give me the evidence he had if I voted against. He'll never be able to use it against you. He doesn't give a damn about you or your past, Cora. He only wants to harm me, and he used you to get to me. I'm sorry marrying me brought you into this."

"You're sorry? Leo"—she very nearly threw herself against him and ran her fingers through his hair—"aren't you upset that I didn't tell you the truth?"

"I was a bit, but I understand. Aren't you upset that I voted against the property act? I knew when I agreed with Bolingrave's demand that the bill wouldn't pass, but I still feel guilty. I broke my promise to you."

She nodded. "Furious," she said, but with a tender smile. "I'm so very angry with you and I'm angry that you were put in that position. But I love that you were trying to protect me and my sisters."

"I'll always protect you, Cora. Always." He drew her hard against him and thanked God that she was safe. But even as he wanted to put this all behind them, he couldn't. He couldn't deny the hurt he felt.

He must have stiffened or given some other indication of his feelings, because she drew back enough to look him in the eye. "There's something else?"

He nodded. "Earlier today on the stairs . . . you said that we should be able to rely upon each other and be honest."

"I did," she agreed, her eyes narrowing a bit in question.

"But you didn't rely upon me. Given the evidence, you chose to believe the worst. You chose to believe that I would harm you."

She nodded, and her eyes became glossy with tears. "I'm sorry. What hurt me most was that you kept it from me, but I promise from this day forward I will trust you and believe you in all things. I love you, Leo."

He let out a laugh that sounded suspiciously like a sob. "You love me?" he asked, repeating her earlier reaction to his declaration of love back to her.

She smiled, and when a tear slipped down her cheek, he caught it with his thumb. "I've never been so angry and so in love with someone at the same time," she said.

"How long have you known?" He had asked it to torment her as she had tormented him, but as soon as the question hung in the air between them, he found that he really wanted to know.

She shook her head and looked down, obviously embarrassed. "I don't want to say."

"Tell me," he prodded gently.

She shook her head again, but said, "Always," with a shrug. "I know that sounds unbelievable, but I felt something that day on the football pitch. It only grew every time I was near you." She met his gaze with a gravity that held him in thrall. "The more I came to know you, the more I admired you. Somewhere along the way . . . that became love."

He kissed her furiously, desperate to consume her. This woman would be the end of him and he didn't care. He was eager to end and become something new with her. He picked her up and placed her on his bed. He couldn't wait any longer.

When they finally parted, she asked, "What of Bolingrave?"

"He gave me the receipt, and I believe that's all he had."

"How are you so certain?" she asked, but her eyes were dilated and she was watching him with longing as he shrugged out of his coat.

"Because he wouldn't have wasted any time in telling me he knew more had he actually known more. Besides, Vining found some information about him. He found evidence that Bolingrave has a child in Northumberland that his wife knows nothing about. That evidence is now in my possession where it will stay unless Bolingrave gives me reason to use it."

She gasped and sat back on her heels, but he kept undressing. "What else did your investigator find?"

"Something about a divorce in Fanny's past and a childhood spent in an orphanage in Chicago." He wrestled with the clingy linen of his shirt as he stripped it off.

"Is that all?"

He had pressed a knee into the mattress—he'd bed her with his trousers and boots on—but paused at that ominous question. "What else is there?"

"Nothing," she answered a bit too quickly for his liking.

He watched her through narrowed eyes as she sidled up to him, her fingers doing their best to distract him as she went for the fastenings on his trousers. "Cora?"

She kissed her way down his chest and then said, "We can talk more about it later."

In that moment, he was certain that he'd likely never know everything there was to know about this stranger he had wed. His last thought, before her warm mouth ensured that he forgot everything but her for the rest of the night, was that for the first time in his life, he was completely at ease with the uncertainty.

EPILOGUE

CORA HAD NEVER SEEN A SUNSET QUITE LIKE A RO-man sunset in summer. The golden light painted the domes, churches, and palaces dazzling shades of orange and red. An evening breeze wafted through the open window of their bedchamber. It was a beautiful end to the most perfect day. It was also their last day in Rome. Their wedding trip was coming to an end, and tomorrow they would begin the journey home. They had been able to make the trip a little bit sooner than planned because Harry had gotten himself into some trouble with the local authorities, which meant Leo had been forced to come down and post his bail. After they sent Harry home, they had stayed longer to enjoy the time alone together.

Home. It still amazed her how quickly she had come to think of home as London and Timberscombe Park rather than New York. Leo would always be her home now.

He came up behind her wearing only his drawers and put his arms around her. She leaned back against him and luxuriated in how good and natural it felt to simply exist with him. The Public Health Act had passed, and Bolingrave had not produced any evidence linking her to the name Lavender Starling, which meant that Leo had found all of it. There was always the chance that something else would emerge, but she knew that Leo would be by her side when the news did leak. She just hoped that Eliza and Jenny were settled before that happened. Eliza's wedding was coming up soon, and Jenny had yet to find a suitable match.

She and Leo had spent the past couple of weeks simply enjoying each other's company and letting the worries back home slip away from them. He was perfect for her in every way. She thought she was perfect for him, too. He wasn't as aloof as when they had first married, and she noticed he often turned to her for advice and approval.

"Here. I brought you something." His voice was low against her ear.

"Hmm." Her gaze still on the sunset, he took her hand.

"I remembered you liked a particular emerald at that shop in Venice."

He slid a ring onto her finger. It fit perfectly. "Emerald?" she whispered in awe. The jewel winked up at her in the gold light of sunset. "This is the one I said reminded me of your eyes."

He nodded and kissed her temple. "The same one. I never got you a proper betrothal ring, because we never had a proper betrothal, I suppose. But you should have one."

"I love it." And she did. She loved even more that it was something special between the two of them.

"I want you to have it because I want you to know that I'd wed you all over again."

She smiled and turned in his arms, holding him with one

hand while she gazed at the beautiful ring. "Even without the money?" she teased.

"Even without the money, though I have to admit it's a nice benefit of the arrangement."

She pulled a face but then rose up on her toes and kissed him. "I would marry you, too, even without the title."

He kissed her back until a knock on the door interrupted them. He smiled at her. "It must be the chocolates I ordered along with your favorite biscuits. Can you believe they found them here?"

"What favorite biscuits?" She didn't know she had a favorite.

"The orange cream biscuits you ate at our wedding breakfast," he said over his shoulder as he went to answer the door. "They were the only thing you ate the entire time."

She hadn't eaten because she'd been too nervous, but she had never realized that he had noticed. She had assumed the biscuits were common enough in England and Mrs. Anderson served them at tea because of *her* personal preference.

"Are you telling me you arranged to have Mrs. Anderson serve me the biscuits every day because I ate them at our wedding breakfast?"

He flashed a grin as he shrugged into his dressing gown and opened the door to a man wearing the hotel's livery.

All this time he had been noticing her, observing the things she liked, and giving her small gifts of them. The chocolates, the fountain pen, the orange cream biscuits, and now the emerald ring. He might just be the most perfect husband in the world.

He closed the door after a quick conversation with the servant. A deep crease appeared between his brows, and he walked over to her holding a folded yellow sheet of paper. She recognized it as a telegram, and her stomach churned with anxiety. This could not be good.

"It's for you," he said and handed it over.

She opened it and read.

```
I have decided I cannot marry Mainwaring STOP I
love another STOP Please advise STOP
From: Miss Eliza Dove
```

"It's a good thing we leave tomorrow."

"Why?" Leo asked. "Is something the matter?"

"Eliza needs us."

AUTHOR'S NOTE

The snowstorm that contributed to Devonworth's need for a wife was inspired by a real snowstorm, which swept through Exmoor in the southwest of England on the evening of March 28, 1878. The severe weather was unexpected after a mild winter. Accounts of the storm record one shepherd losing over two hundred and sixty sheep. The event was noteworthy enough to get a mention in *Symons's British Rainfall*, one of the first published annual guides that recorded weather for the United Kingdom.

The bill that Devonworth is trying to pass in the book is a combination of the Public Health Act of 1875 and the water addendum to that act of 1878. The acts were essentially a consolidation of all the other public health acts that had been implemented throughout the nineteenth century. This century saw drastic changes in the way people lived in Great Britain. At the start of the nineteenth century, most of the population was rural and lived in farming communities. By the middle of the century, people had begun to move to towns and cities in pursuit of jobs, which resulted in over half of the population living in urban centers. As you can imagine, this population shift created unsanitary conditions and health hazards that local governments were slow to address.

Terraced homes were built to accommodate the people who moved into the cities to work in factories and industry, but very little consideration was given to the additional waste and water and food needs of these people. There were still open sewers in many cities and little to no regulations on waste removal or safe food and drinking water. There are reports of rubbish heaps as tall as buildings. As a result, cholera and typhoid were common and devastating diseases that killed many people. This was made all the more devastating because these diseases were and are largely preventable.

Smaller acts were created throughout the decades to address the rapidly changing needs of the growing urban population, but they were piecemeal and more like a bandage to the bigger problem. The 1875 act was the result of a concerted effort by various groups to address the needs of the population. It stated that local authorities were responsible for providing access to clean water, ensuring that safe food was available, and disposing of all sewage. It also required all new houses and dwellings to be connected to the main sewer lines. The Public Health (Water) Act of 1878 went a step further and stated that all sewers should be covered and that every dwelling should have access to clean water. It established distance requirements for water access and created local authorities to enforce them, and also expanded the reach of the act to rural areas, rather than only larger cities.

As you might expect, there had been quite a bit of resistance to these changes, primarily due to the cost involved in creating efficient sewers and upkeep on old sewer systems, along with plumbing each residence with running water. It not only increased local tax rates but shifted the cost of implementing initiatives to landlords and homeowners. These same landlords and homeowners spent a lot of money lobbying to keep the acts from passing. Even when Dr. John Snow proved the physical link between cholera and water sources in the 1850s, and Louis Pasteur scientifically proved that germs, not miasma, caused sickness, people in power were resistant to change laws because of the expense. Because it wasn't convenient to believe, it wasn't until the 1880s and 1890s that the majority began to accept that it was germs and not unpleasant smells and vapors that caused disease, despite decades of proof.

The letter that Bolingrave wrote to the newspaper is based on a paper written by Dr. Benjamin Richardson, a colleague and friend of Dr. Snow. Dr. Richardson presented his paper to the Congress of Sanitarians in Exeter in September of 1880. In the presentation he offers the unfortunate, but typical, argument of many educated and accomplished men and women of the time that women should be allowed an education but only in the sense that it would make them better homemakers and caretakers to their families. These people believed that women wouldn't have anything of value to offer society outside the home. They often argued that educating women would result only in women taking jobs away from men who needed them.

Married women in Britain at this time lived under what was known as coverture. This means a woman was considered to be under her husband's protection and was his property. In essence, when a man and woman married, they became one under the law. What was hers became his, and she ceased to exist as her own person. Women's rights activists fought to change this. They believed that married women and unmarried women should enjoy the same rights. Thanks to their efforts, the first Married Women's Property Act was passed in 1870, but it was a watered-down version of what had initially been proposed. It gave women rights to some of their income, investments, property, and children, but only up to a certain threshold. Obviously, this was a step in the right direction, but it wasn't enough.

Cora and the women's rights group she joins rightfully believe that expanding the rights of married women was an important step on the road to full equality for women under the law. It took over a decade, but the Married Women's Property Act of 1882 finally passed. This act gave married women their own legal identity. They were able to sign contracts; own, sell, and buy property; and keep inheritances without limit. While it did not make women equal to men in the eyes of the law, it was a crucial step in securing a woman's legal identity.

ACKNOWLEDGMENTS

Books are never written in a vacuum. They start out as the result of an author's imagination combined with hard work, and then an entire support system helps bring that book out into the world. I'm so thankful to have so many great people around me.

First and foremost, I have to thank my family for being supportive of my writing. They give me the time (usually) to work on my stories and truly believe in me. Thanks, especially, to my husband, who brings me food when I'm on a tight deadline and listens patiently to me prattling on about imaginary people.

A huge thank-you to my editor, Sarah, who helped me find the heart of this story and cut the excess. She is amazing, and I couldn't write the books I do without her. Thank you to Kevan for being so very supportive of my work. Also, I'd like to thank everyone at Berkley who has a hand in seeing my books through every stage of production and sales. I could not reach so many readers without you. Thank you for your attention to detail and your unwavering support.

Thank you to Laurie for reading the early versions of my stories and finding the plot holes and asking me the tough questions like: Why would he do that? (*Spoiler alert* He wouldn't.) Thank you to Marielle for listening to me grumble about my characters over endless bagels and how they won't do what I want them to do. And a thank-you to all the writers in my life who help me work out plot and historical issues in ways big and small. Elisabeth, Erin, Jeanine, Jenni, Lara, Lucy, Melissa, Nathan, Nicole, Seána, Tanya, Tara, Terri, Virginia, and everyone else . . . thank you!

Keep reading for an excerpt from

ELIZA AND THE DUKE

by Harper St. George

A YOUNG WOMAN IN SEARCH OF A HUSBAND SHOULD not go wandering the halls of Montague Club. This was particularly true if the young woman in question was only pretending to be a gently bred heiress. Any hint of scandal could not easily be absorbed by a centuries-long family lineage that didn't exist.

Eliza Dove knew that. She knew it in her bones. The problem was that, sometimes, once an idea took hold, she had trouble reining it in. Her bad angel always seemed to be more persuasive than her good angel.

This is how she found herself searching for the nearly imperceptible crease where the hidden door that would lead her to the club met the wall. The door was covered in wallpaper and made to look like part of the corridor. She wouldn't have noticed it at all except she'd seen a man in livery pass through it only moments ago. Her fingertips slid over the wall, fingernails trailing over the scarlet and gold wallpaper in search of the break in texture. She found it right at the edge of a section of molding, exactly where she thought it would be. There had to be a way to open it.

Ah-ha! Her thumb brushed against a gilded latch that was disguised in a section of gold pattern on the wallpaper. She very gently gave it a tug and the door swung toward her. Victory pumped through her veins, along with a fair amount of wine from dinner. She paused to make certain no one saw her and to give fate a moment to catch up and intervene. No one happened by and the twinge of guilt that made itself known was so puny it might not have existed at all.

The Dowager Duchess of Hereford was Eliza's sponsor for the season. The widow was engaged to one of the proprietors of Montague Club, Mr. Jacob Thorne, who just happened to live in an elegant home attached to the establishment. The couple had invited Eliza, her sister Jenny, and their mother over for dinner. Eliza had only seen the secret entrance because everyone was enjoying dessert in Mr. Thorne's salon when Eliza had excused herself to use the facilities and then gone exploring on her way back to the group. She probably hadn't been meant to see the servant using the entrance, but now that she had there was no way she was passing up an opportunity to get a glimpse at a real gaming club.

What could it hurt to take a peek, especially if no one saw her?

She hurried through the doorway, making certain that the door shut behind her, and found herself in a service corridor. The narrow hallway was rather plain and unadorned except for gas sconces that dimly lit the space. Her excitement dampened, though it made sense that the corridor would exist if Mr. Thorne utilized the club's servants for his own household.

Luckily, there were doors on the opposite wall, which she was certain would lead her into the club. Now that she had come this far, she couldn't turn back without seeing *something*. The doors on this side had visible handles and were not camouflaged into the wall, since they needed to be seen and easily accessible for the servants who would likely have their hands full. Pressing her ear against the first door she came upon, she listened for noise. There were voices, but it sounded like revelry coming from deeper in the club. She slowly opened the door and peeked inside to find a very wide and extravagant hall.

It was like stepping into another world. The walls were white with opulent, gilded molding and sections of scarlet wallpaper. The molding continued all the way to the recessed ceiling where each section was inlaid with gold. Fine paintings of landscapes lined the wall in either direction.

Like the infamous White's, London's oldest gentleman's club, Montague was notorious for its card tables, smoking rooms, and extensive collection of priceless wines and whiskies. Unlike White's, Montague allowed women into its membership. Eliza had hoped to step into a gaming room or, at the very least, a lounge with men and women draped about in various stages of debate . . . or debauchery. Either would have sufficed.

But all wasn't lost. While one direction led to a window that no doubt overlooked the street, the other way led to sounds of merriment. Male voices rose in excitement, likely at a gaming table. Other voices could be heard singing out of tune, but no one seemed to mind. They kept right on singing. She could see a railing not twenty feet away from her. She'd only take a quick look and then run right back to Mr. Thorne's residence.

The secret door behind her had been made to look like the wall with panels of white wood obscuring the entrance. She made note of the location of the hidden latch and set off toward the railing. As long as she kept to herself and generally out of sight, no one would notice her. She wanted only to observe.

Eliza soon found herself in a gallery of sorts. It encircled the room below it, which was one of the gaming rooms. A quick look over the balustrade revealed the gaiety below. A crowd of mostly men, but a few women, gathered around tables playing various games. The table with the loudest spectators had a wooden wheel set into it. The wheel seemed to be divided up into several sections with painted numbers in alternating colors of red and black. A man wearing his best evening suit spun the wheel and a small white marble bounced around until the wheel came to a stop and it landed in a numbered compartment. Another cheer went up from several of the men while the others exclaimed in dismay.

She watched for two more spins, silently wagering on which number the marble would land on each time. Finally, one of the patrons glanced up and caught her watching. He murmured to his friend next to him, who also looked up at her. She might be impulsive at times, but she was no fool. When one of them stood as if he meant to come upstairs, it was her signal to go.

She sprinted to the secret door and hurried inside. When she pulled it closed, she was shaking with laughter at her own audacity. That might have been the most reckless thing she had done since they had arrived in London.

Determined to make her way back to the residence without getting caught, she turned to dart through the door that would take her back to the dinner party, but ran into a solid wall of muscle instead. The impact nearly knocked the breath from her. The man grunted but didn't move.

"Pardon me," she said and backed up against the club door to create space between them. The corridor was very narrow, not large enough for two people to stand abreast.

The man didn't say anything. In fact, he seemed to be leaning against the wall awkwardly, using it for support. His hat was pulled low over his forehead, revealing only the lower half of his face, which was pale and covered with a slight growth of beard as if he hadn't shaved in a couple of days. His square jaw seemed to be clenched tight. He was dressed entirely in black, from his long coat to his boots. His arms were wrapped around his middle as if he might be in pain.

"Are you injured?" she asked, but he didn't respond.

Where had he come from? He leaned heavily against the door that would take her back to Mr. Thorne's residence, but she didn't think he had come from there. She had no clue where the service corridor might lead or how he had come to be in it. He wasn't dressed like a servant. His coat was finespun wool, and his boots had a sheen that made them appear to be of the highest quality.

"Do you need—?"

Before she could finish, he moved, a sound like a groan rumbling deep in his chest. His steps took him down the corridor away from her, though he continued to lean on the wall. His hat fell to the floor behind him, and she picked it up.

"Your hat!"

He paused again, but she didn't think it was because he had heard her. He rested his head back against the wall, breathing shallowly. When she took the few steps needed to reach him, he didn't acknowledge her in any way. The light from a nearby sconce bathed his face. He was young, likely in his twenties; older than her but younger than Mr. Thorne. A thick shock of dark hair fell over his forehead. Pale skin was pulled tight over a face that was too coarse to be conventionally handsome but too interesting to be common. His eyes were closed in obvious pain.

"You *are* injured," she said.

His eyes glittered when he opened them, but he didn't seem to see her. They were glazed in a look she had seen once before. Years ago in New York, her mother had had a male friend over to visit. He'd spent the evening drinking and smoking a pipe that had left a sweet smell in the air. By the time he had left, his eyes had been glazed like marbles and he had regarded her without focusing on her face. This man's eyes had the same look, but whether it was from intoxication or pain or some mixture of both, Eliza couldn't tell.

The pain seemed to originate from his midsection, so she dropped his hat and gently attempted to open his coat. He allowed her ministrations by easing the grip of his arms, and she parted the wool and gasped aloud. He was shirtless. His chest was broad and solid with well-developed muscles. That alone might have been enough to surprise her under normal circumstances, but it was the gore that made her catch her breath. Streaks of blood crisscrossed his chest and stomach. There were nicks in his skin, but she couldn't tell if those were the source of all the blood. Some of it had dried to blotches of black, but there were crimson smears near his shoulders. His ribs were mottled with what would likely become bruises as the night wore on.

"You need a physician," she whispered. The club must have someone on staff who could be called upon to handle medical issues. If not, then a doctor could be sent for.

The man only grunted in acknowledgment of her words and pushed forward. It seemed it took all of his concentration to stay mostly upright as he continued down the hall. She made to put an arm around him to assist him.

"No." It was the first word he'd said and was spoken in a low and gravelly tone that gave her pause.

"I can help you," she insisted.

"No."

Standing upright again, she looked at him with growing annoyance. "Who are you?"

"Who'm I?" He might have laughed. She wasn't sure how to interpret the chortle that barely made it out of his chest before he swallowed it. "I'm the Duke, milady."

A duke?

He didn't give her a chance to respond as he continued down the hall, his shoulder pressed to the wall to keep himself upright. This time his arm trailed behind him, and she noted his knuckles were scraped.

What had he been up to tonight, and what did he mean by calling himself that? He wasn't a duke. Although his accent was decidedly English, it lacked the crisp drawl she had come to associate with the aristocracy. The word *duke* hadn't been spoken with the *dj* sound that so many of them seemed to use, and the words *who* and *am* had slid into one.

She glanced at the light coming in beneath the secret door that would lead her back to Mr. Thorne's residence. Her good angel was urging her to open that door. It would lead her to safety and to a life where a very well-qualified nobleman would marry her at the end of summer to gain her inheritance.

Her bad angel urged her to follow the strange man. It would take her five minutes to find out who he was and where he was going. He was already halfway down the corridor. His destination couldn't be that far. If she was quick, no one would be the wiser.

Retrieving his hat once again, she followed him.

Harper St. George grew up in the rural backwoods of Alabama and the northwest Florida coast, where her love of history began. She now makes her home in the Atlanta area writing historical fiction romance set in various time periods, from the Viking Era to the Gilded Age. Her novels have been translated into ten languages.

VISIT THE AUTHOR ONLINE

HarperStGeorge
HarperStGeorge
HarperStGeorge
HarperStGeorge.com

Ready to find
your next great read?

Let us help.

Visit prh.com/nextread